余墨三集

陆谷孙 著

復旦大學 出版社

七旬老翁告白

混混噩噩又一年，颓然自放，顽鄙益甚，见者多嗤称爷爷，惟诸君犹有以取之而不弃。诸君所以见爱者，与某之爱诸君实无异也，即所谓“惺惺相惜，心心相应”是也。

古之所谓君子实非真君子。倘不用于世，必寄物以自遣。阮籍以酒，嵇康以琴。阮无酒，嵇无琴，即令其食草木，友麋鹿，仍有不安者矣，躁动也！

独颜回饮水啜菽，居陋巷，无假于外而不改其乐，此孔子所以叹其不可及也。又有东坡病亟时，索沐浴，还清白，后谈笑而化。生死两淡，后来者岂能不瞻望此中堂堂！七十老物谨以此与诸君共勉。

2010年3月2日

出版说明

陆谷孙先生在《余墨二集》的“自序”中写道:“《余墨二集》篇幅比《一集》膨胀不少,原因之一是老之已至,敝帚自珍,巴不得把写过的文字,包括与正业有关而并非余墨的,及早盘点搜辑……”《余墨三集》(以下简称《三集》)秉承这一收录原则,将陆先生“非余墨”的文章也一并选收入集。

《三集》中选收的文章主要有以下三个来源:(1)《余墨集》、《余墨二集》中未收录的已发表文章和《余墨二集》出版后发表的文章;(2)陆先生于 2010 年发布在博客中的博文;(3)陆先生的好友提供的陆先生写于 1960 年代(“Sunset, Mother and Home”,叶扬教授提供)和 1980 年代(“A Cursory Comparative Study of English and Chinese”, “China’s Response to the Renaissance”, 两篇均为 Thomas Creamer 先生提供)未发表的文章。

与前两集相比,《三集》最大的不同之处在于收录了陆先生二十余篇纯英文文章。《三集》的正文分为“谈文论字”、“三尺讲台”、“故人旧事”、“世间百态”四个版块。每个版块中已发表的文章在前,未发表的文章在后,相接处以空行分隔。“已发表”和“未发表”的内部文章均以时间顺序排列。未发表的文章中,文末显示写作日期者为陆先生的博文。

正文注释中,凡未作任何标记者为陆先生本人所注,标“原注”者为原本就有的注释,标“编注”者为此次编辑加工过程中所加的注释。

2017 年 12 月

目 录
CONTENTS

谈 文 论 字

三 尺 讲 台

故 人 旧 事

世 间 百 态

附 录

谈 文 论 字

Translator: A Scholar and a Writer in His Own Right*

Small have continual plodders ever won,
Save base authority from others' books.
— *Love's Labour's Lost*, I. i. 86-87.

Over the past ten years or so there have been several scholarly attempts to rake through records of antiquity and look farther afield for evidence of a longer tradition of translation in China (Ma 1984, Chen 1992), and high-sounding voices are now and then heard arguing for a superior translation theory that is "indigenously Chinese" (Luo 1984). For all that, to me the Shakespearean lines quoted above remain an apt description of what Chinese translators essentially are and what they can aspire to achieve: continual plodders winning at best base authority from others' books.

Neither Fish Nor Fowl. In a historical perspective, translation in China was characteristically part of Lesser Learning (小学), and a very minor part of it at that. A time-honoured empirical and impressionistic rather than theoretical Chinese tradition of letters proved particularly

* 本文是作者于1995年1月在香港城市大学"翻译与语言学国际学术研讨会"上发表的论文。——原注。

unfortunate with regard to translation studies — a virtual wasteland until the landscape was enlivened by Buddhist sutra translators with a scattered spate of comments on translation around the fourth century. Translators as "petty officials who imitate" (象胥), "those who know about the exotic" (狄鞮) or "tongue men" (舌人) were never scholars properly. In fact, quoting Zhang Yuanji, a late Qing (Ching) Dynasty mandarin, "Confucian scholars from illustrious families are always above learning foreign tongues and those who go in for translation are mostly of humble and needy origin and dull in their native wit." (Chen 1992: 141) So persistent was this literary snobbery that translators in modern China were variously dubbed "go-betweens①", "puppets", "parrots"— all in a vein of denigration. Ironically, such unflattering sobriquets often originated with prominent men of letters who practised translation on the side or dabbled in it. Guo Moruo (1921), for one, out of an exaggerated wrath over "sinful" translators "tyrannizing over the literary scene", went so far as to plead for shoving translation to the no man's land beyond the elevated kingdom of creative writing. What he and some of his cohorts advocated boils down to what Peter Newmark (1981: Preface ix) would later call "an adapted Shavianism": Those who can, write; those who cannot, translate. It is but small wonder that ostracized by scholars on the one hand and by writers on the other, translators in China should find themselves awkwardly placed, neither fish nor fowl, belonging nowhere.

By a consensus, spoken or unspoken, translation remains "unscholarly" today, adding little, if anything, to a person's academic

① Guo Moruo may have borrowed this from Goethe in the first place (Qian 1985: 69).

worth when he or she is evaluated for professorial promotion. In one case — my own case in fact, two million words translated over a ten-year period was less of a convincing reference than a fistful of essays, supposedly learned and original, composed in a couple of years and totalling no more than 20,000 Chinese characters. How base borrowed authority truly is or, with a ratio of 100:1, how sadly words devalue in the hands of a translator! In terms of remuneration per thousand words translated, however difficult the SL text is, are paid for at an unchanging maximum of RMB ¥30.00 — hardly enough to "lubricate the translator's ink-brush" (润笔) in view of an ever-worsening double-digit inflation, whereas a breezy essay of the same length carried by a low-brow evening newspaper can bring the writer five times as much. Granting that the incentive growingly lessens and morale stays low, dedicated translators would have gladly "plodded continually" but for the dramatic curtailment of translating commissions as publishers under copyright obligations are loath to pay royalties in hard currencies for foreign books to be translated into Chinese. As matters stand now, publishers of translations either dish out warm-overs, the copyright of which has expired, or flock to hitherto untranslated old titles such as James Boswell's *The Life of Samuel Johnson* and Lord Chesterfield's *Letters to His Son*①; the total volume of translation undertaken diminishes; burgeoning young translating talents are few and far

① Old titles have to be "politically correct", though. The Chinese translation of Mallinaga Vatsyayana's *Kama Sutra*, for instance, an abecedarian book almost every college student in the West reads, still goes begging. Cowering before a heavy-handed but ineffectual censorship on porn, no government-operated publisher would dare publish this sexually oriented sutra although everybody salivates at the prospect of an extremely lucrative bargain of publishing it.

between; old hands are readier to take on proposed projects of translation from overseas than contracts offered locally; and career translators who freelance for a living as Fu Lei used to do are rapidly becoming, as it were, an endangered species.

In brief, as Professor Ji Xianlin of Beijing University sounded a tocsin recently (Zhang 1994), there is a "major crisis" for translators in the Mainland for the moment. To rectify the situation, besides the need to rethink and reshape cultural policies in general, we may want to re-examine translation as a skill, craft, art, discipline or science in its true perspective, using the Western experience as a frame of reference.

Western Experience In Little. It is true that Westerners also coin derisive epithets for translators such as "traitors", "murderers", "slaves", "beggars" and, last but not least, "women" or "wives" with unmistakable sexist overtones. Likewise, it is true that translation in the West is sometimes thought of as "a subsidiary and derivative art" that "has never been granted the dignity of original work" (Belloc 1931: 26). However, as I see it, in the general judgement of letters translation in the West plays a more important role than it does in China, and Western translators are generally more visible and vocal than their Chinese counterparts. This observation is at least true of the Old World — if the Americans are by and large too isolationist and complacent to accord adequate importance to translation (Fischbach 1968).

To begin with, it is not wide of the mark to say "The history of Bible translation is a history of Western culture in microcosm." (Bassnett-McGuire 1980: 46) From its formative stages Western civilization owed a big debt to translators who translated an originally oriental Christian canon first from Hebrew into Greek as early as in the third century BC and then from either Hebrew or Greek into Latin. Among early Bible translators were to be found such great humanist thinkers as Erasmus and pioneer reformers as Martin Luther. In due course translation became not only an ecclesiastical must but also an affair of state plus a kingly pursuit, if one considers that Alfred, the only English monarch to be remembered as "Great", learned Latin at the age of forty amidst "various and manifold cares" of his kingdom so that "he could translate" (McCrum *et al.* 1986: 69). Of so vital an importance, indeed, was translation that translators could be executed for mistranslating and objectionable versions burned publicly. And by the time Latin declined to give rise to distinctive national vernaculars in Europe during the Reformation and the Renaissance, translation had practically assumed the politico-social significance of a revolutionary movement — a circumstance unknown to China at any time in her history.

Except for a basically common biblical tradition, Western civilization, composed of cultures of different emergent nation-states, was perhaps as heterogeneous and several as Chinese civilization was homogeneous and monolithic — one predominantly of the Han nationality. To meet the needs of crossfertilization such as the Chinese didn't keenly feel, translation in Renaissance Europe, according to George Steiner (1975: 247), came to play a role of central importance. Geoffrey Chaucer①, Edmund Spenser and William Shakespeare would not have been what they were and still are in English literature without borrowing

① Whether Chaucer was medieval or Renaissance is moot as the temporal limits of the Renaissance are hard to define.

from, imitating, paraphrasing and translating verbatim from their respective sources. That being a literary giant of genius and originality invariably consists in learning from and reworking upon seminal alien models is further testified by an unceasing intertraffic of translations across the European languages done by a host of talented writers such as Dryden, Pope, Goethe, Stendhal, Scott, Byron, Carlyle, Joyce, Brecht, Pound, Pasternak and Nabokov — to name a few.

Moreover, as scholarly temperaments differed, Western savants were as enamoured with what was apodictic as Chinese mentors were contented with what was empirical: lecturing, commenting or annotating, translating as Confucius, Zhu Xi (Chu Hsi), Xuan Zang (Hsüan Tsang) respectively did without reflecting in scholarly writing upon what they did①. As a result, Western translation theory took its embryonic shape in the last century BC, approximately 500 years earlier than in China, when Cicero and Horace distinguished between word-for-word and sense-for-sense approaches in translation. The Roman legacy was taken over jointly by practitioners of translation as a craft or art pragmatically and by critical minds diagnostically defining translation as a learned discipline, among whom were notably Alexander F. Tytler, Friedrich Schleiermacher, Karl Humboldt, Schopenhauer and Nietzsche. In the twentieth century, otherwise identified as "an age of translation" (Newmark 1981: 3), while growing full-fledged as translatology (Harris 1977: 42) being taught first in Continental European and Canadian universities and then in UK polytechnics, translation theory has been formulated anew scientifically to include,

① Xuan Zang's "Five Untranslatables" were more of an admission of defeat than a positive contribution to translation theory.

among other things, semantic, semiotic or pragmatic studies, discourse analysis beyond the sentence, and a more or less metaphysical probe into relationships between thought and language and between word and meaning. In the meantime, as Eugene Nida (1975: 97) puts it, "the scientific analysis of translation can provide important insights, and even correctives, for various theories of linguistics." Firth (1968) goes further in perceiving modern translation theory not only as the basis of a new theory of language but also as firmer foundations in philosophy.

An Eclectic Scholar. One of the insights one gains from the Western experience sketchily dealt with above is that translation is by nature a dignified intellectual endeavour involving scholarly acumen and artistic sensitivity. The translator, therefore, is ideally a scholar and a writer in his own right.

It is often suggested that any one with a basic grounding in a language other than his own can translate without having to undertake any systematic study of translation. He can, up to a point. However, any translator worth his salt has to be consciously or unconsciously a minimal comparativist in linguistics and/or culture. Those who ill understand or don't understand at all how equivalence is achieved through comparison and contrast are no translators or mistranslators. Added to the boilerplate examples of mistranslations of "the Milky Way" in English as "牛奶路" in Chinese and of "lying on one's back" as "躺在自己背上" (Lu Xun[①] 1931) is a lately circulated wisecracking dialogue between a

① A present-day reader may not feel very comfortable with Lu Xun's often laborious translation and his unscholarly quarrelsomeness in literary polemics. But when he metaphorized a translator into Prometheus stealing fire for man, he made clear a more positive and less snobbish attitude towards translation.

visiting Chinese dignitary (CD) and his English-speaking host (H) through a pathetically amusing "translator" ("T") that follows:

CD: (in polite response to the host's compliments on his wife's good looks) 哪里,哪里!

"T": Where, where?

H: From head to foot.

"T": 从头到脚。

CD: 不见得,不见得。

"T": Can't see, can't see.

This must have been a concoction in poor taste with punch lines bordering on surreal absurdity. But the lesson from such erring over-punctilious adherence to sameness in the surface structure (form) at the expense of equivalence in the deep structure (meaning, attitude, etc.) is no laughing matter. The lesson certainly becomes more widely relevant when one considers realistic instances of mistranslation of a similar kind which occur by no means infrequently. Pearl Buck, for one, who was a Nobel laureate presumably steeped in Chinese culture, rendered "江湖" as "rivers and lakes" and "老百姓" as "old hundred names".[①] More recently, an American Sinologist advising the Mayor of Shanghai in financial matters spoke unflinchingly at a dinner party of "五百千" (five hundred thousand) where he should have said "五十万"[②]

① For all I know, Buck's translatese may have appealed to a Western readership by retaining, word-for-word, an authentically exotic flavour.

② In 1980 on China's National Education TV, based upon a contrastive study between English and Chinese, I dwelled upon at some length what Logan Pearsall Smith called "speech-feeling" or "Sprachgefühl" in German (Lu Gusun 1980). Of the five contrastive consciousnesses that need to be cultivated and sensitivized in bilingual translation is a numeral consciousness as English and Chinese differ in the way of enumerating five figures and more.

of course. Similarly but on the other side of the coin, "Fleet Street" in London translated into Chinese as "舰队街", "a man of God" as "上帝的人" (Zhang, 1994), and an *ad hoc* American neologism FOB (Friend of Bill [Clinton]) as "离岸价格" (free on board) are all instances of mistranslation out of a failure to compare SL and TL or RL — receptor language as Nida (1975: 98) calls it to emphasize the process of decoding at the receiving end — etymologically, idiomatically or contextually.

The question of equivalence, therefore, as well as a whole gamut of fundamental questions involved in translation (e.g. translatability or untranslatability, variance or invariance, loss and gain or omissions and additions, overtranslation and undertranslation) all bear directly or indirectly upon comparative studies. The more comparatively aware a translator is, the better the overall equivalence between the SL and TL texts.

On top of being a comparativist the translator would vastly improve his performance and competence if he could cultivate himself eclectically in, say, linguistics, semiotics, discourse analysis, sociology, psychology, aesthetics, information science and other marginally related subjects for that matter. At a more practical level eclecticism also means a versatility required of a competent translator who tries his hand at a wide range of genres with a great variety of topics; who, for instance, knows not only that the Prince of Denmark's line "Not so, my lord, I am too much in the sun" admits of over forty possible interpretations or that "careful carelessness" in the parlance of literary criticism is a Dickensonian quote, but also what "virtual reality" and on-line "emoticons" in present-day technologese are all about. To be sure, eclectic scholarship is a *Jenseitigkeit*, a shore yonder one constantly gets close to but never quite arrives at. But learning to apply multidisciplinary findings to solving problems encountered during the actual translation process, trying to heighten one's theoretical perceptiveness by bringing one's practical experience to scholarly discussion, and always seeking to know something of everything with a pulsating interest in the new will undoubtedly help in adding a new dimension to translation and making an eclectic scholar out of a translator.

A Straitjacketed Writer. Placed somewhere between imitative art and creative art, translation is a unique kind of writing: "one of the most difficult tasks", as Randolph Quirk (1974: 63) puts it, "that a writer can take upon himself". Translation is difficult because, instead of only having a reader over one's shoulder to worry about as does the writer, the translator by comparison moves in a thornier thicket of having to take care not to betray the original author in the SL on the one hand and not to put off the reader reading in the TL on the other. It is difficult because, unlike a monistic writer freely using an idiolect with aplomb, the translator has to negotiate gingerly between two languages, and write, so to speak, with a straitjacket on. The difficulty grows double, triple or multiple when the translator translates between two lineally unrelated languages and two geographically remote cultures.

The translator's claim to writing well is conditional on how well he adapts to his straitjacket or on the extent to which he approaches the SL text as a judicious reader, incisive analyser, careful annotator, and willing empathizer thinking and feeling himself into the mind and heart of the original author. To be a judicious reader, let alone the rest of the capacity[①], is not so easy as it may sound, especially when the SL happens to be a foreign language or, worse, a particular lingo in a foreign language. I've seen a veteran translator belabouring a realistic dialogue quoted in *The Washington Post* (October 14, 1993: p. cs). A bit of the dialogue and his translation:

A: This jam is thick. Plenty of mad honeys, dope system.	甲：这果酱涂得厚。发疯的姑娘好多,还有毒品。
B: We phat. But I gotta flex. I'll be maxing at the crib.	乙：咱们养养吧。可我得去活动下。我要去小房间睡觉。
A: I'm easin' here. Later.	甲：我在这儿休息。再会。
B: Later.	乙：再会。

The incoherence of the translation is glaringly obvious, for the translator is apparently uninitiated in the slang of America's hip-pop generation by which "thick jam" means "an exciting party", "mad" means "good", "dope system" means "a good sound system or loud music it plays", "to phat" means "to freak out on music", "to flex" means "to go or leave", "crib" means "home", etc., etc. Assuming that correct understanding and thorough digestion of the SL text are indeed a point of departure in the entire process of translation, evaluation of the quality of a translator's writing — and at times even of his work ethics — should be process-oriented as well as product-oriented. And readability in the TL alone doesn't attest to the éclat with which the translator does full justice to the SL text.

---

① Annotation, for instance, can pose untold difficulty in translating literary criticism fraught with quotations and allusions or expressionist literature with a covert message couched in abstruse symbols. The 1994 Chinese translation of Joyce's *Ulysses* by Xiao Qian and Wen Jieruo is commendable in that it is an amply annotated version drawing not only on English sources but also on notes that appeared in previous Japanese translations of the same work.

Yan Fu and Lin Shu are by common consent pioneer translators in modern China who made invaluable contributions to translation and translation theory alike. But judging by Yan Fu's exquisitely voluble style in the TL that was comparable to that of the ancient masters of the late Zhou (Chou) Dynasty (Chen 1992: 129), I suspect he was too elevated a scholar-writer to feel comfortable in a translator's straitjacket. Besides, he might have felt impelled to opt for the style he translated in — if only to cater to an elitist readership at the turn of the century accustomed to a classical Chinese expression. However, rendering nineteenth century English into the Chinese that was in vogue four or five hundred years before Christ is hardly good translation worth emulating. Lin Shu, being the second-hand translator he was, seemed even less patient in putting up with the straitjacket, so much so that Qian Zhongshu (1985: 74), whilst pinpointing his erroneous renditions, omissions and additions, came up with a very interesting generalization based on Lin's case that those who write well "itch" to improve upon the original when they take to translating. Qian, driven doubly by a partiality to Lin Shu whose translations he had read aplenty in his early days and by the characteristic magnanimity of an eminent scholar, didn't say a single unkind word about Lin Shu's slipshodness but argued instead that it is precisely his intentional distortions that made his translations durable. But by stricter criteria today, Lin Shu's freewheeling style, not to say his second-hand approach of taking down what was orally translated to him, is not a profitable example to be followed.

Fu Lei, a contemporary exemplar in readability many Chinese translators look up to, is lately being scrutinized closely for evidence of taking liberties too much with his straitjacket. In fact, as early as in the

1950s Fu Lei's amazing readability in the TL somewhat to the detriment of faithfulness to the SL texts raised a few brows already (Jin 1993: 239-240). Qian Zhongshu, who was called upon to evaluate Fu's translation of Balzac's *Ursule Mirouet*, made quite a few suggestions and comments only to be emotionally countered and defiantly ignored. Fu Lei's case further illustrates that a translator with a strong personality may want to exercise more self-denial in order to be a straitjacketed writer in due deference to the original author.

On the reverse side of the coin, the straitjacket sometimes cramps too much. The result is often a tongue-twisting mouthful of translatese as in the case of multibranching English sentences with complex inclusion relations being clumsily rendered into Chinese. Right at this writing I have on hand an English sentence to be translated into Chinese, although it is not a typical example involving extreme difficulty in sentence structure. A pithy topical sentence highlighting a *Reader's Digest* familiar essay about the authoress's reluctance to sell an old family dinner table full of memories, it reads: "Parting with it means giving part of myself away." A straitjacketed rendition could be: "与它分别意味着交出我自己的一部分", which would appear opaque in meaning plus sounding unChinese. To give all the catchiness due a topical sentence, I decide to loosen the straitjacket a bit and allow myself greater latitude than is normally legitimate by a bold paraphrase: "物去如断肠". Under normal circumstances, however, I don't think a cramping straitjacket spells any great danger. In fact, translatese resulting from too tight a straitjacket, to my mind, grows less repugnant now that an increasing number of readers become bilingual or multilingual in a much shrunk world. Not only do mutual lexical borrowings abound; structural imitations also happen more frequently as in the now perfectly acceptable Chinese utterances "中国过去是,现在是,今后仍将是第三世界国家" (*à la* "China was, is, and will remain a Third World country") and "这事的重要性怎么强调也不过分" (*à la* "The importance of the matter cannot be overemphasized"). In a larger context of growing linguistic cosmopolitanism a right dose of translatese even makes for a stronger sense of like-mindedness in interlingual communication.

All in all, as a writer tackling "one of the most difficult tasks", the translator cannot afford to stop for one moment juggling a personality of his own and a straitjacket imposed on him. Nor can he stop tightroping between a challenging author and a demanding reader.

* * * *

To conclude, continual plodders boasting base authority from others' books have a rightful place on the high benches of scholars and writers. Only by accepting the role of the translator doubling as a scholar and a writer and living it to the full can we look forward to the day when a legion of talents will mushroom who can write well, translate well and theorize about translation with true cogency.

References

All Chinese references have been translated into English. Translations are mine.

Bassnett, S. 1980. *Translation Studies*. London: Methuen & Co. Ltd.

Belloc, H. 1931. *On Translation*. Oxford: Clarendon Press.

Chen, Fukang. 1992. *A Historical Survey of Translation Theories in China*.

Shanghai: Shanghai Foreign Languages Education Press.

Firth, J. R. 1968. Linguistic Analysis and Translation. In F. R. Palmer (ed.), *Selected Papers, 1952–1959*. Bloomington: Indiana University Press.

Fischbach, H. 1968. Translation in the U.S. *Babel 7*, pp. 119–124.

Guo, Moruo. 1921. Epilogue to Three Letters Discussing Translation. In Luo Xinzhang (ed.). *An Anthology of Treatises on Translation*. Beijing: Commercial Press, pp. 328–329.

Harris, B. 1977. *Papers in Translatology*. Ottawa: University of Ottawa Press.

Jin, Mei. 1993. *Biography of Fu Lei*. Changsha: Hunan Literature and Art Press.

Lu, Gusun. 1980. *A Contrastive Study of English and Chinese* (offprint). Shanghai: Fudan University Press.

Lu, Xun. 1913. Letters Discussing Translation. In Chen Fukang (ed.), op. cit., pp. 289–298.

Luo, Xinzhang. 1984. *An Anthology of Treatises on Translation*. Beijing: Commercial Press.

Ma, Zuyi. 1984. *A Brief History of Translation in China: Up to the May Fourth Movement*. Beijing: China External Translation and Publication Company.

McCrum, R. Cran W., MacNeil, R. 1986. *The Story of English*. New York: Viking.

Newmark, P. 1981. *Approaches to Translation*. Oxford: Pergamon Press Ltd.

Nida, E. 1975. *Language, Structure and Translation*. Stanford: Stanford University Press.

Qian, Zhongshu. 1985. On Lin Shu's Translation. In *Seven Patchup Essays*. Shanghai: Shanghai Classics Publishing House, pp. 67–101.

Quirk, R. 1974. *The Linguist and the English Language*. London: Edward Arnold.

Steiner, G. 1975. *After Babel: Aspects of Language and Translation*. London: Oxford University Press.

Zhang, Xinying. 1994. Ji Xianlin Is Worried Sick About Translators Beset with Crises, *Wenhui Daily*. June 13. 3.

(《弦歌集》,朱永生主编,复旦大学出版社,1998)

词典的继承与创新*

在辞书界，我被认为是一个传统派的经验主义者，这与我的如下三点疑虑可能不无关系：

第一，尽管许多人主张辞书学应成为一门独立学科，其理论也可以与语言学一样复杂深奥，我仍认为辞书编纂，就其本质而论，首先是一项实践性的工作。北美辞书学会会长 S. Landau 认为词典编纂者的成长"靠学徒式的方法"，"靠实习而学得这门技艺"。[1] 不论是在 Landau 的书中，还是在其他人的著述中，我时常碰到建立在辞书编纂实践之上的深刻而有趣的观点，这些观点与我这个一直致力于词典编纂的人的亲身感受相吻合，有"似曾相识"之感。我所读到的辞书理论给我的一个总的印象是常识性的东西居多。我这样说可能有些失于简单化了，但词典编纂者为了给自己的职业找出一套理论而力求向现代语言学靠拢的做法恐怕是"一厢情愿"。君不闻，有人说词典编纂乃是"无法赶上理论最新发展而成明日黄花的旧式语言学家的庇护所"[2]？

---

* 本文由于海江译自作者 1997 年 3 月在"第一届亚洲辞书学研讨会"上的英文主题发言，有删节。——原注。

① Landau, S. I. 1984. *Dictionaries. The Art and Craft of Lexicography*. New York: Charles Scribner's Sons, xii.

② Malkiel, Y. 1980. The Lexicographer as a Mediator between Linguistics and Society. In Zgusta, L. (ed.) *Theory and Method in Lexicography: Western and Non-Western Perspectives*. Columbia S C: Hornbeam Press, p. 54.

其次，究竟有多少辞书编纂者有阐发理论的想法和能力，也值得怀疑。理论所需要的是宏观的综合能力，而辞书编纂主要靠微观的分析能力。从性格、习惯和职业训练上讲，称职的词典编纂者是一群特殊类型的人：终年不停地辛勤劳作，或者埋头于堆积如山的资料卡片和手稿中，或者双目终日盯在计算机屏幕上；他们把注意力放在一个个单词、短语和单句上，而不怎么去关注篇章。James Murray 爵士的经验就证明了这种琐细的苦劳。据他本人讲，当他编写像 above 和 art 这样的词条时，资料卡摆满了书桌甚至地板——如他孙女所言，像“缠身在词网里”一样。[①] 我所认识的一些具有献身精神的词典大家也大都如此——只管词语，无暇旁顾。Robert Burchfield 博士就是其中一位。他 1979 年来沪时曾对我谈及他编纂《牛津英语词典·补编》的“秘密武器”——21×25（厘米）的资料卡片。他对辞书理论的贡献在我看来也不过是编选了一些专题文章，而并未去阐述自己的理论。[②] 兰登社已故的 Stuart Flexner 先生认为自己是词典编纂者而不是词典学家，对自己所做工作的学术性保持低调。复旦大学教授葛传椝先生生前曾长期从事词典编纂工作，常常讥刺一些热衷于理论的人是在炒作一些明明白白的常识性的东西。北美辞书学会的 T. Creamer 先生则相信“铁屁股”（意指词典编纂者必须有“坐功”）胜过其他任何精心炮制的理论。

我本人成为词典编纂者也纯属偶然而不是出于有意识的培养。“文革”时期，我受到冲击，我的思想被认定不适合教书育人，于是被罚去做苦差事——编纂《新英汉词典》。我可以说是还未学会游泳就被抛进了辞书编纂的海洋。我在几近溺水的情况中学会了游泳。虽然《新英汉词典》深深打上了“文革”的烙印，据上海译文出版社统

① Murray, E. 1977. *Caught in the Web of Words: James Murray and the Oxford English Dictionary*. New Haven: Yale University Press, pp. 203-204.

② Burchfield, R. 1987. *Studies in Lexicography*. Oxford: Clarendon Press.

计，迄今也已销售达900万册。80年代，当中国的政治气候好转之后，我被任命为《英汉大词典》主编，这部词典在90年代曾迭次获奖。在从《新英汉词典》到《英汉大词典》的二十余年辞书编纂实践中，我极少停笔思考辞书理论问题。我所注重的是我的编纂计划是否经过精心推敲，是否能够准确无误地按其规模、性质编写出来。

第三，从数据库到电子词典，辞书编纂同人类其他智能领域一样发生了巨变，这一点毋庸置疑。但我不认为明天的词典，无论是文本词典还是电子词典，会使传统意义上的辞书编纂完全消失。正如Zgusta所言："计算机将处理那些机械性的苦活，更抽象的工作它却帮不上忙。"[①] 计算机的作用是工具性的，影响及于方法，却不能改变实质。计算机的智能来自为它编制程序的人。但在目前为词典编纂编制软件，特别是为双语词典编制软件，是复杂而又昂贵的。通常词典编纂班子中需要两种不同才能的人：计算机专家（编程人员和打字员）和编纂者。他们之间的作用是互补的，但由于缺乏共同的志趣常常难以很好地合作。

从目前词典编纂和计算机技术所取得的成就来看，在语料库建设方面计算机的作用尤为突出。当年《英汉大词典》的资料卡片仅50万张，全部靠手工摘录。如今当我和我的同仁一起编写《英汉大词典·补编》之时，我们已经有了计算机，建立了计算机语料库。但我有时仍然会怀念从前没有计算机的年代。那时我们可以有选择地将有用的语言材料抄录下来，剔除一些不相关的冗余材料的干扰。眼和手虽然不能与扫描仪和打印机相比，但"湿件"（大脑）总是比硬件和软件更强大、更智慧。手工资料的优点在于精，而计算机语料库中可有可无的资料太多，很容易膨胀得无法驾驭。

显然，上面三个观点相加很可能成为一个保守主义者的宣言。

---

① Zgusta, L. (ed.) 1980. *Theory and Method in Lexicography: Western and Non-Western Perspectives.* Columbia: Hornbeam Press, p. 20.

但词典编纂本质上是传统的、保守的。事实上,从亚里士多德以来,语词定义的原则未曾有根本性的改变;英语词典在二百五十年的历史中变化甚微;近两千年前许慎在《说文解字》中使用的检字法,沿用至今。

词典编纂者在不同程度上都要依赖于前人的成果,这就给我们提出了一个问题:惯于沿袭传统的词典编纂者们,特别是双语词典的编纂者,在哪些方面能够有所创新呢?

首先,英汉双语词典编纂者需要依据某种英文蓝本或者是几种参考本,但为词目寻找恰如其分的、可望在汉语中存活下来的汉语对应词就是一项创造性很强的工作。如皮杂饼(pizza)、朋客(punk)、极可适(jacuzzi)、嬉蹦(hip-hop)等都可谓成功的创造。另外,搜集和选取第一手例句也是需要很高鉴别力的创造性工作。如在《英汉大词典》"a, an"条下就有"a pipe and pouch","a madonna and child","hire a car and driver","a hammer and sickle"等来自一手资料、令人耳目一新的例证。

我还想提出一条对于双语词典编纂者来说更富挑战性和创造性的工作:观察追踪外语中的新词、新义、新用法。这一点听起来似乎不合逻辑,但语言中的一些类似冰河运动的细微变化往往被身居其中的本族人所忽视,而外族人对这些变化却更为敏感。

我的"异族敏感论"形成于1978年。当时我与来访的Lancaster大学教授Geoffrey Leech谈到了几个英语新词语,其中之一就是"an albatross (a)round the neck"。这一用语当时出现频率很高,引起了我的注意,但当时各种词典均无收录。我猜测这个词语来源于Coleridge的诗作"古舟子咏",Leech教授证实了我的推测,并且说他本人也多次见到或听到这个词语,却从未从词典的角度来考虑它。

两年之后,当我在纽约与兰登社的Flexner先生初次相识时,我就一份问卷向他请教。其中有两个问题是:"为什么status的第一注

音是 /ˈsteɪtəs/，但美国人大多读作 /ˈstætəs/？为什么我致谢时餐馆服务员对我的回答是 Sure 而非 My pleasure 或 You're welcome 之类教科书上教授的用法，但在当时词典中却没有涉及这种用法？" Stuart Flexner 先生承认他对这些表达法已习以为常，从未从语音或惯用法的角度去作一番考虑。与此相类，当我被海外的汉语观察者问及汉语的新词时，我或者一无所知，或者突然意识到词典中该收却未收录。例如"嫂"字在汉语中已成为活跃的构词语素，像"空嫂"、"军嫂"、"警嫂"、"藏嫂"。但当 T. Creamer 先生问到我时，我才意识到这个字的广泛使用。

从《新英汉词典》到《英汉大词典》，二十多个春秋中我都在与词典打交道。如今我和同事们又开始了《英汉大词典补编》的编写工作。我们选择的是一条中间道路：一方面继承新词词典编纂的悠久传统；另一方面我们不仅补充《英汉大词典》在收词方面的缺漏，而且将勇于探索英语单语词典尚未涉足的领地。在我们的计算机语料库中，就有不少国外词典尚未收录的新词语，如 HOV（[乘客在三人以上的]多座车），emoticon（情感符，微笑符），sizism（肥胖歧视），shapism（体形歧视），Wimbledon neck（温布尔登脖颈症［因长时间观看网球赛不停转动脖颈而引起的颈部麻木酸痛等症状］），scholarly license（学者特许权），wallet x-ray（钱包透视）等。虽然在这一领域探索要冒风险，但我认为"异族敏感论"是值得尝试的。

（《辞书研究 1998 合订本》，鲍克怡、徐庆凯主编，
上海辞书出版社，1998）

附:

Traditionality and Creativity in Lexicography*

Introduction

I begin with a note of doubt. I doubt three things currently being discussed with gusto in lexicographic circles. The first of these is the claim that lexicography is a discipline comparable to linguistics. The second is that lexicographers in general are prepared and qualified to evolve lexicographical theories about their work. The third is that the use of computers can significantly change the nature of lexicography. Let me look at each of these doubts in turn.

1. A Discipline Comparable to Linguistics?

Firstly then, despite vociferous claims for lexicography as a full-fledged discipline with sophisticated theoretical abstrusities comparable to those in linguistics, I remain inclined to think of it as above all an empirical undertaking. Sidney Landau of Funk & Wagnalls (currently with Cambridge University Press, New York) put his finger on the crux of the matter when he referred to the making of a lexicographer "by the

* This paper was a plenary presentation at the Dictionaries in Asia Conference.

apprenticeship method" who "learned the craft by practicing it" (1984: xii). To be sure, in Landau's book, as elsewhere, I've occasionally come across thoughtful insights and interesting constructs based on lexicographic practice which call forth a feeling of *déjà vu* in me as a practising dictionary-maker. But at the risk of oversimplifying, I'd say the overall impression I receive from reading or reading about lexicographic theory — ranging from the ex-Soviet linguist L. V. Shcherba's "Opyt" (1995) of the mid-century to a more recent attempt at applying a deconstructionist approach of literary criticism to lexicography by William Frawley (1985) of the University of Delaware — is that it is basically synoptic, derivative, or little more than commonsensical.

Modern linguistics, admittedly the most fertile soil whereupon lexicographic theories shoot forth, is to all intents and purposes an exclusively scholarly endeavour of pride and prejudice when it comes to dictionary-making, which they look upon as "a haven for erstwhile philologists who have not gotten into line with the latest turn of the theoretical screw" (Malkiel 1980: 54). As a result, Richard Hudson of University College London has observed: "... linguists in some of the better-known schools ... haven't yet 'got their act together' on a number of questions which are of crucial concern to dictionary-makers", warning lexicographers thereby "against taking too seriously some very general claims of linguists that touch on their work" (1988: 287). Lexicographers, assiduity, therefore, in theorizing their *métier* in linguistic terms, I am afraid, is largely "love's labour's lost" and it is a typical case of unrequited love at that.

2. Lexicographical Theories?

Secondly, I wonder how many practising lexicographers, apart from a few exceptions one can count on one's two hands, are both prepared and qualified to evolve elaborate theories. Among other things, theory calls for macrocosmic synthesis while dictionary-making is essentially microcosmic and analytical. By temperament, habit and profession, lexicographers worth their salt are a special breed: drudging harmlessly for years on end either with their heads buried in a mountain of a citation file and manuscript or with their eyes riveted to the computer screen; attentive to lexical minutiae (or "lexemes" as they are called in shop talk) rather than keeping an eye on the larger picture of discourse beyond the sentence syntagmatically and pragmatically; preoccupied with keeping track of what actually happened and happens in language instead of delving into why and how language behaves in a certain way. Sir James Murray attested to this kind of microcosmic drudgery, according to his grand-daughter Elizabeth Murray's account (1977: 203–204), when he recounted his experience of editing for the monumental *Oxford English Dictionary* such individual words as "above" and "art" with quotation slips spread on a table or even on the floor — "caught in the web of words", so to speak.

Many are such dedicated wordsmiths I personally know who are too preoccupied with words to care about anything else. Dr Robert Burchfield, for one, told me during his visit to Shanghai in 1979 that the "one secret weapon" he had when working on the Supplement to the OED was his 10 × 14 in. citation card and when he dabbled in lexicographic theory (Burchfield, 1987), his contribution, as I see it, was largely secondhand in that he selected and edited monographs rather than set out to expound a theory of his own. The late Stuart Flexner of Random House, with whom I shared many interests, identified himself not as a lexicographer but as a dictionary-maker, downplaying whatever amount of scholarliness there was to his work. The late professor emeritus of English at Fudan University in Shanghai, Ge Chuangui, my mentor and co-worker (who had in the early 1940s convinced Henry Watson Fowler of his inaccuracies and omissions in *The Concicse Oxford Dictionary*, 1911, and who compiled or co-compiled a series of English-Chinese usage and general dictionaries①) used to scoff at "theoretical buffs" for belabouring the obvious and fussing about commonsense. Thomas Creamer of the Dictionary Society of North America, a long-standing friend of mine since the late 1970s who is present at this conference, believes, if I am not misrepresenting him, in "iron buttism" (a literal translation of the Chinese "*tie pi gu*", meaning dictionary-makers must stay put in their work seats with admirable fortitude), more than in any quaint theoretical propositions.

I myself became a dictionary-maker not by purposeful upbringing but by sheer accident. It happened in 1970 during China's Cultural Revolution when I was stigmatized, judged ideologically unfit for teaching, and assigned the punitive busywork of compiling *A New English-Chinese Dictionary* (NEC), on the assumption that, in dealing with words instead of with live persons who were my students, my presumably unorthodox thinking would play less havoc. I was thus plunged into the sea of lexicography without having been first taught

① Among Professor Ge's major lexicographic achievements are *A Dictionary of English Usage* (1942). *A Revised Dictionary of English Usage* (1958), and *A New English-Chinese Dictionary* (with others) (1975).

how to swim. Sure enough, I was all but drowned and had to learn swimming little by little — the hard way.

Though heavily and at times absurdly politicized, NEC turned out to be a remarkable success①, supposedly for want of a better handy English-Chinese reference book in the market. In the mid-1980s when the political climate had considerably cleared up in China, I was nominated editor-in-chief of *The English-Chinese Dictionary* (*Unabridged*) (ECU), which was to win a row of book awards in the 1990s. In the twenty-odd years of my lexicographic career from NEC to ECU I seldom if ever paused to think, for instance, what "circular definition" meant, although I did it all the time. Nor did I care if one lexicographic taxonomic theory was superior to another, so long as my own works were thoughtfully mapped out and executed in terms of size, perspective, focus and presentation. Interestingly, it fell on some of my colleagues who had practically no or very little lexicographic experience to write up a theory for both NEC and ECU②.

3. The Use of Computers

Thirdly, granting that the computer is creating a sea change in lexicography, as well as in other fields of human endeavour (not only by expanding and aligning corpora but also by possibly making dictionaries interactive or, in Atkins' terms, "customized" [1996: 531]), I doubt if the dictionary of tomorrow — be it a virtually real

① NEC has since 1975 sold an accumulative total of over nine million copies on the Chinese mainland according to the in-house 1996 statistical release of its publisher, Shanghai Yiwen Publishing House.

② See, for instance, Chen Bingtiao.

dictionary or held in hypertext — can be so revolutionary as to render altogether obsolete such an inherently slow-to-change business as dictionary-making in the traditional sense. As Ladislav Zgusta has remarked, "The computer will take care of much of the mechanical drudgery, while being unable to help with more abstract work." (1980: 20) Yes, the computer is ultimately instrumental, affecting primarily the hows rather than the whats. The computer is smart only when people who programme it are smart. But, as matters stand, it is commonly accepted, and keenly felt too, that programming for lexicographic purposes and for bilingually lexicographic purposes in particular is horrendously costly and complex, what with a myriad of coding and identifying tasks performed electronically with regard to both format and form.

Moreover, a typical major dictionary outfit today usually consists of two kinds of talent: computer experts (programmers, analysts, and keyboarders) and editors who are complementary but do not always achieve a two-in-one harmony for lack of "a common denominator". It's often the case for editors to explain lexicographic subtleties and dictate to computer experts what they expect each and every program to do, while computer experts try their best to translate editorial dictates into operations. In my own experience, different backgrounds, interests, and focuses do not make for optimal computer performance satisfactory to both sides. Unless and until these two kinds of expertise could fuse comfortably in one person to eventually bring about a new breed of "cyberlexicographers" or "lexicographic computerniks", major breakthroughs in on-line lexicography would remain a futuristic far cry. Considering state-of-the-art achievements in both lexicography and computer technology, it is a truism to say real revolution *has* taken place in the development of a citation file, which I call the infrastructure of a dictionary. Mine for ECU was a pathetically meagre half million cards, all manually done. Today, when my colleagues and I work on a supplement to ECU, we are blessed with computer facilities, rejoicing in the manifold and obvious advantages of an electronic citation file. But funnily enough, there are atavistic moments in which I miss the precomputer ECU days when I took down by hand only those language facts I deemed pertinent and useful instead of being confused by a surfeit of redundancies and irrelevancies. Human eyes and hands are assuredly no match for the optical scanner and the printer, but the "wetware" (the human mind) is always more selective, more cogent and, all in all, smarter than any software. All weaknesses apart, a manual citation file is to the point and lean; all strengths apart, a computerized citation file involves too much that is extraneous and can easily become unmanageable.

4. Occasions for Creativity

I am fully aware that the three doubts expressed above may well amount to a traditionalist manifesto — the manifesto of a lexicographic conservative. But then, both the dictionary and its making are by and large traditional and conservative by nature, especially when they are compared with textbooks, grammars, pedagogic methodology, and linguistic canons. One easily observes that: (1) there has been little deviation in definitional principle since Aristotle (see Frawley 1988: 189); (2) there has been little evolution, not to say radical revolution, in the 250 years of English lexicography (see Bailey 1986: 124); and

(3) there has been little change in Chinese lexicography in terms of an ingenious system of radicalizing pictographic Chinese characters first devised by Xu Shen in *Shuowen Jiezi* ("Defining Characters and Analyzing Their Shapes") in 100 A.D. A time-honoured tradition of lexicography, on the other hand, is reinforced by institutionalized need-based user behaviour which presupposes a dual function of reception and production of a dictionary. The fact that any dictionary, however synchronic it is meant or professed to be, invariably involves the diachronic, and the fact that all dictionary-makers are indeed "a succession of plagiarists", as Frederic Dolezal of the University of South Mississippi calls them (1989: 168), relying to varying degrees on predecessors, combine to underpin an edifice of tradition that is lexicography.

A question then logically arises: Is there any chance for lexicographers, moving more or less on a beaten track, to tread a new path, instead of always following the old footprints? To put it more narrowly: For those of us who go in for bilingual lexicography with English, a foreign language, as the source language, is there any role to play other than that of a copycat or a parrot or a "plagiarist"? Can we aspire to some measure of creativity in our work? Granted that bilingual lexicographers have to have a model in monolingual dictionaries in the source language or, more preferably, an eclectic blending of several models, room for creative work remains ample. Among other things, finding pithy, exact and comfortable equivalents that will hopefully stick in the target language for culturally exotic entry words in the source language rather than supplying a lengthy paraphrase, calls for an extremely strenuous and dexterous effort on the part of a lexicographer as translator.

For instance, I was quite elated when I came up with a Chinese equivalent, my own coinage, *pi za bing* for "pizza" and entered it in ECU, thinking it was vastly superior to the version *bi sa bing* already in vogue in the Chinese lexicon of loan words. *Pi za* in Chinese is phonetically closer to "pizza" and more descriptive of the crust covered with miscellaneous ingredients of the food, while *pi sa*, being a long-standing transliteration of the Italian city Pisa, is likely to give rise to the misconception that the food is somehow associated with the leaning tower. My preference for *pi za*, however, was and is not shared by the pizza huts in Shanghai who have continued to call themselves *bi sa wu*.

Moreover, Yu Haijiang, a PhD candidate I supervise who is also present at this conference, observed recently (1997) that *pi za* is prescriptive and *bi sa* descriptive, and that in the present age of descriptivism a prescribed term, even though it is one with enough presumed rationale and to spare, doesn't begin to compete with a recognized term enjoying widespread currency. Although I concede a point to him in this argument — in fact, I can contribute more examples on his behalf to illustrate the force of habit with which mistranslations in the first place have persisted, e.g. Fleet Street in London with Fleet as the name of a creek having nothing to do with a naval fleet but translated into Chinese as *jian dui jie* — I nevertheless delight in the creative triumph of coining, by partly transliterating and partly translating, a row of exotica, such as *peng ke* for "punk", *ji ke shi* for "Jacuzzi", *xi beng* for "hip-hop".

For authenticity, bilingual lexicographers, as a rule, rely on monolingual dictionaries in the source language for illustrative examples. The ECU has raised quite a few disapproving eyebrows by quoting liberally — some verbatim — illustrative examples from a host of monolingual English dictionaries which it doesn't forget to acknowledge in its prefatory matter. A Hong Kong *Ming Pao Daily News* columnist Gu Deming pinpointed some of these examples and rancorously identified the ECU as a typical case of "Commie outlawry". But a closer scrutiny would also reveal a number of firsthand examples in the ECU, roughly one tenth of the total, such as "a pipe and pouch", "a madonna and child", "hire a car and driver", and "a hammer and sickle", alongside the more conventional and secondhand "a cup and saucer" in the entry "a, an". Albeit to a lesser degree, being firsthand in culling examples involves a discriminative eye and a creative effort on the part of a bilingual lexicographer.

Translation of illustrative examples is a speial kind of translation, with the translator having to move in a thicket of contextlessness, straitjacketed, as it were. Often, clipped examples are nonspecific, admitting of more than one interpretation, challenging the translator to figure out what is unsaid from what is said by a creative stretch of the imagination. By my own experience, such ambiguous examples occur aplenty in the entries of functional words. A very simple sentence "That's about it", for instance, under "about", or "Henry didn't run home" (see Frawley 1988: 191) under "not", can respectively mean different things if contextualized differently. For the former, wordings of translation must vary when it is used either, say, toward the end of a letter when the writer feels he/she has mentioned nearly everything and is about to sign off, or as a response to an invited guess which is close enough; for the latter, meaning varies with the ambulant focus of negation expressed by "not" with the result that three renditions in Chinese are both possible and probable: (1) *pao zhe hui jia de bu shi Hengli*; (2) *Hengli bing wei pao zhe hui jia*; and (3) *Hengli pao zhe bu shi hui jia qu*.

In addition, how to juggle succinctness in translation on the one hand (dictated by such lexicographic constraints as maximum information in minimum space) and readability on the other, taxes to capacity a lexicographer's creative potential. A William Faulkner quote "His determination to have my company bordered on violence" in the entry "border" as a verb in the ECU (with the translation *ta ying yao wo pei zhe ta cha bu duo yao dong wu le* in Chinese) may offer a convincing example of overall equivalence and good readability with a suspicion of overtranslation (fourteen Chinese characters for nine English words). Fortunately, though, translation of illustrative examples in the ECU has received little if any critical fire. In fact, such distinguished men of letters as Cai Siguo and Dong Qiao have written kindly, also in *Ming Pao Daily News*, about the ECU in terms of translation.

But most of all, I would make bold to suggest, creative work on the part of a bilingual lexicographer is to be carried out in connection with watching and detecting neologisms in the source language. Skeptics would counter by asking: "Wouldn't it be more logical for native speakers to watch and detect, close-up, their own neologisms, while bilingual lexicographers as non-native speakers mind their own business?" Allowing for their apparent powerful logic, one must not lose sight of the infinitesimal and glacial changes in a language that serve as a backdrop for neologisms which native speakers, living amidst them, more often than not take for granted. A Chinese saying about chess games embodies a paradoxical wisdom: "Those who play can get lost in the midst of the game whilst an onlooker often sees the most of the game." This onlooker awareness, if you like, is analogous to the "alien sensitivity" I argue for.

5. Alien Sensitivity

I first formulated my theory about "alien sensitivity" in 1978, when I discussed a number of neologisms with the visiting Professor Geoffrey Leech of the University of Lancaster, among which was a lately voguish allusive phrase, "an albatross (a)round one's neck". As a regular word watcher, I had been alerted to a high frequency of occurrence of the phrase and was dismayed by the fact that it had been conspicuously absent from any phrase or quotation dictionary available at the moment. Professor Leech, confirming my speculation that the phrase might be an allusion to Coleridge's *The Rime of the Ancient Mariner*, observed that he himself saw or heard the phrase a lot but hadn't got round to examining it from a lexicographic point of view.

Two years later, in 1981, when I was introduced to the late Mr. Flexner of Random House in New York, I asked him for enlightenment on a questionnaire I had with me. Among the questions were: "Why is 'status' phonetically transcribed /ˈsteɪtəs/ as first choice while in actual American English I keep hearing people say /ˈstætəs/?" and "Why do restaurant waitresses respond to my thanks with a 'Sure' while no dictionary makes a mention of the usage?" Mr. Flexner admitted to the effect that he and "those he heard talking"[①] had lived

① See his *I Hear America Talking*, published in 1976 by Van Nostrand Reinhold Company, New York.

with such usages long, but few had paused to ponder over them phonetically or in terms of idiomaticity. Similarly, but on the other side of the coin, when I am approached for tips on Chinese neologisms by regular watchers of Chinese abroad, I either draw a blank or am suddenly made aware of the lexicographic failure to report them. The word *sao* (literally "elder sister-in-law"), for instance, is becoming a highly active combining form in present-day mainland Chinese usage, as is found in such compounds as *kong sao* (a laid-off woman in her thirties or forties retrained to assume the job of an air hostess), *jun sao* (wife of an armed forces man, living away from barracks on her own), *jing sao* (wife of a policeman who is away from home on duty a lot), and *zang sao* (wife of a city person sent to work in faraway Tibet leaving her behind). The extended application and quick proliferation of this word were first brought to my notice by queries from Thomas Creamer (above), who, watching the Chinese language from across the Pacific, was apparently more sensitive to it than I was. This is what "alien sensitivity" is all about.

Language is inexhaustible and a-changing; dictionaries are never complete or up-to-date in the true sense of the word. Working intensively on a supplement to the ECU, a glossary of 3,000 new words, new meanings and new usages (with a few occasional hitherto untranscribed pronunciations[1] thrown in), my colleagues and I opt for a middle-of-the-roadism between traditionality and creativity. On the one hand, we stick to the "new word" tradition, an old tradition recently strengthened and enriched by, say, the Barnhart dictionaries of new English of 1963

① e.g. *endurance*, normally transcribed as /ɪnˈdjuərəns/, is heard pronounced /ˈendjuərəns/ on CNN and on a number of American TV tire commercials.

and 1980, and several slim Merriam-Websters since 1976 as supplements to *Webster's Third*. On the other hand, we aim not only at making up for the deficiencies and omissions of the ECU, but also at venturing into ground as yet untrodden by monolingual English lexicographers, trying to be creative with our sharpened "alien sensitivity" to the extent that we do not overstep the bounds of the lexicographic norm.

Among the entries we are editing on the basis of a sizable computerized citation file are those that are, as far as our available reference resources are concerned, not verifiable in monolingual English dictionaries compiled by native speakers — such as *HOV* (for *high occupancy vehicles* as a road traffic sign), *emoticon* (emotive+ icon), *sizism* or *shapism*, *à la sexism* and *ageism*, *Wimbledon neck* (a sore neck from turning from right to left non-stop when watching a tennis match), *boot camp* (a correctional facility for juvenile offenders), *scholarly license* (by which scholars break the society dress code and go casual on formal occasions), and *wallet X-ray* (as verb or noun in the sense of finding out a patient's solvency before admitting him/her to hospital). There is thin ice, to be sure, on this untrodden ground and we stand an equal chance of reward and penalty in our venture. But at any rate our alien sensitivity is worth trying out if only to prove the two constantly warring but essentially complementary factors in the making of a lexicographer: traditionality and creativity.

References*

Atkins, B. T. S. 1996. Bilingual Dictionaries: Past, Present and Future. In

* References in Chinese have been translated into English.

Gellerstam M. et al. (eds.) *Euralex '96 Proceedings* Ⅰ-Ⅱ. Göteborg: Göteborg University, pp. 515-546.

Bailey, R. 1986. Dictionaries of the Next Century. In Ilson R. F. (ed.), *Lexicography: An Emerging International Profession*. Manchester: Manchester University Press, pp. 123-137.

Burchfield, R. 1987. *Studies in Lexicography*. Oxford: Clarendon Press.

Chen, B. 1991. *An Introduction to Lexicography*. Shanghai: Fudan University Press.

Dolezal, F. 1989. Introduction: The Bibliography of Words and Notions. *International Journal of Lexicography*, 2.3: 167-195.

Frawley, W. 1985. Intertexuality and the Dictionary: Toward a Deconstructionist Account of Lexicography. *Dictionaries: Journal of the Dictionary Society of North America*, 7: 1-20.

Frawley, W. 1988. New Forms of Specialized Dictionaries. *International Journal of Lexicography*, 1.3: 189-213.

Hudson, R. 1988. The Linguistic Foundations for Lexical Research and Dictionary Design. *International Journal of Lexicography*, 1.4: 287-312.

Landau, S. I. 1984. *Dictionaries: The Art and Craft of Lexicography*. New York: Charles Scribner's Sons.

Malkiel, Y. 1980. The Lexicographer as a Mediator Between Linguistics and Society. In Zgusta L. (ed.), pp. 43-58.

Murray, E. 1977. *Caught in the Web of Words: James Murray and the Oxford English Dictionary*. New Haven: Yale University Press.

Shcherba, L. V. 1995. Opyt or Toward a General Theory of Lexicography (tr.). *International Journal of Lexicography*, 8.4: 314-350.

Yu. H. 1997. Flamboyance Reduced to Simplicity: A Comment on *The English-Chinese Dictionary* (*Unabridged*). *Fudan Journal* (*Social Sciences Edition*). Shanghai: Fudan University Press. 11: 99-103.

Zgusta, L. (ed.) 1980. *Theory and Method in Lexicography: Western and Non-Western Perspectives*. Columbia: Hornbeam Press.

[*Lexicography in Asia*, Tom McArthur & Ilan Kernerman (eds.), Password Publishers Ltd, 1998]

两部词典两重天

造化弄人。“文革”期间，我被判定为“白专”，不宜从事自己比较感兴趣的外国文学研究，不宜“与人（指学生）打交道”，因而给罚下讲台，专门去“跟字打交道”，去做一件完全陌生的工作，从此阴差阳错地走上英汉词典编写的轨道。从1970年到1991年，我先后参加或主持了《新英汉词典》和《英汉大词典》的编纂，历时二十年有奇。

恰恰是在这二十年当中，以真理标准的讨论和中共十一届三中全会为转折点，国家经历了从“文革”到改革开放的历史性巨变。词典是工具书。与其他文科课题相比，词典编写是个技术性较强的领域，双语词典编写尤其如此。但就在这看似远离意识形态纷争的一隅，我们对这场历史性巨变的认识同样痛切而深刻。从“文革”时期的《新英汉词典》到改革开放时期的《英汉大词典》，可以说是两部词典两重天。

允我从头道来。

我是1970年5月从“一打三反抗大式学习班”（变相隔离审查）直接发配去参加《新英汉词典》编写的。那正是文化专制主义横行的年代，在工宣队领导的词典编写组里出现了许多今天看来是违反常识的“荒诞派”一类事情。譬如说，编词典要以“大批判”开路，于是远至《牛津》、《韦氏》，近到“文革”前出版的英汉词典，都要用“照妖镜”检视一番，把“We need a Lincoln”（我们需要一个林肯式人物）之类的所谓“毒素”像剔核桃肉似地深挖出来。我师葛传椝先生因在英汉词典编写方面颇多建树，就被作为“反动学术权威”的活靶子批判再三。葛是个向来不问政治的“字迷”先生，实在没有多少把柄留给批判者，那就抓住他在英汉词典的例句中最好用“Henry”、“Beth”等英语人名而不用“老张”、“小王”等的主张，把所谓“洋奴哲学”狠批一通。我的另一位老师林同济先生从《毛选》英译本中摘录了一个英汉等值佳译的词组“seething popular discontent”（民怨沸腾），当即被火眼金睛们认为“心怀叵测”而拍桌打凳声讨一番。谁做到“sleep around”（中文意思“找异性滥交”）之类的词条，谁必倒霉，因为把此种词义形诸字面，乃是“黄色阴暗心理大暴露”。所谓的“全面专政”除了导致泛政治和泛意识形态化，还必然戕害实事求是的原则，戕害词典的科学性。Confucius 是“孔夫子”的音译，但当时“批林批孔”正酣，岂可再尊孔丘为夫子？任你把道理说得唇焦舌敝，领导照样明令写上“孔老二”，与之形成驴唇马嘴的“对应”。Pekingese 由词源决定，既作“北京人”又作“狮子狗”解。但堂堂伟大首都的人岂可与小狗为伍？于是，非得人为地分列 Pekingese[1] 和 Pekingese[2] 不可。不破不立。“大批判”是破，破了以后立什么呢？一些激进派甚至提出英汉词典应当把以字母顺序列条的传统编排和检索法兜底推翻，代之以两份“红”与“黑”对立的词汇表。更有甚者，毛泽东思想工人宣传队把全体编写人员集合在一起，夜以继日地“研讨”全部例证应当容纳多少条毛泽东语录，应当如何宣传“样板戏”、“赤脚医生”、“五七干校”、“上山下乡”等所谓新生事物，应当如何保持批判苏修、美帝的大致相同比例。记得当时流行的豪言壮语中有一句“一不怕苦，二不怕死”（“Fear neither hardships nor death”），往哪个词目放，真是难煞编写人员。放“fear”（怕）条吧，说的明明是“不怕”；放在“neither ... nor ...”（既不……又不……）下面吧，一个虚词词组又何能显出伟大世界观的熠熠光辉……至于早请示、晚汇报、斗私批修、民兵操、深挖洞(参加挖防空洞劳动)、下干校、野营拉练之类的仪式和功课,编写人员更是一点不能疏忽,战战兢兢唯恐不逮。但是,另一方面,知识分子们总要顽强表现自己,又很善于钻工宣队领导不识英文的空子,所以就千方百计找来各种英文书刊,有的还以无偿的业余翻译劳动去换取借书和读书之便,从阅读材料中贪婪地吮吸语言营养,勤奋地挖掘语言信息,“走私”似地把这些东西纳入词典,“曲线”救书。我和其他几个屡教不改的“走私犯”常被詈骂,经手的校样因为添加内容分用红、蓝、绿笔勾划,被斥之为“打翻墨水瓶”,因而被遣往印刷厂端搬字盘,体验排字改样的艰辛,兼作惩罚。

实践是检验真理的唯一标准。1975 年,《新英汉词典》出版。国外旋有评论说,词典像是一篇“文革的政策声明”;国内也有读者在翌年“四人帮”倒台后投书高层,控告编者传播极“左”毒素,要求追究政治责任。另一方面,“曲线”救书也有成效,《纽约时报》发现《新英汉词典》收了大量英语国家政治、外交、经济、军事、文化、科技领域内的新词,就连一些四个字母的粗俗词也未忽略,由此认定“在中国观察美国的人就像在美国观察中国的人一样,正密切注视着对象国”。撇开“文革”烙印不说(1983 年对《新英汉词典》动过一次“整容”手术,把大部分有烙印的例证剔除,补以字数间距大致相仿的新例,另附 4 000 余条新词、新义、新用法的补编),读者发现《新英汉词典》还是一部有用的工具书,特别是在改革开放之初的“英语热”中连年畅销,迭次获奖,迄今累计印数已逾 900 万册。

我是在继《新英汉词典》之后的《英汉大词典》编写组内经历“四人帮”覆灭、真理标准讨论、“凡是派”下台、十一届三中全会召开等重大历史事件的。如果说《新英汉词典》的编写过程充斥了“文革”政治,充斥了无知、偏执、轻率和荒诞,编写人员在苦涩和无奈之余只能消极抵抗、“曲线”救书的话,《英汉大词典》则是真正遵循实事求是的原则,按照工具书编纂的客观规律,在建国以来最自由、最开放、最祥和的学术气氛中,由一批深感身心解放来之不易的知识分子勠力编成的。我所说的两部词典两重天也就是这个意思。

编写人员不再是全面专政的对象,而是工人阶级的一部分,不必再偷偷摸摸搞“走私”,而是可以理直气壮又心情舒畅地充分施展自己的聪明才智,正是这种从对立面转化为自己人的主人翁意识,使他们定下独立研编(而不是从一部或几部英文词典译编)《英汉大词典》的方针,定下超过相同规模的英俄、英日和海外出版的英汉词典的目标。《英汉大词典》包含约十分之一自行搜集而未见于英美原文词典的例证;《英汉大词典》详释详解一般英美原文词典相对从简处理的功能词词条;《英汉大词典》兼顾历史和现状、语词内容和百科内容、共核域和各种语用域;《英汉大词典》出版后即被联合国翻译处推荐使用,并被英国《牛津英语大词典补稿》主编 R.伯契菲尔德博士称为“远东最好也是全世界较好的一种双语词典”——所有这些事实说明编写人员的目标至少已部分达到。

泛政治和泛意识形态的干扰被排除之后,编写人员才得以奉行国际辞书界客观描述、如实记录的通行做法,在实用性、学术性、信息性之上保证词典内容的稳定性,而不必在书成之后因时势人事的变化忙着挖补修订甚至“整容”。词典内容的稳定性实为工具书科学性的一个指标,《英汉大词典》中对一些历史事件和人名条目,如朝鲜战争、红卫兵或赤卫队、斯大林、杜勒斯、叶利钦等的释文证明是站得住脚的;一篇既高屋建瓴又实话实说的前言,在港台分出繁体字本时可以不改一字而为海外华人一致激赏。

在英汉词典里,英语是来源语或译出语,汉语是目的语或译入语,因而在当年的《新英汉词典》中收录的诸如“喜儿打了黄世仁一记耳光”和“半夜鸡叫说明地主的贪婪”之类例句以及大量如井冈山之类汉语拼音的专名词条,不但毫无必要,更是错把英汉当汉英,违反了双语词典的本质规律。《英汉大词典》坚决摒弃了“为工农兵所喜闻乐见”等似是而非的“文革”功利政治，坚持“解必有据”，一应例证全部采自英语本土环境中的真实英语资料，引用需经删改时必须由以英语为母语的专家认可，从而对《新英汉词典》的“中国式英文”来了个拨乱反正，正本清源，为改革开放新形势下学习和使用英语的读者提供了背景真实、语言地道的英语资讯。编写《新英汉词典》时还有一个貌似堂皇而实则荒唐的口号，叫做“以我为主”，即要把据认为是先进的中国科技成就往外宣传。于是，又误把英汉作汉英，不但有“针刺麻醉”，更有“万吨远洋轮”、“人工合成胰岛素”等误作固定复合词的自由合成词组，违反了收词立条原则。《英汉大词典》采取开放态势，重在“知彼”，从外部世界摄取了数以万计的科技新理论、新发现、新工艺、新材料、新产品的专名术语，分请各科专家考究译名或释文，不但为读者释疑解惑，帮助开阔视界，对术语标准化也大有裨益。

新时期的新领导，从校到市，放手委托主编和编委会负责《英汉大词典》的编写工作，同时力荐将《英汉大词典》列入国家哲学社会科学“七五”规划的重点课题，引导传媒关心十数年如一日埋首蝇头小字的词典编写人员，并在经费拨放、人员抽调、后勤保障、编写出版排印三个环节的协调诸方面做了大量创造性的工作。尤其是电脑照排的决策，说明领导不但懂行，更具魄力和前瞻性，为《英汉大词典》从简体到繁体的转换以及后续派生作品的生产作好了技术准备。《英汉大词典》编写之初曾荟萃了沪上和外地的百余名专家学者，后出于种种原因逐渐流失，但一个 20 人左右来自不同高校和出版社的骨干班子始终未散，并共享各单位的图书资料和咨询信息资源。要是没有上海市委宣传部的多方协调和切实保障，这种社会主义大协作是很难想象的。

《英汉大词典》出书迄今已获“中国图书一等奖”、“上海市哲学社会科学优秀著作特等奖”等多个奖项。但以日益深化的改革开放形势的要求衡量,以语言学、词典编纂学、计算机科学新发展的学术和技术标准衡量,以广大读者多方面的需要衡量,这部书还有许多缺陷,已发现的错误比设计时预定的每50页出一错的容许比率要高,只能算是"比较有用,基本成功"。复旦外文系自老一辈专家葛传槼先生始,就有一个比较悠远的双语词典编写的传统,乐于此道的同仁不少,近年又招了以双语词典编纂为培养方向的博士、硕士研究生,形成一股新锐少壮力量。有了十一届三中全会以来的正确路线和宽松的学术环境,有了从《新英汉词典》到《英汉大词典》的经验和教训,有了传承和创新的双重势头,我们正在从事的《英汉大词典补编》工作进展顺利,为此而建立的电脑语库不但是英汉词典编写的基本建设,更可为教学和科研提供多功能服务。拟议中的《大中华汉英词典》兼收并蓄,收录大陆、香港特别行政区、台湾和海外华人社区的通用词语,解剖阐释汉字字形,可望突破现有汉英词典的窠臼,现正与美国一汉英语料库商谈合作事宜。这几项工程无疑将进一步促进复旦外文系的学科建设,使教学和科研更直接为改革开放和现代化事业服务。

在这篇文章行将收尾的时候,我想提到一个始终萦回脑际的疑问:为什么实事求是这样一个基本原则会多年横遭践踏?从大端言,使国家和民族在极"左"时期付出如此惨重的代价;从小处说,使英汉词典编写走过如此曲折的弯路。这难道也是树欲静而风不止的历史必然?给上述问题找到一个确切的答案,以史为鉴,保证实事求是的原则不再遭到践踏,也许这才是对真理标准讨论和十一届三中全会20周年最好的纪念。

(《与历史同行——复旦大学哲学社会科学研究的回顾与展望(1978—1998)》,施岳群、周斌主编,复旦大学出版社,1998)

进二言

——写在《译林》出版百期之际

《译林》出满一百期了，主事者邀约写篇短文，本想拼凑几句“米汤大全”式文字应景交差。落笔前打开李景端同志赠我的《波涛上的足迹》一书翻翻，李详写了《译林》初创时的酸甜苦辣，倒也勾起了我的一些感慨，于是决定还是写几句寄托腹心的实话。

拟向《译林》进二言。其一叫做保持本色。这儿所说的本色自然不是指刊物的外观和内质——此两者迭经改良优化，早非当日可比；我指的是“译林人”在刊物草创时期那种不为困而改节的凌霜志气。记得是在1978或1979年，经学生倪俊介绍，初识《译林》编辑金丽文女士，复由金引见拜识李景端。《译林》当时处境困难，庄子所谓的“人之生也，与忧俱生”用在这本新生刊物上尤为剀切，如果说“围剿”属用字太过，那么说被人封杀则是完全合乎实情的。我就曾亲耳听到有人以不屑的口吻谈到《译林》，说是搞外国文学翻译，北有××，南有××，市场两分，天下早已底定，其他外省出版社想要打破这格局，还是“识相一点”为好。呜呼！我这人浑身上下都是缺点，自问只有同情弱势群体的平民意识还算个优点——当然在某些人看来可能正是更大的缺点。不管怎么说，恰恰就在《译林》面临困难的当儿，我成了《译林》的译者、读者和友人。

毕竟时代不同了，当年上海的旧《译林》于1940年5月创刊，仅见两期便无疾而终；今天，江苏的新《译林》不但站稳了脚跟，而且飚尘疾进二十多年，与兄弟刊物已成鼎立之势，而从近年来出书的种类、质量和速度看，我和不少书友都感到译林出版社正大有后来居上之势。人一变阔，或者一种刊物被供入庙堂，最难保持本色，守其初心。看来继续保持当年创业时的理想主义和道德激情，不做“超级大国”，不追求话语霸权，这才是真正涅而不缁的《译林》！

进言之二与翻译评论甚至学术民主有关。记得那年《译林》搞翻译竞赛，用的原文是美国作家John Updike的短篇小说《儿子》。原作在写到父母龃龉不断，甚至端着咖啡杯在客厅奔逐追打时，有这样一个句子：“It is the mother whose tongue is sharp, who sometimes strikes.”在《译林》的专家委员会（记得由编委会扩大组成，内中包括一位华籍英人）提供的标准译文中，这句话被译作：“做母亲的说话尖刻，有时还出口伤人。”按我的理解，whose与who两个从句并置叠加，有明显的语气递进关系，也就是说“说话尖刻”应是常态，sometimes才有超乎口舌之争常态的暴烈举动；再者，英文中要表示口舌伤人的意思，一般似更可能用上sting, lashout, bite之类的动词，而不大会用strike。据此，并且考虑到上文奔逐追打的情节，我提议把“有时还出口伤人”这半句改译为“有时还动手打人”。可是那专家委员会却讲究定于一尊，因此我呼吁了半天，只换来某老前辈“hair-splitting”的呵责。所谓“hair-splitting”者，是把细细的发丝再去剖分，显然是不足取的，但若是以“hair-splitting”表示翻译时必须对原文作穷原竟委的推敲和钻研，我以为不但不应诘责，反应提倡。关于上例究竟是“出口伤人”还是“动手打人”，我求教过多位高明，直到今天也没有定论，由此我悟到英文里单词个个识得而对整句“能指”多有歧解的情形常有发生，一个人的学养和识见总是有限，因而要否定一种可能的译法确宜慎重再慎重。（Never is a long word!）今天，

《译林》适换上第二届编委,又正好举行另一轮翻译竞赛,特将旧日公案重提一遍,警策自己,并与编委会诸公共勉,相信不会是完全多余的。

(原载 2001 年 12 月 25 日《光明日报》)

Foreword to *From Poem to Poem: An English Translation of Classical Chinese Poems*

Robert Frost said, "Poetry is what gets lost in translation." Not necessarily: that thousands upon thousands of poems get translated back and forth in the world is evidence enough to the contrary. And if you, dear Reader, take a look at the poems translated in this book, you'll find the meaning conveyed faithfully, cultural milieu kept intact, and the poetic ethos enriched. Little, if anything, is lost.

Nevertheless, nobody has dwelt with greater cogency upon the enormous difficulty involved in poetry translation than Frost in the above-quoted remark. As I see it, translation of poetry requires that the translator has the makings of a poet in him or her. He/She absorbs the source poems with innate poetic sensibilities until they become part of his/her aesthetic being. The empathy is such that the absorbed poems stir, agitate, even haunt him/her, making the utterance of them an absolute must as Jin Shengtan (a literary critic of the Ming Dynasty) said. By now the translator has to turn to be a poet in the target language in his/her own right, relying on an abundance of prior poetic experience in it. A songster, as it were, cannot enjoy a minute of peace of mind unless the song is sung. Poetry translation worth its salt invariably involves such a receptive-productive process.

Professor Ren Zhiji or Charles Jen as he is known in the US, an old friend of mine since the 1960s, from whom I've learned a lot as it was our wont to discuss matters concerning English and other subjects so much so that during the "cultural revolution" in China we were accused of "scratching each other's back in a coterie like the Hungarian Petöfi Club", has enough qualifications of this kind and to spare. He was born an Odysseus, not that he seeks adventures, but that he is a nostalgic by nature. I remember swapping writings in English with him for comment or pleasure reading in the early 1960s. One sentence in one of his essays has never escaped my memory: "Suddenly a cuckoo called. The only audibility in the mountains. And we were thinking of mother."

For Ren, emigration happened when he had outlived an ardent age. What remains now is no longer the ecstasy of new horizons but rather the apotheosis of memory. No wonder he has zeroed in on ancient Chinese poetry mostly with a motif of nostalgia and homesickness. People notice that unless he/she is a *dolce vita* in the mainstream, a feeling *emigré*, like Milan Kundera, cannot but look back and sing with a heart throbbing with emotion worthy of a Homeric epic: "Alone, in a sadness sublime, /And tears come." (see page 6) Greater pathos is couched in seemingly light-hearted lines such as "Kids … /And asked me smiling where's my home." (see page 4) I feel my old friend is tackling a reconciliation with the finitude of life with these lines. In this sense, the value of Ren's translations far exceeds poetry alone but is a good sample of diasporic literature.

Technically, Ren's preference to condensed, succinct phrasal utterances instead of to drawn-out, grammatically viable sentences shows how well he grasps the quintessence of poetry. Stylistic devices like synesthesia (e.g. "Green moss lit up by the echoing flare", see page 17) abound only where they are comfortably apt. Rhythm and rhyming are continuously a Kierkegaard Either/Or proposition in poetry translation. Ren handles both with aplomb: unrhymed but pleasantly rhythmic lines are fully justified especially when the translator aims at an English-speaking readership accustomed to a time-honored poetic tradition traceable to Shakespeare's blank verse.

Mr. Yu Zheng, the other translator, is but a slight acquaintance. He did excel among his age peers when he studied at Fudan University Shanghai, in a class which both Ren and I taught. He has since been remembered as an assiduous and affable young man — with few words but a lot of promise. If he doesn't feature prominently in this foreword, I sincerely beg his pardon.

(《从诗到诗：中国古诗词英译》,任治稷、余正译,
外语教学与研究出版社,2006)

“What Is Out of Sight Is Lost Forever?”: In Lieu of a Preface to *The English-Chinese Dictionary* (2nd Edition)

I begin by quoting Samuel Johnson’s remark when he commented on the widespread rural illiteracy in Scotland in his time (Vincent, 1989: 48), suggesting that those who knew nothing of written language were doomed to live only in the present tense. With a twist — I have changed Dr Johnson’s full stop to a question mark — the remark is hereby quoted with a view to showing that although a tradition, that of Samuel Johnson’s included, is often “out of sight,” it percolates down and is not “lost forever.” Time being a continuum, willingly or unwillingly, consciously or unconsciously, all vagaries of fashion notwithstanding, we live to some extent in the shadow of what is “out of sight.” In the field of lexicography we therefore write, using a *double entendre*, in the past as well as the present and future tenses.

However, if one cares to look ahead across the lexicographic landscape, what catches the eye, I presume, is the future tense writ large. Living in the computer age, when we consult a dictionary most of us “click, look and listen.”① True, the trend unmistakably and

① See back cover of *The Random House Compact Unabridged Dictionary* (Special Second Edition, 1996).

irreversibly makes for dictionaries whose information is transmitted through such electronic media as computers, CD-ROMs, the Internet, or plug in memory chips. A good many of them enable a speedier look-up of a wealth of data and are much user-friendlier with a multimedia combination of texts, graphics, images, video clips, audio clips, and animation, allowing greater user autonomy in virtual space or even soliciting user participation in or interaction with the dictionary text by cutting, copying and pasting, indexing, bookmarking, hyperlinking, up- or down-loading, deleting, adding or fleshing out entries with a click of the mouse or a turn of the track ball in real time. No wonder when the Second Edition of *The Oxford English Dictionary* was published in 1989 in both p- (ink-and-paper) and e- (CD-ROM) forms, the sales ratio of p- to e- was approximately 1:10 (Mai, 1994: 123). Taking one step further from there, the *OED* Online which was made available in March 2000, boasting some twenty search options, not only incorporated its sizeable *Additions* in three volumes, but also ruled out the problem of CD-ROM wear and tear, creating in addition more look-up options by numerous pop-up windows for the purpose of customization. Therefore, it is hardly an overstatement to say that from now on practitioners of lexicographical art and craft will primarily "write in the future tense" and it is predicted with assurance that the dictionary market for tomorrow will teem with works like the *OED* Online. But the "future tense" lexicography, as it were, looks backward as well as forward — no mistake about it. The December 2003 *OED* Online Update, for instance, pinned quite a number of words down etymologically by antedating, say, "nit-picking" from 1970 to 1961, and "noisy" from 1693 to 1609.

Machines are made by man. So are computers with their programs. However state-of-the-art the computer ware is, be it hard or soft or firm or whichever, in the final analysis it is always the wizardly liveware (people working the computer) or the "wet ware" (jocularly the human brain) drawing unceasingly on an accrual of human wisdom that ultimately counts. Put another way, he who writes in the future tense cannot do away with the present and the past tenses, and whatever is "out of sight" is NOT "lost forever." Johnson, for instance, is very much alive not in that as a cultural relic his *Dictionary* sells at 10,000 to 30,000 USD (Hitchings, 2005: 229n) apiece today, but in that as recently as in February 2000 seventeen U.S. Congressmen brought a federal lawsuit against the then President Bill Clinton, who, according to them, had no constitutional right to bomb the former Yugoslavia without Congressional authorization. An issue at stake was the exact meaning of "to declare" and that of "war." A decision was thereupon reached to appeal to nonpareil dictionary authority and this authority was none other than Samuel Johnson of course! (O'Hagan, 2006: 12-13) More interestingly, perhaps out of a propensity to revive inkhorn archaisms, the owl in the hit novel series about Harry Potter is named Pigwidgeon (meaning a teeny thing), one of a panoply of quaint entry words Johnson's *Dictionary* abounds in.

Most dictionaries of today — and of tomorrow presumably for that matter — provide grammatical and pragmatic information such as parts of speech, irregular inflexions, usage or register labels which are all taken for granted. But has any one ever paused to think who initiated the paradigm in the first place? In the 150-odd years of English lexicographical chrysalis prior to Johnson there had been some twentyish works ranging from Robert Cawdrey's *Table Alphabeticall* to Henry Cockeram's glossary of "hard words" (who was the first to call his work a dictionary) and to Nathan Bailey's *An Universal Etymological English Dictionary* of 1721. It is interesting to note that the above-mentioned *Table* contained no entry words in the W, X and Y sections while the last left behind the perpetual laughing stock of defining "cat" as "a creature well known" and "black" as "a colour" and of circular definition or of *ignotum per ignotius* ("definiens" befogging "definiendum" in technical parlance or, plainly, explaining the difficult with the more difficult) aplenty so that "to wash" was "to cleanse by washing" and "to get" was "to obtain." The learned world had yet to wait for Samuel Johnson to introduce grammar and pragmatics in his *Dictionary* of 1775, to which we are indebted even today after the lapse of nearly 250 years, although we may offer to disagree with him upon his legendary truculent diatribes about Whig politics and about oats being a Scottish human staple but an English horse fodder. The liberally used but sometimes misplaced "cant" label of his has spawned a multitude of usage or register labels we apply and will continue to apply in dictionary-making. *Plus ça change* indeed!

The Johnsonian lesson, as I see it, lies first and foremost in the lexicographer's fervour in reading. Johnson had meant to plunder the wordlists from predecessors such as Nathan Bailey and Robert Ainsworth[1]. But the more he read with a view to ransacking quotable nuggets, the more was he carried away by reading over 500 authors spanning more than 200 years, so much so that his own wordlist —

---

① Johnson referred to Ainsworth 584 times and to Bailey 197 times (de Vries, 1994: 64).

especially in the latter letters — eventually was generated in a large part by illustrations he had gleaned from reading. For a total of 42,773 entries he supplied approximately 110,000 quotations — only half of all he had collected, thus winning himself a fame of "a robust genius, born to tackle with whole libraries" (Boswell, 1831: 78). Johnson, having made a point of regulating an "undefiled" [*sic*] English language rather than indulging it, read eminent authors of a past age such as Shakespeare and Milton, setting an example of what I call "literary realism" (using REAL English from the assembled matter of literacy and canonicity) to be taken over by Sir James Murray's *OED*①, who even went so far as to identify lexicography in terms of "a department of literature" (Hitchings, 2005: 81). And it was his wide-ranging interest and unquenchable curiosity that induced Johnson to read vastly and variously about not only, say, Aristotle, Isaac Watts and John Locke, but also about exotic flora and fauna and about the then novelties such as coffee houses, spa towns, cricket, ginseng and tea. Living contemporaries usually didn't pass muster with him, although later he relaxed his rule a little bit and even smuggled in some thirty of his own written samples marked as "anonymous." His was not the kind of leisurely reading on the part of a connoisseur making fetishization of books, but that under an oil lamp in the prison house of learning for the specific purpose of enriching his dictionary with refined elegance of a bygone age occasionally interlaced with a smattering of novel "otherness" (according to him, for example, the

① Murray, being a like-minded man of letters, copiously quoted Johnson in over 1,700 places in his own work. The Herculean work he didn't live to see accomplished in entirety contains 414,825 entries with 1,827,306 illustrative examples out of a total of five million.

number of possible combinations of the letters of the English alphabet is 1,391,724,288,887,252,999,425,128,493,402,200!) — a tradition reinforced by the *OED* afterwards.

Today we are wont to speak of corpora painstakingly developed by teams working with scanners. To be sure, what we have in the end is a massive cache of riches. But remember: many men, many minds and many criteria, and scanning by machine is more often than not indiscriminate. Coming across such useless examples as "He is a muppet" under the entry word "muppet" in a prestigious British dictionary of the 2000s and a dubious one "I don't want a cigar now, thank you, but I'll take a rain check on it"① under the entry "rain check" in another — both claiming to have derived from well-stocked corpora — we would undoubtedly be nostalgic about Samuel Johnson's selective acumen in providing apposite illustrative examples. Quoting literary giants verbatim may appear DWEM-ish and snobbish by present-day standards, but in the age of ours when science and technology dictate, Johnson's compendium of examples gives the reader a sense of transcendence over what is mundane and mechanical, adding credit to the sagacity of remarkable "wet ware" and breathing some uplifting air into the ambient feculence.

With your permission, dear reader, a tangential word or two by way of digression. "Reading maketh a full man." While the Baconian saying still rings mellifluously in the ears of superannuated people of my age, it gives rise to a hackneyed ennui among modish computer-savvy young men and women who would rather spend days and nights

① The example, as I see it, is both possible and probable — but atypical if it is taken out of its social etymon. Can one take a rain check, for instance, on a slap in the face?

browsing BBS websites or other web pages, emailing, chatting, blogging, googling, playing games on the computer. When they encounter an unknown word in English, they will simply highlight it and click on an electronic dictionary for an equivalent in Chinese. The result of using some low-quality handheld electronic bric-a-brac and, worse, developing a learning strategy thereby, can be disastrous. Some of the grossly mistranslated English store signs and menus such as "Japanese Arrangement" for "Japanese Cuisine" and "cloud swallow soup" for "wonton soup" that are uproariously notorious internationally are a case in point. As a pedagogue, I keep advising my students to read variously and viscerally so as to ensure a minimum of information input of a million words a year while using a sizeable enough decoding dictionary and an annual output of at least 10,000 words with the help of a "radioactive" encoding dictionary. Learning means, above all, an adequate amount of reading plus writing using two different kinds of dictionary, or, in a nutshell, making one "fuller" in the Baconian sense of the word.

Besides being a purposeful reader with scholarly talons laid on every available book, what other qualities are required of a lexicographer? Using Samuel Johnson as an exemplar once more, he or she has to be a bibliophile or a man or woman of letters, not only keen on reading with gusto but also capable of writing with brio. Johnson himself declared that he WROTE a dictionary instead of compiling one. Approximately sixty percent of all Johnson's learned quotes in the dictionary and elsewhere were taken from Greek or Latin savants, with Horace accounting for the most of them (Hitchings, 2005: 103). And his writing career began as early as when he wrote for Edward Cave's

Gentlemen's Magazine in 1731, and, working to order, he could produce as many as — wow! — 10,000 words at one go a day. He edited a complete Shakespeare with a now world renowned preface and proceeded to work on *Lives of the English Poets* otherwise known as Johnson's *Poets*. His most learned essays appeared in the six-page *Rambler*, a magazine underwritten by the said Cave and a few others. It is in these essays that Johnson tried out a Latinate style fraught with words from his *Dictionary*: "adscititious," "efflorescence," "equiponderant," "quadrature,""terraqueous," and "to superinduce."

Last but not least, integral to the *Dictionary*'s appeal is decidedly Johnson's letter written on the 7th February 1755 to Lord Chesterfield, a disdainful lip-server of a patron who was now prepared to partake of the success of the project, a letter to salve the writer's own acrimony as well as to admonish the imposter. Deservedly, it is a masterpiece of English prose, a sample of controlled rage and epistolary satire — satire in prose rather than in its Johnsonian definition of being always in verse. Being so regularly and enthusiastically given to words is admittedly going a long way to being a wordsmith worth his salt. But Johnson was a wordsmith of common sense rather than abstrusities. His observations about it being easier to translate homelier words like "bright" and "sweet" into another language in a bilingual dictionary than explain them in the mother tongue in a monolingual one and about linguistic corruption happening most frequently and flagrantly as a rule at the extremes of the social spectrum are worth more than tons of the now voguish academic gibberish. To me at least.

Part of being a wordsmith is to know as many languages as possible. Johnson was conversant in eight while James Murray allegedly knew twenty! A few years ago a Chinese dictionary-maker claimed to know thirteen. He was scoffed at all around but I kept wondering why he was never put to test to see if he was a really worthy polyglot. Yours humbly (that is the present writer) knows only Chinese and English, with six years of Russian in secondary school and one year of college German to boot. However rusty and paltry my knowledge about the latter two languages, it comes in handy in dictionary-making. For example, it was my knowledge of Russian that helped to decide if the plural form of Bolshevik was Bolsheviks or Bolsheviki, depending on whether the entry was treated as a totally naturalized English word or a Russian loan. As this preface is being prepared, it is the Christmas season of 2006. I have always heard sung and seen as a lighting ornament the word NOEL but had to look it up in a dictionary to know that it comes from Latin "natalis" to refer to the birth of Jesus Christ. Similarly, when I perspired profusely sitting in a sauna, I didn't know the word had originated in Finnish, the language of a very, very cold country. In such circumstances I would wistfully lament that I didn't take the trouble of learning more languages in order to be a well-equipped lexicographer. An indefatigable and vocal critic of the first edition of *The English-Chinese Dictionary* (*Unabridged*), of which I was editor-in-chief, knew Chinese, English, Russian and Japanese. His scathing criticisms offended a no small number of my dictionary colleagues, but I always take my hat off to him and his quirky gibes never fall on deaf ears.

Another requirement is an extraordinary resolve and unusual fortitude plus pliant mutability when and where necessary. It is known to everybody that Johnson identified dictionary-making as " low drudgery" and the illustrative example he supplied for the entry word "dull" was "To make dictionaries is *dull* work." On another occasion he was quoted to say:

> The uncertainty of our duration ought at once to set bounds to our designs, and add incitements to our industry; and when we find ourselves inclined either to immensity in our schemes, or sluggishness in our endeavours, we may either check or animate ourselves by collecting ... that art is long and life is short ... [Whoever has] trifled away those months and years, in which he should have laboured, must remember that he has now only a part of that which the whole is little; and that since the few moments remaining are to be considered the last days of Heaven, not one is to be lost.
>
> (Hazen & Middendorf, 1958-: Ⅲ, 97)

Johnson's initial ambitions were towering but hardly realistic. He dreamed that he could do the dictionary in three years single-handedly with the help of several amanuenses. Reality taught him a lesson the hard way that history of dictionary-making is one of deficits and delays. By Christmas of 1750, three years from when he first made his *Plan*, he had done from "A" to the twenty-first sense of "to carry"— a total of 280 pages. Fortunately he was now made excruciatingly aware of the excessive "immensity" of his proposed project, a project that had taken forty French to spend forty years on it[①]. He was sane and pliant enough to change tacks, shrunk his expansive strategies, sacrificed numerous good enough quotations, loosened the rule about incorporating living

① A commonly accepted story. In fact, it took the *Acadèmie française* fifty-five years to accomplish the dictionary in 1635. Who knows if the long delay wasn't the downside of teamwork and the "too many cooks" syndrome?

authors as it was mentioned above, and so forth. As a result, to an experienced eye, the letters A to C are disproportionately more circumstantiated than those that follow.

A late teacher of mine, a famed dictionary man, Professor Ge Chuangui (or Hertz C. K. Ke by Wade-Giles) by name, signed a contract with the Commercial Press for *A Large-size English-Chinese Dictionary* in the early 1960s. Assisted by a few junior teachers and graduate students, Professor Ge ground away at it for five or six years and ended up finding himself still lingering in the A section. Take alone for instance the gathering of evidence of whether English nouns beginning with the letters "h" and "u" are preceded by the indefinite article "a" or "an"— so I am told — the cards Professor Ge and his men made exceed fifty! Regrettably, the *magnum opus* aborted. Professor Ge was a deeply revered and loved person, a perfectionist. I remember writing to him in his twilight years quoting Samuel Johnson: "To pursue perfection, like the first inhabitants of Arcadia, is to chase the sun." Bless his soul chasing the sun in Heaven!

It is common sense that the dictionary is not an anthology of literature or of any other one subject. Nor is it a monograph on it. Knowledgeable persons tend to look at it as "a mine of information, an encyclopedia in disguise" (Eco, 1984: 49). Johnson's is no exception, offering a miscellany of knowledge rather than an overarching system of it. The nature of the dictionary has decided that a lexicographer be a Jack or Jane of all trades: to name a few — an untiring word-muncher, a discriminate microstructural editor, a hair-splitting meaning explicator, a fault-finding proof-reader, and also, when the work is completed and published, a punching bag for rancorous attacks like

Johnson was by Noah Webster on the other side of the Atlantic (Hitchings, 2005: 244-246). (But Johnson, living in a haughty time, would rather be a "cudgel" than a "punching bag" because of his pride and prejudice.) Johnson's was basically a one-man show, yet he had to coordinate with his amanuenses. Later, in Sir James Murray's case, he had to work with a fistful of philological stalwarts no meaner in academic standing than himself, not to mention the demanding Delegates of OUP and two thousand-odd outside readers including the "mad professor."① An able editor-in-chief, therefore, needs to be equipped with managerial prowess, knowing about the strengths and weaknesses of every member of his team, tapping his/her potential to the full so as to ensure optimal work efficiency. Vis-à-vis publishers/booksellers, he becomes a hard-driving bargainer like Samuel Johnson, who committed himself to the proposed job over breakfast on 18th June 1746 only on condition of getting paid a considerable sum of £1,575, roughly equivalent to £150,000 today. True, there were giants in those times, as the proverb says. But these same giants found an added secretarial dimension to their dictionary work, lugging heavy books, cutting up quires of paper into copy slips, stamping serial numbers on them to prevent misfiling, and so on and so forth. In short, traditional lexicography is the kind of work into which a dozen labours and chores roll, calling for a kind of *esprit de corps*. He/She who master- or mistress-minds a dictionary project and executes it must needs be a lexical steeplejack/jane and a grassroots word hod-carrier at one and the same time. It is by no means an armchair job, hands down, as some

① See Simon Winchester's *The Professor and the Madman*, published by Harper Perennial in 1999.

visualize it to be. And it goes without saying that with the advent of the computer, a lexicographer's functions have further multiplied as a programmer, an interface designer, and a cyber-CEO perhaps.

Samuel Johnson is phenomenal. Having dwelt upon what ramifications his tradition has held out for posterity, I feel obliged to hasten to add as an afterthought his obvious inadequacies and limitations. In the first place, feedback to his dictionary was and has been controversial (Hitchings, 2005: 240–241). To a modern person, 42,773 including some verbal rarities and curios doesn't account for anywhere near being adequate when we consider that the English language at the time comprised over 300,000 words, not to mention the present-day vocabulary tally of World English as a common denominator. Secondly, as was pointed out in the preceding context, Johnson's personal prejudices are manifest in some of his definitions and are ethically unacceptable. Thirdly, yes, there are piquant wordings of definition such as "uxorious" as "infected with connubial dotage" and other pithy sallies ("Patriotism is the last refuge of a scoundrel"!) that Macaulay, Coleridge and Lamb spoke highly of. Alongside them, however, there exist definitions that are inaccurate, esoteric and obscure, some of which simply err ("leeward" = "windward") or border on being absurd ("defluxion" = "a defluxion"). The gap between "the past tense" and "the present tense" also bears negatively upon the quality of definitions: for instance, we do not go to Johnson for the contemporary meaning of "penthouse," "car," "urinal," "rapper," "jogger," or "barbecue." Being a cynosure of British letters, Johnson wasn't prescient enough to see that "the American dialect, a tract of corruption" (Hazen & Middendorf, 1958–: X,

202), would one day become a global tongue a third of the world's population now have some command of and the other two-thirds aspire to learn. Furthermore, instances of inconsistency are numerous such as "uphil" but "downhill" and "instal" but "reinstall." To me, technicalities aside, the most objectionable is a professed tendentiousness that attests to Johnson's fusion of a tool book with moral didacticism. All the seven illustrative examples for "to instruct" are quotes from the Bible and for his own preferred ends he even felt free to change them at will at times. Thus, when Caliban in *The Tempest* by Shakespeare actually said "I know how to curse," Johnson unflinchingly added a NOT to make the utterance negative: "I know not how to curse." This is something a lexicographer should never do — whether in the past, at present, or in future. In my humble opinion, it is a matter of professional ethics although Johnson might have regarded lexicography as above all a consecrated vocation or even avocation rather than a profession.

On balance, none the less, Dr Johnson's *Dictionary* is not an ossuarium but a receptacle of good taste in *belles-lettres*, magnetic effusion, ennobling endeavour, propitious tradition, and creative lexicography, the memory of which hopefully will be kept alive long.

References

Boswell, James. 1831. *The Life of Samuel Johnson. LL. D.* (5 vols.) Ed. John Wilson Croker. London: John Murray.

de Vries, Catharina M. 1994. *In the Tracks of a Lexicographer: Secondary Documentation in Samuel Johnson's Dictionary of the English Language.* Leiden: LED.

Eco, Umberto. 1984. *Semiotics and the Philosophy of Language.* London:

Macmillan.

Hazen, Allen T., and John H. Middendorf, eds. 1958–. *The Yale Edition of the Works of Samuel Johnson.* 16 vols. New Haven: Yale University Press.

Hitchings, Henry. 2005. *Defining the World: The Extraordinary Story of Dr Johnson's Dictionary.* New York: Farrar, Straus and Giroux.

Mai, Zhiqiang. 1994. Multimedia Technology and Dictionary-Making. *Lexicographical Studies*, 6: 121–129.

O'Hagan, Andrew. 2006. Word Wizard. *The New York Review of Books*, April 27.

Vincent, David. 1989. *Literacy and Popular Culture: England 1750–1914.* Cambridge: Cambridge University Press.

[《英汉大词典》(第2版),陆谷孙主编,上海译文出版社,2007]

指尖薄技，还是工倕之巧？

——漫论手机语言“现象”

曾撰文介绍过我的同龄人、英国“水晶”（David Crystal）先生近年作品的两个“兴奋点”，前端是莎士比亚，尾端是今日英语（见《上海书评》3月1日）。对于后者，感兴趣的读者可找他的《语言和因特网》（*Language and the Internet*，剑桥大学出版社，2001年）、《絮说英语》（*The Stories of English*，综观印书社，2004年；文题显然沿袭1986年的《话说英语》——*The Story of English*，因从story到stories，故试以一“絮”字应译）和《网络和手机短信用语一览表》（*A Glossary of Netspeak and Textspeak*，爱丁堡大学出版社，2004年）等书来延伸一读。

本文评介的是此公2008年新书《手机短信：大辩论》（*txtng: the gr8 db8*）。这是一本200多页的小书，正文仅175页，一两天就可读完，可作者抱负不小，据称写作本书的念头在2002年已经萌发，要把手机短信英语“现象”（加引号，系从英语借用，指难得一见的特殊人物或事情）评述一番，深究其来龙去脉和是非曲直。这样的事情，这样的英语——如书题所示——经院派那些写惯高头讲章的语言学家们必不屑为。其实，任何学问都是“以不息为体，以日新为道”，“苟日新，日日新，又日新”，更何况聚蚊尚且成雷，发送手机短信业已成为涉及世人一半（30亿，见本书第5页）的每日功课，再不是什么秋毫之微。

手机短信其兴也勃。记得七八年前鄙人学会这套“拇指功”后，几次出洋，那儿的人手机使用虽已相当普及，但即使持有的是“黑莓”之类的新款，多数只用来打电话或收发电子邮件，问津短信的极少（这当然跟与我交往的多数是成年人有很大关系）。据“水晶”先生的跟踪观察，还有高德纳（Gartner）咨询公司的统计，自1992年芬兰人最早试发长度不超过20字符的手机短信以来，头十年发展相对缓慢，世纪转折的2000—2001年像是个分水岭，移动通信的短信服务技术已使信息长度扩展到160个字符，因此，2000年全球收发的短信总数为170亿条，次年即猛增至2 500亿，而预计到2010年会“大跃进”到24 000亿之数。比较而言，美国人采用个人电脑早于他国人，习惯于在大键盘上敲打电子邮件或电子聊天；又因为驾车人口多，成天手握方向盘（按游记作家比尔·布赖森的统计，美国人离家出行，不管距离长短，目的何在，93%都要开车。见 Bill Bryson：*A Walk in the Woods*——笔者不知道这位“俏胡子”是怎么统计出这个百分比来的），“单脱手”用手机或车载电话与人通话都足够便利，不可能也无耐心查摁小键发短信；加上美国电话通信业竞争剧烈，一月免费60分钟之类的套餐服务种类繁多，结果“Talk is cheap”（通话便宜），座机已经够用，短信收发便相对滞后。但是根据2006年的统计，全年也有1 580亿的短信收发，较之2001年猛增了95%。至于咱们中国的情况，读者诸君耳闻目睹身受，这儿可以略过不提。

“gr8 db8 = great debate”，“c u 18r a3 = see you later, anytime, anywhere, anyplace”，“xxxx = 告别时 kiss 4 次”，“：）@ smb = smile at somebody”，在双方默契交流互动过程中问：“did di(ana) like ham(let) j(ust) 4(for) f(un)?”……手机短信星火燎原，站出来痛斥的人占多数，其中攘袂切齿的是媒体，当然也不乏教师、家长和语言学家，詈辞至今不绝于耳。根据“水晶”先生转述的有：手机用语“贫

瘠，荒芜，可悲”，是“魔鬼的创造”，是“数字病毒”，是“杂交速记”，是“致瘾的语言大麻”；收发短信一族都是公元 5 世纪劫掠罗马并恣意毁坏文物的“汪达尔人”，是横冲直撞的“成吉思汗铁骑”，不是“脑懒”就是“文残”（dyslexic）；还有从医的专家证明，短信发多了会影响睡眠，甚至诱发 TMI（拇指伤害）。这儿，“水晶”先生又用上了他的“一英镑”论（详见拙文《莎士比亚真的不难读吗?》，《上海书评》3 月 1 日）：“说技术发展带来语言灾难，每听到一次这样的预言，如我可得一英镑的话，那么这会儿肯定已是大富豪了。如果计入中世纪的印刷术和后来的电报、电话、无线电广播等等，我的银行存款不撑破大天才怪哩。”

“水晶”先生随后从社会、心理、商业、技术、语言等不同层面论证手机短信勃兴的必然性和优势，认定这一“现象”不但不损害语言文字，反而有助于启智，提升信息传播速度和效率，加快生活节奏，更为语言发展另辟蹊径。不假，短信一族多青少年（挪威的一项调查显示：年过六十七岁还收发短信的只占 2.7%），这些人不甘传统戒律的约束，急于创建本身年龄段的集群个性，在人际交流中追求“一步到位”式的直率、简捷。“prw = parents are watching”（指家长在近处监视，要对方注意）在青少年短信中出现频率之高，足以说明这一集群的心态。另外，2007 年 4 月，美国弗吉尼亚理工大学发生亚裔学生射杀 32 人事件后，学校当局急向全校学生发出电子邮件示警，但因许多人未必适在电脑前坐候，警告所起作用有限，当局这才续发手机短信，警告因此方始奏效。从商业角度说，“水晶”先生握有数据，说是 2005 年各家移动通讯公司赢利超过 700 亿美元，比当年好莱坞的票房收入高出三倍之多。

从语言层面，“水晶”先生引用撒切尔夫人时代英国教育和科学部下属专门委员会的调查报告，指出英国学校语文水平的下降早从上世纪 70 年代中期就已开始，与手机完全无涉。他继而引用考文垂大学心理系2006—2007的一份调查报告，证明就总体而论，青少年早日拥有手机开始收发短信，对语文的兴趣和文字敏慧反倒发生得越早，创造欲加上顽皮心理会使这些孩子中的一些人成为很出色的语文学生。如2007年纽约举行过一次短信大赛，共有250人参加，结果头奖25 000美元被一位十三岁小学生揽得，此人一个月发8 000条短信。发短信的吉尼斯纪录为一名十六岁的新加坡少年所创，此人在43.44秒钟之内发成160个字符极限，其中包括Sarrasalmus和Pygocentrus这样长而难的鱼类属名。短信英语中最受人诟病的是缩略语泛滥，“水晶”先生劝世人莫大惊小怪，须知我们生活的时代本身就是个“缩略的时代”，用语不但有全社会认同的缩略式，还有行业、技术、产品、论文等特有的缩略式，甚至还有个人的创造。举个近例，“世博”已是中文缩略，可笔者在跟友人收发短信时更习惯于用“wx”（World Expo，由于Expo本身已是缩略，再缩作“x”，以一个字母代替“ex—”，自我感觉更简）。“水晶”先生强调，缩略始终是英语造词途径之一，从书证确凿的借自拉丁的“pm”（1666年）、“NB”（nota bene=note well，1673年）等，到后来的“IOU”（I owe you，转义至“欠条”）、“RIP”（rest in peace，墓碑用语）、“aka”（also known as）、“FYI”（for your information）、“btw”（by the way）、“asap”（as soon as possible）、“c/o”（care of）等，乃至今日那些被替代的原词常常已被遗忘的“laser”（镭射）、“DVD”（影碟）、“AIDS”（艾滋病）等等，以及大量今日手机短信中使用的截缩音变词（注意：与以上首字母缩略不同），如“agn = again”、“coz = because”、“luv = love”、“thanx = thanks”等等，其中许多早早就被记录在《牛津英语大词典》和/或Eric Partridge 1942年的《缩略语词典》中了。即便是口语、方言中的缩略句，如“wotcha = what are you”，读者只须稍加注意，在狄更斯、马克·吐温、司各特、哈代、劳伦斯等大家的作品中，都不难发现类似的句例。

反对手机短信用语一派还对“存辅(音字母)去元(音字母)”深恶痛绝。其实,语言学家在研究阿拉伯、希伯来等语种之后,早已从信息论的角度认定,辅音字母传达的认知信息多于元音字母。譬如:this sentence hasn't got any vowels 可分别化作:

ths sntnc hsnt gt ny vwls

i eee a o a oe

显然,“全辅音字母”的第一句尚可勉强认知,而“全元音字母”的第二句则绝对认知不能。所以,手机短信中常常略去元音字母不是没有认知理据的。还有一个滥用感情符问题——“水晶”先生考证,这东西青少年和女性用得最多——这不怪诸如“空景”(Skype)等的设计人员弄出了64个表情符,诱惑生性顽皮的主顾去选择,而是因为象形满足人的需要,尤其是当你有复杂的情愫急于即时表达之际。早在1605年,因循法古的英国历史学家 William Camden 曾批评某些作家,“[they] lackt wit to express their conceit in speed; did vse to depaint it out (as it were) in pictures, which they call Rebus”(“阙智思以急表垂光思理,乃借图[不妨如此形容]勾勒,是为画谜”)。画谜者,源于埃及象形文字,达·芬奇玩过,写《爱丽丝漫游奇境记》的 Lewis Carroll 玩过,现在轮到21世纪的手机短信作者们玩了,只要玩得表情达意,无可厚非。

短信时代的困惑

说到一个玩字，填字游戏、猜字谜、“避字文”（lipogram，源自希腊文，指通篇有意避用某个字母，如美国作家 Ernest Wright 1939 年的小说《盖兹比》[Gadsby]，全书五万余言不用一个“e”字母；三十年后有法国人学样写出《空白》一书，三百页中无一“e”字母；据说还有人悬赏征求《哈姆雷特》的重写本，全书只能用同一个单个元音字母）等无不属此。“水晶”先生早些时候写过一本《语言游戏》（*Language Play*，1998 年，伦敦：企鹅出版社），录述趣闻不少，值得一读。发送手机短信的人群中颇不乏这样的“玩家”，“掺码”（code-mixing）似乎可算比较常见的玩法。如中国人要说的明明是个“晕”字，打上手机的却是“ft”（= faint）；德国人祝贺圣诞快乐，手机短信上不出德文 Frohe Weihnachten，而是“mx”（= Merry Christmas）；日本人不说“ぉはょぅ”，而是打上 0840 即 ohayou 的读音。

手机普及，短信满天飞，会动脑子赚钱的主儿忽发奇想，主办一场短信诗歌比赛如何？不曾想参赛者踊跃，“穿着紧身衣”的诗人，还确实写出一些佳作，有人得了“短信诗桂冠诗人”的雅号，在荷兰还评出过“金手指”。请看下引参赛某原诗和笔者的译文：

his is r bunsn brnr bl %,
his hair lyk fe filings
w/ac/dc going thru,
i sit by him in kemistry,
it splits my @toms
wen he :-) @ me.

双目像本生实验灯般幽蓝，
发如铁屑
交流/直流电通过点燃，
化学课上我坐他身边，

浑身原子被击散
当他向我露笑颜。

除了诗歌,写散文、小说、短剧、布道文的都有,就是没见十四行诗。

中国手机业的兴旺颇受作者注目,附录11种语言中的短信用语表中就有一份是汉语的。“水晶”先生还专门提到中国有职业短信写手,负责创作段子和贺辞之类的内容。“飞信”技术沟通了短信和电邮两个渠道;初级的“predictive txting”(即打出一字,频用程度最高的后接字在下一键搜索时首供选择)智能技术也在中国开始普及,而这些正代表了短信技术下一步的发展:凭着苹果iPhone、“黑莓”、PDAs等的改进——有待改进处尚多,如英语中最频用的“s”非至7键摁四次始能屏显,而最罕用的“q”摁两次即得——以及这类新一代产品之用于连接多媒体群发,短信收发行为在可预见的将来当有所改变。

从语言学视角展望,“水晶”先生一方面不主张夸大手机短信用语对整个语言的影响,也指出短信用语中一些语标(logograms)指代并非惟一而可能引起的误解(如“m8=mate”中的“m”读作/m/音,而在“mbrsd=embarrassed”中非读作/em/不可;又如“lol”既是“laugh out loud”又是“lots of love”的缩略),另一方面并不否认手机短信语会促进英语的拼读趋同(如以“f”字母取代“ph”)、元音字母减少(如“xlnt=excellent”)、缩略语激增,甚至影响句法(如“8-9 r paw hrs=8-9 are parents watching hours”),英语作为国际通用语的地位也将继续加强。但从总体说,英语毕竟已是嵯峨高山,峥嵘岩峣,任风雨溥畅,无损固本,所谓的“手机语言学”(cellinguistics)高论似乎可以休矣。

最后,说个有意思的巧合。“水晶”先生在他的近年“兴奋点”首尾两端有个发现,都与五这个数字有关。说到莎士比亚和同代诗人为什么像他们的希腊、拉丁先行者那样,多用“五音步诗行”(pentameter),

按普林斯顿大学认知心理学家乔奇·A. 米勒（George A. Miller）监听实验对象一般对话作出的统计结果，据说95%以上的人可以毫不费力摄取并存储的信息往往只含五个重读音节——这里说的是首端。漫论手机短信英语时，“水晶”先生本人的另一发现是：英文单词所包含的字母，平均为五个左右。他分析自己这本小书短短581词的前言，共计2 744字母，每词平均含字母4.7个。这两个“五”对于醉心于英语从词到句组成规律的人来说也许不无一定的启发。

笔者1995年学用电脑，2002年10月27日在宁波受教收发手机短信，除向青年学子学习外，自问也有点小发明，譬如在美国曾与上海的朋友以全拼音书写互通电邮，前后鼻音拿捏不准时，用上个“（g）”表示或有或无；又会从小字辈处学他们短信中标新立异的“色艺=适意”，“组撒=做啥”，在我是“txting adultescence”——“短信装嫩”；还会视短信接收对象不同，在汉语、英语文字中掺杂拉丁化写法的上海话，我称之为“txting aloud”——“读出式短信”，前提是对方与我交谈时必都说上海话。譬如说在普通话的文本中，突然不厌其烦转换语言选择，打上“m me”，即“呒没”，这样似乎会产生一种更浓厚的“实时”亲近感。但我又是保守的，电脑操作只求指尖薄技，不图工倕之巧，小遇故障，即发SOS找门生；用惯了一款不带摄影功能的黑白诺基亚，说什么也不肯换彩屏，因为换机意味着重新熟悉功能和工序。“老狗不学新招”，有这点薄技可以了。

有位老友与我同龄，也置备手机，但就是不肯学短信收发，连当作移动电话使用，也有点“茄门”。我说这手机可有用了：约会、通知、寻人、协调、迎送、祝寿、贺年、问候，甚至交流“不折腾”的译法。他回答说：是啊，还可以骚扰、作弊，甚至搞恐怖主义。这次我希望他能读读“水晶”先生这本小书，看能不能起到洗脑作用，毕竟人家也是这把年纪了。现代技术就在你的指尖,放过不用,不但可惜,而且迹近 sinful（犯罪）呢——我准备这样开导他。

（原载 2009 年 3 月 8 日《东方早报》）

《胡诌诗集》译者絮语

若干年前，正在编辑《万象》杂志的陆灏老弟，约我翻译爱德华·里尔（Edward Lear）的《胡诌诗集》（*A Book of Nonsense*）。诗不可译，方家之言（个别驯手自然不在此列）；信口胡诌之诗，似更无从着手，因为一看内容，诗人所记地点、人物和题材，如“山花趁马蹄”般随性发散，兴之所至，无中生有，插科打诨，虚无谲诡，有时近乎独家放言狂欢，而读者则不知所云。果然，鄙译发表若干之后，即遭批评甚至詈骂，说是“两个姓陆的（陆灏‘陪绑’）吃饱了饭没事干似的”（“豆瓣”网友语）。另一方面，英国文学中向有童谣儿歌传统，这胡诌打油诗，初兴于18世纪，越百年，到了里尔手中，势更大炽，因当时多用于幼儿教育，严格讲究格律：五行之中，第一、二、五行一般含三音步而较长，同押一韵；三、四行含两音步而较短，另押一韵（若用公式表述更可一目了然，即3/3/2/2/3的音步和aabba的韵脚）；诗行内，音步构成的节律可以是轻—轻—重，也可以是轻—重—轻，且不排斥用词的重复。（也有将三、四两行接排作一行而以四行排印的，公式相应改作3/3/2—2/3和aa/b—b/a。）胡诌诗的这种音乐感，对于矫正幼儿音素误读，对于幼儿体验英语的节律，习惯成自然，逐步形成敏感，进一步发展到理性认知，大有裨益。举个例子说吧，谁能把“Chippy-wippy sikky tee / Bikky-wikky tikky mee / Skippy-chippy wee”说得极溜，那么非但/ɪ/和/i:/两个元音音素能够读准，英语的节奏意识也会大大增强。《胡诌诗集》之所以一度受到欢迎，这形式上的长处功不可没。更何况里尔本人还是画家——传说曾教过维多利亚女王作画——为一诗配一图(都是漫画),当能进一步激发学童兴趣。

一经翻译,特别是从一种分字连写成词的表音语言,译入另一种单字分写表意和/或意音语言,形式上的转移,已经使音步、格律、韵脚等诗的技术性元素对新的译入语受众失效,因而也才会受到部分读者对译出《胡诌诗集》必要性的质疑。试设想如果拘泥于形式,把下面这样的“胡诌诗”

There was an Old Man of Melrose,
Who walked on the tips of his toes;
But they said,'It ain't pleasant,
To see you at present,
You stupid Old Man of Melrose.'

刻板地译作:

有个梅尔若斯的老头,
他用脚尖把路走;
可别人说:“这可不像样,
看你现在这模样,
你这梅尔若斯的笨老头。”

而全书一百多首的胡诌诗又都是按大致雷同的体例写成的,要说个性,大多被掩埋在共性之下,那么,这样一个译本绝对是平淡寡味到极点的“泥车瓦狗”,说“两个姓陆的吃饱了饭没事干似的”也很在理。现在,我们把英文原文五行或四行实录,维持上述公式,供有兴趣的读者吟诵练舌或遥想当年学童的语言习得;同时,既然是“胡诌诗”,译出内容时,干脆挣脱形式的紧身衣,放开手脚,允许有限度的“胡诌”(包括变换句序、避免重复、参画改诗、打破单调等)。用心在于:从内容到形式用汉语尽量保存爱德华·里尔《胡诌诗集》的精萃。这是一种尝试，能否得到读者认同，我们静候指教。胡诌打油，积靡使然，作为一种传统，并未绝唱于里尔，时至20世纪，还有作家续写，如以小说《南风》著称的英国作家乔治·诺曼·道格拉斯（George Norman Douglas）。只是风俗与化移易，胡诌诗在新一代手中，常多色情内容。

说到里尔一生以及《胡诌诗集》的内容，如今是电脑时代，搜索引擎五花八门，读者自查可得，毋庸赘言。这儿只想就里尔和胡诌略说几句。里尔虽自称“要给千万人送去无害的笑”，本质上却毕生与笑无缘，只是个独行的“他者”：癫痫、独身、气喘、半盲、种种社会钳制形成的离群恐怖、维多利亚时代特有的对非理性和暴力的焦虑、对荒诞的彻骨敏感、对意义的无谓追求、对约定俗成各种语言规则的大不敬戏仿和蔑视——这一切大凡愿意细细咀嚼《胡诌诗集》的读者，多少都会有所体认。而所谓 nonsense（胡诌，无意义），往深里想去，其实就是一个变形人间的 good sense（常识，正常意义）。在荒诞与常识之间打上一个等号，是多少现代派到后现代文学作品的主题？只不过里尔是采用诉诸视觉的夸张方式表达，先走一步而已；而由于漫画的受众主要是儿童，也较易被人忽略。不过，里尔及其作品在英国文学史上也能占一席之地，这恐怕是很重要的一个原因，而绝不只是因为他反映了有闲阶级的英国特征（Britishness）。

我这儿“东施效颦”，也来上一首“胡诌”，打油之余，看看荒谬与常识之间的关系：

> There were in Henan pigs very lean,
> They are good to look at than to eat;
> Due to a chemical powder, added to the fodder,
> The athletic pigs poison and cheat.

自由试译：

> 河南地方健美猪，

中看不中吃想得出；
化学品，瘦肉精，
拌进饲料毒害吃肉人。

里尔是个悲剧人物，一生与胞姐为伴，虽也不乏丁尼逊这样的文友，同他关系最契的却是他的厨子，而落葬时居然没有一个吊客到场，可谓生也柔脆，死也枯槁。悲剧作家需由悲剧人物翻译。笔者自知在这一方面还不具备充分的资质，那就继续努力吧。

最后，推荐西班牙阿利坎特大学学术年刊 *Revista Alicantina de Estudios Ingleses*（1993 年第 6 期）的英文论文"Rule-Breaking and Meaning-Making in Edward Lear"，有兴趣的读者更可根据此文所附文献目录，扩展阅读，进一步理解里尔及其作品。

（《胡诌诗集》，[英] 爱德华·李尔著，陆谷孙译，海豚出版社，2011）

志虽美，道难达

事情发轫在香港，当时我刚编完上海译文版的《英汉大词典》，五十出头的年纪，寓居香港一年，总觉得自己还能做些什么。经朋友撺怂，拿林语堂、梁实秋等老前辈的作品摆出来刺激我的虚荣心，要我效颦，又恰与喜好向洋人介绍中国文字的安子介先生有过几席谈，兼之美国朋友有个汉英语料文档（复旦的薛诗绮同志和我曾为他们剔除大量不成词的自由组合），说是可供我们无酬使用，作为原料，便生发了编写一部汉英词典的念头。在这之前，也多次出入海外华埠的书店，发现读者对英汉词典的需求，远远低于汉英，心想若继英汉之后真能编出一部汉英，出版商或可创相当利润，也算是件好事。这一切都是上世纪90年代的事，器识赫赫的"大外宣"什么的，当时还没人提，我辈小巴拉子自然更加想不到那上面去。

注意到的事实，只是大陆以外的华人用辞与我们有显著的区别，因袭前朝各种用语不说，大量吸纳外来语，如"卖点"（selling point）、"贴士"（tips）等等，今日在大陆也已是耳熟能详，但对更多的用法，犹觉陌生，连专名翻译有时也鴃舌不通，如Sierra Leone，大陆取音，译作"塞拉利昂"，海外取意，译作"狮子山"。要是把这些熔于一炉，收词涵盖中华本土及海外华人社区，以简繁字并列参照的形式，如实收录各社区特有的高频词语，使之通过同一种译入语（英语）的媒介，渐趋互相认同而凝聚，兼收扩大现代汉语词汇共核域之效，有何不美？所以，不自量力地暂时给这部汉英词典起了个书名，叫做《大中华汉英词典》(*The Greater China Chinese-English Dictionary*)。安子介先生尤其希望一部汉英词典除为汉语读者服务外,对于学习汉语的外国人也会有益有用,这才定下了音义之外,形训兼顾的原则,就是用最简英语说一说汉字何以写成现在这模样的故事,如"寳"字就是"屋顶下面有钱币和玉器藏于缸"(书中自然用最简英文写出)的意思。

编着编着,有感于大陆读者——尤其是青年读者——对汉字、汉文的兴趣不再像上几代人那么浓厚,知识似也渐变浅薄而对此又并不在意,所以词典还决定增加汉字通假内容,并纳入大量成语、古谚、警句等等,尽我们之所能,译成过得去的英文。以下是从鄙人正在审读的稿子中抽出的数例:"燕雀安知鸿鹄之志[<idiom>(how can a swallow know the soaring ambitions of a swan goose) how can the mediocre know the minds of great men]";"人之将死其言也善(truth sits upon the lips of dying men,原系 Matthew Arnold 言)";"偏听则暗(heed only one side, and you are benighted)";"功败垂成(to fail when success seems within reach *or* to fail in the eleventh hour 或 a slip twixt the cup and the lip)";"人头攒动(a mass of bobbing heads)";"恶有恶报(as he sows, so he shall reap 或 there's no leap from Delilah's lap to Abraham's bosom)";等等。

当然,收词收例也要适当照顾古今平衡。古代帝王宝座旁边的"宥坐之器"(或称"宥坐器"),今日青少年不看下面的英文释义可能还不知道是个什么东西:"tilted container for holding water placed on the right-hand side of an emperor's throne [served as a reminder that the last drop makes the cup run over, a reminder of always doing things with moderation]"。与此同时,"不求同年同月同日生,但求同年同月同日死"(<familiar> although we could not have chosen an identical moment of birth, we are prepared to die at one and the same time [oath taken by a devoted couple or sworn brothers］）和今日口语中常说的“博眼球”（［usu. by going out of one's way］to attract the eye; to say or do an eye-popping thing）以及衣食住行中老百姓常用的大白话，如“这米出饭”（this rice rises well when cooked），“去你的！”（get out of here; buzz off; beat it; get lost）等等自然收得更多。身处高科技时代，百科术语的收录更成为重点之一，词典使用的科目标签逾90；实在找不到英语俗名的特定地域动植物，交代拉丁学名，以供识者或有兴趣的读者有个追查线索；大陆译法与海外社区译法不一致的，以大陆译法为主词条，其余译法参见至此，如“云计算”（［Comp］cloud computing）作为主词条的同时，“<non-M>［指非大陆用法］（Taiwan）云端运算”另列互参。有些新出现的西方理论，汉语译法犹在流动未定状态，是否一定要以“先译为准”，如queer theory港台文评界和“同志”亚文化群译作“酷儿理论”，大陆跟风者不乏其人。在收录此条的同时，能不能以譬如“另态［故意不用一个“畸”字］属性理论”、“多态性征理论”之类的措辞，求教于专门家和识者，以求少些轻薄味。如蒙同意或以更佳译法教我，能不能即以大陆译法作为主词条，让“酷儿”互见至此，即便前者一时尚不广为人知？如此，斟酌乎质文之间，隐括乎雅俗之际，高头讲章和雕虫小技互为调剂，有常与无方结合，是否可能更受读者欢迎？这通假和互见，虽是技术操作，要做得比较圆满，却是非花大工夫不可。

一些网友热衷于按英语规律自造的时髦词，由于不无创意，眼下风行，有人希望我们能率先收入（其实收不收中国人新造的英文词，主要是英汉而非汉英词典编者的决策）。这类汉语用词，如“给力”，虽说美国《市井词典》这样的洋人辞书网页也已收入gelivable，但毕竟到目前为止，仍限于我们自娱自乐，要像“关系”、“劳改”这样被英语作为成熟的借词吸收，也许尚待时日。这样，对于“给力”，我们还是宁可注释成：“<colloq> 1. boosting, stimulating：这番话真给力啊

these remarks are a real pick-me-up | 前冠军咋这么不给力 the ex-champion is but a let-down 2. cool, awesome, nifty 3. bravo! phat! far out!”似更能达到言语乃至文化转移的目的。至于“gelivable”等英文词能否存活并登堂入室，拭目以待吧。

志虽美，达不易。某种意义上说，词典是同样苦煞编者和出版人双方的项目，所以被我戏称为“3D”，即 deficiency（缺点多多），deficit（蚀本生意）和 delay（一拖再拖），三者似乎已成规律。这部汉英词典拟收单字、词、词组及词化成语等 18 万条以上，估计总字数在 1 600 万字左右，将由复旦大学出版社出版。但是“苦莫苦于多愿，悲莫悲于精散”，由于自知之明不足，目标定得太高，既没有专职的编写人员，已经介入的（包括本人），要他/她全心全力投入枯燥的编写工作且持之以恒，也难；毕竟事竣稿费有限，且一般又不作学术成果计入；二是长期惨澹经营，对讲究“性价比”的出版一方来说，历来是个大忌，从代表牛津出版社的衮衮诸公催逼牛津英语大词典主编杰姆斯·穆雷开始，一向如此，什么项目最好都要在自己这一任内完成。所以这部汉英词典，弄得不好，怕会成为当年我师葛传椝先生为商务印书馆编写的那部“永不完成的‘杰作’”；即便终善有时，书成，可能已是人事皆非，“出师未捷身先死”的先例还少？果能一代又一代前仆后继，坚持到底，估计最早也该到庆祝复旦出版社成立 35 周年的时候了——他们目前正在庆祝建社 30 周年，这才要求我写这篇小文。

（原载 2011 年 11 月 6 日《东方早报》）

《生活曾经这样》译者后记

正读 *Tolkien's Gown & Other Stories of Great Authors and Rare Books* 的时候,译文出版社来人了,要我就格雷厄姆·格林的《生活曾经这样》(*A Sort of Life*)写篇译后记。前书的中译本《托尔金的袍子》,他们已经出版了,我想编辑们和读者必已注意到,1988 年,纳博科夫的首版签售本《洛莉塔》被书商以 3 250 英镑(相当于 5 900 美元)的价格,上榜出售。几星期后,格雷厄姆·格林致信书商说,上榜的并非《洛莉塔》首版,他手里有奥林匹亚公司真正的两卷本首版(其实未必,在宽容的法国,此书 1955 年已出版),上有作者题签:"书赠格雷厄姆·格林,弗拉基米尔·纳博科夫。1959 年 11 月 8 日。"题签下方,纳博科夫绘上他那招牌式的蝴蝶,附言:"齐腰处蹁跹的燕尾翠蝶。"作者把纳氏这段签赠文字影印于书名页左上方,以为佐证。(纳氏那字迹使我想起咱们中国的英语大家王佐良先生的书法。格林本人的蝇头小楷至少同样眇细难辨。)格林后来还把纳博科夫此书推荐为 1955 年度首选佳作,在检禁制度尚未完全退出历史舞台的英美社会,激起一番小小的骚动。

书商跟格林边呷伏特加,边谈价钱,最后以 4 000 英镑成交。有意思的是,谈兴一浓,说起对作家的评价,格林承认:"康拉德和(亨利·)詹姆士是一流小说家。本人属二流。"

这个格林好有自知之明!从伍尔芙和乔伊斯,到艾丽斯·默道克到金斯利·艾米斯,这些作家的作品都难入格林法眼,这会儿才难得说了句自谦的话。格林多产,从 25 岁发表第一部作品,到 2005 年(死后 14 年)最后一部出版,很多时候是一年写出一部甚至多部作品。评界承认格林有“编织”(“文本”者,text 也,源于拉丁语的“编织”)故事的出色才能,但对格林创作成就的评价历来不乏争议。一说多少倾向于贬,鉴于作家写了太多的悬疑类间谍小说,说格林有点像个娱乐读者的 melodramatist(译不好,被迫“夹心”),因而由文字改编成电影者尤多。若论文字,实用有余,可动俗眼,但工而入逸、自成一格的妙品寥寥(格林密友 Evelyn Waugh 语);左翼人士,如特里·伊格尔顿,不但谴责格林加入共产党仅 6 周即匆匆回归体制的政治取向,更指出如此朝三暮四必然在作品中表现为是非和善恶的淆错。另一说强调他的文学性,特别是他擅写创伤心理、生死象征、善恶隐喻和宗教焦虑;而英国式的冷嘲文字,也被他用得淋漓尽致。美国性感女星媚·维思特(Mae West)是二战时期飞行员的救生“小背心”,说话也特别泼辣、慧黠,留下名言不少。强中更有强中手。格林说她忸怩作态的模样,活像“一条吃撑了的滚圆肚子大蟒”(overfed python)。至于评论童星秀兰·邓波儿小小年纪就会“若真若假卖弄风骚”(dubious coquetry),更给他惹来官司缠身。

特别是格林的短篇,早期评家都不看好,认为大多是为长篇热身暖笔。尽管格林自称为取悦未来的妻子,同时也为“打发时光”,才受洗入教,尽管一生与教廷摩擦不断(保罗六世可谓例外),早期评家宁可集中注意力于格林作品中罪孽与救赎的宗教主题,把格林认定归类于“天主教作家”。可是值得读者和出版人注意的是,如评家 Richard Kelly 所言,短篇可能成为日后格林研究中的重点:“作为一个总体,格林的短篇是部长达一生的心理剧,反映出他嗜刺激、旅行和写作三者如命。更有甚者,这些故事表现出格林在永无休止地与童稚时代的心魔搏斗,还显示他把这些鬼魅化作笔下角色和主题以及再往后塑造成宗教、政治和社会问题的能力。”格林自己也说(见

1967 年《短篇小说集》前言）:“我认为与《破坏者》、《勒佛先生的一个机会》、《花园底下》和《八月贱卖》（笔者注：四种皆短篇）相比，本人没写出过更好的作品。”

这儿译出的《生活曾经这样》是格林自传的前半部分。作者的元初回忆是童车（象征禁锢）和狗尸（象征死亡）。所以，第一，读者可以此为线索，随着作者一起探索缠扰格林一生的“躁郁症”（bipolar disorder，也有专业人士译作“双极性情感疾患”，指周期性情绪过度亢奋或低落）的成因和发展。成因中是否既有祖上行为乖张拗捩，脉络未断，又有父母近亲结合，遗下骀荡浮漫性格？躁郁袭来时，甚至异想天开要去开家妓院。还有，独特的寄宿学校特别是公学制度、鞭笞学童、恃强凌弱，有人说这些曾是英国民族性的一部分（详见 Peter Mandler 2006 年所著《英格兰民族性——从伯克到布莱尔》），是不是也会导致躁郁以至于小小年纪六次自杀未遂？其实格林父母并不特别悍鸷，躁郁和孤僻之所以日甚一日，更多来自寄宿学校猥鄙环境中的格格不入和被同学孤立凌虐的经历。笔者当年在中国国民小学的经历也差不多，挨了“打手心”和“立壁角”的惩戒之后回家，老祖母居然叫好不迭，说“老师打，讨来打”（指付了学费买回），倒也不曾因此寻死觅活。反而是体罚已经基本成为历史的今天，过分的课业压迫和升学焦虑，是不是也会导致性格畸形，甚至造成青少年自杀的社会问题？——虽说拿支左轮手枪玩“俄罗斯轮盘赌”的创意，非有格林式的想象力不可。

第二，除了“躁郁症”这条线索，格林记忆的蜂巢里还有众多童年读物营造的巢脾：哈葛德、司各特、斯蒂文森、布肯等等。独自躲进故乡公地的草莽，一边读冒险传奇故事，一边自导自演一幕又一幕的心理剧，追求刺激的性格由是养成，而一生气运终归于此，也就没什么奇怪了。鄙人幼时也爱拿扫帚当宝剑，持厚重的门闩当大炮，游戏效摩书里读来的情节，一会儿扮演法国剑客，一会儿反串“荒江女侠”,惹得二姐嗤笑。“以他人自居”(identification,业内亦称“定向统合”),据说是儿童从“性蕾期”开始就萌发的心理活动,其陶铸功能不可低估,又一例也。只看日后环境如何冶炼儿童了。是把儿童投入自由天地,还是放进高压锅烹煮,结果可能大不相同。

第三,读者不妨等待格林自传续集 *Ways of Escape* 译出,再来重读《生活曾经这样》;或者找来为格林本人认可的传记作家 Norman Sherry 教授的三卷本《格雷厄姆·格林的一生》,对照着读,方可对本书的价值作出比较客观的判断。大凡自传,不可能只是普鲁斯特所说的 *mémoire* involontaire(非意愿记忆),而是像格林在起笔之首承认的,“必有选择性”。贤明的读者自能从已经写下的内容中去挖掘作者有意遗忘或忽略的内容,也就是从回忆探究遗忘(to infer what is unsaid by what is said)。譬如说,格林可以把老家花房里的一把椅子描写得具体而微,儿时的性萌动和婚前艳遇也交代得巨细靡遗,但是对于如何追求 Vivien,如何写过数以百计的情书(有时一日三封,用词重彩浓墨,称呼对方是“You glorious, marvelous, most beautiful, most adorable person in the world. You are simply the symbol of the Absolute”或“Dear love, dear only love forever, dear heart's desire”——详见 Richard Greene 所编 *Graham Greene: A Life in Letters*),直到最后结婚的这一段经历却语焉不详。在他笔下,婚姻只是格林皈依天主教的引渡由头,至于婚后生活更是一笔带过:“I married and I was happy”。一个躁动的灵魂试图泊停在婚姻和信仰的港湾,谁知亢奋过去,随后是更深沉的抑郁,于是分居,信仰则是从一开始就带有怀疑主义(格林自称“天主教不可知论者”[Catholic agnostic],而 Walpole 等人称,格林更倾向于接受 Quietism[静修主义]甚至 Deism[自然神论])。无怪乎,格林求爱之初以及提出与妻子分居之际写去的信中,歉疚之意跃然纸上。前者用“I really am very sorry”,后者用“I can't tell you how sorry I am”。业镜高悬,人命有数，毕竟躁动的秉性是世间任何东西都擒拿不住的。

读这部格林自传，是否可从以上三点契入，意浅识薄，试质之读者诸君，或有会乎？

本书翻译过程中，同仁沈黎教授谦虚，索去译稿对照原文阅读，说是“学习”，结果指出数处漏译，又对译文提出一些宝贵修改建议，谨表感谢。

（《生活曾经这样》，[英] 格雷厄姆·格林著，陆谷孙译，上海译文出版社，2012）

“食莲”还是“吞枣”*

安迪公子真能缠人。时值溽暑，正想“逸游自恣”几日，他那边又是短信，又是快递，非要我译篇毛姆不可。余姚话说“像前世欠伊个”一样，拗不过他，只好上电脑。而我这个人的毛病在于，单打一犹可，若头绪纷繁，心理压力必定陡增(玩电脑也是这样，这边下载如要十分钟，宁可枯等，不像学生那么善于 multi-tasking，鼠标乱窜的同时，在键盘上噼里啪啦一阵击打，早就把几件事情一举完成)。所以对我来说，事情要么不做，做了就追求个“快”字，最好一蹴而就，早早脱手，转骛其他。约稿的公子可以证明，这上万字的短篇，不数日即译出。我这么说，非为自炫，而是立此存照，给自己一个参照系，看看效率这东西如何衰减，会不会像这篇故事里威尔逊购买的保险年金，受到期限的制约，过了一定的年龄，总有一天，变成枯木朽株，任你安迪公子十二道金牌催逼，就再也榨不出多少汁水来了。

就文题“The Lotus Eater”的翻译说几句：

香港的董桥兄在一篇文章中，从早年曾虚白、周作人对 lotus eater 的讨论说起，典引丁尼生的诗和大英百科的释文，认为《食莲人》是“漂亮”的“求诗意”的译法。盖 lotus 一词多义，遍查牛津、韦氏、大英、维基等纸质和电子资源后，总括起来，大概能指三“莲”一“枣”。三“莲”者，“亚洲莲”、“埃及睡莲”、“佛座莲”也，显然都与文

---

* 本文是作者为译文《吞食魔果的人》撰写的译后记，原附于文尾。——编注。

本用意不合，剩余的唯有一“枣”，即希腊神话中奥德修斯的随从，在北非某岛被岛民怂恿而误食的所谓忘忧花果。这种果子具有“莲”所没有的致幻和致瘾效应，看维基提供的照片当属枣类无疑。有鉴于此，“食莲”虽美，是否信译，似成问题了，而判断译文良窳，区区素以一“真”二“美”（如果“美”得起来的话）为准。复从拉丁学名返查到1963年中国科学院编写、科学出版社出版的《英拉汉植物名称》（试用本），这才找到《英汉大词典》采用的“落拓枣”之名。至此，究竟是“食莲”还是“吞枣”，基本上有了答案。根据上述求证，不取“食莲人”，改译“吞枣人”，另加脚注？如是，不但“诗意”荡然无存，叠床架屋，递相模效，不足为训。为防谬计，鄙意文题翻译用词中既不出“莲”，也不出“枣”，避实就虚为好，好在原文中主人公入魔也没写到吃了什么。

避实就虚，说说容易，做起来难。原因是神话里的 lotus eaters 一族“花头经”实在太多。吃下何种花果之后会陶陶然酣睡一场，然后“此间乐，不思蜀”，非要奥德修斯绑着他们回去不可。知足忘忧，终日倦慵，耽于逸乐，摒弃劳作——要把这些特点归纳到一个词，殊非易事。根据毛姆故事主人公威尔逊的个性特征，我曾想译作“散淡人”，但马上自我否定了，因为“能指”和“所指”俱狭于英文原文，又怕读者跟诸葛孔明和卧龙岗发生联想；接着想到“幽遐人”，一查《汉语大词典》，说是“幽遐”二字一般只用以修饰地点，只好放弃；继而想到四字成语“逸游自恣”，用来描摹主人公好像还算贴切，却又太酸；搔头半天，又试用过“着魔人”，怕有人回译过去，成了英文里的 the possessed，导致毛姆与陀思妥耶夫斯基撞车；译“入魔人”吧，生生把“走火入魔”四字拆开，于心不忍；还想到过“忘川中人”，那是 paraphrase，而非翻译，更何况尽管两者都源出希腊神话，意象已由 lotus 偷换作通往地狱的 Lethe，诚属张冠李戴。最后决定半实半虚，于是有了现在这个差强人意的文题译法：“吞食魔果的人”。“莲”

啊,“枣”啊,全避开了。以上文字也算是给董桥兄一个解释,兼及自辩,只是写了一大通,仍难自恕。董兄精通中西,当代超迈高士,商榷云云,我不敢也。

“工作的目的乃是赢得闲暇”,安迪公子识人深眇,知道我这人老是把“Not working is the real work for me”(不工作才是真正受罪)挂在嘴上,或许这才派我翻译此文,给我洗洗脑子——人家以最后六年为代价,也要换得前二十五年的 carpe diem,人生深厉浅揭的真谛即在于此。毛姆这个短篇,文字清通易译,但翻译时总觉得这位高寿老人由远及近,娓娓道来,有点啰唆,行文的进展速度犹如卡普里悠闲生活的节奏,特别是跟当时开始在文坛崭露头角的现代派作家一比,尤觉他有曲写毫芥的毛病。如酒店老板娘与三位食客完全无涉,也要来上一段“天后赫拉”、“水汪汪的眼睛”之类冗笔。对话本是小说诸多元素中的一种,这儿却多少成了叙事主体(是否与作家本人生活中出语艾艾口吃有关?);而身在卡普里这样的风景胜地,大有象征意象可以挖掘利用,可是每逢写景段落,莫不一语带过,唯有故事最后主人公“死于月皎时分嵯峨之美”一句耐得咀嚼。我本人倒宁可读他的阿申敦间谍短篇。不好,一时笔滑,闯进文本评论的领域来了,赶快就此打住。

(《毛姆短篇小说精选集》,[英] 毛姆著,冯亦代等译,译林出版社,2012)

啥都可以?

——谈谈语言的“污秽”化倾向和趣味编词典

文题是从英文的 anything goes 翻译过来的，四个音节照应四个汉字，说的是在高容忍的语言环境中，禁忌大可破除，标准随意颠覆。追踪历史，可能有的禁忌原不应该成为禁忌，而是虚无；至于遣字造句的高容忍，极易滑入安那其（anarchy）式的狂欢。这种态度，扩而大之，是整个社会后现代性格的一种表露。这类取“啥都可以”态度的人，英文中姑且称之为 whateverists，即“啥都可以”一派。

举个例子说，因为美国的《市井词典》（*Urban Dictionary*）收了条“no zuo no die”（不作不会死——哂人爱“作”），有人就推波助澜，把这句据说源自动漫的话炒作而激起一场小狂欢（我译 minicarnival）。三个英语词加一个汉语拼音的混搭，核心词“作”仍然无解，语言如此“活”法，笔者至今懵懂，就连年龄小去几茬的“潮友”也未必果真明白，确实应了“啥都可以”一问。记得在网名作“老神仙”时代的微博讨论中，我曾建议把“作女”译作“high maintenance girl”，那至少还部分解释了“作”的意思。

再举一例。一位朋友把 snobbery 译作汉语的“装 B”，而非传统的“势利”。这译法果然准确，更是生猛鲜活，确是某公子所说的“活的语言”。眼下，那个以英语 B 字母置代汉字，又好像是一场语言狂欢，损人时自然通用（我被人骂时，什么难听的名字都能容忍，唯独被叫做“傻 B”受不了），就连正面褒引最近上市的某款手机，也要说到机器的“B 格”如何如何——当然也是为了与“bigger than bigger”谐音。这叫做语言的“污秽”化倾向。都说使用污秽语，一开始会给人在压抑之际“一吐为快”的宣泄和震撼效应，一传十，十传百，说得多了，也说得溜了，效应开始减弱，直到成为空心化的虚词。一般说来，一个人大约从高小到初中时代，对于污秽化最易接受，从众是个因素；另外，青春期也会导致过剩的语言能量发泄——现在叫“吐槽”（源自台湾用法）。要是可行，有志者不妨做个统计，语料库中的“B”使用的总量有多少，若能分析出使用者的年龄、身份、职业、教育/教化程度等等参数，更是对社会语言学研究的贡献。同理，英语里的以f 打头的或其他四字母污秽语，你若看惯美剧，可能整体的英语还没来得及学好，四字母倒是白牙红口张嘴就喷。一个“绝望主妇”跟与自己差不多年龄的朋友说话，即使是无害絮叨，可以大剌剌地喷出四字母，而对自己年幼的子女说话，纵有强烈的詈骂冲动，可能会上齿接触下唇，发音部位调整就绪，口腔部位的表情肌使力不少，只是不去震动声带，毕竟这种语言还是幼儿不宜。可见“啥都可以”未必都可以。

我是主张撇除渣秽，不纳腐朽这条底线的，不能像上述美国《市井词典》那样有太多诲淫诲毒的白描内容，这不但是为了表明社会的品行公约，也是编者尊重读者的一种价值取向，更何况我们这儿说的词典编者，大多是学语言的过来人，身为家长和教师，对于后来者和自己的子弟以接触何种语料为宜，自有一种天然的关注。

所谓啥都可以，与英语世界描写主义与规范主义的对抗有关。自 17 世纪中叶开始，规范主义曾大行其道，谁造个生鲜新词就像“铸假币”一样可恶（笛福［Daniel Defoe］语），“王者英语”（包含Royal, King's 或 Queen's 等名目）之类的社团踵趾相接，层出不穷，直到 2011 年尚未绝迹。上世纪，自英国亨利 · W. 福勒（Henry W. Fowler）的《现代英语惯用法词典》和美国的小威廉 · 斯特伦克及其弟子 E. B. 怀特（William Strunk, Jr. and E. B. White）的《风格的要素》（亦译《英文写作指南》）以降，乔治·奥威尔（George Orwell）、金斯利·艾米斯（Kingsley Amis）、欧内斯特·高沃斯（Ernest Gowers）、威廉·赛菲尔（William Safire）等作家名士，一直强调规则的作用，提倡清丽、优雅、特别是所谓“得体”的英语，描写主义者基本上是被边缘化的，充其量只有如埃里克·帕特里奇（Eric Partridge）这样一些专注研究俚俗英语并把不登大雅之堂的语料编入词典的有数几人。直到上世纪 60 年代韦氏三版问世，原先大量的语用标签被斧削，不但收了“ain't”、“irregardless”和“like”（用作连接词），还有“drownded”、“hisself”等内容，打出了描写主义的高牙大纛，一时曾引得舆论大哗，贬评如潮，仿佛英语从此将受尽溷乱。记得当时笔者曾写过一篇小文抱不平：“韦氏三版未必就是‘韦带布衣’”（取“韦”字字头谐趣，与锦黻相对）。事理穷尽，止于两端。果然，规范主义很快卷土重来，《美国传统词典》可算一个对付韦氏三版的显例。他们的一个做法就是特邀专家，组成评判委员会，判别有争议词语用法的正谬、清浊、高下、娴媸。时至今日，特别是上世纪 80 年代出现“政治正确”之后，新保守主义可以在政坛一时回潮，但语言层面上描写主义似已占定上风。读者对此如犹有疑问，可读英国 1970 年代后作家亨利·希金斯（Henry Hitchings）的诸种近著。更有意思的是《美国传统词典》的转舵，编者始而改组评判委员会，把描写主义学者聘入，与规范主义分庭抗礼，以求公正互补，而到了最新的第五版出书时，前言竟有两篇，分别出自斯坦福和哈佛两位教授之手，前者继续强调规则，后者则把规则看作老得没牙的“bubbe meises”（old wives' tales）。

尤其需要说一说，中国读者不属印裔美国学者布拉·卡奇鲁（Braj Kachru）首创的所谓“世界英语”（World English）——*World-English* 一书书名古已有之，那是 19 世纪有人为倡导英文拼写改革所著，宏旨却非今人之所谓——三个同心圆中的内圈，即以英语为母语的人群，也不属于包括英国前殖民地等的中圈，而是处在最外圈，因此在中国教英语似更不能完全撇开规范，一味描写，放任语言无政府主义和虚无主义。毕竟我们读、听到的“内圈”英语，并不完全等同自己写、说的“外圈”英语。当然，人在“外圈”，有些不尽规矩的英语表达，例如“to discuss about”和“to emphasize on”这类违悖及物动词惯用法的实例，因为相应名词“discussion”和“emphasis”的“传染”，“about”和“on”纯属多余，但并不影响实质交流，小疵而已。我们教书匠的手中肯定都积累了不少类似的小疵：human resources 遗漏复数词尾，younger generation 遗漏比较级词尾，in charge of 似乎不足以表示中文“主要负责”的意思，而非加进一个 major 不可，等等。不是讨论“啥都可以”的“世界英语”吗？谁知道“外圈”人不会由于习惯成自然，某一天把“内圈”人表达的小疵逐渐视作合理合法？前几年坊间出现一批“外圈”英语新词，据说是南京某位英语高人仿“内圈”构词法的首创，如 shitizen（屁民）等，相信“内圈”人都能见词会意，更像是活的语言，可接受程度应该大大高于前文说过的“no zuo no die”。“瓷器店里的公牛”（bull in a china shop）是固定熟语，如果恰好碰到左冲右突、毛手毛脚的主角/主语是女性，“外圈”人追求戏谑的修辞效果，兼顾暗讽疯牛病，斗胆改作“瓷器店里的疯母牛”（mad cow in a china shop），又如何？

除了活的语言，人们又在兴趣盎然地讨论活的词典。所谓“活”，受“维基百科”的启发，我的理解是词典采录的内容“上不封顶，下不保底，四周无墙”，可删，可增，可改，可置换，读者同时又是编者，真正做到开放式的互动。如影随形的纸质词典的篇幅意识，随着电脑帧面的自如滚动，绝不再是一大掣肘。当然，参与编纂的读者诸君最好不要轻浮衍言，把词典网页当作涂鸦场。但即使到了数字化时代，词典的本质依然有保守的一面，因为描写和记录，永远滞后于语言实际。所以,再"活"的词典,是做不到"实时"而只能是"历时"的。

如此说来,所谓活的词典,其宏纲大要看来就是建一个可靠又丰富的语料库。早在1970年代早期,"文革"时编写《新英汉词典》的同仁,已有朦胧的语料库意识,只不过当时,唯有极个别的编者已从自己的阅读中搜取材料,添加新词、新义、新用法,就我回忆,如词条"streaking"(裸跑)、"plumber"(水门事件中大行其道的堵漏防漏的所谓管子工——还记得美刊当年一篇报道的题目:"Officially Inspired Leaks and Plumbers"[官方授意泄露的机密和管子工])、"schmaltz"(滥情感伤,还有犹太裔知识分子多用的其他意第绪语词)、"-in"(作后缀,指集体抗议形式,缘于1960年代后期美国"反文化"潮流的sit-in, sing-in, love-in, be-in,等等)、"defoliant"(越战中美军直升机为开阔射界用的化学品"除绿叶剂");又如"prewar"用作副词而非形容词(记得仔细查过,这在当年的"内圈"词典中均付诸阙如,"外圈"人却有书证在握而添加了);更多的第一手例证被采用,记得有"the sky is thick with flying foreign ministers"(典型的所谓新闻体:空中,外长们来回飞行忙)、"do you really want to come or are you merely being amiable?"(你是真想来,还是敷衍应景?)、"she modeled between husbands"(那女人在离婚后再结婚前做模特儿)、"消暑旅游只需打个电话"(summer is only a call away——典型的广告体)等等。朦胧的意识在之后的《英汉大词典》编写时,渐趋清醒,编写组终于设立一个资料组,把撷取语料的工作制度化了。1976年的同仁们虽还来不及侈谈"语料库",也已开始把"引语档"(citation file)一语挂在嘴边,手工做成50万张卡片。虽是区区数目的小儿科,而且阅读并无系统,从上图去借原版英文书的那位并不懂英语(辛劳的老顾——上天保佑他的灵魂!),原来设想的有声资料更未涉及,重要的是,"引语档"必须以"内圈"真实的英语,也可以说是活的英语,作为根据,再没有"文革"时期《新英汉词典》那样的"喜儿打了地主一记耳光”一类“外圈”自造英文例证;更重要的是,若干采自书证的第一手内容,未必都已经被“内圈”辞书收录,若可证其频用,“外圈”人凭自己跟踪语言的“异族敏感”,胡不捷足先登?事实也证明,像 jacuzzi 这样的漩涡浴缸,“外圈”词典收得早于“内圈”——抑或同步?《英汉大词典》还曾设法给那种意大利新产品冠以“极可适”的汉文!词典要激“活”,编者除了长年累月地徜徉活的语言之外,个人的性灵和机趣似乎从未见人提过。牛津补编的 Robert Burchfield 倒是说过,编英语词典的人大可以把全书的最后一条落在 zzz 之上作结,兴会大功告成,呼呼睡觉去也。“啥都可以”意味着语料库里多些插科打诨的歇后语、趣双关、文字游戏之类,供编者长时间正襟危坐之余莞尔调剂,供读者在娱乐中养成语言机敏。举几个例子:1)名人怎么才能一直装酷/冷冰冰的?他们有许多粉丝/扇子啊 how do celebrities stay cool? they have many fans(可入英汉“stay cool”);2)问题很菜,回答更二 the question is puerile and the answer lower-IQ(可入英汉“puerile”);3)seckill(ing), instantkill(ing)(eg in e games) 2. to outbid others at the click of the mouse; to speed-shop (eg in online business):最牛秒杀书店 a peerless online bookstore with numerous titles at a bargain price(自然入汉英“秒杀”);4)we aim to please. you aim too please 我们让你方便。请你瞄准了方便(可入英汉“aim”);5)最先抵达且贡献至巨者说了算 whoever arrives “firstest with the mostest” has the say(可入英汉“superlative degree”);6)(a floor covered with chicken feathers) a bad litter of trivialities/trivia; bothersome day-to-day life; a can of worms; an omnishambles of a situation:小夫妻俩吵得不可开交,弄得一地鸡毛 the young couple traded zingers, opening a can of worms(自然入汉英“一地鸡毛”),等等等等。此类语料极大丰富之后,编者再不是寻章摘句的老雕虫,选词设例,通透活络,游刃有余,甚至可以体会到一点语言玩家的乐趣。

看来,活的词典唯有基于活的语言,否则就是植木无根,生意无从发端,本地单薄的,也只能华尽一朝。共时性的学生词典暂且不论,一部大型的综合性词典,既是共时的,必然同时也是历时的。我常胡思乱想,一部大词典究竟有多少内容是“备而需查”,又有多少内容是“备而待查”的。前者可能是无穷大人次寻常频繁查阅的,而后者之中有没有零人次所需的条目?想来也总有吧。即便仅为录而备忘,那也是有价值的。不怕“啥都可以”,不怕庞杂,查得率第一,或许这正是词典追求的目标。

(原载 2014 年 10 月 17 日《文汇报》)

《中华汉英大词典》前言

大约 1/4 个世纪之前,好像也是这个季节,曾为自己参与编纂的《英汉大词典》写过一篇前言。那时年未及艾,矜愎不知自敛,声势过大,逸辞过壮,特别是第一段,什么要把词典献给中华祖国,献给世纪交替的新时代,等等。时至今日,开卷重读这等文字,只剩下条风时丽之感。第二版的前言,虽是用英文写的,依然还是有藻绘的毛病。

那么这部《中华汉英大词典》的献辞该怎么写?平实点说,就我个人而言——不代表积极参与编纂并做出巨大贡献的兄弟院校同仁——权作献给母校复旦大学吧。我 1957 年入校,迄今五十年有奇。优劣不论,可以说我这个人主要是在这儿养成的,理当为母校留下一点物理形式的东西作为纪念,尽管可能只是雪泥鸿爪,甚至恍若蚊虻一过。

回归常识。当然,更重要的是供读者使用,不但是国人,还有老外。早在上世纪 80 年代初,我在美、英、加等国的华埠书店就发现,有意购买汉英词典的华洋顾客远多于购买英汉者,只是因为汉英的种类偏少或不甚合用,常失望而去。国人中凡对汉语字词(尤其是今人已不那么常用或熟悉的)感兴趣但苦于知之不多,或时被大陆以外汉语社区常用字词困惑者,以及在全球化大背景前有志于不同民族语言交流,特别是汉英和英汉翻译的,也许会发现这部《中华汉英大词典》尚有用处,释文大致易解可读,例证包含不少新鲜信息,也还有趣;外国读者把这样一本除了音训和义训还有部分形训内容的汉英词典买回去使用,可能也还差强人意吧。

设计《中华汉英大词典》的几条大原则,亦即编者的着力重点,在于:

(一)在英语世界描写主义和规范主义之争的大背景前,采用一种不妨称之为“有保留的描写主义”(descriptivism with a grain of salt)的编纂方针(其实所有的描写主义都不认同 anything goes),亦即在描写语言实际用法为主的同时,绝不纯客观地“有闻必录”,而是奉行取舍必经汰选的原则。例如撇除渣秽,不纳腐朽,不但是为了表明社会的品行公约底线,也是编者尊重读者的一种价值取向,更何况我们这儿的编者大多是学英语的过来人,身为家长和教师,对于后来者和自己的子弟以接触何种语料为宜,自有一种天然的关注。倘若因为我们的取舍,被责“已经沦为规范主义的描写主义”,我们也一无憾恚。再就语言表达而论,所谓“有保留”,我们也非随你怎么使用英语,一律照录不误的一群,不是人称 whateverists 的一群。

毋庸讳言,在英语世界,自 17 世纪中叶开始,规范主义曾大行其道,谁造个生鲜新词就像“铸假币”一样可恶(笛福[Daniel Defoe]语),“王者英语”(包含 Royal, King's 和 Queen's 等名目)之类的社团踵趾相接,层出不穷,直到 2010 年尚未绝迹。上世纪,自英国亨利·W. 福勒(Henry W. Fowler)的《现代英语惯用法词典》和美国的小威廉·斯特伦克及其弟子E. B. 怀特(William Strunk, Jr. and E. B. White)的《风格的要素》(亦译《英文写作指南》)以降,乔治·奥威尔(George Orwell)、金斯利·艾米斯(Kingsley Amis)、欧内斯特·高沃斯(Ernest Gowers)、威廉·赛菲尔(William Safire)等作家名士一直强调规则的作用，提倡清丽、优雅，特别是所谓“得体”的英语，描写主义者基本上是被边缘化的，充其量只有如埃里克·帕特里奇（Eric Partridge）这样一些专注研究俚俗英语并把不登大雅之堂的语料编入词典的有数几人。直到上世纪60年代韦氏三版问世，原先大量的语用标签被斧削，不但收了“ain't”、“irregardless”和“like”（用作连接词），还有“drownded”、“hisself”等内容，打出了描写主义的高牙大纛，一时曾引得舆论大哗，贬评如潮，仿佛英语从此将受尽溷乱。记得当时曾写过一篇小文抱不平：“韦氏三版未必就是‘韦带布衣’”（取“韦”字字头谐趣，与锦黻相对）。事理穷尽，止于两端。果然，规范主义很快卷土重来，《美国传统词典》可算一个对付韦氏三版的显例。他们的一个做法就是特邀专家，组成评判委员会，判别有争议词语用法的正谬、清浊、高下、妍媸。时至今日，特别是上世纪80年代出现“政治正确”之后，新保守主义可以在政坛一时回潮，但语言层面上描写主义似已占定上风。读者对此如犹有疑问，可读英国1970年代后作家亨利·希金斯（Henry Hitchings）的诸种近著。更有意思的是《美国传统词典》的转舵，编者始而改组评判委员会，把描写主义学者聘入，与规范主义分庭抗礼，以求公正互补，而到了最新的第五版出书时，前言竟有两篇，分别出自斯坦福和哈佛两位教授之手，前者继续强调规则，后者则把规则看作老得没牙的“bubbe meises”（old wives' tales）。

尤其需要指出的是，中国读者不属印裔美国学者布拉·卡奇鲁（Braj Kachru）首创的所谓“世界英语”（World English）——*World-English* 一书书名古已有之，那是19世纪有人为倡导英文拼写改革所著，宏旨自不同于今人所谓——三个同心圆中的内圈，即以英语为母语的人群，而是处在最外圈，因此在中国教英语似更不能完全撇开规范，一味描写，放任语言无政府主义和虚无主义。毕竟我们读/听到的“内圈”英语，并不完全等同自己写/说的“外圈”英语。要是我们的学生张口闭口都是英语的“四字母词”，浇风易渐，待到形成习惯，怕是淳化难归，“当如后患何”了。

（二）具体说来，《中华汉英大词典》在收词方面，古今兼顾，中华本土（大陆以及港澳台）和海外社区兼顾，多少可算是这部词典的特色之一。即以海峡两岸和香港、澳门乃至海外的词语为例，试设想，同样一个专名，如 Sierra Leone，一处取音译“塞拉利昂”，另一处取意译“狮子山”，如何认同；即便同取音译，因用词习惯加地域方言的影响，写成汉字读出来也会嗒舌不通，如 Trinidad and Tobago，我们这边译的“特立尼达和多巴哥”（近见媒体嫌长而缩作“特多”，倒也有趣），到了大陆以外成了“千里达”，何以对应？说到非专有名词，近年来，大陆以外汉译——有的意译，如“卖点”（selling point）、“愿景”（vision）等；有的音译，如“贴士”（tips）、“车厘子”（cherries）等；有的音意兼译，如“幽浮”（UFO）、“迷你”（mini-）等——被大陆采用的不在少数，但歧异仍多；如科技术语，虽然也有互相袭用的例子，差异仍比比皆是。除了已为大众熟知的“软件”和“软体”（software）、“鼠标”和“滑鼠”（mouse）、“激光”和“镭射”或“雷射”（laser）之外，最近被称为现代物理学“圣杯”的“上帝粒子”boson 被发现，大陆译为“玻色子”，而台湾某些行业则有通译作“玻子”的，虽非迥别，亦无伤互解，毕竟相类而非。商业经管，不论你喜欢不喜欢，似乎已成百工之首，但就是对这个领域中最常用的缩略语之一的 CEO，不同华人社区就有不同译法，诸如“首席执行官”、“行政总裁”、“执行长”等等 。另一方面，大陆用语同样也有向大陆以外华人社区扩散的趋向。当我看到港澳台报刊上屡屡出现“话题性”（topicality?）、“认问性”（accountability?）之类前所未见的词语时，不由得想到大陆用词中相当于英语-ness 的后缀“性”字，频用之极（此间人交谈，往往不用清楚直白的“一般”，非说“一般性”不可），难免不习染其他华人社区？于是，编者们设想：要是把这些熔于一炉，收词涵盖中华本土乃至海外华人社区，以简繁体字并列参照的形式，如实收录各社区特有的高频词语，使之通过同一种译入语（英语）的媒介，渐趋互相认同而凝聚，兼收扩大汉语词汇共核域之效，有何不美？

近年来提倡文化传统继承，第一步自然要读懂古文献，识得其中的字和词。而坊间的汉英词典多以《现代汉语词典》为母本，收词对古籍的覆盖面自然甚有局限。为古今兼顾计，将《汉语大词典》作为必要参考书之一，从中收词，很有必要。同时，在精力可及范围内，重温古汉语的若干种笔记、尺牍等，搜辑第一手语料（如古人说西湖、蛾眉之"妙"在景色或名字之柔美，而"病"在寓讽不够阳刚的高论），译成英语，俾使内容也有超出《汉语大词典》窠臼之处。事实上，即使如笔者这种年龄和文化程度的人，说来惭愧，对博大精深的汉语文化，认知只及非常有限的局部，以管窥天，以蠡测海，未知远大于已知，已知又常非确知或真知。就拿本词典所收的"宥坐（之）器"这么个实物为例，不查《汉语大词典》并写出"tilted container for holding water placed on the right-hand side of an emperor's throne [serving as a reminder that the last drop makes the vessel run over, a reminder of always doing things with moderation]"这样的英语释文，笔者依然懵懂不知为何物。逾"而传"之年，尚且如此无知，遑论今日读者中的幼稚少年。古人云：一字之褒，宠逾华衮之赠；片言之贬，辱过市朝之挞，也从一个侧面说到文字的重要性。收录"宥坐（之）器"等词的启示是：读者说不定还能从词典的英语释文，识得一些古色古香的汉语文字呢。而要让中国文化"走出去"，岂可坐视古籍覆盖面的缺失？古文典籍不少已有训手名家译成英文，原本撷来录入即是，但典籍皆是语篇逐译，诗词类的翻译还有韵律方面的技术要求，与出现在词典里的单句孤例不完全相同，所以有时我们会自行另译，非为斗胆偏离桃蹊李径，只为提供栀子红椒之类的另一种选择而已。譬如李白名句“安能摧眉折腰事权贵”，我们把宾语“眉”和“腰”都避开了，译时只用上英语惯用法的“bow and scrape to”，不知读者是否可以接受？

说到现当代汉语，自然不能不提计算机、手机等科技手段扩散之后对语言文字的影响。我们对所谓的“互联网汉语”，在坚决排除污人耳目的用法的同时，总体上采取较为包容的收词策略——亦即上述“有保留的描写主义”。诚然，我们知道文字与人一样，丰悴有时，一来一去而不可常。一个时期的高频字或词，进锐退速的例子多的是，特别是在词汇平均寿命较短的网络语言中。然为词典的查得率计，复从共时和历时互为依存又不无相互包容的角度，对待所谓“阶段有效词”（period terms），适当放宽尺度收录，我们并不以为就是降低品味哗众取宠，毕竟词典的主要使用者若不已经是也必将是越来越依赖“两机”（计算机和手机）——日后或许还有眼镜、手套、手表、义齿等可穿戴高科技物件，甚至使用寻常灯泡（Li-Fi）并随身随地联网（mi-fi）——来获取并传送信息的新人。附带说一句，正是基于此种考虑，我们在选词时，还特别注意加重科技用词的分量，部分国外新产品、新工艺、新技术、新理论的名称，即使国内尚无标准化译名，我们也先试译作汉语，然后以汉-英形式呈现给读者，亦即由译入语（英语）出发，到译出语（汉语），进入词典，再从译出语（汉语）重回译入语（英语）的倒序。衣不经新，何由而古？相信这样做，符合国人对科技新时代的要求，有一定的前瞻效应。有人说词典的本质特征之一就是保守，因为描记永远落在语言实际之后，但不同类型的词典，根据各自承担的使命，在某一方面尝试突进，如对读者有用，对译出语（汉语）词汇的补遗、纳新、扩充有益，又何乐不为？更何况即使倒序，描记其实仍然落后，只不过语言实际暂时还未发生在汉语领域而已。拿个非科技的极限运动用词 skydiving 为例，跃出飞行器，延缓开伞那种“碧云深处共翱翔”的空中动作，大家在电视上见得多了，可是如用汉语描述，大多数人仍会用上英语“夹心”，或是解释性

(paraphrase)的“花式跳伞”。为翻译而非说明这个词，想在网上找到一个与汉语相应的译法，至今不得。“凫空”二字，姑且收入，以试试上述逆序作业是否可行。

（三）释义方面，强调“等值”不仅仅是扣准语义（字面的和比喻的），也要针对语用，在做到“等值”的同时还力求超越。编者们常在追求等值的同时以“超越等值（beyond equivalence）”自勉，也就是尽量在译入语释文中扩大语词的文化适用阈，使词条的对译，除去犹如穿上紧身衣的严格技术作业之外，只要有可能，还有一点涵化(acculturation)或本人称之为文化漾溢的作用。试以一些成语、谚语、熟语为例。譬如在“一地鸡毛”条，在“(a floor littered with chicken feathers) a confusion of trivialities/trivia; bothersome day-to-day life”之后，再漾溢引渡到所指都还接近的“a can of worms; an omni-shambles of a situation”；在“木已成舟”条，对应之后，涵化如下：“one cannot unring a bell”或“one cannot unscramble eggs”(unscrambled eggs 在西方已用作书名)；在“屋漏偏逢连夜雨”条，对应之后，漾溢如下：“it's a perfect storm”(perfect storm 虽古已有之，经 1997 年用作书名和 2000 年用作影片名渲染推广，几乎尽人皆知)；在“功败垂成”条，对应之后，漾溢如下：“there is yet a possible slip twixt the cup and the lip”；在“人之将死其言也善”条，对应之后，采用 19 世纪英国诗人兼文评家马修·阿诺德(Matthew Arnold)的原文句“truth sits upon the lips of dying men”；在“水涨船高”条引用美国前总统肯尼迪(J. F. Kennedy)的“a rising tide lifts all boats”；在“猫哭老鼠”条，直译之后，加上西谚“carrion crows bewail the dead sheep and then eat them”；在“会哭的孩子有奶吃”后，配上意象明显发生“基因突变”的“the squeaky wheel gets the grease”；在“害人之心不可有，防人之心不可无”条，在“削足适履”条等不少词目的释文中,也是在直译之后,分别加上西谚"every Caesar has his Brutus"和习用语"to put a quart into a pint pot"等,其中意象的变换可能有损"等值"这一金科玉律,但一部双语词典要起到在两种文化间穿梭摆渡的作用,这儿提到的涵化和漾溢,只要不是钻奇凿诡,笔者以为只会有助于保持语言的元气。古语今用的跨文化翻译是个棘手问题,如汉语成语"醉生梦死"或熟语"今朝有酒今朝醉"一译入西方语境,对应之余,立刻就会碰到那儿的颓废派常用语"YOLO(you only live once)"——有庙堂中人称之为2013年"最丑陋的词"——且不管其生命是否须臾奄忽,暂且收入又何妨?这种漾溢已属语用变化范畴,实际上已损及"对应"(至少是形式对应),我们也不以为忤。当然,在字和词的层面,这样的穿度和呼应自当更加普遍,譬如以英语套语"at the end of the day"对应汉语"总之"二字(纵然又有规范派不以为然,认作"滥用");在用直译达到"等值"之后,再以西方超感官心理学和神经科学正着力研究的"clairvoyance"和"clairaudience"分别对应汉语神话里的"千里眼"和"顺风耳",可能更给人一种语言玩家的乐趣。诚然,不同语言间的翻译活动有一种与生俱来的"彼岸性",涵化也好,漾溢和穿度也罢,词典中未臻脱化境界之处尚多,只能怪编者能力有限了。

给汉语中大量的新生"文化局限词"用英文释义,可能是最耗费心力的工作。对于这类字和词,能够用来参考的虽也有数种英文报刊和几家翻译网站,但往往收录有限,译文时而生涩甚至失真,如把"黑车"译作"black taxi";"捣浆糊"译作"to give a(该用a或the恕笔者存疑)runaround, to run wild, to act restlessly";"调酒师"译作所指的宽狭并不完全对等的"bartender";"包二奶"等同于旧时"纳妾"而译作"to have a concubine"等等,就是信手拈来的数例。近年来我国公示英语译文中时常出现令人啼笑皆非的大错,已引得众口哓哓,识者呕哕,甚至有人说已影响到国家的"软实力"。想来,纠正明显的错误，改进翻译，编出一部释义比较精准，译入语比较符合异族语言习惯的汉英词典，应当也可以在文化“走出去”方面发挥一定的作用。为响应“拯救方言”的呼吁，我们比较注意收录粤、闽、吴等方言词语，而因为在上海编这部词典，近水楼台先得月，沪语中的语言现象出现得可能更多一些。

近年来国人学英语的兴趣大增，其中多有不甘蹈袭、热衷于利用英语构词法则自造新词来翻译汉语的高手。一些网友自造的时髦词，由于不无创意，眼下相当风行，有人希望我们能率先收入（其实收不收中国人新造的英文词，主要是英汉而非汉英词典编者的抉择）。这类汉语用词，如“给力”译作 gelivable，虽说如美国《市井俚语词典》这样的洋人辞书网页也已收入，《纽约时报》做过专门介绍，但毕竟到目前为止，仍限于我们自娱自乐的层面，要像“关系”这样被英语作为成熟的借词吸收，也许尚待时日。这样，对于“给力”，我们还是宁可注释成“<colloq> **1** boosting; stimulating: 前冠军咋这么不给力 the ex-champion is but a pathetic let-down | 这番话真给力啊 these remarks are a real pick-me-up **2** cool; awesome; nifty; bravo: 这首歌太给力了! this song rocks!”之类，似更能达到言语乃至文化转移的目的。至于“gelivable”这类英文形式的词能否存活并登堂入室，拭目以待吧。

（四）配例方面，与其他词典一样，《中华汉英大词典》配例的一大目的在于佐证释义，补足释文“言犹未尽”的部分，因此力争例证译文措辞与词目释文措辞既略有别，又有呼应，能够成为释文的延续或扩展。有些词目的内涵和外延绝非一个译名可以穷尽，对于其中某些我国读者一时还比较生疏的内容，通过适当例证予以揭示，笔者以为很有必要。例如美国嚣嚣一时的“另类医学”，汉英词典做到 = alternative medicine 之后大可就此搁笔，读者尽可二次查阅百科全书或作网上搜索。鉴于另类医学包含的内容繁多,涉及多项术语或专名,如果我们的词典能把“chiropractic, naturopathy, homeopathy, herbal medicine, holistic medicine, acupuncture, Ayurveda, spiritual devotions, etc.”这些难词收入条内作为例证,译出“脊柱推拿、自然疗法、顺势疗法、草药、整体医疗、针刺、印度草药疗法、精神祈祷,等等”,是否可为一般读者提供足够的关连信息,又为专业读者勾勒了一张继续搜索的粗略的路线图?至少得以在一定程度上减轻读者下一步的劳动量。当然,语词词典与专业词典更与百科全书不同。例证作为释文的延续做到什么程度,提供何种以及多少额外的信息,其中分寸需要妥然把握。而若不是词典编纂数字化的终极愿景始终萦绕心头,实现有望,词典编者的纸张篇幅意识也会极度掣肘此类扩写式的例证。不过,“再生医学” = regenerative medicine,“大数据” = big data,想来只是一牖之开,一般英语水平的读者不查词典也知道。若求大致照通(不是至察!),前者如辅以“虽说有些简单化,再生医学无非就是干细胞研究和组织工程学两大块 though a bit simplistic, regenerative medicine consists of stem cell research and tissue engineering”,后者辅以“大数据是信息技术业界的一个新词,可与现在已为人熟知的‘云’字相提并论。巨量数据之大有三个方面:总量达到万兆字节,速度剧提,多样性激增 big data is a new term in IT industry comparable to the now familiar term cloud. it is threefold big: in volume in terms of PB (petabytes), in velocity, and in variety”,是否可收相对洞明之效?配例的另一目的,在于提供常识和知识。如在“血压”条下把收缩压(systolic)和舒张压(diastolic)120 至 80 的读数录以备忘[我本人的查阅习惯就是权把汉英当英汉,去“血压”试查有无表示上下血压读数的两词,得则幸甚;同理,读者也可能去“地震”条查寻“里氏震级”(Richter scale)英文怎么说,去“手机”条查各种制式的对应英文]。在个别情况下,例证包含的信息,在编者眼里可能比之释文更有价值。拿个单字条“不”为例,按说有一个 no 和 not,或至多配上 to be not 和/或 to do not 的例证,理当足矣。编者们恰好找到一个“真实英语”的用例,其中有三个 don't,又惟妙惟肖写出今人的某种消费陋习,虽略嫌长,仍决定取作例证收入:“他们毫不含糊地透支购买奢侈品,只为在不认识的人面前显摆 they buy things they don't want with the money they don't have to impress the people they don't know”。笔者个人的认识是,这样的例句,有心的读者可能会过目成诵,用作词典例证,也无不可。当然,配例的词汇学价值(如词源、语义、语用、同义——包括辨异——反义、上位、下位等)始终是编者选择的着眼点,譬如利用复现和对比效应,努力诠释 perfect 一词的内涵和外延:“十全十美的完人没找到,我却学会了看透不完美的常人(或于不完美处看完美)instead of finding a perfect person, i learned to look through an imperfect person perfectly”一句,有助读者吃透何谓“perfect”;而“我们从存在化为乌有实在是太容易了 how easily we slip from is to isn't”[Thomas Lynch 语],使人由“verb to be”及其口语变异形式的自由发挥,联想到哈姆雷特的“To be, or not to be”。当然,与丹麦王子的独白相比,殡葬师/诗人语录可能蓑不如裘,但寻常口语中还是可以用上的,甚至还带一点现代存在主义的意味。

本质上,词典当然是为释疑解惑的目的供人查阅的工具书,而不是适合从头至尾阅读的作品。不过,从古到今,阅读词典,从中学习语言的中外奇人还真偶有所闻。我的老师葛传椝先生就曾通读过英国福勒兄弟的词典,还找出错误若干,写信指谬,得到编者回复,称英国之外有如此深谙英语习惯用法者,实属难得云云。我国鸿儒钱锺书先生据说暇时也喜闲读词典,吸取语言营养。(至于外国通读词典的字迷,读者可参阅笔者 2008 年 9 月 28 日载于上海《东方早报》“书评”版的旧文《真有这等“痴人”?》)今天,生活节奏加快,学英语的途径和手段大增，但问道学生中还是有人想知道："背词典，记生词，是不是一个好办法？"窃以为（用时髦话翻译：IMHO）单靠词典当然不是个好办法，甚至不是办法。不过在发生查阅需要时，在使用词典解决手头某一特定问题的同时，发现前后左右有精彩的例证，顺便背下，我看仍不失为辅助学习的良策。基于这样的认识，《中华汉英大词典》收入相当数量比较短小的例证，其中有警句、箴言、妙语一类（如反衬实干精神的"喋喋不休而不肯动手 long tongue but short hands"，"落后就要挨打 laggards are beaten"，"知识越多，方始明白自己其实缺乏知识 the more i know, the more i know i don't know"等），也有名人名言（如"炉火纯青的极致就是简单 simplicity is the ultimate sophistication [Leonardo da Vinci]"，"我们从历史学到的就是我们从不接受历史教训 we learn from history that we learn nothing from history [George Bernard Shaw]"等），偶尔还有诗句入例（如"焉知我见人，人见我/皆非梦中梦？ is all that we see or seem/but a dream within a dream? [Edgar Allan Poe]"或"死亡是癫狂的暗夜，未知的新路 dying is a wild night/and a new road [Emily Dickenson]"等）。笔者是兴趣学习的鼓吹者，故而特别注意例证的趣味性，如"为什么都把酣睡说成'睡得像个婴儿'，而实际上婴儿一小时要醒十次？ why is it that people say they 'sleep like a baby', while a baby wakes ten times an hour?"，"别为今天是世界末日烦心了，在澳洲此刻已经是明天了 stop worrying about the world ending today. it's already tomorrow in Australia"，"你难道不知死亡是遗传的吗？ you don't know death is hereditary?"或"诺亚怎不把方舟上那对蚊子拍死？ why didn't Noah swat those two mosquitoes?"等等。虽说大俗未必即雅，涉及生理功能的内容，在严格控制的同时，也不能一律排斥，如男士便池警语："我们要为您提供方便，请您也要瞄准了再方便 we aim to please; you aim too please"，虽有类似文字谜语之弊，但不能否认是极简主义的实用例子，是“瞄准”条的合适例证。兴趣常常是学习的推动力和滑润剂。编者们从自己的经验出发，相信经典例证和趣味例证，往往过目不忘，积累多了，何患求业不精？

这么大一部词典，必然问题成堆。其中，笔者絓结最甚的，一是汉语字、词、语的划分处理必有失当之处。也许是因为我们考虑实用尤其是查得率居先，怯于介入尚无权威定论的汉语词汇学的学术讨论，条目的取舍——尤其是像“说他胖，他还喘”之类熟语的收录——必定留下许多可供质疑、挑剔、批判的疏漏；而由于简体和繁体、异体和变体以及因声调不同致字义变异的单字和词组大量存在，词目数量急剧膨胀，查阅难度大为增加（如同一写法的“假日”会复现在不同声调的“假”字头之下），读者难免对词典有“庞杂”、“芜累”之责。其实，任何一部大词典——除去共时的学生词典——既是“备而需查”又是“备而待查”的工具，其中大部分内容是无穷大人次寻常查阅的，也有若干内容不太为人所需，甚至可能是零人次查阅的。有鉴于此，笔者对于“庞杂”、“芜累”就少了一点顾虑。在词典即将编成之际，实有“信当喜极翻愁误，物到难求得尚疑”之叹，并恳请读者诸君贤能容愚，博能容浅，粹能容杂。二是在这数字化时代，笔者受了“维基百科”等的启发，非常属意于互动式辞书。即这儿采录的内容，“上不封顶，下不保底，四周无墙”，使用这些内容的读者同时又是编者，可删，可增，可改，可置换——当然最好不要轻浮衍言，把词典网页当作涂鸦场。要做成这样一部开放式的辞书，目前我们的人力和技术资源尚嫌不足，那就只好留待下一版去设法解决了。

最后，笔者要特别感谢香港邹嘉彦教授主持的LIVAC语料库为我们比照、核对海峡两岸和香港、澳门汉语用词提供了大量权威性的数据，给予我们巨大的支持和帮助。LIVAC 语料库也为国内其他几种汉英词典提供支持，此举理应成为中国双语词典编纂事业中的佳话。

编写之初，美国原 MRM（Mathias Research Management）公司同意我们无偿使用他们积累多年的中文词库，给我们提供了一个原初的始发点。Jim Mathias 和 Tom Creamer 两位先生在三十多年前与本人结下的友谊，由英汉而至汉英，终成全璧。

复旦大学前校长杨玉良院士关心这部词典的编写。我们不但讨论过“烤羊肉串”用于纳米技术等具体问题，还从梵蒂冈举办干细胞研讨会，谈到理工科和人文伦理交叉等问题；林尚立副校长和外文学院褚孝泉前院长为《中华汉英大词典》的立项，勠力推毂，编写组和我本人对此不敢稍忘。

还要感谢以各种方式为这部词典提供素材并随时提出修改意见的个人：他们是范家材（燕京校友、复旦学长）、沈黎（复旦）、杨韵琴（联合国）、张楠（复旦）、陆雰（美国）等女士和先生。

2013 年 8 月初稿
2014 年 10 月定稿
于复旦大学

（《中华汉英大词典（上）》，陆谷孙主编，复旦大学出版社，2015）

A Cursory Comparative Study of English and Chinese*

In December 1979, I spoke on China educational TV about some of the most marked differences between English (as target language) and Chinese (as source language). The audience feedback, as ensuing mail indicated, was generally favorable. It is assumed, therefore, that a similar comparative study (with target and source duly reversed) might likewise be of some practical use to American learners of Chinese at the intermediate level this side of the Pacific.

That English and Chinese are two most extensively used languages in the world is never a controversial point. Nor is it open to doubt that the two languages, unrelated in any way by kinship, are vastly different in idiomatic vernacular. So the quest we are embarking upon by this talk is to find out how wide apart they are from each other and to what extent an adequate awareness of differences on the part of a learner of the one can help improve his language proficiency in the other. But as one or two speeches are always limited in available space, an elaborate comparison with scope and system is out of the question; what is aimed at instead is a few practical points haphazardly brought up for a cursory comparative study.

---

* 本文是作者 1981 年 2 月访美前所写，由作者的好友 Thomas Creamer 先生提供。——编注。

But as no comparative study could claim to be optimally balanced if the student failed to dwell upon similar as well as dissimilar aspects between the languages under review, I would in the first place offer to account, very briefly, for some apparent similarities in expression between English and Chinese. Such similarities, as I see it, do not on any account point to affinity in origin or later evolvement, but are rather accidental parallels resulting either from inherent linguistic processes common to all human languages or from mutual conscious borrowing. Let's take for instance the process of synesthesia—transference mentally of one sense-impression to another. The distinction made between the "cold color" and the "warm color" is valid in English and in Chinese alike. Thus "hánbì"[①] (meaning literally in English "cold green") and "nuǎnhóng"[②] (meaning "warm red") are two frequently employed descriptive epithets in ancient Chinese poetry. A similar pair of common-core modern Chinese expressions "lěngjìng"[③] (meaning literally in English "cold and quiet") and "rè'nao"[④] (meaning "warm and noisy") are presumably derived from the same process of synesthesia. Speaking of transference of sense-impressions, I might mention another example: I understand that native English speakers often use the adjectival modifier "loud" (sense-impression by hearing in the first place) to describe colors (sense-impressions by sight) that are overly flamboyant. The same modification pattern can likewise be found in classical Chinese poetry, e.g. the Northern Song Dynasty poet Huang Ting-jian's line

① 寒碧。
② 暖红。
③ 冷静。
④ 热闹。

"Carriages shuttling, horses jostling, lights beginning to go loud"①. Allegorization, metaphorical or otherwise, we may say, is another process inherent in human speech. It is out of similar human thinking behavior that English proverbs like "To strike while the iron is hot" and "Man proposes, God disposes" happily coincide with Chinese proverbs like "Chèn rè dǎ tiě"② and "Móu shì zài rén, chéng shì zài tiān"③. Besides abovementioned and/or other built-in factors responsible for accidental concord in expression between English and Chinese, there has been a "cross-fertilizing" mechanism operating over long years between the two languages, thus producing more similarities. Linguistic loaning, we know, occurs mostly in the field of vocabulary in the form of sound or sense borrowings; facts attesting to this convenient method of acquiring new words are positively too numerous to need citation. The point supposedly worth mentioning in this context is that over recent years Chinese borrowing of English ways of expression, or of commonly applicable ways in other European languages for that matter, seems to be spilling over to fields beyond that of vocabulary. Although purists have all along frowned upon "Europeanized" usage in Chinese, expressions like "Shùnbiàn tí yī-jù"④ (the prototype in English being "by the way" or "incidentally") or "Jùyǒu fěngcì yìwèi de shì..."⑤ ("ironically" used as an attitudinal adverb modifying a whole

① 黄庭坚(1045-1105):《次韵公秉、子由十六夜忆清虚》中句:"车驰马骤灯方闹"。Transference of sense-impressions also makes possible such English expressions as "The truth shouts to his face" and "The headline screams." However, there are no Chinese equivalents I can think of.

② 趁热打铁。

③ 谋事在人,成事在天。

④ 顺便提一句。

⑤ 具有讽刺意味的是……

statement), and sentence patterns like "... zài qiángdiào yě bù guòfèn"[①] ("... cannot be over-emphasized") and "Nǐ guòqù shì, xiànzài shì, jiānglái réng jiāngshì wǒ-de lǎoshī"[②] ("You were, you are, and you will remain my teacher"), keep on cropping up in standardized modern Chinese. Most of the Chinese college students I have approached for comment on such borrowings do not find them exotic or quaint any more. Unfortunately, I have not had experience enough with English-speaking people in their mother-tongue environment to judge if there are in English equally liberal borrowings from Chinese of bigger linguistic units than individual words like "cheongsam", "chop-suey", "paper tiger" and "consciousness-raising".

We then proceed to relate to some of the most salient dissimilarities (or differences) between English and Chinese. To compare the two languages with any relevance, we need to examine both morphology and syntax, and finally we will also need to delve a bit into the cultural background against which a national speech takes shape and develops.

The overriding impression one receives from a comparative morphological study of English and Chinese is that while the former is only slightly inflectional[③], the latter, being an agglutinative language, is non-inflectional altogether. This fundamental difference serves to account for a major portion of mistakes Chinese students of English are liable to commit with regard to grammatical agreement and to the English tenses. That is why in my TV talk back in China, I called the

① ……再强调也不过分。
② 你过去是,现在是,将来仍将是我的老师。
③ The English language abandoned most of its inflections during the early Middle English period.

attention of my audience to the inflectional patterns of their target language, prioritizing acquisition of a tense consciousness, of the past tense consciousness in particular. On this side of the Pacific, where people are accustomed to inflect their verbs to distinguish between tenses, I assume that a native speaker of English who is beginning to learn Chinese would do well to keep in mind that "Chinese tenses" (if there are such grammatical categories in the language) are in most cases contextually implied rather than morphologically indicated. Therefore, an English speaker needs to suppress his built-in tense consciousness lest he should produce dubious sentences in Chinese like "Tā zuótiān lái guò kàn wǒ le"[①] (its English equivalent being "He came to see me yesterday"). Similarly, to attain idiomaticity in Chinese, a native English speaker would have to take pains to change his speech behavior in terms of nominal plurality and verbal passivity where more inflections take place in English. Otherwise utterances such as "Niǎor men jiào")[②] (Birds chirp) and "Tā bèi dāngxuǎn le"[③] (He was elected) would

① (?)他昨天来过看我了。The sentence is problematic because the speaker is too tense-conscious, lavishly using tense-denoting functional particles "guò"(过) and "le" (了). As a matter of fact, except in cases where an effort must be made to avoid ambiguity in time reference, native Chinese speakers use such tense markers but sparingly. A more acceptable rendering of the sentence, therefore, would have been "他昨天来看我", or "他昨天来看过我了" with a clearer view to emphasizing completion of the encounter.

② (?)鸟儿们叫。The number-denoting "men" is superfluous. It might be interesting to note that in early Chinese báihuà, writers, including some fairly distinguished ones, did cultivate a habit of appending "men" to inanimate as well as animate objects to indicate plurality (e.g. 星星们 — stars). But the practice never "went big" with Chinese reading public at large.

③ (?) 他被当选了。As "dāngxuǎn" (当选) is a passive verb in its own right, the passivity-denoting "bèi" (被) is absolutely excrescent. Foreign students of Chinese would presumably benefit to a large extent from a note of caution: use "bèi" only when they have to. In point of fact, a good many Chinese verbs are at once active and passive. Therefore, in sentences like "Chéngshì jiěfàng le"(城市解放了 — The city was liberated) and "Màizi gē xià le"(麦子割下了—The wheat has been cut down), no passivity markers are used.

sound far too conscious of the plural number and of the passive voice to pass for accepted Chinese usage.

Another point to consider morphologically is while the English language has an elaborate system of parts of speech for words, a similar word-classifying apparatus is yet to seek in Chinese. In fact, there has been a sustained discussion going off and on in Chinese academic circles, a discussion to decide if there are clear-cut lines of demarcation between various parts of speech for minimal meaning entities in the Chinese language, and if there are, how to attach part-of-speech labels that fit. Related to and contingent on this discussion is another arduous probing effort to tell apart independent words (or "bound forms" like "zǒudòng"①) from less tightly bound collocations, mostly "vb.+obj." collocations (or "free forms" like "zǒu lù"②), and one-character meaning entities like "jiā"③ from pure morphemes like "ā"④. Often, there are frustrating fuzzy areas in between these categories. As a result, a beginner in Chinese from English-speaking societies is apt to mistake one for the other and get confused. Always tending to apply the handy part-of-speech mechanism in his native language to Chinese meaning entities, he is inclined to interpret contextually viable collocations in terms of a single bound form and equalize "zǒu lù" to "zǒudòng" in actual usage. Moreover, based on his knowledge about

---

① 走动: 1) to be up and about; 2) to exchange visits.

② 走路: 1) to walk; 2) to walk it; and in Southern dialects possibly 3) to beat it.

③ 家: 1) home; 2) family; 3) school of thought; 4) a measure word for a shop, a restaurant, a bank, etc. But when "specialist" is meant by it, it is a morpheme, similar in meaning to the English suffix "-ologist".

④ 阿: Devoid of any lexical notion, it is never used independently except in some Southern dialects where it serves as an interrogative.

Chinese verbs (mostly one-character verbs) being capable of occurring twice in duplication, reasoning by analogy from idiomatically possible "zǒudòng zǒudòng" (as in the imperative sentence "Qǐ lái zǒudòng zǒudòng"①), he is tempted to say grotesque sentences like "Ràng wǒmen qu zǒu lù zǒu lù"②. Similar labored things foreigners have been heard uttering in Chinese are "dǎ jià dǎ jià" and "tán huà tán huà"③.

Over recent years a commendable attempt has been made to mark Chinese dictionary headwords with parts of speech④. Utmost caution should be exercised, however, in doing so while compiling Chinese dictionaries specially designed for foreigners, because, as was mentioned above, the lexical status and grammatical function of many meaning entities in Chinese remain doubtful or controversial.

A closer comparative scrutiny of various word classes in the two languages will provide further insights into the subject under discussion. Let us first take verbs for instance. English verbs are subdivided into minor groups, each showing an idiomatic usage pattern of its own⑤; in American English such a division can be made finer as there has always been a fondness for hooking with considerable freedom adverbs or prepositions to verbs. Chinese students of English I teach have repeatedly made it clear that English verbs and verb phrases are

---

① 起来走动走动: Get up and about.

② (?)让我们去走路走路: Let's go and take a walk.

③ (?)打架打架: to fight and fight; (?)谈话谈话: to talk and talk.

④ But according to an informed source, as many as 90% of entire entry headwords in a medium-sized Chinese dictionary, mostly national items, would possibly defy proper marking.

⑤ One comes up with twenty-five such verb patterns in A. S. Hornby's *Advanced Learner's Dictionary of Current English* (3rd edition, Oxford University Press, London, 1974).

treacherous "blunder-traps", and one can never tell with assurance if "to inspire somebody to do something" is acceptable usage in English. Likewise, errors of expression are frequently in evidence at the opposite extreme: English-speaking students of Chinese are likely to transplant, unconsciously, their naturally implanted verb patterns to Chinese, thus coming out with sentences such as "Tā xiào le yīge tiánmì de xiào"① and "Tā shǐ zìjǐ máng-zhe xǔduō shìqing"②. These sentences are weak, to say the least of it, in that the first is a word-for-word surface translation of the English cognate verb pattern and the second that of the English reflexive verb pattern. Neither is idiomatic Chinese, though.

A comparison in the pronominal reference and application reveals other interesting things. In the first place, the English anticipatory "it" is sometimes wrongly thought of by English speakers as being more or less the counterpart of the Chinese demonstrative "zhè"③. By this doubtful analogy English-speaking students of Chinese are prone to trot out telltale speech specimens like "Zhè shì hěn hǎo-de, zǒu zài yángguāng-li."④ As a matter of fact, "zhe" in Chinese is more often than not a far cry from the anticipatory "it" in English in that the former is primarily anaphoric with reference made to an antecedent item, whereas the latter is always cataphoric, referring to an item structurally posterior to it. So an improved version of the above sentence would have been "Zǒu zài yángguāng-li hěn shūfu"⑤ or "Zǒu zài

① (?)她笑了一个甜蜜的笑：She smiled a sweet smile.
② (?)他使自己忙着许多事情：He occupies himself with many things.
③ 这
④ (?)这是很好的，走在阳光里：It is nice to walk in the sun.
⑤ 走在阳光里很舒服。

yángguāng-li, zhè hěn shūfu"[①]. Speaking of the difference in pronominal application between the two languages, I am put in mind of an amusing episode. Years ago I was invited to dinner in a restaurant with a Canadian teaching English in the lakeside city of Hangzhou. Sitting down at a table in the restaurant, this Canadian said to me in a very gracious manner (and in tolerable Chinese too!): "Zhè dùn fàn shì wǒ-de."[②] Apparently, he was being nice trying to tell me that he was going to foot the bill. But the regrettable fact was that he was not aware that the English pronoun "my" is much broader in both connotation and denotation than its counterpart in Chinese "wǒ-de", which expresses possession exclusively. Under other circumstances I have heard English speakers remarking to me in a car "Guānshàng nǐ-de chēmén"[③] or asking me in a hotel "Nǐ-de lóu shì nǎ-yi céng?"[④] Again, on such occasions I have to point out to them that the vehicular load of pronouns is different between their language and mine. Also worth noting is the fact that in written Chinese, personal pronouns are used much more sparingly than in English, especially when two or more than two persons of the same gender are involved in an integrated discourse. Where an English writer would unhesitatingly use the same pronoun to refer to two or more persons of the same gender, a Chinese writer chooses to repeat all along proper person names or identifying appellations like "fùqin" (the father), "guówáng" (the king) and so

---

① 走在阳光里,这很舒服。

② (?)这顿饭是我的: This is my dinner.

③ (?)关上你的车门: "Shut your car door" in the sense "Shut the car door on your side".

④ (?)你的楼是哪一层? "Which is your storey?" in the sense "On which storey is your room?"

on, in a deliberate attempt to avoid ambiguity in pronoun reference. Following are two quotations taken respectively from the eighteenth-century Chinese baihua novel *The Dream of the Red Chamber* by Cao Xue-qin and from the nineteenth-century English novel *Vanity Fair* by William Thackeray. Studied in unison, these two passages will hopefully serve to bear out the advisability of using reasonably fewer personal pronouns on the part of an English-speaking student learning to write in Chinese.

Quotation (Ⅰ)

宝玉举目见北静王世荣……真好秀丽人物。宝玉忙抢上前来参见,世荣从轿内伸手搀住。见宝玉……面若春花,目如点漆。北静王笑道:"名不虚传,果然如'宝'似'玉'。"问:"衔的那宝贝在那里?"宝玉见问,连忙……取出,递与北静王细细看了,又念了那上头的字,因问:"果灵验否?"贾政忙道:"……未曾试过。"北静王……亲自与宝玉带上,又携手问宝玉几岁……宝玉一一答应。北静王见他语言清朗……又向贾政笑道……

Personal pronouns on the one hand and proper person names or identifying appellations like "北静王" on the other constitute a ratio of 1:15.

Quotation (Ⅱ)

Well, meanwhile Becky was the greatest comfort and convenience to her, and she gave her a couple of new gowns … and showed her friendship by abusing all her intimate acquaintances to her new confidante … and meditated vaguely some great future benefit — to marry her perhaps to Clump, … or to settle her in some advantageous way…; or at any rate, to send her back … when she had done with her…

Personal pronouns on the one hand and proper person names on the other constitute a ratio of 11∶2[①].

English differs further from Chinese in the number and frequency of occurrence of measure words. Relatively speaking, English measure words (such as "piece") are fewer and occur farther between than Chinese measure words. This is because the English indefinite article "a" (or "an") generally serves unit-denoting and measuring purposes admirably. Therefore, when an English speaker switches to Chinese, he is understandably puzzled by the absence of a near all-purpose indefinite article as well as by such a profuse variety of measure words instead. Suppose he began by learning that "a car" in English changes to "yī liàng chē"[②] in Chinese. The measure word "liàng" was therefore imbedded in his consciousness. Next time when he came up with "a train", "a locomotive", etc., he would readily appeal to it and forthwith say "yī liàng huǒchē"[③], "yī liàng jīchē"[④], etc. However plausible it is logically, this method of extension does not always work, for in Chinese one uses measure words different than "liàng" in connection with "train" or "locomotive". The correct choice would have been "yī liè huǒchē"[⑤] and "yī tái jīchē"[⑥]. Another fact English speakers might feel interested to know is that in expressions "yī tóu niú"[⑦] and "yī pǐ mǎ"[⑧]

---

① I wish to present a general picture with these statistics. Meanwhile, I think it is safe to add that the same ratio varies with authors employing different styles. To tell their stories in an elaborate manner, earlier and more scrupulous English writers like Henry Fielding would presumably have used more proper person names.

② 一辆车。

③ (?)一辆火车。

④ (?)一辆机车。

⑤ 一列火车。

⑥ 一台机车。

⑦ 一头牛。

⑧ 一匹马。

the measure words involved "tóu" and "pǐ" are not interchangeable.

Syntactically, the easiest-to-detect difference between the two languages lies, if anywhere, in the degree of structural compactness of the sentence. In English, sentences logically related to one another are usually cohered by connective words or other devices, their conjunction in meaning taking the physical form of conjunction in structure. In Chinese, interrelated sentences are generally stuck together in an apparently loose manner often with no structural conjunction indicated somehow. Sometimes, one comes up with two or more Chinese sentences running parallel which are in fact components of a larger, logically integrated sentence unit. Subordination or whatever syntactical relation hidden among them is rather to be deduced from the meaning than to be appreciated by examining the form. As a result, connective words are often suppressed and the focus of the sentence more diffused. For instance, a native Chinese speaker says "Zǎo zhī-dao zhèyàng, wǒ jiù bù qù-le"①, whereas a native English speaker, drawing instinctively and heavily on his indigenous English subjunctive pattern, would have surely used the connective "if" and phrased the first part of the sentence as a distinctively subordinate clause of hypothetic condition, saying in Chinese "Rúguǒ wǒ zhī-dào shì zhèyàng de-huà, wǒ jiù bù qù-le"② ("If I had known, I would not have gone" in English). More examples for comparison:

Idiomatic Chinese: Nòng diū-le, xiǎo-xin nǎo-dai.

---

① 早知道这样,我就不去了。

② 如果我知道是这样的话,我就不去了。

If the sentence is grammatically workable — it probably is given the ever increasing influence on the Chinese language by the English language — it is correct to a fault — the fault of being redundant.

Anglicized Chinese：Rúguǒ nǐ diū-le zhè dōng-xi，yào xiǎo-xin nǐ-de nǎo-dai.[1]

(If you lose it，take care of your head.)

Idiomatic Chinese：Dāo gē-zài bózi-shang，yě bù qūfú.

Anglicized Chinese：Zòngrán nǐ bǎ dāo gē-zài wǒ-de bózi-shang，wǒ yě bù qūfú.[2]

(Even if you lay a knife on my neck，I will not give in.)

Idiomatic Chinese：Tā bù chàng zé-yǐ，chàng zé fēicháng dòngtīng.

Anglicized Chinese：Dāng tā chàng-de shí-hou，tā chàng-de fēicháng dòng tīng.[3]

(When he sings，he sings beautifully.)

Idiomatic Chinese：Wǒ tài lèi-le，zǒu bù dòng-le.

Anglicized Chinese：Wǒ tài lèi，yǐzhì zǒu bù dòng le.[4]

(I am too tired to walk.)

As subordinate clauses appear less manifest in Chinese，Chinese sentences tend to be shorter in length and more split in structure. Compare，for instance，the following two versions relating to the same idea.

English：He went into the room where they were having a meeting.

(An eleven-word one sentence.)

Chinese：Tā zǒu-jìn fángjiān，tā-men zhèng zài nàr kāi-huì.[5]

(Two sentences comprising seven words.)

---

① “弄丢了，小心脑袋” vs “如果你丢了这东西，要小心你的脑袋”。

② “刀搁在脖子上，也不屈服” vs “纵然你把刀搁在我的脖子上，我也不屈服”。

③ “他不唱则已，唱则非常动听” vs “当他唱的时候，他唱得非常动听”。

④ “我太累了，走不动了” vs “我太累，以至走不动了”。

⑤ 他走进房间，他们正在那儿开会。

Should an English speaker learning Chinese cling tenaciously to his English syntax, the sentence he says in Chinese would in all probability run to such unconscionable length by Chinese standard and be ill balanced: Tā zǒu-jìn nàge tā-men zhèng-zài lǐmiàn kāi-huì-de fángjiān.① Similarly, "John, who comes from a lower-class family, enrolled in college this fall" is a well organized English sentence. Rendering it into satisfactory Chinese, one needs to loosen the compact structure by splitting the sentence up in two, the possible wording being tantamount, upon back translation, to "John comes from a lower-class family; he enrolled in college this fall", which would certainly have been condemned as being structurally untidy and weak, a negative example at any rate in English rhetoric.

For compactness, English conveniently resorts to non-finite forms of verbs which occur alongside principal verbs. This device of deploying verbs with one of them as the predicate and the rest as subordinate elements is again unknown to Chinese syntax. Therefore, the English sentence "Expecting trouble, the soldiers were fully armed", when properly translated into Chinese, would call for re-ordering of the different parts in the sentence. "Shìbīng-men liào-dào yào-chū luàn-zi, suǒyǐ dōu quánfù wǔzhuāng"② would have been a much happier rendering than the laborious word-for-word translation "Liào-dào yào-chū luàn-zi, shìbīng-men quánfù wǔzhuāng"③.

① (?)他走进那个他们正在里面开会的房间。
② 士兵们料到要出乱子,所以都全副武装。
③ (?)料到要出乱子,士兵们全副武装。

English, the written language of it especially, makes heavy use of abstract nouns. It is but a deplorably false notion to think that for English nouns ending in -ness, -ibility and so on there has always been a ready-made Chinese equivalent "xìng"[①] (meaning in English "quality" or "character"). Thus "to doubt the effectiveness of the policy" is converted to "huáiyí zhèngcè-de yǒuxiào-xìng"[②] in Chinese; "to question the wisdom of staying" to "huáiyí liú-zhe bù-zǒu-de míngzhì-xìng"[③]; "to claim infallibility" to "shēngchēng zhèngquè-xìng"[④], and so on and so forth. Such Chinese expressions, however, are either awkward with too strong a flavor of English or scarcely intelligible. More acceptable ways of saying these things would have done away with the suffix "xìng" and have amplified the English abstract nouns into phrases or clauses[⑤], thus loosening the sentence structure a bit.

Another note of caution for English speakers learning Chinese syntax is that they had better guard against an excessive use of linking verbs. If we roughly divide Chinese affirmative sentences in the indicative mood into two types — definitive statements and descriptive statements, we will easily find that the Chinese linking verb "shì"[⑥]

---

① 性。

② (?)怀疑政策的有效性。

③ (?)怀疑留着不走的明智性。

④ (?)声称正确性。

⑤ The above three phrases would then be re-worded respectively as "对政策是否有效表示怀疑","对留下不走是不是明智提出疑问" and "声称一贯正确"。

⑥ 是。

(verb to be) mostly occurs in the former (e.g. "Jīntiān shì xīngqītiān"[1] — "It is Sunday today"), while in the latter it is as a rule omitted. So syntactically speaking, except in unusually emphatic and assertive statements, "Jīntiān tiānqì shì hǎo-de"[2] (meaning "It is fine today" in English) would sound more English than Chinese. By analogy, as ordinary matter-of-fact statements, the following three utterances — all being actual speech samples produced by English speakers learning Chinese — are problematic to a varying extent.

(1) "Wǒ-men shì máng-de yào sǐ."[3]

(We are terribly busy.)

(2) "Wǒ bù-shì tài cōngmáng-le."[4]

(I am not in too much of a hurry.)

(3) "Huār shì gèng hóng-le."[5]

(The flowers become redder.)

Yet another syntactical difference worth probing into is that of negation focus. In English, except in sentences where the inverted word order is introduced for emphasis, negative particles (most frequently "not" and "no") are made to appear in as close proximity as possible to the principal verbs. This usage form determines word order in sentences such as "I doN'T think he will come" and "I didN'T see the film because he told me to." In Chinese syntax, no such proximity is called for; instead, negation is focused in most cases on the elements

---

① 今天是星期天。
② (?)今天天气是好的。
③ (?)我们是忙得要死。
④ (?)我不是太匆忙了。
⑤ (?)花儿是更红了。

logically needing to be negated. Consequently, a Chinese student of English is strongly tempted to shift the negation focus in the above two sentences by saying "I think he will NOT come" and "I saw the film NOT because he told me to." Both sentences, unless coupled on by antithetic elements, sound a bit lame in English. Likewise, if he failed to keep in mind such a shift of focus as being necessary, an English-speaking learner of Chinese would readily convert the first of the above two sentences to "Wǒ bù rènwéi tā huì lái"[①], or simply err with the second one "Yīn-wèi tā duì wǒ shuō-le, wǒ méi qù kàn diànyǐng"[②], which, though communicative in another context, grossly distorts the original fact of "me having actually gone to the movies" into its diametrical opposite, and would read, upon back translation into English, "I didn't see the film because he told me not to." While we are about it, it might as well be mentioned in passing that native Chinese speakers have considerable difficulty getting accustomed to English negative structures like "The meeting did not begin until seven o'clock" to the same extent that native English speakers find it hard to develop linguistic acumen geared to the Chinese habit of matching the "not ... until ..." structure with an affirmative. I once put this assumption to test by calling upon an American friend to say the above sentence in Chinese. Sure enough, communicatively competent as he is in my language, he unhesitatingly handed me a negative: "Zhí dào qī-diǎn

---

① 我不认为他会来。At this point I feel I am obliged to add that over recent years owing to an expanding influence of the English language sentences with negation focus shifted to principal verbs have been increasingly in evidence in Chinese expressions (e.g. 我不觉得这有什么好笑的。— I don't see anything funny in it.). Granting such sentences are perfectly intelligible and therefore acceptable, they smack in a large measure of "translatorese".

② (?)因为他对我说了,我没去看电影。

méi kāi-huì"[①], to which I said I would decidedly prefer an affirmative: "Zhí dào qī-diǎn cái kāi-huì."[②]

A few other differences I can think of before we have done with the syntactical aspect of our study are: 1) The English "end weight"[③] principle does not appear to be applicable to Chinese sentences, in consequence, sentences with the inverted word order like "Gone are the days when my heart was young and gay" or "Here comes the bus" are hardly legitimate in Chinese unless a very special stylistic effect is intended; 2) In polite speech, fewer disjunctive and/or alternative questions with rhetorical queries involved are used in Chinese than in English. So, for instance, "Nǐ bù hē chá-ma?"[④] (Won't you take some tea?) would sound as though the speaker had taken for granted that his guest did not care for a cup of tea, and therefore convey much less invitational meaning than in English. And "Nǐ bù zài-hu wǒ zài fàng diǎnr yán, shì ma?"[⑤] (You don't mind me putting more salt in it, do you?) would in all likelihood confuse a Chinese interlocutor untrained in "Anglicized Chinese" awhile before he can bring himself to answer to the point; and 3) In colloquial speech, English is richer in conversational fill-in clichés such as "I think", "I suppose", "I figure", "I presume" and "you know", which can occur as attitudinal sentence beginners, mid-way inserted gap-fillers, or afterthought tags

---

① (?)直到七点没开会。

② 直到七点才开会。

③ By "end weight" is mean the English disinclination to speak or write "top-heavy" sentences. Instead, the lengthy, the weighty, the substantial and/or the hitherto unknown elements are stowed at the end of a sentence to achieve proper balance.

④ 你不喝茶吗?

⑤ 你不在乎我再放点盐,是吗?

of statements. In ad-lib spoken Chinese, if and when the speaker hems and haws and such clichés have to occur, they are generally not allowed to take place mid-way through, still less at the tail-end of, a discourse lest the normal speech flow be interrupted.

Lastly, as we all know, English and Chinese having sprung and later evolved from radically divergent cultural backgrounds, either of the two boasts a rich stock of imagery peculiarly its own. The English, for instance, has historically been a sea-faring nation, while China has had a long tradition of land agriculture and self-sustaining small-farmer economy. As a result, English abounds in maritime terms and idioms, "to know the ropes", "to see how land lies", "to sink or swim", to name only a few, just as in Chinese there are modes of expression aplenty related to farming. It then logically follows that to describe a thirsty person guzzling avidly, a native dweller of the British Isles would automatically think associatively of fish — an object the sailor is at home with — by saying "He drinks like a fish." In China, where "niú"[①] (an ox or a buffalo) has always been a highly valued animal of draft in tilling and ploughing crop fields and where the agrarian Chinese used to be affectionately watchful of whether their cattle were feeding properly to keep in working shape, the analogy is understandably traced to "niú", hence the metaphor "niú-yǐn"[②] (meaning literally in English "the buffalo drinks"). Proceeding further along this pattern of comparison, a native English speaker would invariably be struck by the presence of a large number of bovine idioms

① 牛。
② 牛饮。

in Chinese, such as "niúpí-qì"[1] (meaning in English "mulish stubbornness"), "niújiǎojiān"[2] ("an unsolvable and often meaningless abstruse problem", or "a blind alley" figuratively), "niújìnr"[3] ("an enormous effort" or "a Herculean effort"), and "niúpí"[4] ("boastful talk", or "a bull session" in present-day American slang[5]) — all being authentically Chinese expressions with no image parallels available in English. Likewise, a traditional Chinese small farmer living more or less in self-sustaining isolation was characteristically attached to his poultry as well as to his cattle. Looked at in this context, it is but small wonder that the white goose, symbolic in English of ungraceful movement (e.g. "goose step") and of stupidity (e.g. "to make a goose of somebody" in the sense of making a fool of him), used to pass for an elegant bird in agrarian China. The Tang Dynasty poet Luo Bin-wang composed an ode to white geese[6], which people of my age used to chant as a favorite nursery rhyme, and the famous Chinese calligrapher of the Jin Dynasty Mr. Wang Xi-zhi, keeping a pond for his geese to swim in, was said to have drawn artistic inspiration from looking at their movements. Modern Chinese may not take kindly to these web-footed noisy creatures, but in established Chinese usage a

---

① 牛脾气。

② 牛角尖。

③ 牛劲儿。

④ 牛皮。

⑤ I understand that "a bull session" is in turn derived from a modern vulgarism "bullshit", while the Chinese expression presumably takes its rise from "inflating with one's breath a container made of oxhide." Nevertheless, the accidental coincidence is interesting to observe.

⑥ Luo Bin-wang's ode reads as follows:"鹅,鹅,鹅,曲项向天歌,白毛浮绿水,红掌拨清波。"

daintily light yellow color is referred to as "éhuáng"[①], which has so high an aesthetic value that it frequently stands as a poetic portrayal for a wide range of visually pleasing objects, such as drooping willows, autumn chrysanthemum blooms, rice shoots and a mellow wine[②].

Speaking of divergent values centering around animals and birds, I think I might as well mention for further comparison the dog and the crane. Dogs are good hunting companions for English people, in whose language, therefore, one doesn't have to go far to find canine idioms. A considerable number of such idioms concede to dogs a near human status in a manner often more friendly or affectionate than depreciatory (e.g. "Love me, love my dog", "an old dog learning new tricks", "a jolly dog of a companion"). Dogs, always mean and lowly creatures, fare worse in China, where they are never entitled to a near human status. In China, if anybody is addressed to as a dog, downright insult is meant. An interesting exception is the older practice of presenting one's own son to others modestly as "xiǎo-quǎn"[③] ("my little dog" in English), which usage, however, has practically died out today except when the speaker is being funny. As for cranes, English people think of them matter-of-factly as mundane birds with long necks so much so that the word "crane" is made to designate a long-arm lifting machine. In other European languages, in German and French for instance, the same pattern of meaning extension is discernible, too[④].

① 鹅黄。
② "弄日鹅黄袅袅垂"(王安石);"都胜出陈州,开以九月末,鹅黄千叶"(刘蒙);"秧田百亩鹅黄大"(林逋);"应倾半熟鹅黄酒"(苏轼)。
③ 小犬。
④ German: Kran; French: grue.

For the Chinese, however, it seems next to impossible to borrow this pattern[①]. I figure it is largely because in traditional Chinese imagery the crane is a divine bird, pulling a vehicle ("hèyù"[②] — crane vehicle) for gods or habitually kept by ancient transcendental hermits, in any case symbolic of longevity (e.g. "hèshòu"[③] — literally crane's long life). It would be blasphemous, therefore, to associate this sacred bird with a noisy machine of the modern world.

Peculiar fauna and flora supply another answer to the difference in imagery. Lions, for instance, are mostly taken in India and parts of Africa, which Britain used to colonize. As a result, the image of the lion is frequently employed to suggest might, hugeness and ferocity (e.g. "a lion's share", "to show somebody the lions", "to lionize somebody", "to beard the lion"). For native inhabitants of the Chinese landmass, lions are relatively recent imported zoo exhibits[④]. And the elevated position of "king of animals" the lion occupies in the framework of English imagery has traditionally been accorded to the tiger, in China, where these sinewy, black-striped beasts are to be found in several provinces. Hence an anticlimax is described in Chinese as "huà hǔ lèi quǎn"[⑤] (meaning in English "to begin by trying to sketch a tiger but end up presenting a likeness of the dog"). Numerous

① Although other meaning extensions patterned on various European languages are by no means rare in Chinese. "Shé-tou" (舌头), for one, with its meaning extended from "tongue" to "an enemy officer or soldier captured alive to supply military information, is patterned on the Russian word Язык.

② 鹤驭。

③ 鹤寿。

④ The Chinese equivalent to "lion" "shī-zi" (狮子) or its earlier form "suānní" (狻猊), is a borrowing from old Persian or Sanskrit.

⑤ 画虎类犬。

are other idioms with the tiger as the central metaphorical figure of speech.

As for how the two languages are further at variance in imagery or expression because of different religions and different mythological traditions, the difference is self-evident and hardly merits citation of examples, I think I only need to interpolate a few remarks by way of debunking the fallacy of taking for granted some erroneous translations across the language barrier. For years now, few people, either Chinese- or English-speaking, have ever come to question the felicity of making comparable a Chinese "hé-shang"[①] to a monk, a Chinese "nígū"[②] to a nun, the legendary Chinese auspicious animal "qílín"[③] to the English unicorn, and the "fènghuáng"[④], queen of birds in ancient Chinese fables, to the phoenix. From Chinese into English or the other way around, each of the abovementioned pairs hardly consists of happily matchable components. A "hé-shang" or a "nígū" is, among other things, characterized by a "bald head" as it were, while a Catholic monk or nun has his or her hair intact. The difference is too visible for anybody not to see. So an immensely more preferable approach, it appears to me, is to find auricular equivalents in English for such Chinese expressions with footnotes attached explaining them at adequate length. If conveyance of meaning is insisted upon, restrictive modifiers must be added to distinguish between the English and the Chinese species, such as "a Buddhist monk (or nun)" for "hé-shang" (or

① 和尚。
② 尼姑。
③ 麒麟。
④ 凤凰。

"nígū"), "a Chinese unicorn" for "qílín". With "fènghuáng", however, one finds himself at a greater loss, because while the two characters combine to form a meaning entity in its own right, either is meaningful when taken asunder: "fèng" — a male bird of the species; "huáng"— a female.

Some time ago a New Zealand Chinese teaching English in Shanghai delivered a lecture at the city's foreign languages institute, reflecting upon some usage differences between English and Chinese that had been brought under his notice. Basing his theory on typical "Chinglish" (Chinese + English) mistakes his students were in the habit of making, such as addressing him who teaches them as "Teacher So & So" and him whom they are apprenticed to when they do a stint of manual work in factories as "Master Worker① So & So", the New Zealander argued that Chinese is less specific than English as far as forms of address, direct or indirect, are concerned. It is true that to precede proper person names with such generic nouns as "teacher" and "master worker" is too general an appellative practice to conform to idiomatic English usage. But to say thereby that Chinese as a rule tends to be less specific than English when it comes to interpersonal appellations is certainly, as I see it, far too sweeping a conclusion. For not all Chinese forms of address are that unspecified. In fact, in Chinese one makes much finer distinctions of interpersonal appellative epithets than in English, especially of those reserved for members in a family circle or among kith and kin. Hence the English word "uncle" has to be

① "shī-fu"(师傅), when used as a direct form of address in accosting a stranger among men, is a relatively recent development; in Shanghai dialect it is perhaps only second to "tóngzhì"(同志) in frequency of occurrence and width of application.

broken down in Chinese respectively to "shū" (father's younger brother); "bó" (father's elder brother), "jiù" (mother's brother either younger or elder), "gū-fu" (father's sister's husband), and "yí-fu"[①](mother's sister's husband). So do other English words like "aunt", "cousin", and "niece". Also, I have always wondered if one can ever find in Chinese perfectly happy equivalents for English interpersonal appellations like "parent" (and "grandparent" by inference), "brother" and "sister" and "brother-in-law" and "sister-in-law" by inference), because with us Chinese a parent is always sexually definitive, either father or mother, and a brother (or a sister) is always indicative of seniority or juniority, either an elder or a younger brother (or sister). Moreover, when there are more than two siblings involved, one has to attach ordinal numerals (like "first", "second", "third" and down the line) to appellations to make the sequence clear. This very sophisticated system of very specific forms of address and interpersonal appellations, I understand, had come into being over long long years when Chinese society remained feudal-patriarchal in character. Incidentally, in present-day China, where the nuclear family is the order of the day and with it the clannish bond becomes increasingly loose and weak, it takes the younger people a long time and pains-taking effort to decide where they stand in this highly complex appellative maze. For an English speaker, it undoubtedly poses greater difficulty.

* * * *

Before bringing to a conclusion the present comparative study, I

---

① 叔,伯,舅,姑夫,姨夫。

see fit to extend two pieces of advice to those who are either learning Chinese or working with the language.

First, as English and Chinese are quite different in certain respects, guard against a punctiliously rigid word-for-word approach in translation. I have come across a no small amount of instances of English translations of Chinese expressions being faithful to a fault — some of them by professionally authoritative translators in English-speaking societies. Take as an example Pearl Buck's translation of the famous Chinese novel "shuǐhǔzhuàn"①. For all her adept and liberal rendering of the book's title into ALL MEN ARE BROTHERS (The John Day Company, 1933), her translation is never short of unprofitably scrupulous instances of putting into English "river and lake" for "jiānghú"② (meaning in English "everywhere in the world") and "one's hands and feet were all in confusion" for "shǒumáng-jiǎoluàn"③ (meaning "terribly confused and busy"). Such renditions almost always sin in being over-precise to the detriment or conveyance of inner meaning. Likewise, translating "hányā"④ (a special kind of raven, smaller in size than a common crow), a recurrent figure of speech in ancient Chinese poetry, into "winter crow", and "líuhuǒ"⑤ (the intervening period between summer and autumn, somewhat analogous to "Indian summer" in English) into "flowing fire" are all objectionable instances of taking at face value separate Chinese characters which should have been treated together as

① 《水浒传》。
② 江湖。
③ 手忙脚乱。
④ 寒鸦。
⑤ 流火。

meaning entities not to be broken asunder. Back in China I was once shown a Hangzhou tourist guidebook, in which the city's suburban scenic spot "Jiǔ-xī Shíbā-jiàn"[①] is entered literally in English as "Nine Streams and Eighteen Rivulets". The scenic spot is in fact a secluded vale where are to be found many (certainly more than nine!) streams and more rivulets (my latest counting put the number at thirty-odd)[②]. The translator was apparently unaware of the fact that in Chinese enumeration the numeral "jiǔ" (nine) is sometimes not taken at face value; instead, it is made to designate an infinite number. So the highest heaven and the abysmal netherworld are respectively referred to in Chinese as "jiǔxiāo"[③] (or "jiǔtiān"[④]) and "jiǔquán"[⑤]. To indicate further lengthening or proliferation, "jiǔ" is multiplied to "shíbā" (eighteen) as in "shíbā bān wǔyì"[⑥] (meaning literally in English "eighteen knacks in martial art") and "shíbā céng dìyù"[⑦] ("the eighteenth layer of hell" literally). In this light it is not difficult to see that the translator of the said tourist guidebook would have done immensely better if he had done with the two numerals "nine" and "eighteen" — both being matter-of-fact face-value words in English — and replaced his version with a freer rendering like "Murmuring streams and Winding Rivulets" I would tentatively suggest.

---

① 九溪十八涧。

② To describe the expansive and uplifting scenery of this vale, the Qing Dynasty poet Yu Qu-yuan(俞曲园)composed the well-known poem：重重叠叠山，曲曲环环路，丁丁东东泉，高高下下树。

③ 九霄。

④ 九天。

⑤ 九泉。

⑥ 十八般武艺。

⑦ 十八层地狱。

Secondly, I should advise against anybody going to the other extreme by misfitting exclusively English allusions to typically Chinese ones in an attempt to strive for seeming equal value in translation. Allusions to events, places and characters in history or legends vary from one national language to another; if there is any thing peculiar in a national speech that is not to be shared with others, these allusions are. In this sense, I venture to say that allusions, for the most of them, are virtually not translatable unless treated very punctiliously from surface to surface and then complemented with notes providing indispensable information. So, "to carry coals to Newcastle", a commonly accepted translation of the Chinese proverb "Bān mén nòng fǔ"① (meaning literally in English "to wield an ax in front of Lu Ban, a master carpenter", is absolutely too heavily British in flavor to be an apt equivalent to the Chinese original. Still wider of the mark is saying in English "to offer the peace pipe", an American Indian expression derived from the tribe's traditional peace-making gesture, to bring it in correspondence with the Chinese allusion "Fùjīng qǐng-zuì"② (literally "to ask for forgiveness with a wood stick strapped to one's naked back"). Other Chinese four-character proverbs in Chinese that would call for rigidly faithful renderings on the one hand and amplifying footnotes on the other hand are many, among which "Dōngshī xiào pín"③ (meaning literally in English "Dōngshī, an

---

① 班门弄斧。Ban being the name of the master carpenter.

② 负荆请罪。A proverb distilled from a historically well-known quarrel between the prime minister and the commander-in-chief of the State of Zhao (赵) during the period of the Warring States. The quarrel was finally settled by the latter asking the former to forgive him.

③ 东施效颦, from Zhuang Zi (《庄子》), a proverb satirizing those who imitate indiscriminately with a disastrous effect.

ugly woman, imitating the beauty Xīshī's finicky frown") and "Sàiwēng shī mǎ"[①] (literally "the frontier old man losing his horse") are two that readily come to one's mind.

So, the final conclusion is: as a competent translator, one needs, among other things, to examine comparatively both his target and source languages in a historical perspective as well as in the light of day-to-day communicative practicalities.

① 塞翁失马, from Huainan Zi (《淮南子》), an allusion to an old man in ancient times at the frontier who lost a horse only to find it return bringing back another horse to him. The allegorical message is that a seeming mishap may eventually turn out to be a blessing in disguise.

China's Response to the Renaissance

— A Renaissance of Her Own*

The dynastic history of China can be traced back to a remote recorded past long before Christ. Covering no fewer than three thousand years[①], it is adequate proof that the feudal system was longer-lived by a wide margin at both beginning and end in China than in Europe. Therefore, a period roughly contemporaneous with the Middle Ages in European history, i. e. the period from the Southern and Northern Dynasties (南北朝) of the fifth and sixth centuries down to the heyday of the Ming Dynasty (明代) in the fifteenth century, accounts only for a third of entire Chinese dynastic feudalism. During this period, as was always the case under the feudal yoke, landlord exploitation and oppression persisted, giving rise to frequent peasant uprisings; seigneurial wars went on and off, never really stopping; from time to time class animosities were aggravated by racial contradictions as during

* 本文是作者于 1983 年 3 月在马里兰大学"文艺复兴时期的城市生活研讨会"(Urban Life in the Renaissance: A Symposium)上宣读的论文，由作者的好友 Thomas Creamer 先生提供。——编注。

① How long Chinese society had remained feudalistic is a matter of academic controversy. To the writer's knowledge, there have been at least five different schools assigning five different dates to the start of Chinese feudalism. Here we are going by the theory advanced by Guo Moruo (郭沫若) that feudalism began in China as early as the Western Zhou Dynasty (西周)(approx. 1046–771 B.C.).

the conquest by the Mongols in the thirteenth century. For all that, from a historical point of view, those were not in any sense particularly gloomy times for the Chinese: no asceticism or obscurantism dictated by a despotic church; no Inquisition nightmares; not the "Dark Ages" anyway. Similarly, when the Europeans rejoiced over the rebirth of man during the Renaissance, exuberantly and exultantly referring to it in terms of a "new era", Chinese society had remained practically the same. Changes, if any, were infinitesimal and glacial. No spectacular expansion of secularism. No urgent need for overhauling the existing value system — yet. So, before we can gauge Chinese response to the Renaissance with any accuracy we have at least two long centuries to wait, i.e. till the mid-nineteenth century.

In the modern intercourse among nations, nineteenth-century imperial China was relatively a late arrival, and she arrived reluctantly. For one thing, an agrarian economy characteristic of the Asiatic mode of production and operating across an extensive and continuous landmass under one centralized jurisdiction had enabled China to stand self-sufficiently on her own and smugly apart from others for thousands of years. Secondly, in conformity with the established economic pattern a typically Chinese world view had long taken root, a world view that is basically secular and sets great store by restraint, moderation, and self-centered contentment① rather than by unscrupulous egoistic assertions or self-aggrandizement. So when the doors were forced open

① This world view is variously expressed in familiar Chinese quotations such as *Zhizu chang le* (知足常乐)— Contentment is a source of constant joy, *Mingzhe bao shen* (明哲保身)— A sage knows how to protect himself, and *Ji suo bu yu, wu shi yu ren* (己所不欲,勿施于人) — Do not do unto others what you would not like others to do unto you.

in the 1840s by foreign gunboats and when the *status quo* was compelled to change *vis-à-vis* an ever increasing foreign impact, shock was enormous, resistance manifest and stubborn. Meanwhile, a serious effort to understand Western civilization began.

At an early stage, however, the effort was a more or less utilitarian affair with the focus on the then more advanced weapon-oriented Western technology. To the handful of court reformist zealots headed by Kang Youwei（康有为）and Liang Qichao（梁启超）, the effort meant, above all, transplanting the Western model of constitutional monarchy in an essentially unchanged framework of the Chinese political apparatus, whereas for reasons self-evident foreign missionaries and their Chinese protégés were trying to shunt the effort onto a religious track by financing a Bible industry. As for understanding Western thought and culture in any real depth, the effort did not begin in earnest until the turn of the century when two eminent men of letters Yan Fu（严复）and Lin Shu（林纾）took to translating works such as Thomas Huxley's *Ethics and Evolution* and Mrs. Stowe's *Uncle Tom's Cabin*, with some Renaissance works like William Shakespeare's thrown in for good measure. In a traditionally Chinese attempt to make exotic things appear indigenous, both gentlemen used a highly stylized classical Chinese as the target language in translation with the result that their renditions could easily pass for being the original writings of ancient Chinese masters[①]. Elegant as they may have read, such translations

---

① In a preface to Yan Fu's translation of *Ethics and Evolution* (1897) Wu Rulun wrote as a complimentary comment: "The flow of composition is so effortlessly swift that Yan's scholarly translation is as good as the original writings of distinguished masters of the late Zhou Dynasty."(吴汝纶《〈天演论〉序》:"严子一文之,而其书乃骎骎与晚周诸子相上下。")

only catered to an elitist few and failed to reach the man in the street.

Then broke out the Revolution of 1911 led by Dr. Sun Yat-sen (孙中山), which toppled the last imperial court and turned a republican new leaf in Chinese history[1]. The overthrow of the emperor, or of the *tianzi* (天子) — Son of Heaven — as he had always been reverently called in China, was a breakthrough in Chinese experience which set off a chain reaction. If the absolute authority of *tianzi* could be demystified, what else, including a patriarchal-feudal ethical code at large, could not? Likewise, with the abolition of imperial examinations it followed logically that old-fashioned learning and culture previously required of the candidates for His Majesty's civil service should have fallen into disrepute. As doubts mounted, enlightenment deepened, leading to a kind of awareness that any time-honored institution, however awesome and apparently absolute, is capable of change. This awareness of possibilities of change is presumably one of the most important ramifications of the Revolution of 1911.

To complement such a subjective awareness there were on the other hand circumstances in objective realities calling for change. As the economic foundations of the feudal rule remained largely unshaken and the forces of the warlords intact, the Revolution fell through halfway — way short of its professed goals. The political power was seized by military autocrats to whom democracy was sacrilegious heresy and the nation's sovereignty a mere joke; the transformation of the Chinese from "subjects" to "citizens" was but nominal; foreign powers

① In after years there were a couple of attempts to put an emperor back to the throne. However, as absolute monarchy was definitely out, all such attempts only proved to be short-lived farces.

continued to lay harsh demands or impose more unequal treaties on China. As a result, resentment seethed, culminating in a massive anti-imperialist and anti-feudal movement which took place on May 4, 1919 in Peking in the form of an indignant protest march of the students and which soon spilled to other major cities involving more and more people from other walks of life.

Thus, the awareness of possibilities of change and circumstances necessitating change combined to pave the way for the growth of a New Culture movement, the significance of which, from a Chinese point of view, is comparable to that of the Renaissance in Europe. As the movement surged ahead, for the first time in her history, China, and a radicalized segment of her *intelligentsia* in particular, responded to the Renaissance by bringing about a renaissance of her own. It was an animated response, to be sure, though a bit belated. And a cursory glance would reveal that to this renaissance movement of twentieth-century Chinese vintage its European precedent had a no mean contribution to make.

With the rise of the New Culture, "Renaissance" became an instant catchword of a kind in China. *Li Nai Shuang*, a Chinese transliteration of the term, kept appearing in New Culture publications as a cute pen name (with certain orthographical variations in the three component characters, though) favored by different contributors who wished to jump on the bandwagon yet stay incognito. About the same time The Renaissance came out in print as an English subtitle of a popular periodical *Xin Chao* (《新潮》)— The New Wave — edited by a group of activist students of Peking University. A prestigious seat of higher learning in China, Peking University was at that time a fountainhead from which came a steady flow of newfangled ideas expounded in liberal publications such as *Xin Qingnian* (《新青年》)—*The New Youth. Among the faculty members active in the operations of Xin Qingnian* were notably Chen Duxiu (陈独秀), one of the founders of the Chinese Communist Party in 1921 who later pushed a rightist policy of compromise and collaboration with the Nationalist Party, Dr. Hu Shi (胡适), who ultimately ended up identifying himself with the ruling Establishment by turning against the Communists, and Lu Xun (鲁迅), pseudonym of Zhou Shuren (周树人), an indisputably literary giant of modern China.

Just as humanism had played a vital role during the European Renaissance[①], in order to elicit maximum participation the New Culture in China needed an ideological stimulus, a rallying banner to make the movement relevant and appealing. Thus, "two gentlemen" arrived on the scene: a Mr. *De* and a Mr. *Sai*, *De* and *Sai* being first-syllable shortenings respectively of *Demokelaxi* (transliteration of Democracy) and *Saiyinsi* (that of Science). As Chen Duxiu put it, "To support Mr. *De* we must oppose Confucianism, feudal rites and laws, women's self-sacrificial chastity, dated ethics and politics. To support Mr. *Sai* we must oppose old arts and religions. And to uphold both, it is imperative to wage war on the cultural quintessence and the worn-out literary practice."[②] So clay Buddha statues were demolished alongside the memorial tablets in honor of Confucius enshrined in *Wen Miao* (文庙)— temples sacred to the supreme deity of literacy. The order of importance or seniority in human relationships consecrated by Confucian tenets was held in blasphemous ridicule — cheap junk on sale, as it

① Cf. Walter Ullmann, *Medieval Foundations of Renaissance Humanism* (1977).
② *Xin Qingnian* (《新青年》), Vol. VI, No. 1, p. 10.

were, in a "Confucian market". Patriarchal ethics had to be done away with; ritual reforms became a must; women, with their bound feet and all, had as much human dignity to assert as men①. In a general climate of pulling down old idols and debunking fetishes, superstitious fallacies came under heavy attack, too. It was widely accepted that Chinese society needed science as badly as democracy, not only to motivate and speed up a tangible progress, but also to help fashion a modern consciousness and cultivate an inductive method of inquiry. As a result of a long metaphysical tradition, abysmal ignorance was then ubiquitously in evidence beside abject poverty. For instance, talk of the earth moving around the sun in a Copernican light, a fact long taken for granted elsewhere, could still raise many a skeptical brow in China as late as the early nineteenth century. Even among some of the well-educated people like above-mentioned Liang Qichao there existed an anti-science prejudice so ingrained that they would conveniently attribute all modern evils including the First World War to the advance of science②. Therefore, to render a stagnant Chinese society dynamic, an energetic role of Mr. *Sai* was absolutely called for.

Thus, from a comparative perspective, a surface parallel can be readily drawn between the Chinese New Culture and the European Renaissance in so far as both demanded a reappraisal of the basic formula of man versus cosmos. However, *au fond* there lies a discernible difference. What is "cosmos", for instance? The medieval

① See, for instance, Hu Shi's essays published in 1919 My Reform of the Funeral Ceremony (《我对于丧礼的改革》), On Chastity (《论贞操问题》), and On Women Victimized by Outrage (《论女子为强暴所污》).

② See, for instance, Liang Qichao's *My Impressions of Europe* (《欧游心影录》) appearing in his *Recent Writings* (《梁任公近著》) (1919-1920), Vol. 1, Part One, pp. 19-23.

Europeans tended to equate the cosmos to *Christianitas*, to papal ecclesiasticism especially, which was brought into fierce antagonism with *Humanitas*[①] during the Renaissance, whereas in China *tian* (天)— the cosmos — and *dao* (道)— the way — in opposition to *ren* (人)— man — had all along remained fundamentally earthly concepts. Unlike most European countries, at no time in her history has China ever been monotheist. Confucianism, though it was exalted to the status of a near religion in the sixth century, had started as a mundane doctrine governing man's conduct in this world. Daoism, for all its frills such as enigmatic diagrams used in divination, was in effect an epiphenomenon of Lao Zi's (Laotse's) philosophy of letting things take their own course, chiefly concerned with an equilibrium of body and mind in actual existence. Buddhism, since its first introduction about two thousand years before, had undergone a process of "Sinicization" and was in due time able to co-exist peacefully with Confucianism and Daoism. If and when stripped of all paraphernalia, Hinayana Buddhism as it was practised in China by clergy and laity alike was more of a cultural constituent exercising an influence on ethics, art, and literature than as a rigid church hierarchy aggressively tampering with the body politic[②]. Consequently, the archenemy that stood in the way of the Chinese New Culture was not so much as a number of clerical thou-shalt-nots as an encrusted system of secular usages and conventions with all its taboos. In this context it is but small wonder that while stories of, say, Boccaccio's *Decameron* could by and large succeed in tickling the

① Cf. Wallace Ferguson, *Renaissance Studies* (1970), p. 101.

② See Ren Jiyu's *A History of Buddhism in China* (任继愈:《中国佛教史》), Vol. I (1982).

Chinese fancy as well, the anti-clerical message embedied in them was not always fully appreciated by a readership accustomed to Chinese monks and friars presented in traditional literature either as transcendental hermits with exemplary virtues and steeped in high learning or as just-minded rebels excelling in martial prowess. It is all a matter of different aesthetics presupposed by different historical and cultural ingredients.

A picture of the New Culture in China can never be complete unless the *baihua* (白话) — vernacular idiom — movement, an important integral part of the New Culture, is taken into consideration. In this respect another close analogy can be traced between early twentieth-century China and Renaissance Europe. In fact, there was a conscious effort on the part of the New Culturists to pattern the philological reform then afoot in China on an European model several centuries earlier that relegated Latin to a secondary place with its prevalence giving way to that of a modern vernacular idiom, ethnic or national. Dante, Chaucer, Rabelais, and other Renaissance big names were frequently cited as path-breakers in philological innovation, their precedents good enough to go by if a language reform was to be launched in China. More convincing, of course, was the Italian example, for of all the European countries if Latin had to be abandoned in Italy as well, where it originated, why shouldn't a similar process happen in China? As it was, fervent New Culturists of the time were invariably staunch advocates of *baihua*, bent on having it institutionalized as a legitimate idiom of literary composition. For one thing, *baihua* as a plebeian medium whereby daily oral communication can be most realistically reproduced in a written form, is by far easier to understand, to learn, and to teach than *wenyan* (文言) — stylized literary language — which, having evolved out of a copious corpus of classics, is not actually "speakable"— all in all a stereotyped ivory-tower affair. In a Chinese context of low literacy at that time, therefore, introduction of *baihua* was decidedly a giant stride making for progress in education. Furthermore, it supplied a viable solution to the long-standing separation of the writtern form from actual speech in the Chinese language. It is true that in a long literary history of China there had always been a trickle of *baihua* novels since the Tang Dynasty (唐代) in the seventh century, which would now and then swell to major pro-portions of a full-fledged genre in its own right. For all the popularity they enjoyed among common readers, such works of fiction had been as a rule kept outside the parameters of the so-called *belles-lettres*. Unwarranted as it was, the conviction that held sway among *literati* has been one of snobbish dismissal, of rejecting the *baihua* novel as though it were inherently inferior to other genres such as classical poetry and rhythmical prose characterized by technically impeccable parallelisms and antitheses. Moreover, there arose from those who would have found the New Culture otherwise acceptable a vehement clamor that *baihua* was nothing short of "bewitching demagogy"①. As a result, the *baihua* movement, perhaps more than

---

① See Yao Meng (《妖梦》) — The Nightmare — an allegorical essay written by Lin Shu (林纾) which appeared in *New Shanghai Daily* (《新申报》) in 1919. Lin Shu was so irreconcilably hostile to *baihua* he even appealed in an open letter to Cai Yuanpei (蔡元培), President of Peking University, demanding that Cai should call a halt. Also joining in the clamor were some musty academicians at Peking University who published *Guogu* (《国故》) — The National Legacy — and *Guomin* (《国民》) — The Citizen — in an bigoted attempt to bear down on *baihua*.

Mr. *De* and Mr. *Sai*, had had a really formidable obstacle to remove before it gained a *force majeure* in 1919 when the total tally of *baihua* publications, by my own estimate, ran up to over four hundred in the nation. The following year saw the *baihua* camp winning more scores: textbooks of Chinese were overhauled; a new punctuation system analogous to its European prototype found wider and wider acceptance; a plan of using thirty-nine symbols for phonetic transcription was adopted and a standard pronouncing dictionary published. When in the end it was accepted as *Guoyu* (国语) — National Speech, the further ascendance of *baihua* became a matter of course. Lashing at a calcified aesthetic structure as it swept along, the *baihua* movement helped in a large measure to give a specific complexion to the age.

Yet another happy coincidence is detectable when we search the *baihua* landscape for prominent figures and find that just as Dante had been adroitly "bilingual" in Latin and in vernacular Italian①, many accomplished *baihua* writers were capable of a felicitous expression and a facile style in *wenyan* as well as in *baihua*. Visible among them were above-mentioned Lu Xun, Guo Moruo, poet, playwright, and historian, and Mao Dun (茅盾) — pen name of novelist Shen Yanbing (沈雁冰). Thanks to a perseveringly assiduous effort of experimentation jointly undertaken by these dedicated people, two major trends took shape in *baihua* literature: 1) works of fiction of a hard and poignant realism; and 2) poems composed in an extravagant romantic vein and unfettered by old rules with respect to line length, tonal pattern, rhyme scheme, and so on. The trend of realistic fiction may be best

① Cf. B. Pullan, *A History of Early Renaissance Italy* (1973).

represented by Lu Xun's short story *Kuangren Riji* (《狂人日记》) — The Madman's Diary (1918) and by his later novelette *A Kiu Zhengzhuan* (《阿Q正传》) — The True Story of Ah Q (1921). Both works are noted for being a scathing critique of the old system with a tocsin-like message that the powers that be, ethical or otherwise, with the Revolution of 1911 or without, had remained cannibalistic. Lu Xun's attitude as evidenced in these two stories is one of a bitterly somber exposure, of an uncompromising revolt and wrathful protest, and of a passionate sympathy for the poor downtrodden. As for new *baihua* poetry, in which, incidentally, Lu Xun had tried his hand with considerable achievements too, it fell on Guo Moruo to set a dominant motif and mood of the time with his first fifty-odd poems collected in *Nüshen* (《女神》) — The Celestial Lady. Take Guo's *Fenghuang Niepan*(《凤凰涅槃》) — Nirvana of the Phoenix, for instance. The poet presented nirvana not as silent extinction but as resurrection symbolic of a new China which would eventually rise from the ashes of the old. The tone was ecstatically uplifting, imagery rich and novel, calling upon the benighted Chinese to strive confidently ahead. Other *baihua* poems such as Shen Yinmo's (沈尹默) *Renli Chefu* (《人力车夫》) — The Rickshaw Man① — were less romantic, but had a more direct bearing on exigencies of life, alerting the disadvantaged to a sordid day-to-day lot.

In retrospect, however, for all its positive ramifications and implications, the New Culture in China had its limitations as well. For instance, among some of its most ardent champions, a judicious

① The poem appeared in *Xin Qingnian* (《新青年》), Vol. IV, No. 1.

discrimination was often conspicuously absent. In consequence, a formalistic nihilism would lead to a total and uncritical acceptance of whatever is Western to the exclusion of anything Chinese. Take Dr. Hu Shi for example. Lying prostrate before European dramatists from Sophocles, Aeschylus, and Euripides all the way down to Ibsen and Shaw, he summarily condemned the whole tradition of Chinese drama by unduly magnifying its unactability, its "crude cumbersomeness", and its "built-in lack of a conception of tragedy"[①]. Any essentially valid point, we know, can entail absurdities if it is stretched too far. So did a commendable point at that time of emancipating women which was in some cases made tantamount to giving vent to carnal desires. A plethora of love poems in *baihua* were thereupon written, all preoccupied with the purely sensual so much so that statistics show a kiss occurs in every four poems throughout a poem anthology[②], a phenomenal incongruity in view of Chinese manners. For a while, even graphically pornographic literature threatened to come back, such as *Jin Ping Mei* (《金瓶梅》) — Plum Blossoms in a Gilded Vase, a sixteenth century novel, and *Pin Hua Baojian* (《品花宝鉴》) — Magic Mirror for Appreciation of Flowers, a heavily homosexual book of the early nineteenth century. Last but not least, a rank-and-file consensus was yet to be enlisted by the New Culturists, some of whom could have dispensed with part of an emotional or sheerly academic debate with the old school and been more intimately concerned with bread-and-butter

① Cf. Literary Evolution and Reform of Drama, *Hu Shi's Manuscripts* (《文学进化观念与戏剧改良》,见《胡适文存》), Vol. I, pp. 195-214.

② Cf. Liang Shiqiu, *The Romantic Trend in Modern Chinese Literature* (梁实秋:《现代中国文学之浪漫的趋势》)(1926).

actualities of life instead.

It is only predictable then that such a defective aspect of the Renaissance-inspired New Culture would result in a split soon. Already, truly probing minds were turning elsewhere for a therapy of greater efficacy. Ultimately, a Marxian solution was opted for and tried with success. Thus a new chapter in Chinese history began.

如何走出去?

孔子学院在海外办得有些时日了,提升文化软实力的口号也已耳熟能详,但是我们究竟走出去了没有?只要实话实说,也许这个问题由前不久浩浩荡荡参加法兰克福书展的 VIPs 来回答,最有说服力。一说中国已是世界最大外汇储备国,是排名第二或最低不次于第四的经济实体,走出去还这么不易,是欧美发达国家特别是其中敌对势力的封堵,此话可能部分有理。我曾在美国一家 Barnes & Noble 书店浏览终日,查过门口电脑以后又用笨办法,一个个书架扫瞄过来,只发现七种与中国题材有关的读物,却又都是属于我们海关要查抄的问题书,想找一本不久前出版的司徒雷登回忆录都没有。我又曾在佛罗伦萨的中心广场歇脚,坐在长椅上看那边的万国旗,"膏药"、"八卦"都有,就是没咱们的五星。说这些都与意识形态有关,我信。

那就不妨把目光转向第三世界,就拿我们出大力援助的非洲为例吧。据不完全统计,走出去的中国人在那儿已有百万之众。黑兄弟对我们的接纳程度又如何呢? Made in China 改称 Made in China with the World 之后,黑人兄弟姐妹对中国商品的质量仍多疑虑,对某些中国商人"和尚打伞"式的金融和商业文化颇多微词,罔顾公德又缺少教养的行为举止又被诟病不断。我们可以说,有些黑兄弟或许患了殖民主义的后遗症,可他们就喜欢把走出去的中国人跟那儿的欧美人作疵谀之比。要是当年曾被人当作奴隶买卖的一群,对我们五千年的悠久文化都背毁不已,我们岂能不恻痛于心?

所以,走出去前,不能不针对外部世界的“傲慢与偏见”谋定而动。要突出围城,事涉国本自然动不得,但必须拆迁的墙还是得拆迁,而已经走出去的中国人先得记住:不可旷职偾事。

其次,说到翻译。年前,上海译文出版社的《外国文艺》叫我写几句话。我是这么写的:“天上九个缪斯,无一职司翻译;地下学人万千,皆视译事为末技。天眷人顾两阙,译人惟有自娱自爱自尊自强。”这第二句话用的是“学人”二字,其实当时心目中展现的是那些拥有话语权的学界判官。译文酬金 n 年不变,致成爝火;译著一般不计入学术成果,即得百万之数,不及谈玄说虚千百字,风成化习,译道渐芜,自属必然。而没有汉外佳译,中国文化如何走得出去?外汉翻译对中国文化的推动力,特别是在社会巨大转型时期,先例累累,已毋庸多言。现在的问题是,上述拥有话语权的学界判官,有几位从头至尾读过几部译作,更遑论自己动手翻译,其经历和器识甚至远不及当年主管文宣的周扬们——周扬等人还在 1965 年前后阶级斗争的“休耕期”策动过西方文论及批评史的系统翻译。对翻译工作的报酬和学术确认问题不解决,定位失正,“蒋介石”变“常凯申”式的悲喜剧还会上演;更可怕的是,翻译人才枯竭,恐怕不久就会成真。

要走出去,还有一个汉外翻译的选题问题。笔者曾参与香港三联版王世襄先生的《明式家具》英译工作。我的两位定居国外的弟子曾联袂译出并由两家美国大学出版社分别出版冯梦龙的白话小说《古今小说》和《警世通言》。我不知道这类书在国外售出过多少册,问出版社也以商业秘密为由,不肯明确相告。估计成百上千到顶了,而且买家肯定以花费公帑的图书馆为多。为什么成不了气候?译者不是大家肯定是个原因。可就是杨宪益先生夫妇翻译的名著《红楼梦》,销量能有多大,我亦存疑。看来,要走出去,非先造成一个“势头”(momentum)不可。选题时适当多拆几堵墙,延聘高手——最好是洋人,即使像“中国制造”斥重金往 CNN 投放广告那样也在所不惜——用洋文写出译著的书评,先瞄准大众报章杂志书评栏,继而力争刊布于国外有影响的专业化书评报,也许能够蓄势瞻程,一步步造成“苟日新,日日新,又日新”的局面。

最后,还有个心态问题。老子所谓“自伐无功,自矜不长”,说说容易,做起来难。提倡谦虚,不是妄自菲薄,更不是鼓励多出“汉奸”,而是充分估计到历史的、传统的、社会-政治的,乃至文字语言的诸种因素带来的困难,放低身段平等融入,而不是居高临下地去空降。这样,走出去的路子是不是会平坦一些?

2010 年 1 月 26 日

子非鱼，子非我

昨天写到《论胡扯》(*On Bullshit*)那本小书，书里有个情节颇带哲学意味：路德维希·维特根斯坦的俄文教师动过扁桃体摘除手术后卧床恢复中，维氏去探望，问术后感觉如何，对方说糟透了，“就像一条被车碾过的狗”。维氏说你又不是狗，更没被车碾过，何来此比？瞧，哲学家诠释语义就是和旁人不一样。我联想到庄、惠二子游于濠梁之上的对话：一个问：子非鱼，焉知鱼之乐？一个反问：子非我，安知我不知鱼之乐？俄文教师不是被车碾过的狗；你不是鱼；你不是我——寻常人往往无视个体与个体之间的不可比性，用特殊代表一般，唯有哲学家是[动词]是[名词]非非，至察必多疑于物。所以说，我们之不断地“被代表”，而终不自觉，从哲学上说，应该对貌似正常的东西开始问一个“为什么”。常识的回归始于对常识的怀疑。

夜里躺在床上，被迫承受迎财神的全城鞭炮噪声污染。因为睡不着，就试着设想那些放鞭炮的都是什么样的人。是“被车碾过的狗”，还是“出游从容的鲦鱼”，还是看着鱼儿乐游的庄子？是股民在泄愤？是小民憧憬工资多年不动之后“加两钿”？是老板祈财运？是贪官求保佑不被叫去喝咖啡？子非鱼，子非我，想像总是不准确的。只是全城陷入这“史前”般的集体疯狂，而且年甚一年，不知哲学家们又作何解？要是世博期间，也来这么一下子，中国文化是不是顷刻间即可走向世界？

庄子与惠子游于濠梁之上。庄子曰：“鲦鱼出游从容，是鱼之乐也。”惠子曰:“子非鱼,安知鱼之乐?”庄子曰:“子非我,安知我不知鱼之乐?”惠子曰:“我非子,故不知子矣;子固非鱼也,子之不知鱼之乐全矣。”庄子曰:“请循其本。子曰‘女安知鱼乐’云者,既已知吾知之而问我。我知之濠上也。”

2010 年 2 月 18 日

In Answer to Tom Creamer's Request in His Left Message Commenting on "子非鱼 and So Forth"

遵命议一议网络和手机通讯常用的语言,用英文说就是cyberspeak+textese,搜索枯肠,中文里找不到词语对应;再说,这种语言中的不少元素正在潜移默化地进入报刊甚至书籍文字,所以想不出一个妥帖的文题。看到不少年轻朋友爱用JP,虽有友人告我,这两个拉丁化拼音字母一般用以指人,权且挪用一下来谈谈语言吧。

问一位大家闺秀+乖乖女式的学生,对某某老师有什么评价,回答不但让我大惊失色,甚至有点替说话人脸红:"哦,某某老师啊?闷骚。"作这篇短文时,说到这两个字还栗栗危惧,不敢再书写一遍,因为在我们读书那年代,用这两字来形容人,丑笃矣!当事的这位老师为人正派,俨然一恺悌君子,只不过平日里不苟言笑,稳定持重。后来问了好几个学生,始知这两个字早已不按字面意义解释,"脱敏"之后,只是拿来说人少言寡语,多少给他人留下"酷"感而已。所以,即使从女学生嘴里说出来,也一点不打格愣。再往后才知道,这两个字可以算是眼下JP用语的一部分了。

我于是觉得自己有点像华盛顿·欧文笔下的瑞普·凡·温克尔,长梦醒来,许多世事都看不懂了。因为不甘心就这样做了JP用语的"文盲",就去学着上网,碰到问题先自己练练"脑子急转弯",实在不行,就向年轻人请教,这才慢慢看懂同音异写(如"叫兽"="教授",沪语"色艺"="适意")、拉丁化汉语拼音缩写("ZF" ="政府")、洋文缩写("gf"="女友")、洋文直译(如"干物女"="[日文]ひものおんな,读作/himono onna/")、洋文变义("BMW" = "大嘴巴(话匣子)女人,即 big-mouthed woman")、数字表意("286"= "慢速,迟钝——从电脑最早主板版本号化出")、字母象形(如"Orz"="屈膝跪地姿",疑与北京奥运图有关)、复古字(如"囧"、"槑")、惊叹语(如"汗[颜]"、"赞"、"顶",现在又出来一个"排"字 —— 没抢到"沙发",排队读好文之意?)和词缀(如"……[一]族"、"……门")等等的用语花招。还有一类典出时政的流行词语,如"X 跑跑"、"楼倒倒(或歪歪、脆脆)"、"俯卧撑"、"躲猫猫"、"跨省追捕"、"含泪劝告"、"开胸验肺"、"酒桌烈士"、"我佛上市"(指要出卖少林寺赚钱)等 —— 正写此文时又蹦出一个"纸币开锈"—— 莫不"雷人",不解其意者,肯定被认作"SB"(骂人话,恕不译)。尤其可以注意的是,这种 JP 用语已有从词汇层面向语法层面推进的迹象,最明显的例子便是被动语态的畸形扩用:"被自杀"、"被潜规则"、"被脑残"、"被人肉(搜索)"等等。

就像所有亚文化群落的俚俗用语一样,这类语言之得以形成并渐渐推广的最大主观动因,就是挑战主流,颠覆传统,蔑视规范,戏弄尊严。美国黑人俚语用一种双唇紧张而非放松的一个"bad"来指"good";青少年群落用"awesome"(原意"叫人敬畏的")和"wicked"(原意"邪恶的")等,来表示"呱呱叫的"意思,就是这种词义故意倒错的例子。今日中文网上把"悲剧"写成"杯具","喜剧"写作"洗具","惨剧"写作"餐具",我看就有把原来的文学词汇"去魅化",拿文人来"开涮"一番的用意。我试过电脑的汉字输入程序,键入"beiju",首现的是"悲剧",即使为便利计,也不应再去找来"杯具",除非你要有意冒犯崇高,与规范等标准对着干。当然,也不排斥首用"杯具"者个人的一种狎弄文字的心理,同时彰显独特。

也不能完全排除JP的外部因素,即上网发文,发帖,稍犯禁忌,易遭网上的隐身人斧削,毕竟你的IP地址是掌握在别人手里的。凭着现在的科技手段和隐身人群的数字、嗅觉和热情,要找到你的真身,并不太难。不过也有例外,某次饭桌上听说,一句“拥护GCD的领导”,屏上显示时成了“拥护敏感字的领导”,难道是隐身人打瞌睡了?

使用JP的人跟工体看足球时集体以国骂爆粗口的观众不同,也同外文俚语中污言秽语泛滥的情况不同,即便口水仗打得难分难解,开骂时仍不忘常用婉语,如上面提到的SB,还有“考”(代替/cao/音),“草泥马”什么的。骂对方“你丫”,不操京片子者如我,还得去百度一下“丫”的辞源;自谦是小民一个,常用“p民”,那“p”字是代表吃了五谷杂粮以后下行之气。在暴戾恣睢的上下文中,何以非要避免一些过于龌龊的字眼?这是一个很值得研究的心理现象。

语言在社会剧变时代流动性最大,而这种流动首先一定表现在变化最活跃的词汇层面。今天熟人相见,说一声“你好”,已是常规。我虽没有深入研究语料,但印象主义地觉得,在解放前,这样的招呼语似乎难得一闻。不知是不是与翻天覆地的1949年以后“一边倒”时全社会大学俄语,一见面必说“Здравствуйте”有关。(就像改革开放以后,从台湾或者不知道什么地方引进的“不好意思”今天常常挂在人们嘴上一样。)至于那个“搞”字,既可用于“搞运动”,又可用于“搞女人”,简直是个万应动词,那更是当年社会剧变时的语言创新,可能是从老区带来。因为政权出自枪杆子,一时,中文带上浓重的军事色彩,什么“大兵团作战”啦,“集中优势兵力”啦,“战略上藐视,战术上重视”啦,“精兵简政”啦,“打一场人民战争”啦(最后一语近出动员市民参加2010年世博的上海市长之口),等等。“文化大革命”可算是另一次剧变吧?好在离我们还不算太远,“炮打”、“揪出”、“砸烂狗头”、“扫地出门”、“自绝于人民”、“不齿于人类的狗屎堆”

之类用辞,应当还不致已集体失忆。今日里 JB 大行其道,是否足以反证中国社会也正处在所谓的"转型期"剧变之中?

外行人议论 JP 用语,肯定有许多错误,欢迎读者"拍砖"。但我不认为语文界不去理会它,或是拼命把它边缘化,这种用语一定就会自动退出历史舞台。写这篇小文时正读香港作家陈冠中的小说,其中"小小嗨"一语,开始完全看不懂,"急转弯"一下,始辨出那是"小小 high"即"high lite lite"的意思,不免莞尔。看来 JP 用语的影响也不是完全消极?

2010 年 2 月 23 日

248 人骂 144 人：毒汁四溅？

英国记者兼作家盖里·戴克斯特（Gary Dexter）不是什么文坛大腕，一共才出过三本书——准确点说，应作原创一部，编撰两部——可绝对是个有趣的怪才，英国文学中模仿戏讽（parody）的技法学得尤为老到。就说原创的小说《牛津大盗》（*The Oxford Despoiler*）吧，看介绍是对福尔摩斯和助手华生的刻意模仿，只不过书中的大侦探同时又是英国头号性学专家，那八个维多利亚时期的案件背后都有“孽癖”（perversion，“孽癖”者，笔者信手胡译也，我们的“80-90后”肯定称之为BT）作祟。订购的这本书尚在邮递途中，待读完再给安迪公子写上几句覆命。另一本《为什么不叫第21条军规？》（*Why Not Catch-21?*），写了50部作品的书名由来，兼及诸多文坛轶事趣闻，也很想一读。

这儿要介绍的是2009年由英国弗兰西斯·林肯有限公司出版的《笔端溅毒：从艾米斯到左拉，文坛出言伤人大观》（*Poisoned Pens: Literary Invective from Amis to Zola*）。进入正题之前，有一点说明和一个疑问。说明：编者显然在戏仿英文里的习用语from A to Z，故有我“大观”一译；艾米斯指的自然是被某些评家归于英国“愤青”一派的Kingsley Amis。疑问：明明是从美国上网向Amazon订购的书，投递逾两周，版权页上却赫然印着“Printed in China”字样，亚马逊在中国开印刷厂了？

言归正传。这是一本关于欧美文坛作家贬评、苛责甚至谩骂其他作家的书，施事者凡 248 人，受事者，或用大白话说，挨骂者 144 人。此乃笔者采用最原始的笨办法，从正文之后的索引中计数所得。全书按时序分五大阶段：古典时代、奥古斯都时代、浪漫主义时代、维多利亚时代和现代主义时代。

嫉妒、睥睨、奋矜、歹毒、以人之卑自高、同行相轻——这些可能是人性弱点冲破世俗禁锢迟早非暴露不可的恶，表现在作家的笔墨官司里，有时严肃，言类悬河，让当事人额汗泠泠若雨；有时轻薄，黄口号嗄，显得孩子气十足。本文暂时撇开古代大家如苏格拉底、西塞罗等前几个时段，专就一般中国读者比较熟悉的欧美晚近作家作品举例若干如下。

第一，说说义正辞严类的批评。

大概也是因为“不做不错，少做少错，多做多错”的规律起了作用，我发现多产作家往往受诘责最多。说到多产，首先会想到安东尼·特罗洛普（Anthony Trollope），作品主要是长篇小说，还有短篇小说、游记、传记、戏剧、散文等总共一百多种，虽说中国读者未必熟悉这位邮局小职员出身、做事一板一眼的人（每天定时写作，时限一到，即使稿纸上最后留下的是个逗号，也绝不续写），近年来由于英国首相带头读他，影响回归。在《笔端溅毒》中记录的批评家中有斯温伯恩、亨利·詹姆斯、托马斯·卡莱尔、乔治·艾略特、亨利·哈葛德等人，代表性恶评如：“特罗洛普的生殖能力特别旺盛，又行事无度。批评家们说，他为了数量而牺牲质量，这没有什么不公平。丰产本身当然是个优点，但特罗洛普的丰产就是缠着你唠叨，叫人作呕；而他自己，我们相信，还沾沾自喜，因为比同代人给了这世界更多印刷了文字的书页。他的小说一部接着一部，非但没有明显的幕间休息，一味重叠，互踩脚跟，而且每一部大多都是超长类作品……他是近年来写到哪儿算哪儿的伟大作家。”（亨利·詹姆斯语）

特罗洛普之后，有狄更斯、萧伯纳、夏洛蒂·勃朗特等。狄更斯的作品被乔治·艾略特称之为“朽败,粗俗,窳劣……要是小说家不会写作,谁去做乞丐呢?”乔治·梅瑞狄斯断言:“传世的狄更斯作品不会很多,因为与生活太不相符了。他充其量是伦敦东区文化的化身,粗线条勾勒几笔就想学做道德家……世人决不允许在我看来一肚子木头的低能匹克威克先生与堂吉诃德共享荣誉。”前面刚被人数落过的特罗洛普,也来加入合唱:“对于狄更斯的文风,不可能提出表扬,惟有批评:痉挛式的,违反语法,不按规则的滥造。对于教育自己必须看重语言的读者来说,这种文风特别讨厌。”

有“悖论王子”之称的英国作家 G. K. 切斯特顿,批评萧伯纳痴迷超人,以为希腊神话里的巨人布赖厄鲁斯有一百只手,世人只有两只,那么世人一定个个是残疾了;阿尔戈斯有一百只眼睛,世人只有两只,在萧看来岂非个个成了独眼龙? H. G. 威尔斯说得更不客气:“萧是个战时(当然指第一次世界大战)写写传单一类的脚色……像个在医院里大呼小叫的弱智儿童,妨害别人,无法忍受。”

值得注意的是,在《笔端溅毒》中,勃朗特姐妹中的妹妹艾米丽和她的作品《呼啸山庄》没有受到片言只语的攻讦,而对夏洛蒂那“伟大的简·爱,一个瘦小的女人”(萨克雷讽刺语),乔治·艾略特说:“我读过《简·爱》了,很想知道读者诸君欣赏这本书的理由。所有的自我牺牲都是好事,只是大家希望,牺牲是为了一个比较高尚的目的,而不是为了一条匪夷所思的魔鬼法律,是这条法律把一个男人全身心地拴在一具腐烂中的躯体上……我更希望书中人物说话时,别像警察案情报告中的男女。”D. H. 劳伦斯自有他独特的批评视角:“我敢肯定,可怜的夏洛蒂·勃朗特决不有意激发读者的性感情。可我发现《简·爱》已处于色情的边缘,而对我而论,薄伽丘永远是清新而健康的……瓦格纳和夏洛蒂·勃朗特两者都处于某种最强烈的本能崩溃的状态。性成了有点龌龊的事物,虽可沉浸其中,却又遭到鄙视。罗切斯特先生的性激情不‘值得尊敬’,一直要等到他被烧伤,瞎了眼,破了相,沦落到依赖别人的无助状态。这种失去了尊严又受人耻笑的性，到此时也才可以只在嘴上说说而已。”平素显得敦厚的弗吉尼亚·伍尔芙女士也以为维多利亚时代女作家有性压抑的毛病，她针对简·奥斯汀的《傲慢与偏见》，而非《简·爱》，发表过类似于劳伦斯的观点：“不论‘布卢姆斯伯里’怎么看简·奥斯汀，她绝非我喜爱的作家。在我看来，她全部作品的价值不及勃朗特姐妹们作品的一半（笔者注：间接反映伍尔芙对《呼啸山庄》有好评？）。倘有时间读她的信件，我会进一步发现她未能取得更大成就的原因。我估计，这与性有关。信件中多的是暗示，在小说里，她把自己的一半强行压抑了。”

第二，歹毒促狭的詈訾。

最有代表性的是，1912 年出版的《马克·吐温传》中引述的第 13 号吐温信件：“我没权利批评作品，通常我也不这么做，除非真是恨死了那书。对简·奥斯汀，我常想批评几句，她的作品激起我的狂怒。每次读《傲慢与偏见》，真想把那女人从坟墓里掘出来，取过她的股骨狠狠敲打她的骷髅。”D. H. 劳伦斯把奥斯汀叫做“老处女”，“以负面、卑劣、势利表现英国，而不像菲尔丁那样以正面、宽容表现英国”。

伍尔芙女士在私密的日记里说到自己的密友凯瑟琳·曼斯菲尔德时，似已超出文字优劣判断的范畴，迹近人身攻击：“但愿对于此人的第一印象，不会使人联想到，呃，一只黄鼠狼（笔者注：原文为 civet cat，即前几年引起萨斯时疫的罪魁祸首‘果子狸’，为顾及国人接受习惯，译作‘黄鼠狼’，其实两者也确是同属动物）上大街，臭得够呛。”在其他场合，伍女士把曼女士称作气味难闻的猫。据考证，这跟曼斯菲尔德使用廉价香水有关。

英国二三流的文评家西里尔·康纳里（Cyril Connolly）——伍尔芙女士一生同他吃过一餐饭，见面“看相”即不喜此人——说起乔治·奥威尔也够刻薄的：“只要他擤鼻涕，他就想到手帕工业的现状。”因为在法庭上为《查泰莱夫人的情人》辩护（其实是来法庭路上刚从别人那儿听来的意见）而小有名气的理查德·贺伽德（Richard Hoggart）说奥威尔是“洗脑大家”，说奥氏用来用去无非是“dreadful”、“frightful”、“appalling”、“disgusting”、“hideous”这么几个“可怕”的词而已。

女诗人、爵妇伊迪丝·西特韦尔（Edith Sitwell）说D. H. 劳伦斯“活像公园里石筑毒蘑菇上的干瘪小老头”，又像“梵·高的一幅蹩脚自画像”，接着就拿查泰莱夫人的老公跟劳伦斯作比较。人家毕竟“在第一次世界大战中曾像猛虎一样英勇作战”才落下性残疾，你劳伦斯呢？安全躲在后方家里，跟女人私通，扯着嗓门叽叽喳喳！

萧伯纳是爱尔兰人，批评詹姆斯·乔伊斯，特别事涉都柏林，好像有更多的发言权，于是提出，他要封城，然后让每个从15至30岁的都柏林男子读一读乔伊斯的“脏嘴巴和脏思想”，且看其中是否有任何有趣的东西。“本人20岁时从都柏林逃到英格兰，难道今天一切都还和1870年时一样？”美国诗人庞德在收到乔伊斯寄来的新作《芬尼根守灵夜》后，写信给作者：“如此曲里拐弯的文字，其价值也许可以跟发明了一种新的花柳病治疗法相媲美？”

第三，互出洋相，形同儿戏。

自以为了不起的海明威教诗人庞德拳击，恰逢英国画家兼作家温特汉姆·路易斯（Wyndham Lewis）来访，海明威于是大骂庞德手脚笨拙，同时也不放过来客，说对方长了一张“蛙脸”，巴黎对这只青蛙是个过大的池塘。海明威想就此停止拳击训练，可是路易斯不让，非要看到庞德受伤不可。后来，三人饮酒。海明威仔细“看相”，发现路易斯的脸容邪恶，那双眼睛像“强奸未遂犯”。再后来，同一位文坛友人说起路易斯，对方曾见画家老是拿支铅笔在帮助目测距离和体积等等，亦即不住地measuring，这个单词后面加上个worm，即成“尺蠖”。自此，可怜的路易斯就变了一条虫。

海明威恶毒，其他文坛朋友也不逊色。纳博科夫把他称作“三

b”，即 bells（钟），balls（睾丸，化出勇气的意思）和 bulls（公牛），曾拒绝把《老人与海》译成俄语。托洛茨基的朋友、美国作家迈克斯·伊斯特曼（Max Eastman）嘲弄海明威的“伪阳刚”，说他的文风使人联想到“前胸装上假毛发”。海明威听了怀恨在心，时隔四年，犹耿耿于怀，这时，正好两人在一家出版社碰上了，海明威二话不说，便脱去衬衫，叫对方验看胸毛真伪，过后还坚持要伊斯特曼也敞开怀来，让人看看有无胸毛。最后两人像孩子一样扭打起来，按海明威的说法，对方“像个老娘们一样”要抓他的脸，最后被他摔倒在地！

上文提到过的 G. K. 切斯特顿看着精瘦精瘦的萧伯纳，曾说过著名的笑话：“看你那模样，谁都会以为英国发生饥荒了。”切斯特顿本人脑满肠肥，无疑就给了萧伯纳一个极佳的反击机会：“看着你的样子，谁都会以为大饥荒是你引起的。”

* * * *

戴克斯特为这本书写了一篇短短的前言，列举文人相轻的三个理由的同时，提出一个很有意思的理念，那就是书评文字中往往惟有贬评方是的评，而作家也惟有在跟人打起笔墨官司时往往有特别出彩的文字。他引用英国诗人和文评家埃德蒙·高斯（Edmund Gosse）的话：“决不要在乎你要去褒扬什么人，但要你去贬评谁时必须非常当心。”这个理念，还有这条引语，对书评类刊物的编辑，真是法语之言，能无从乎？

最后，说点小小的意见。可能是因为作者刚刚出道，大编辑们不太把他当回事，《笔端溅毒》这书的印刷错误不少，包括书尾索引中有两个 F 字部而缺了 G 字部。封面设计非常幼稚，初看还会以为这是本儿童读物呢。

2010 年 3 月 19 日

修改后的“发刊辞”

复旦外文学院翻译系出了本“以书代刊”的《翻译教学与研究》，遵命写了一篇“发刊辞”。书出，发现编者有所删节，又因近日见闻益多，所以修改扩写如下，欢迎批评：

办学刊是件大好事——只要(1)不为争夺话语霸权；(2)不为揾银。除去这两端，办刊物还有什么目的？有的。顾炎武说过，独学无友，则孤陋而难成；久处一方，则习染而不自觉。复旦就是局促“一方”。办个刊物，经营自己一亩三分地的同时，把门打开，看看其他地方的学友都在做些什么样的功课，甚至可以包容少量古人与稽的内容，这才是博学审问，我们自己也不致变成一群面墙之士。

刚有学生从外地参加学术会议回来，都说“接轨”无处不在，中国的所谓学人开会，现在也有点像戴维·洛奇笔下的“小世界”了，当然还增添了若干中国特色(譬如贵为学会会长在主旨发言中把朱生豪这样几乎家喻户晓的名字误做“朱豪生”；又如承担多项外国文学国家项目的教授把海明威小说的英文书题叫做“For Whom the Bell Rings”)，那就是一家独大，唯我独尊；或者一两家默契联手，对于非我族类者，畏才忌强，冷落排斥。记得许国璋先生生前给我的最后一封信中曾告诫，不可成为“不学有术”之人，谁知道这样的人在金钱拜物教盛行的形势下，再加上什么“导弹”捣蛋，茂密繁衍，不但已有群体效应，都快要自成特异物种了。上面说到的情形，我称之为“学术辛迪加”，我意复旦人不必等人来封杀，早一点自觉置身圈外为好。

被逐出重点，揽不来项目，没经费干不了事，提不上职称，受 publish or perish 的规律支配，你说再不委曲求全怎么办？我说那就跟自己作一点纵向比较，不要左顾右盼跟别人作横向比：想我陆某人当年蜗居 15 平方，一张写字桌要一家三口轮流着用，还要给拘入“抗大式学习班”变相隔离。今天的青年少壮境况再惨烈，也到不了那地步吧？我不是提倡开倒车，大家回到过去，而是觉得这种纵向比较虽说好像没出息，却容易使人安贫乐道，就像苏格拉底看着雅典市场上琳琅满目的商品，感叹道：“这里有多少我用不着的东西啊！”最多像我钦佩的中文系严锋老弟那样，不提职称也罢，自顾自做学问，造福学生，对得起家长就是了。你若不让我在学店里干了，咱出去自己玩学问，多写几篇文章，make ends meet 大概不成问题吧。

同理，办刊物也不必横向朝别人看齐，才不去管自己是不是御批钦定的“权威”或“核心”，只要胸有定识，目有定见，口有定评，倔强地按照一定之规去办，若遭人暗算挤压而致“短命”，自认倒霉之余，不折不弯，设法东山再起就是。对所谓“小人物”的来稿，看它是否言之有物又言之有益，切勿一概弃若瓦砾；挺起脊梁来坚拒关系稿；守节不移不索版面费；就是要让学界看看渣秽溷乱之中，这儿还有一小撮人在清白办刊，清贫办刊。做得到吗？

除了清白和清贫，还要愉快办刊。我学了外语，发现最大的愉快就是翻译——当然要与外部世界对话，翻译不只是愉快还更是有用的。这本翻译刊物如要介绍西方的译论，能否以“达”为先？“达”者，让人读懂。选题不要跟风。像前几日逝世的老寿星列维-斯特劳斯，他的结构主义影响所及主要在人类学，而在文学领域渐呈式微似已有多年。我如有资格决定翻译选题，肯定朝前者倾斜，偏偏有些喜欢跟风的外国文学类编辑一时言必称此公。晦涩的论文体作品当然不可能拒不采用，但希望灰色的理论发表出来也有出彩的时候，让读者虽艰难但又不失愉快地吮吸新鲜的理论营养。尤其要防止西文原文本来还勉强可读能懂，译写成汉文后则实在不知所云。本人读到过一个把修饰语和从句从洋文逐一照译而成的34个汉字的无标点句，后来不经意间读到了英文原文，经过对照，别的不说，足证写下这句话的译学学者，有必要从头学习翻译。你就不能“稀释”一下，化整为零，脱化作几个句子，免读者诘屈聱牙和手足胼胝之苦？说这话肯定得罪人，或许是自我放逐，即自绝于某些理论人孤芳自赏的小圈子。但我自问是有些看透个别理论人的。说白了，洋文、汉文都不怎么高明（听到过“理论人”说“he was bornd”以及类似滚滚而出的错误吗？），域外出现一个什么新奇术语或说法，赶在他人面前，一把拽来，来不及嚼烂消化，囫囵呕哕，先抢占制高点再说。还是就列维-斯特劳斯说事，不知从什么时候开始，可能同翻译他老人家的人类学著作有关，“field studies”在汉语里被新派人物译作“原野研究”。其实好多的调查研究工作都是在逐人访谈的户内进行的。“原野”二字就因为新颖一定比“现场”或“实地”准确？办刊要愉快，希望严肃的学刊也能容下一些实际内容，甚至可辟个“难译之隐”一类的栏目，譬如说为什么“负迁移（negative transfer）”等于“母语干扰”，是谁在何种学术领域首先提出来的？又如，何谓 think-aloud protocols？实时记载译者在换码时大脑认知的“出声思考程序”？有更妥帖的译法吗？既然“set theory”通常译作“集论”，为什么用来解释宇宙存在的 superstring theory 不能译作“超弦论”而要译作“弦理论”？（英文里的 super-哪去了？）理论物理学家们近年来又把“弦理论”的第十维空间扩大为十一维，于是就有了“膜理论”（membrane theory）。不能相应简约作“膜论”吗？在文评界和“同志”亚文化群里已是耳熟能详的“酷儿理论”是“queer theory”的佳译吗？在我看来，音不像音，字不及义，实在不是可取的译法。福柯和他的追随者们煞费苦心发展出这门理论，会不会觉得中国香港和内地人这样的译法太轻佻而不如“畸态属性理论”更像门严肃的学问？“难译之隐”不限于外语习得、翻译、认知等学科范畴，完全可以扩大到其他方面，像老是在困扰我的美国社会少数族裔反歧视（其实本身也是一种歧视）用语“affirmative action”怎么译？“偏帮”、“维权”、“纠歧”、“认肯”行动？甚至还可延及更加实用（虽然并非长久）的时事用语：如眼下热议中的“倒钩”怎么译？to frame sb. up 还是 to plant a provocateur 或 stool pigeon？等等。斟酌乎质文之间，隐括乎雅俗之际，高头讲章和雕虫小技互为调济，有常与无方结合，是否可能更受读者欢迎？

读书人办刊，还要讲究饱读办刊，就是要有深度地介绍新书和有关网站。写书评不能单靠从《泰晤士报文学增刊》和《纽约时报周六书评》作二手转移，而是要提倡书评人必须亲炙作品（最好是原文而非译本，更不能只读高山杉君戏称为“书皮”[blurb]之类的东西）之后有感而发。前两种刊物当然也有用，特别是对于了解世界书情，如英国格拉斯哥大学斯图阿特·吉尔思派编写的《翻译和文学》（爱丁堡大学出版），煌煌 17 卷本，如何可能全读？只能有的放矢查阅或写个第二手的简介；还有，此人与人合编的《牛津英语文学翻译史》，预定明年出书，发个预告，我看也有价值。说到书评，我发现“含金量”高的长篇书评，抽取几个关键词，引文后面注出处，文后附上参考书目，剔除作者个性化过强的闲话，改写作论文也不难，拿去参评职称可能有用，何乐而不为？检验饱读的标志之一还看你有几副笔墨，是否正言精义，抒发情性两宜。为世用者，百篇无害，不为用者，一章无益。至于如何熟悉并利用——注意：不是滥用——网站，青壮学者肯定胜我，就不啰嗦了。

2010 年 4 月 10 日

Fish Fished

It may have been the most difficult title I have ever translated, difficult mostly because of the numerous long passages about fly-fishing therein. I thought of quitting as I found it contrary to my conviction that one only takes to translating material 95% of which one understands. The copy editor representing 文景（I guess）was then kind enough to clear a hurdle for me, assuring me that there was hopefully little if any more fly-fishing in the remainder of the book. She was, however, hoping against hope as I had to belabor fishing technicalities all the way down the line. Honestly, after "the fish is fished," the translator remains quite hazy about, say, how a fisherman "throws a line into the rod." In other words, he doesn't know for sure about the relationship between a fishing line and a fishing rod.

Honestly again, I had known nothing about the book or the writer except for the fact that there is a dorm building at the University of Chicago I had visited years earlier bearing the name of Maclean. But as I worked along, Norman Maclean gradually unfolded: it seems that he is writing in the tradition of American Nature Writing; he has apparently opted for a virile he-man way of writing since the story has tough guys to deal with against a Montana background; he strikes one as Hemingway combined with Thoreau; he can be loquacious in identifying interlocutors in a dialogue or monologue with numberless tags like "he said," "he asked," and "I thought/guessed/supposed" but would reduce the essentials to a lean minimum. All this made translating moderately interesting.

But I had to be punctilious, leaving myself very little room for verbal manoeuvre when it comes to fly-fishing since finally the translation is to be published side by side with the original — a "bugbear-reflecting mirror," so to speak. As a result, I didn't dare to break away from the straitjacket that tethers all translators until either at the beginning or at the very last. At the beginning is the title *A River Runs through It*. The copy editor told me the movie adapted from the book starring Brad Pitt and others is entitled 大河恋 which is widely accepted as *fait accompli* in China. Is it feasible then to change it back to "一江流过水悠悠"? At the end of the story is a one-sentence paragraph: "I am haunted by waters." Having had enough of the said straitjacket, can I enjoy the freedom of paraphrase just for once by rendering it as "水啊,我的梦!"

I await blue- (or is it red-?) penciling of the editor.

11 April 2010

狗血喷头

今天看到一段英国作家 D. H. 劳伦斯痛骂他的英国同胞的一段话,正应了我们中国人那句成语"狗血喷头",摘引并试译如下,供英四同学参考:

"Curse the blasted, jelly-boned swines, the slimy, the belly-wriggling invertebrates, the miserable sodding rutters, the flaming sods, the sniveling, dribbling, dithering, pulseless lot that make up England today."(诅咒那帮构成今日英国天打五雷轰的家伙,一个个都是软骨猪猡,污秽龌龊,肚皮贴地扭行的蠕虫,眼巴巴求偶交配的兽类,淫火烈烧的相公,抽抽搭搭,嘴角流涎,抖抖索索,连脉搏也搭不出了。)

劳君为什么破口大骂同胞?原来是因为英国一家叫 Heinemann 的出版社曾拒出他的一本书——还不是后来遭禁几十年的那部《查泰来夫人的情人》。

劳君爱上比自己年长 6 岁的导师夫人,双双私奔。一战爆发,导师夫人是德籍敌国公民,其兄又是德方王牌飞行员,两人于是迭遭英国政府骚扰,甚至指控两人在英国康沃尔海岸给德国潜艇发信号。加上劳君本人的书,还有画,屡在英国遭禁。这可能就是他仇视英国的原因?劳伦斯有个短篇小说集叫《英格兰,我的英格兰》,当年看到这书题,曾以为他下半生自我放逐在外,开始想念故国了？读过之后，不对了，那集子完全像一本“丑陋的英国人”之类的书。

2010 年 4 月 28 日

谁知道中国的“灰姑娘”?

前面提到过 Gary Dexter 的《书名杂谈》(*Why Not Catch-21?*),的确,未知新鲜信息不多,不甚耐读。像《等待戈多》里的戈多到底是谁,《洛丽塔》有无同名蓝本,《莫比 · 迪克》是否那条原叫“莫查 · 迪克”的太平洋凶鲸?《尤利西斯》,作为一个神话人名,在全书几不出现,之所以被选作书题,是不是因为尤利西斯从小就是乔伊斯心目中的头号英雄?《乌托邦》的序诗是否提纲挈领地解读了书名的意义(Utopia + Eutopia,即理想国+乌有乡)?根本不叫鲁滨逊的瑞士人一家孤岛经历,为什么叫作我幼时读得津津有味的《瑞士鲁滨逊家庭漂流记》?(虽把译者的大名忘了,可至今还记得中译本里那些精彩的插图。)这以后的《泰山》、《蝇王》等等是不是都可归作“鲁滨逊体裁”?……

钩隐抉微某些书题时,鄙人还可不揣谫陋,给 Dexter 提供一点新的线索。像《哈姆雷特》的书名来由,作者从丹麦古书说到法国译本,再说到疑为 Thomas Kyd 所作的《元始哈姆雷特》。莎翁本人夭折儿子名叫 Hamnet 等脉络都也交代清楚了,但就是忽略了莎士比亚十五六岁时在邻城有个名叫 Katherine Hamlet 的姑娘溺水而死,现场也有垂柳,究竟是爱情出了问题自杀,还是意外,舆论存疑。鉴于 Katherine 和剧中人 Ophelia 一样遭遇“a muddy death”,又恰姓 Hamlet,难道不也是解题的线索之一吗?(当然,我这儿提供的线索也是二手读来的,嘻嘻。)

比较有兴味的内容是对《灰姑娘》的解题。据说这个故事的不同版本有345种之多,多数在欧洲口口相传。到上世纪50年代,数量又激增至700种,有“爪哇灰姑娘”、“前哥伦布时代美洲灰姑娘”、“非洲灰姑娘”等。特别引我注意的是,还有“中国灰姑娘”。故事成于9世纪,比欧洲流行的文字作品早去约七百年。说“小脚的故事”源于中国,作者认为是说得通的。中午,蒋天枢先生的一位弟子来访,问他古籍中有没有什么“金莲记”之类的篇什,他一时也想不出,因而在此求教于网友,大家一起把“中国灰姑娘”找出来。

2010年5月11日

蒲松龄写举报信

开玩笑吧，专写狐魅花妖的蒲松龄写举报信？读读学林出版社的《蒲松龄全集》就知道了，这位浪漫派其实现实主义得很，对康熙年间的大饥荒、清代漕运、考试等腐败，都有过白描式的记录，对贪官恶吏更是猛烈抨击，如在写给“给谏”（言官）孙蕙的信中，直指对方“重利盘剥，武断乡曲”，百姓“咋舌咬指，良可骇叹”，而孙蕙还曾是蒲松龄的发小！《聊斋》故事里，更以“鳖也‘得言’，龟也‘得言’”的一则对仗工整的下联，径将“得言”指言官孙蕙，把他骂了个酣畅淋漓。当然也有人说，蒲是为孙的侍妾受到虐待打抱不平，而那位侍妾正是蒲暗恋的对象，连《聊斋》都是为她而作的。

至于这封写给也是儿时朋友、时任刑部尚书王士禛的举报信，就绝无个人意气的纠葛了：“适有所闻，不得不妄为咨禀。”举报对象是漕运经承（经办官）“积蠹”（对胥吏中积恶者的鄙称）康利贞，“欺官虐民，以肥私囊，遂使下邑贫民皮骨皆空……渠乃腰缠万贯。”更恶劣的是，康贪官到王士禛那儿去了一次之后“扬扬而返，自鸣得意”，称已得你个昏庸的“老先生”——王士禛长蒲松龄七岁——荐书。“学中数人，直欲登龙赴诉，某恐搅扰清况，故尼其行，而不揣卑陋，潜致此情。”原来有人想集体上门投诉康贪官，蒲怕发生群体性事件，这才悄悄写了封举报信。至于举报信是否有用，下文不详。鉴于清朝的官场语境，我看可能是泥牛入海。

2010年5月16日

两位留洋生

一个在澳洲留学的学生“闪电”突击回沪。她做的论文涉及汉语构词，很微观，从“的”、“底”、“得”、“地”开始考察，直到外来的“—化”、“—性”、“去—”等，从语言的“small change”（“找头小钱”，即鸡零狗碎）看古文时期小品词泛滥的汉语，如何在近现代容忍并接纳欧化词缀。我刚改完她的文献一览一大段，今天又深谈汉语的小品词问题以及语言的规范和描记之争。她在重温文献时有个特别强烈的感觉，就是：谁说中国没有语法？中国语法界曾有多少出色的前人，从瞿秋白到黎锦熙、赵元任、高名凯、王力、吕叔湘等等，从不同角度生产了多少出色的成果，可惜到“文革”前后一下子出现了十余年的空白，致使她这个年龄的新时期学生，做学问时往往首先想到搜寻洋人怎么怎么说，而不知好好利用我们自己的文化资源。“老”字一定就是“置于指人或动物的名词前”的前缀？“老鼠”=鼠，“老虎”=虎，“老百姓”= 百姓，没错。但适用面有多广？能说“老狮”、“老群众”吗？对我，这充其量只是个适用面高度局限的“去书面化”的小品词而已。汉语之丰赡，大半不正在于小品词特多，语义隐淡，功能模糊吗？

她的感慨引我回忆起昨晚葛兆光兄饭局上另一位留洋学生（现已做到哈佛教授）。我们讨论到西方的“新左”对中国的影响。其实西方“新左”反对的是他们殖民主义、帝国主义的老祖宗，出发点是平等，不成想中国的某些“新左”不许非议老祖宗，说起平等，也要讲中国特色。这样,西方的激进主义成了咱们这儿形左实右的保守主义,真是有趣得——用个小青年的词,我看新《三国》里也用——“紧”。受了西方“新左”的影响,某位中国“新左”问过我对“鞍钢宪法”的看法。“两参一改三结合”,好听得“紧”。干部参加劳动,即使在当年可曾能保证制度化而不是走个过场?还是仅仅停留在口号?较长时间下过厂的老大学生都知道怎么回答。工人参加过管理吗?党的领导和政治挂帅,不都是“鞍钢宪法”的前提吗?

2010 年 5 月 18 日

上海的文化身份?

从今天报上看到,有人在那儿热烈讨论上海的"文化身份",还把"纽(约)巴(黎)伦(敦)"提出来,说这是世界的"三大文化之都"。"纽巴伦"是否受得起如此溢美,暂付不论,倒是此"伦"使我联想到彼"伦"。我宁可把上海称作"现代巴比伦"(为读者搜索方便,英文叫做 modern Babylon)。

说到文化定位,有人总要把上海的海纳百川提出来说事。我所认识的洋人中,喜欢上海的也确多于喜欢北京的,认为上海 more cosmopolitan。如果有人说北京"土",吃大蒜的多,我倒认为北京虽然有点"老迈",却是的的确确具有"文化身份"的,而上海惟有一种本质上的猥琐、浅薄和油滑。最近世博施行优待轮椅人的入园措施,上海居然有人入园前冒充残疾,进得园里,轮椅一丢,健步如飞。你说这是机智?我看是十足的猥琐!再说怀旧,首先得有旧可怀吧。就文学的"根"而言,是民国初年的鸳鸯蝴蝶,还是名门之后的张爱玲?要不,就剩下一个鲁迅?就广义的社会文化而论,现在把旧时的法租界(即上海人所谓的"上只角")都搬出来做卖房的促销号召了,怎不见愤青骂"汉奸"又在那儿怀念不平等条约下的租界时代?西风东渐的日子里,"洋泾浜"大流行,就像沈昌文君对人说过的,他是从"生发油买来卖去=thank you very much"开始学英文的。有人说,这说明沪人善学,我看是油滑成性。上海人"头子活络",善学"夷之所长",取来为我所用。"文革"时代,将提升式电线抢修车开上街头,把曹荻秋像珍稀动物般示众,市民引颈围观叫好,这一幕非常容易让人联想起阿Q里的情节。还有,全市电视批判陈(丕显)曹(荻秋)大会也很有创意,据说曾得到过毛主席的赞赏。

英国诗人W. H. Auden把人分作两大类,一种是“阿卡迪亚人”(Arcadians),怀念古希腊阿卡迪亚田园诗式恬静的人,另一种是“乌托邦人”(Utopians),希望出现新的耶路撒冷式的城市。前者怀旧,从大片绿色而不是亭子间或D.D.S.咖啡馆寻找文化归属;后者的文化视角贯注明天,有政治理想和追求这种理想的活力。试问不论回顾还是前瞻,上海人能摆脱无根漂流而为自己准备好一个“文化身份”吗? 倒是有位上海青年,人家外国杂志捧他,他却坚称自己是个“农村的孩子”。要是上海人都这样,也许再谈文化身份不迟。

2010年5月27日

破碎的心是种看不见的疾病：简介《殡葬》一书

英四要停课了。“Book of the Week”无法再让你们复印，只得借博客简单介绍这本书了。书初版于1997年，我读到的是2009年的纸面新版。你们刚刚读了“Rest in Pieces”，再读本书，两相比照，一定有趣。

“破碎的心是种看不见的疾病。患病的人并不瘸行。也见不到疤痕。不发停车证，难以探病。碎的是心，溃烂的是灵魂。伤口不加治疗，准保致命。”这是美国密歇根州一个殡仪馆老板兼诗人Thomas Lynch在他的散文集子《殡葬》里的一段话，我故意给译文押了韵，为的是凸显这个从事阴森森行当的人的诗性特质。

真是个怪异的集合体：生与死，哭与笑，短暂与永驻，现实与玄思，爱尔兰与美国。一般人都把殡葬商人自然而然地跟残忍无情或麻木不仁相联系，特别是一个在美国中西部小城里操此营生者。谁也想不到，就是这样一个人，会从“殡葬”(undertaking)这么个英文词想开去，试问世人，为什么不把词儿拆开，把殡葬业者认作“带往下面去的伴送者”？这不就有了点“人文关怀”的意思？因为经手处理的尸体多了，他开始追问死的意义。以日瓦戈医生为例，在莫斯科电车上看到拉拉，一步跳下，向心爱的人追去，不料心脏病突发而在大街上猝死。所以死亡常常是在追逐爱的过程中发生的。(当然，作者只能写到个体的爱，写不出许多人集体赴死时追逐的大爱。)正如《时装》杂志评论的那样，“［这个集子］给我们的启示在于生和死，而最重要的，还在于爱”。

还有意外的死亡。行车在州际公路上，顽童把上方墓园里的大块墓碑推下砸中汽车，后座女儿因此死去，而父母为爱女购买坟地时，恰恰与那块大墓碑的主人做了冥界邻居。于是，行车时分的一家人的“生”成为一种嘲弄，因为“上帝之手”或“万有引力”始终支配人间，“生”所衬托的应是“死”的偶然还是必然？

Lynch 笔下的死亡充满了玄思：死亡永远是孤独的，就像抽水马桶发明之后总是一个人独自如厕一样（笔者注：说抽水马桶由 Thomas Crapper 发明似有误，英国早在 18 世纪就有虽非利用虹吸原理但可冲水的便器记载）；又说在英语中“death”和“sex”同韵，是叶芝还是庞德把两者相提并论来着？而对他本人的一女三子说来又绝对是同义词，都是某种赌博的结果。

Lynch 看来还是个文字好手，不但分析“mortician”和“funeral director”（认为前者词尾带“专门家”意味而太“潮”，宁可别人称他后者）之别，还用上“kevork”这类难得一见的词，这词是从美国一个专门从事助人自杀的“医生”Jack Kevorkian 的名字化出的，意指“杀死”。

2010 年 6 月 5 日

笑煞人

从《咬文嚼字》看到,虹桥机场附近有家“航友宾馆”,英文招牌是“Hang You Hotel”。咱们用的是拉丁化拼音,碰巧要是老外把两个词当做英文读出,不就成了“吊死你”? 真是吓死外国人,笑煞中国人。

设在机场旁边,想来主要是为中转旅客以及航班延误或取消的旅客为主要服务对象的。也不知空中交通出了什么问题,最近有过飞行经历的朋友,都抱怨航班延误或取消几乎已经成为常态,晚点一两个钟头,“小意思”啦;什么时候喇叭里要你领盒饭去,那就惨了。在国内旅行,也许有人会把世博会提出来,作为空中交通混乱的理由,可是远在美国的空中旅行,也好不到哪里去,连国会都给惊动了,要讨论立法保护旅客利益。

空运现状如此,滞留旅客激增。有鉴于此,把“航友宾馆”译作“Hotel for Strandees”? 恐怕不行,一是用上 strandees 把住店顾客局限死了;二是滞留的人原已心中有气,一见 strandee 不是火上加油? 那么用“In-Transit Hotel”如何? 也不行。有的明明是在上海登机始发飞出,并非中转。想来想去,“for friendly fliers”可不可以?(联合航空不是用 Friendly Skies 做过广告吗?)勉强可以,虽说 fliers/flyers 一般只做“飞行员”解。那就用“Passengers Home Hotel”怎么样? 用 passengers 而非 passengers',是因为现在词尾变化倾向于减少或脱落,如 teachers college 都不加 apostrophe 了。

借此机会，敦请诸位常读《咬文嚼字》，那里头除了益智，好玩的内容特多，像作家硬把“蜀道难”之叹从李白转嫁给杜甫；婚礼上文绉绉的司仪爱用的“执子之手，与子偕老”，实际上会给新人结婚之后马上就要长期分离、苦苦思念的联想，弄得不好，男方还可能成为“可怜无定河边骨/ 犹是春闺梦里人”呢，等等等等。杂志小巧而便于携带，坐上地铁，驶过五六站即可读完，带着好心情上班去，岂非美事。

[注：我与该刊没有利益共需关系。本文不是软广告。]

2010 年 6 月 7 日

端午节可以叫 Dragon-Boat Festival 吗?

据说,英语教材里说到中国的"中秋节",必须按照中国政府网站的译法,称作 Mid-Autumn Festival,而不得用外国人常用的 Moon Festival。这背后的逻辑,正如 NBC,WTO 等洋文缩写不得在播报中出现一样。你说当官的有时糊涂,什么都要"以我为主"和"一切惟我是从",大家也见怪不怪了。编英语教材的老师们怎么也开始采用"一切惟官是从"的思维了。一个普通的节日,与领土所属之类的重大问题完全无涉,固执于这种思维,我看这教材编出来也大告而不妙。

Mount Everest 应按官方网站叫 Qomolangma Peak 自然是有道理的。说到中秋,我个人倒觉得 Chinese Moon Festival 不但点出"月亮"、"月饼"等节庆主题,也更有利于向外人介绍中国文化。Mid-Autumn 反倒是趣味和个性全无的字面直译,何况东南亚有不少也在这天吃月饼过节的邻国,并不都采用"中秋"说法;更何况美语里虽然也用 autumn 指秋天,文化程度不太高的美国人可能还是听着 fall 更自然(虽说美语将 fall 作秋天解,回溯上去,还是离不了英语老祖宗 at the fall of leaves)。要不,教我们的学生对英人说 Mid-Autumn,对美人说 Mid-Fall? 对着东南诸邻讲 Moon Festival?

我于是又想到了端午节的译法 Dragon-Boat Festival,回译过来便是"龙舟节"。这显然也是洋人始用的译法吧? 现在也有保守的时髦人开始用 Duanwu Festival 了,可总也普及不开。教科书里采用哪一种? 其他的还有“清明”、“重阳”等等。

可怕的不在于具体节气的英文说法,而是那种清末民初就流行过的“以我为主”、“惟官是从”的思维。当年,对于从东邻日本传入的“日制汉字词”既害怕,又抵制,说是用了“取缔、取消、引渡、目的、宗旨、权利、义务、卫生”等近60个词就会“灭国灭族”。这些词后来用了吗? 中华民族灭了吗?

同样可怕的还有,教材编写找人指导,必须雅贿,礼品不到一定级别,受贿人还会公然索取厚酬。只不知指导员们自己的英文水平又如何。听说有专家反馈意见说“No interesting, no impressive”,编者听了诚惶诚恐,都来不及想一想“No interesting, no impressive”是什么英文?!

2010年7月2日

“耳聋判决之后”

这是我给 David Lodge 2008 年的小说 *Deaf Sentence* 提议的书名翻译。本来两个英文词够简单的，可是“sentence”是个可数名词，既不在前面加个“a”，又不是复数形式，弄啥玄虚啊？是要读者联想到“death sentence”？此公喜欢玩文字游戏，像现实生活中的出版社 Mills & Boon 到他笔下成了 Bills & Moon；给角色 Arthur Kingfisher 起名不忘植入亚瑟王传奇的典故，等等（均见《小世界》）。果不其然，作家像是已经预料到读者的疑问，开宗明义，向准备将此书译成其他文字的人打个招呼，警告书名难译，继而引用《新简编牛津词典》给“sentence”所下的定义，其中既有“句子”又有“判决”等常用义项，又有“way of thinking, opinion, mind ...”这些直接来自拉丁辞源 sententia 的意思，跟汉语里的“思路”、“观感”等相近，用上“……之后”就是为了与此呼应。在这“一锅粥”似的义群当中搅拌多时，想出上面这个译法，什么叫“耳聋判决”？是够生涩的。如何把书名译好，当是译者的事情；我这儿为了写书评方便，暂时也只能勉强对付着这样用了。

虽说 David Lodge 文学成就的顶峰只不过是两次进过布克奖提名的第二榜，他却一直是我喜爱的作家。早在上世纪 80 年代改革开放之初，他的所谓卢米奇（虚拟大学名）三部曲就引起了我极大的兴趣。佐证有二。一是，后来一位学生译他的 *Changing Places*（《换位》）时，发现我参与编写的《英汉大词典》里有好几个例证，原封不动地引自这部作品。我一点不怀疑,那是我在当年读书时信手摘下供词典使用的。译者在词典中发现了三条,焉知没有其他?二是,我记得读完 *Small World*(《小世界》),大概是在80年代中后期,曾在书信中向钱锺书先生推荐这部“现代西人版《围城》”,钱回信说,我是向他介绍此书的第一人。说到David Lodge作品的主题,三部曲之三《好工作》在嘲讽女权主义批评的同时,又以精妙的“换工”结构,描写学界与业界的嵌接以及撒切尔夫人时代英国保守主义与自由主义的小步接近;三部曲之前和之后的《不列颠博物馆在坍塌》和《灵与肉》揭批天主教的生育教规;《治疗法》将医学与宗教对峙,探索人的生存困境,引入存在主义讨论时,大费周章给克尔恺廓尔的姓氏拆字;《思想……》则把上述讨论推到认知科学的层面……然而David Lodge为读书界所熟知——也是我喜欢他的理由——可能主要还在于他的“学院派小说”(campus novels),那种由C.P. Snow, Kingsley Amis和Malcolm Bradbury等所开启的文学样式,即便在讨论社会价值观时,始终不忘以闹剧手法戏仿“学院派”,抨击教师的虚荣、知识缺陷和勾心斗角,学生的伪激进与肤浅。

岁月不饶人。长我五岁的David Lodge虽从照片上看还不怎么见老,毕竟耳背多年,如果上述三部曲还是“青壮学院派”作品的话,《耳聋判决之后》可算是“退休学院派”的天鹅之歌了。可老年Lodge并不认为自己已经灯枯油尽,眼下犹笔耕不止,只是不到作品写成,不想过早“让猫儿(实应作施刑鞭子,但一般人都误以为是猫)钻出袋子”(见英国文学网站The Book Depository上Mark Thwaite对他的采访记)而已。且让我们等着看他的下一部作品。

时而采用日记体手法,时而跳出第一人称叙事,《耳聋判决之后》的情节相对简单,再没有Henry James“旧大陆,新美国”那种越洋比照的手法,也无亚瑟王骑士寻找圣杯的隐喻,倒是对一对二婚夫妇,连带着他们各自家人的寻常生活,着墨颇多。小说主人公、英国北方某所大学的语言学系主任 Desmond Bates 自觉听觉日衰,“自己讲得太多太多……听了半天不知道争议的焦点是什么,于是只好沉默,不敢贸然发言……接着就看见某人嘴角隐约挂笑,或是围桌而坐的人们交换调皮的目光,这样他才知道自己听错什么了。”经医生诊断,这种病叫做“高频失聪”,症状为嘈杂环境中特别难辨辅音音素,原因是二十年来,内耳毛发细胞一直在逐步减少。全小说的第一长句就定下了“耳聋是喜剧,眼瞎是悲剧”(以俄狄浦斯的故事为例)的基调,把这句话译成汉语是这样的:

> 这个戴着眼镜的银发高个子,站在主展厅大群客人的外围,俯身与那位穿红色丝绸衬衣的年轻女人靠得很近,头部低垂,角度却是背离着她的脸部,贤明地点头,不时吐出含混不清的声音作为交流。你可别以为他是被女人劝来,在大庭广众之下听她忏悔的下班教士,也不是给骗来提供免费咨询的心理医师。他之所以采取这样的姿势,也不是为了便于偷看女人衬衣前部的内里,虽说这是他眼下处境偶有所得的一点收获,惟一的一点收获而已。

俯身低头原来只是因为耳背而想听清楚对方所说的话,聚会场所则是妻子与人合伙开的一家室内装璜公司的主展厅。渐入老境,兼患耳疾,Desmond 提前退休,在家里当上了多少有些像“买汏烧”的角色——虽然跑商店主要是“为了练身体,而非出于必须”,虽然他的思维一点没有萎缩,只要给他机会,照样可就“语篇分析”、“言语行为”等专题滔滔不绝。丈夫衰落,老婆 Winifred(自寄宿学校时代起人称 Fred。忘记是哪位作家说过,女人若是使用男性名字,读者必须警觉,就像下文那美国女生名叫 Alex 一样)却焕发了第二春,事业有成,成了家庭的经济支柱,而经济基础带动了上层建筑的改变,对着丈夫叫“darling”时的口气再不像从前,而是时而愠怒,时而烦躁,时而表示怜悯,时而隐含讥笑。角色的变换,加上 Desmond 同样患耳疾的伦敦老父,固执独居,不肯听从儿子劝告,雇人照顾。小便失禁,儿子只好停车用个吹风机替他把内裤烘干。一个退休人的苦恼,大到名根未除却无复人理,小到手忙脚乱摆弄不听话的助听器,写得巨细靡遗。成天读着《泰晤士报文学增刊》打发时光,或是去"唇读班"自寻乐子,好不容易遇上个美国来的女生,缠求自己帮她写出一篇关于"自杀遗书"的博士论文,Desmond 不免心猿意马,想入非非,但是就像 Lodge 笔下的不少男角那样,为了维持婚姻,终究还能自持,只不过是给了读者一个悬念而已。

David Lodge 擅写"学院派小说",固然与他二十七年的大学教师生涯有密切关系,更重要的是他洞察"学院派"的名利追求和伪善等人性弱点,都是在高端精英文化的掩盖下,曲折地暴露出来的。低劣弱点与高端虚伪的对衬,乃是讽刺喜剧取之不尽的资源。在 David Lodge 笔下如此,在当年钱锺书笔下如此,在我们今天的校园生活中又何尝不是如此?这种对衬惟有学界中人参透最深,但也惟有学界中人在辛辣讽刺的同时,毕竟耳濡目染已久,并不会因此去全盘否定高端精英文化,从而陷入反智主义的极端。David Lodge 就是这样,几乎在每部作品中,用典极丰,以《耳聋判决之后》为例,他试改弥尔顿笔下力士参孙的诗来制造幽默效果,又多处引用 Thomas Hardy, Philip Larkin, Thomas Hood 等人的诗句(后者的 A Tale of a Trumpet 对一般读者来说相当生僻),复以贝多芬和西班牙宫廷画家戈雅(Goya)耳聋为例,说明听觉丧失本身,实际上也是一种对生活的激敏知觉。即使写到高频失聪最易错失辅音音素这样一个细节时,Lodge 也要引用《爱丽丝漫游奇境记》中的柴郡猫(Cheshire cat),说它因为听不清爱丽丝说的是 pig 还是 fig,也是聋猫。然后从/f/音联想到"F—k you",而在英语中与这句骂人话相当的应是"Damn your eyes!"而绝不能以 ears 去置换 eyes。瞧,学院派作家在鞭挞学院派时,绝不尽失自己学院派的所有特征。我觉得"学院派小说"之所以好看,这是一大吸引。换了个根本与所谓的“风雅”完全隔膜的人来批评风雅,写什么《风雅颂》来反讽,能如此挑战或激活读者的智力而让他们深有会意吗?我看至多只能流于浅薄的脸谱化,遂意辱骂几句而已。

“deaf sentence”毕竟与“death sentence”只有一个辅音之差。这部小说也因此带上生命危浅的悲剧意味,就像 Desmond 所说的,“耳聋是一种‘前死亡’,一种漫长的过程,导向你我大家最后总要陷身其中的永远的寂灭”。寻访奥斯维辛的一日游回来,Desmond 仿佛收到了“死亡判决”,更意识到“我们死死抓住生命,可力量却那么脆弱;而要擦去我们在地球表面留下的印痕,又何其容易”。全书中除了“自杀遗书”课题的研究,Desmond 的前妻和他父亲之死,都给作品增加了阴郁的色彩。父子情深的描写,包括 Desmond 与前妻之子 Richard 的圣诞谈话,在我读过的 Lodge 以前的作品中,似乎难得一见,仿佛作者难得抛开犬儒主义的一贯姿态,向着含蓄的情感表达(男子汉只握手,不拥抱),战战兢兢迈出了一小步。无怪乎,2008 年 5 月 2 日《电讯报》曾刊出一篇苏菲·莱特克里夫(Sophie Ratcliffe)的书评,题目叫做“拔去了利牙的 David Lodge”。然而,Lodge 很快收住了脚步,就在与 Richard 交流感情之后,那边老父亲忍不住内急,在花园里随地解决自然的召唤,就此吓跑了来参加圣诞聚会的宾客;同时,作者又开始玩世不恭地自嘲,就听觉错误大做文章,诸如把“long stick”误作“non-stick”,把“Carcasonne”(一种名叫“攻城拔寨”的地砖棋盘游戏)误作“our arses on”(我们屁股朝上),把“crap and sargasso”(多愁善感的胡说八道)误作“Braque and Picasso”(法国画家普拉克和毕加索);人家历史系主任太太明明说屋外太热,大家“... cowering indoors behind the shutters”(缩在百叶窗后面的屋内),在他听来却变成了乔姆斯基式形式至上的“... the cows' in-laws finding they stuttered”(母牛姻亲们发现他们都结巴)。此类误听妄听的例子俯拾皆是，足证前面说到过的“耳聋是喜剧”一语。这种板着面孔的文字幽默——而非夸张的动作幽默——恰恰就是英国式幽默的招牌特征。

毋庸讳言，我之所以晚去几年才读《耳聋判决之后》，与作品问世后读者贬评甚多有一定关系。有人说，David Lodge 采用日记体，是“最偷懒”的写作方法，可见年事渐高，不免气短；又有人说，在从耳聋到死亡的阴影底下，展开滑稽故事，不伦不类，说明作者江郎才尽。我的看法是，作者随着父亲离世，本人耳背日甚，感到老之已至，不知不觉之中，笔法开始变得醇和浑朴。书中自问：“今天我有什么事情可做呢？”还有老父的告诫：“别就这么老去”，相信都会引发老年读者共鸣。而退休教授与美国女学生那一段若接若离又渐行渐远的纠葛，与其说是“学院派小说”的应有元素，不如说是“后伟哥”时代文学中新出现的一种 buffer-babe（老幼恋）现象。读者看看 J. M. Coetzee 的 *Diary of a Bad Year* 以及 Philip Roth 的 *The Human Stain* 和 *Exit Ghost* 就会明白了。

2010 年 8 月 10 日

语言学家“玩”语言

长假的头几天读了 David Crystal 2009 年 Routledge 版的一本“职业自传”*Just a Phrase I'm Going Through*(暂译《经历微言而已》)。我曾把作者的姓译作“水晶”,在“豆瓣”上被网友拍砖:“他[指陆某]的一些怪癖总是无法接受。翻译人名不按照通用译法,譬如 David Crystal,偏偏要称之为‘水晶’先生。这并非有性格的表现。”“怪癖”也好,“性格”也罢,“水晶”实在不是我的发明,那是当年葛传槼老先生率先叫上口的。葛先生爱“玩”语言,拿人名开玩笑,起绰号的例子,不胜枚举,我在多处写到过,这儿不再重复。他只是跟几个学生或朋友“玩”语言,没有恶意。你新理了发,特别是刮了脸,他就叫你“容再光”(外文系一教师名),容本人听了哈哈大笑。“水晶”本是好东西,自然更不在话下,所以我也便将它搬上书面文字;即使他私下把 Leech 叫做“蚂蝗”,Quirk 叫做“怪癖”,似也无伤大雅。那位网友如听说人名可以这样翻译,可能要扔耐火砖了。我倒觉得,专名究义,说不定对二语习得者记洋人名字还有点好处,至少写“蚂蝗”名字时不会误拼作 Leach。社会多几个语言“玩家”,对成天练这个“主义”那个“模式”的语言学,也不会有什么坏处吧。

书中,“水晶”先生罗列对语言的常识定义之后——诸如“工具”、“媒质”、“技能”、“禀赋”、“艺术”、“游戏”、“社会力量”、“人性化力量”等等——引用罗兰·巴尔特给语言学下的定义“一张皮”;英国那位写了《发条橙》的安东尼·伯吉斯说是“一嘴巴的空气”;美国的爱默生称之为“化石的诗歌”和“历史档案库”；德国印度学家缪勒说是“人脑自传”；德国哲学家海德格尔的定义可以让人咀嚼老半天：“‘存在’之屋”。作者本人给了一个最不浪漫的俗套定义：语言的科学，然后就科学两字大做文章。在他看来科学最激动人心的始发点是“寻问”，是“探究”，其中包含的内容是态度谦恭地遵循规律，排斥先验，遏制主观，按部就班，验练为鉴，寻根究底。研究对象不问大小，探究人必然从中体验痴迷的快感。“水晶”先生一次坐出租汽车，碰到一个说话带 Leeds 地方口音的司机，他马上动员起自己所有有关 Leeds 方言的知识，与之攀谈，从中试验，求证，结果谈得忘情，司机忘了转弯，“水晶”误了火车。某保险公司小姐打电话来找“水晶”夫人谈业务，妻子外出，接电话的是丈夫，问对方是谁。对方报上芳名“Aniela”（听上去像/ann-ye-la/），还把全词拼了一遍。接电话的语言学家来了兴趣，因为他从来没听说过国人当中有叫这名字的，于是说“小姐的名字太有意思了”。两人居然撇开汽车保险，就这个名字谈了 20 分钟。先是对方坦承不知名字的意义，只依稀记得是从祖母那儿传下的，而她这一家子又是波兰移民；接着，“水晶”叫对方别挂电话，他这厢飞快翻书，终于在一本人名词典中查到，源出波兰语无误，相当于英语中常见的 Angela，“英语世界中偶用”。“水晶”亲历一次“偶用”，好不荣幸。这时，对方感兴趣了，问这名字可与 angel（天使，安琪儿）有关。这问题简单，“水晶”先生不用查书就可答善，还回溯到希腊文 angelos，那是“信差”的意思。对方说，妙哇，她的第一份工作就是当听差。对方一来劲，又问了自己老板和挚友名字的意义……

如果说以杜撰“无色的绿念愤怒沉睡”（Colorless green ideas sleep furiously）的模式句来说明意义和形式分离的是语言学家，那么上述坐出租、打电话的能不能算是语言“玩家”？语言这一人类社会现象，有人称之为“变色龙”，又像个捉摸不定的“小精灵”，除了干巴巴的教条，就不需要活泼泼的“玩家”？当然，“玩家”也不好做，要善于疑问,勤于探寻。“水晶”先生查阅《剑桥英语大百科》,发现美国第33任总统 Harry S. Truman 姓氏中居中的那个 S.代表什么,没有交代。续查三四种参考书后,仍无答案。他的鼻子像是嗅到了什么。当代人可上电脑顷刻间解决疑问,但“水晶”起疑是在1992年。于是只好跑图书馆搜罗杜鲁门的传记,翻阅好几本后悬疑犹在,一直读到杜女写的那本才知道,哈利·S. 杜鲁门的祖父名叫 Shippe,外祖父叫 Solomon,为一起尊奉内外二祖,这才有了个二祖共享的 S 字母。最后写上大百科的不过寥寥几笔,查证却花去整整两天!还有,语言“玩家”如果欠缺语言知识,也有被人“玩”的时候。1970年初,“水晶”被英国文化委员会派到智利演讲,主办方决定公开演讲逐句而非同声传译。他刚说了第一句“有幸到贵校演讲不胜荣幸”之类的客套话,那译员叽叽呱呱说了半天,其中演讲人只听懂一个西班牙文用词“语言学”。第一句译完,掌声雷动,“水晶”一头雾水:智利人那么热爱语言学?事后才知道,是那译员掺杂了私货,把第一句话加工成了:“这位支持我们选举阿连德先生当总统的来自英国的杰出的教授要讲语言学。”这不是“玩家”遭“玩”是什么?

看看,听听,我们的周围语言如何在悄悄地变化中。“小姐”、“同志”的意义狭化中,正在变的还有“专家”、“教授”、“精英”;“和谐”作动词不稀奇了,最近看到,在一篇讨伐南方报系的檄文中,“普适”也成及物动词;“民主”被写成“民煮”,“自由”被写成“渍油”;沪语中“我”字的发音/wo/可以有助于你辨别说话人是否90后;自从某位80后办起了“最小说”致富,世博的大人语言也迅速跟上,说中国馆开馆日“最中国”;等等等等,不一而足。汉语“玩家”们可“玩”的余地大着呢!

2010年10月3日

三 尺 讲 台

人事校园里的管理

有些时日了,管理——狭义的和广义的——一直是门显学。于是管理部门像一个个八爪章鱼,应运而生,大盖帽和各色制服成为一大中国特色。即使在高等学校这样的地方,管理虽别称职能部门,不时还自谦两句“我们是为广大师生服务的”,可说出话来毕竟有强势心理作后盾,也是一言九鼎,令我等侧目噤声。

说件小事:去年苦夏,正是宋朝朱淑真所谓的“困人天气”。为赶项目,还文债,一日不停地开着空调干活;虽说有几天看英超到凌晨,白天还是不敢怠慢。一日,突接某职能部门电话,指定日期召开项目负责人会议,届时有领导莅临指导。本来是个寻常的会议通知,可线路那边的“职能人”(听声音是毕业不久找到职能部门就业的一大批新人中的一位,据说此类新人中有不少利用“近水楼台”的优势,成为硕士、博士的优先候补)口口声声强调“领导到场”,引得我很是反感,不免随口讽刺了一句:“嚯,领导到场?可见会议重要。”对方懵懂,对讽刺并无反应,反复强调“领导到场”的重要性之后,挂了电话,让我独自在那儿生闷气:领导怎么啦?能事必躬亲,研经铸史做项目,还是会自掏腰包,发放项目经费?须知那经费可全是纳税人的钱!哦,是了,领导可以对你提出的项目说“yes”或“no”,也可算是操着生杀大权吧,看来这个会还得去捧捧场才是。

谁知当日夜里又接职能部门电话,说你陆某已结项,开会就不必来了。我刚想松口气,不料电话那头突然变得似乎正言厉色起来:

"你报销了出国签证费(注：我是去香港中文大学,这叫出国？小小一个学校的职能部门胆大妄为,想把香港特别行政区划出中国版图？另外,办证的另一职能部门明明说过可以报销,还有责任人背签),那是违规的,要吐还出来;另外有'正大'就餐费,好在次数不多,算了,不计较了!"我这人自知浑身上下有数不尽的缺点、弱点,常惹得领导不开心,但不敢化公为私,最恨揩油。因此在电话上我就声明不可能有就餐费这项支出,哪知对方言之凿凿,我生怕是哪个参与项目的弟子曾犯馋而背着去大啖,于是只好诺诺。

第二天,心存疑惑的我拿出经费本逐页检查,从头到尾也没见一项餐费纪录。在"正大"的开销倒是有的,那是酷暑期间某日宿舍突然停电,曾花100块钱躲到招待所空调房去工作一天的费用。我知道,学校里手握巨额项目经费的大户有的是,本人这个到位仅56 000元(规定拨款额70 000元)、经两年花去13 000元且已结项的"小儿科"项目,尚且受到如此鹰瞵鹗视,可见职能部门管理的力度于一斑了。项目大户们,小心啊!而对那些焚膏继晷或费尽心机还揽不到一个项目的广大师生,也就是大学的主人翁们,咱们的管理部门更不知是以何种目光看待的。譬如说,校长论坛上没有一位不说必须着力培养"个性"学生的。只是当学生真的显示出一点与众不同的淋漓元气时,有关学生管理的部门往往就要挠头蹙眉了,非刓方为圆,拉回到"批量化"的一统标准不可。

管理当然是必要的：规圆矩方,权重衡平,这学校才办得下去。可是近年来的管理膨胀,我以为是对上述规矩和权衡等管理理据本身的颠覆!我不知道现在一所大学里,职能部门与教师在人数、工薪、职称方面的比例是多少,不过膨胀会不会带来文牍主义,带来有悖环保的A4"纸张爆炸",我想大家有目共睹。至于膨胀有没有其他恶果,诸如尸位素餐、老鹤乘轩、近水得月、朵颐酬酢等等,兹事体大,容不得我等置喙,还是再说件小事。学生成绩单是个微不足道的教学细节吧，教师评分有诸如 A-、B+等之别，其中如 B+与 B-之间可能有十数分的上落，可是经职能部门电脑处理，成绩送到学生手里，+-之差居然常被抹煞！小小一张成绩单可以实行“双重标准”，何谈管理的规范化？夸大一点来说，又何谈“争创一流”？

管理在英文里叫作 management，我真害怕管理膨胀会导致 mismanagement 和/或 micromanagement 呢！如近来报道的某省考试院可以扣押高校的录取通知书“留中不发”，除非高校掏出“买路钱”来，荒唐不荒唐？真个应了“利令智昏”四字！从报上还读到管理部门“检查卡拉 OK 曲目哪些可唱，哪些不准唱”之类管头管脚的奇闻。咋不干脆把歌厅舞榭统统关了，不就太平了吗？莫不是怕 GDP 因此下跌？我想花在管理曲目方面的时间和精力，要是改而投入到追查“办证”等非法造假上面来，则社会幸甚。

记得诺贝尔文学奖得主、英国小说家威廉·戈尔丁透过作品《蝇王》里荒岛小霸主之口说过：“管理、约束、控制、干预，方见威权的力量。”另一方面，岛上自也有懦弱童子甘受管束，甚而至于不受管束就不自在。这样，双方一拍即合，自然而然形成了一个“蝇王”社区。记得故事里惟有一个“小四眼”匹基（意译可称“小猪”；目下大红大紫的哈利·波特也戴眼镜，据说“眼镜童子”已成文学“图符”）崇尚理智和人性，不服威权高压管束。面对管理膨胀，校园里甚至社会上是不是也宜提倡一下这种“小四眼”精神？

以小见大，漫说管理，意在表达一名教师深深的忧虑而非浅薄的嗔怨，识者明鉴。

（原载 2008 年 1 月 3 日《南方周末》）

我们需要精英主义*

这样的演讲每年都做，上座率还不错，那是因为新同学入学对复旦的 Who's Who 还有些好奇。我敢说今天在这屋子里的听众多数是一年级同学。到了高年级，自己的事情还忙不过来，兼之 Familiarity breeds contempt（熟生狎——熟悉了就轻视了），谁来听我啰嗦。

说到"啰嗦"，豆瓣上有个批评我的帖子，说这个陆某人讲来讲去总是老一套，什么提倡人文关怀，缅怀民国大师的学问和风骨，讽刺拜金主义，反对功利主义学英文等等，抽剥出几个关键词很容易；对我写的文章，说是一派"遗老风"，很不喜欢，甚至有骂我"傻×"的。我觉得批评挺切中要害，谩骂当然不好。说批评有道理是因为自己也觉得与 80 和 90 后交流缺了个"公分母"，有点像"祥林嫂"了。所以从 2009 年开始，决定除去"雇主"分派的任务，再也不到其他学校去演讲丢人现眼；另外，今天也要试图讲点新的内容。不过，话说回来，一个人成天思索的内容，特别在特定阶段，总有一定的连贯性，就像龙应台的台湾悲情主义，你要完全摆脱开"关键词"还真不太容易呢。

以前的讲题不外乎"学好外国语，做好中国人"，"身在丝绒樊笼，心有精神家园"，"日常生活是草根的，精神世界是精英的"，"知之者不如好之者——英语学习中的 Pressure and Pleasure"等等。其

* 本文是作者 2009 年 11 月 6 日在复旦大学"星空讲坛"的演讲稿，有删节。——编注。

实主旨和用意都是不错的,希望大家在铺天盖地的功利拜物教中,给自己划出一条底线,有一点坚守和担当而已。你要拜倒在功利面前,或是缺了一点定力,身不由己地被铺天盖地席卷而去,我也理解,因为我相信“你活,也让别人活”(Live and Let Live),也叫做“和而不同”吧。只是高等教育批量生产出拜物教徒,而培养不出哪怕是个位数、两位数的知识人、思想人、道德人、性情中人,我看这教育也够失败的了,跟中世纪的思想屠宰场没啥区别了。

我刚读完 Dan Brown 的《失落的秘符》,正借给学生传阅。(我以每周一书的方式把自己最近读过的英文新书与学生共享。上周是 Frank McCourt 2005 年的自传体小说《教书匠》[*Teacher Man*]。)读了《达·芬奇密码》作者新书,对欧美共济会(freemasonry)以及这个准黑社会对政治的操控作用,入会仪式如何,对我本已熟悉的华府地理、民情,国会山何以仿古罗马建在潮汐盆地,共有 580 多个房间等等,都成了知识储存的一部分,晚上做梦也会梦见用骷髅盛着红酒喝。再一本是龙应台的《大江大海 1949》,国共内战中的小叙事,专写“一将成名万骨枯”中后三个字的。读了这样的书,看到《建国大业》中战报淮海战役歼敌 50 余万人,不禁会想到 50 余万个家庭的悲剧,而且是在抗日战争中国人死伤四五千万人之后,同胞自相厮杀啊。还有,国家利益真的高于一切吗?爱因斯坦可不这么看,他最后是放弃了德国国籍的,但德国政府却把他下面这句话镌刻在政府大厦里:“在人生丰富多彩的表演中,我觉得真正可贵的不是政治上的国家,而是有创造性的、有感情的个人,是人格。”想到所有这些千百万死去的同胞,你会体会到一种大悲,人也会变得谦卑,发生敬畏。你说咱们这位赵大叔会去积累这样的智慧、悟解和感情吗?随着爱因斯坦说下去,那就是赛义德说的“有倔强性格的彻底的个人,处于几乎随时与现存秩序相对立的状态”。也有人把这类人叫做“牛虻”。我说的知识人、思想人、道德人、性情中人，也就是这个意思。

不看重豪宅、名车、名牌，也不要绿卡和外国国籍，可能跟我喜欢读书，读了书总爱想一想有关系。现在有些作家写作品，包括我的学生写英文作文，老爱描述白领生活怎么开车上班，如何交代秘书，怎么在俯瞰城市的摩天大楼办公，怎么喝咖啡，不但开会讨论项目颐指气使，夜里还没完没了打 conference calls，浓浓透出一股艳羡的味道，以为这就是精英主义生活方式，而少有像这次得诺贝尔文学奖的 Herta Müller 那样写“被剥夺”、“恐惧”、“少数族裔的异质文化”等等题材的。这文学价值的深浅，不用我说，一望即知。

有人可能因此说我势利。非也。赵大叔自有在他那一领域里特别的追求和感悟。我要说的是：赵大叔、我、你们 —— 任何人，都要像 Matthew Arnold 说的，“让每个人变成一个更好的自己”（let every individual become a better version of himself）。请注意“更好”两字，而不是“最好”。这是一种强调个人终生修养并提升自己的“精英主义”，如果让我来解释，就是三句话：“追求超越 —— 注意：是‘超越’而非一定是福家兄所谓的‘卓越’，超越的当然是自我”，“求智向善”，“不断抵近——抵近的目的地自然是彼岸”。如果我说我们需要这样的精英主义，在座的“愤青”会反对吗？

我的三句话当中，“求智向善”最带价值判断的味道，何谓“智”，何谓“善”，肯定标准不一。那就求最大公分母吧。“大智闲闲，小智间间”，在大学里求学，深谙自己专攻学科的各种知识，兼顾常识，那就是求智。总不见得英文系读了四年最后连 Cain 跟 Abel 谁杀了谁，David 与 Goliath 决斗是怎么回事都不知道吧？（其实这已不算专业知识，而是常识。）我们现在讲国学，到外国大办孔子学院，难道天命的、血缘的、等级的、人治的儒家就是中华文化的唯一源头？别忘了我们有诸子百家呢。国内 900 万儿童读经，我倒宁可让他们看看丰子恺的漫画，像《妈妈不要走》之类的，唱唱李叔同的“长城外，古道边”，读读朱自清的《背影》，老舍笔下的北京，沈从文的湘西，张爱玲的上海，读读鲁迅怒不可遏的匕首和投枪，胡适心平气和的实证，当然，还有1949年以后的顾准《文集》和《日记》，陈寅恪的密码诗，古华的《芙蓉镇》（看谢晋导演的电影也行啊），从维熙的《走向混沌》等等。同样，说到西方文明的源头，从希腊城邦到罗马帝国，从宗教改革和文艺复兴再经新古典到启蒙运动，从法国大革命到二次大战，希腊城邦流动的爱琴海文明，海上契约必须共同遵守的约定；罗马的公民社会和法制原型；讲究个人尊严以及权利和义务平等的日耳曼骑士精神；提倡节俭和积累的清教文明，要好好理出个头绪来为我所用，绝不是“西方文明的主要资源是个人主义”一句话就解读清楚了。智与知两个字在汉语中是通假字，意义相通。在我看来就是truth-seeking，当小老百姓的追求真相，历史的和现实的；掌权的公开真相，即便有所顾忌，至少不掩盖、歪曲真相，就算做得不错了。至于“向善”，像上面提到过的骂七十老者“傻×”，总不能算“善”吧，这点共识想来不像白毛女应不应该嫁给黄世仁那么难以达成。再看这张照片，想想梁启超对国人的评价：“私德居其九，公德不及其一”，再想想对环境的影响，“善”还是“恶”应该一目了然。

这个房间里的都是读书人，我们需要的精英主义，主要营养只能来自书本，而且不能因为“政治正确”反对DWEMs（死白欧男）就不读经典。学英国文学的，从莎士比亚到《尤利西斯》和《荒原》这样的文本属于必读，阅读中追求大悲大喜，大彻大悟，还有自怡、陶冶和精

神狂欢,不但要博览,还要沉潜精研——那是对特别打动自己的作品而言的。从文学到文学批评,再从文学批评到知识分子的思想史演变,这是读书的轨迹和必然指归,最后落实到制度思索和社会批评。就这样,读书,思索,“不逾矩,不从众”(虽然我反对儒家独大,这句话还是愿意引用的),每日超越一点,向着彼岸无限接近,做个“绝对独立的”知识人,思想人,道德人,性情中人。这就是我今天想跟各位分享的一点体会。

期终学生来信

改完考卷,填入成绩,统计等第百分比,写出阅卷总结——总算把期末工作的大头对付过去,可以长出一口气了。想想吧,那是 69 份试卷,每卷又含 3 道 essay questions(问答题),把个老头子累得够呛。

卷子汇总到教务员处的次日,就收到学生电邮。第一位是质疑我分数给低了。老朽不敢怠慢,立刻回信,答应周一(那天是周六)一早即去复查,叫她静候。周一早上 8:30,带好私章(万一要改分须由教师签章确证)到得系办,赶快调卷复查。果不其然,4 小部分得分的加法做错了,少给了 10 分,忙不迭改正并电邮当事人道歉。那封信是这样写的:"果然是少加了 10 分,现已改正。你的得分是 82,属 B+。只是教务网上的改正要在新学期开始后 1—2 周始能显示。给你造成精神损害,非常之抱歉。不过复看你的卷子以后,还是要请你以后写英文时留心下面这些问题……"(这种时候还不忘把学生的错误罗列一遍,乘机敲敲木鱼,"好为人师"确已病入膏肓。)那天深夜,对方回一短信,表示谅解和感谢。

第二封电邮不知怎么埋在 spam(垃圾邮件)中间,过了几天给电脑打扫卫生时方始看到。来信先是说考后自我感觉不太好,但希望打分时高抬贵手,因为发信人正申请出国留学,而人家又是很看重本科成绩积点的。可惜读到此信时批阅已经结束,即使想帮帮那位小字辈,心有余而力不逮了。

第三封同样给埋在垃圾堆里，调出一看竟是封长信，与我讨论精英主义等重大问题，而且对我前不久的一次演讲的动机揣摩得十分准确。信写得十分精彩，讨论的都是大问题。我们的90后有此等洞察力和识见，还有担当，我这做老师的读了非常欣慰，还有一丝钦佩。只是，“大江阔千里，孤舟无四邻”，这位学生并不愉快，尤其反感“娱乐至死”哲学的横行，时有自己是不是“BT”的惶惑。一言不合，好朋友会绝裾而去，“好像我是个‘鬼’似的”。我恨我这电脑乱扫垃圾，感到迟迟不答不仅失礼，而且非常有负学生推诚置腹的信任，于是赶快复信，一封写完，言犹未尽，马上又追去第二、第三封。要点是鼓励对方走自己认准的路，即使因此做个“异类”或“老哈姆雷特”式的鬼魂又有何妨！

2010年1月26日

二十年后成一流?

中国大学二十年后可成世界一流?谁给卜的卦?日前在南京,据报道多所外国名校校长不约而同如是展望。我印象中,最早说这话的是耶鲁大学现任校长 Richard C. Levin。洋大人们当然也挠痒痒地说一些中国大学存在的问题,譬如培养学生的批判精神(主要针对教师而言)不够,师生缺乏互动和交锋,等等,但就连中国人今天自己也并不回避的体制问题,譬如“去行政化”,则只字不提。我怀疑这些人串通好了,集体来给中国人“灌迷汤”。我人在高校,可能当局者迷,但我绝对无法共享洋大人们“二十年成一流”的乐观主义。在这么个社会大环境内,只要当局下决心,出狠手,好好查查高校的招生、提职、教学、科研、评估、基建等各个环节,那种可怕的积重难返,不把人吓死才怪呢。

好笑的是上海某校一位副校长发言,原意是为了驳斥“大学生一代不如一代”的谬论,却被媒体报道成相反,实在有些冤枉。副校长还举出他们那儿近年来的优秀产品,一个以剽窃“出道”的文学青年,如何制造出大批“粉丝”,其作品又如何以副校长读不懂而证出色,由此说明一代胜似一代,而且为此质疑大学还有没有传承衣钵的必要。鄙人虽非汉语教师,但如看到那位文学青年“最小说”这样的三个汉字结合,而且大喇喇作为刊名,而且张牙舞爪荣登榜首,非当作语病抓出来不可——即使因此被愤青骂死,虽千万人,我往矣。除了那位说现在是文学“盛世”的“最作家”称赞这位文学青年的语言有“陌生化”之功,我看该校百万身价的文学院院长也不会认同如此“创新”汉语吧?既然衣钵毋需传承,我等还是早早告退,“寄愁心与明月”去吧。

2010 年 5 月 5 日

教授不治学干什么?

近来常听到“教授治学”的说法,好像这说法还体现了某种政策进步似的。也许是我“下愚不移”,怎么品来品去,觉得这话其实就是最最直白浅显的常识,作为一个口号,成天在高校嚷嚷,快要变成超级废话了。

教授不读书,不写文章,不做实验,不上课,不造福于学生,不参加学术活动——一句话,教授不治学,能干什么?叫他们去治政法,治 GDP,治世博和亚运,治房价,治股市,治菜篮子?僭越之余,那可真成了“名存实亡,失其所业”。依我看,之所以提出“教授治学”,是生怕当年的所谓“右派”主张“教授治校”复活,是要给大家击一猛掌:教授不能治校!

与“教授治学”相关联的是学校“去行政化”的提法。如果说“去行政化”只停留在切断学校主管与官本位级别之间的比照等等,我看不出这会给教育带来多少好处,更何况,连这一刀子都还难以切割下去。只要学校组织部门的一定之规或学校招办的一张条子,比之尔等教授们唇焦舌敝的进言,更加有效,“去行政化”就是空谈。

“教授治学”可以换种角度解读,即把四个字读成命令句,我倒觉得这可能还不失现实意义。也就是说,现在的教授当中并不是个个以治学为重。有的不自量力,要做什么公共知识分子或是什么大人物的幕僚策士;有的炒房炒股,买官鬻爵,就是没法全神贯注坐定在书桌旁,站定在讲台前。无怪乎,教授常被网民哂称“叫兽”。所以我宁可从“回归学术”的意义上来理解“教授治学”,亦即“教授们,治学去吧”。

2010 年 5 月 7 日

做 PPT 有感

大概是因为开世博会的关系，听课学生大减，往日布置 presentation 的活儿时，志愿者踊跃，这次居然一无响应，这才自己动手，介绍的对象是 D. H. Lawrence。

实话实说，学生做的 presentation 虽然图文并茂，但往往是各种网上资源的撷秀，散乱有余而概括不足，也不太能看出个人对作家、作品的真实观感，疑问更是鲜有。这次由教师本人做 presentation，共 3 帧：(1) 围绕 Lawrence 生平，用上友人对他一生的生动描记，短短一段，绝无人人皆可上网查得的生卒年月等枯燥内容；(2) 引他本人小诗一首，加上翻译，强调 human touch 对人际交流的重要，凸显 Lawrence 对机器文明异化本真人性的厌恶，注解课文对“本能”和“直觉”的推崇；(3) 引他信件中的一段话（见本书“狗血喷头”一篇），附加翻译，不但说明作家的 Anglophobia（仇英）态度，更让学生直接体味此人用辞汪洋闳肆、震骇耳目的手法。好像效果还不错。

接着要教关于死亡的一篇课文。说到死亡，让我大惑不解的是一种奇崛的对比：一方面，眼下清明尽孝，给先人上坟的后代如过江之鲫，其势可与春运一比；另一方面，媒体上关于儿女在老辈生前弃养或不孝的报道，几乎无日无之。扫墓时花样百出，据说有焚烧美元、欧元冥币的，还有纸糊的豪宅、房车、小秘等，太有中国特色了。这次做 ppt 准备用西汉杨王孙提倡“裸葬”（“布囊盛尸，入地七尺，既下，从足引脱其囊，以身亲土”）的材料，既对比中美的殡葬观，又让学生读一点点《汉书》，有何不美？

2010 年 5 月 11 日

最后一课

今日是这届英四散文的最后两堂课，我称之为"最后一课"，小朋友可能觉得"最后"二字有歧义，又不太吉利，给我加了"本学期"这个限定语，用心良苦，我很感激。恰恰也是今天，收到1980年代同编《英汉大词典》一位姓杨的故旧的来信，说起我曾"花了一个午休的时间"助他写成一篇有关会计学的论文，1981年在美国发表，而就是这篇文章，据他说，"改变了我的后半生"：去Berkeley访学；又在香港科技大学任教十年；现定居于阿拉斯加颐养天年。这封信，写于2007年，杨君一直保存在电脑里舍不得删除，直到最近偶遇复旦会计系人，问得我的电邮，才投发过来。那是一封充满了感情的长信，我发给技监读过了。

上完最后一课，祝同学们事事顺利，长进一生，又联想到杨君的信，直到此时，我才意识到自己在人世间盘桓得确是够长久的了，到了bow out的时候了。很可能自己不意识到，我的存在业已堵塞了别人攀登之路。背后骂我"学霸"和"垂帘听政"，自然是出于歹意，但部分原因可能也是由于我堵路。于是，我就设想，鄙人即使为君把座位腾出，从此大道通天，凭着钧座的学养和人品，虽可一路送礼登高，最后能成何种"霸业"？

最后一课总带有一丝伤感的意味。我看着一张张耀若白日、皎如明月的脸，有本校的，也有外来的，心底涌上殷殷期盼，但愿这一年16篇精讲课文，连同每周1-2本新书的课外阅读，达到了毕业离开复旦前“恶补”英语的预期目标。谢谢你们送我阵阵掌声,我愿把掌声送还,为的是预祝你们在今后的生活道路上,走得步步坚实。成功了,没什么了不起,须知 The grass is greener on the other side of the fence; 一时遇到挫折了,吟吟勃朗宁下面几句诗如何?

One who never turned his back but marched breast forward,
Never doubted clouds would break,
Never dreamed, though right were worsted, wrong would triumph,
Held we fall to rise, are baffled to fight better,
Sleep to wake.

2010 年 6 月 10 日

车棚画展和草坪足球

今天散步自觉收获甚丰。一是在光华楼右侧的自行车棚里,看到学生的一个抽象派画展。我对色彩之美还算有点感觉,对线条之美最为迟钝,所以仔细看了刻把钟也无多少领略可言。打动我的是画展的场地:这个自行车棚因为离教室较远,学生宁可冒着座骑被偷的危险(一说大学四年,累计自行车被偷不达三辆,不算毕业),把车泊在楼外露天,因此车棚使用率一直不高,前一阵子,曾见老年员工在此跳舞自娱。今天,一批可能是既无钱又无权的学生,仅从共同的爱好和自我表达的愿望出发,把个高雅的画展,低调地办在这里,颇令人对他们刮目相看。当然,也不排斥主办者读过凡·高传记一类的书,故意“波西米亚”一把。但不管怎样,有这样一个画展比没有要强,说明我们的学生有着精神世界的能量崇拜。就像杨玉良校长最近接受《中国青年报》采访时说的:“我反对任何形式的在学校中莫名其妙地闹哄哄,鼓乐齐鸣,因为这会降低学校的高雅性。高雅不是培养精神贵族,而是要培养精神境界高的学生。”我惟一与校长有些不同看法的是,只要生活永不脱离草根平民——这个前提十二万分之重要——精神上追求脱俗超凡,即使被人叫骂做打引号的“贵族”,也没什么不好。

继续前行,来到逸夫楼前的草坪。七八位男生用书包垒作球门,在这儿分两队比赛足球。球员中有好几位是鼻梁上架副眼镜的书生。他们踢得很投入,突然变向拨球过人,脚跟蹭球,临门怒射,一招一式,都挺像那么回事的。我忍不住走上前去搭话。

问:“你们都看世界杯吗?”

答:“当然。”

问:“你们看哪支队伍夺冠?”

答:“巴西。”

问:“有外文系的吗?”

答:“没有。都是理科的。”

我好失望。

可能他们怕我是个什么纠察之类的角色,会指责他们损坏草坪,就抱怨说复旦之大,无处可供他们踢球。我说不至于吧,就我所知,穿过邯郸路就有个使用率很低的操场。其实,即使他们在这里损坏草坪,我仍觉得他们可爱,因为他们在用一种非常健康的方式,释放自己的能量。他们至少知道自己爱好什么。我走远了,身后传来他们的欢笑声。

2010 年 6 月 22 日

言犹未尽

不知是官办的还是学生自己民办的,一次毕业生民意测验给了七十老物一个荣称,还要我留言。本来打定主意,做“穴居野人”,少与世接。倒是远在异国的前学生劝我多为学生着想,就算满足一下他们的好奇心总可以吧。我这人就这样,要末不说,真说起来,又陷入另一“多语症”的极端——特别是因为正改考卷,发现答卷错误很多,既是学生努力不够(有的明显是因为不来上课而答不上来),更怪自己没有能耐把他们教好。

对着摄像机说了几句现代人都听得懂的话,待学生辞出之后,又颇有些老生常谈的遗憾,觉得言犹未尽。这时我想起本人幼时父亲嘱咐我牢记的做人之道。在此补充转赠给毕业生们,有用无用,他们读到这篇博文后自己判断就是。因为先父当年引用的是明代尺牍,允我稍作注解。

那是万历年间一个叫支大纶的进士写给儿子的信中的几句话:

丈夫[今天的人该叫“大丈夫”吧?]遇权门须脚硬,在谏垣[规谏朝政和监督官行的部门]须口硬,入史局[编修历史的部门]须手硬,浸润之谮【读作 zèn,谗言】须耳硬。

我斗胆给进士再加一条:察人真伪须目硬。

引用支大纶，不是说他的"四大硬"我都做到了。远远没有。脚、口、手俱不硬，耳朵根子更是软得可以；看人须目硬，也是因为自己瞎曚失误太多而提出自诫的。相信年轻人今日起飞远翥，一定会在各方面胜过我的。

2010 年 6 月 23 日

复旦校歌里的两句歌词

毕业典礼上，集体站起唱校歌，那歌词打出在大屏幕上，我是第一次窥全豹，知其详。（这是我个人玩忽的问题，歌词早已在校刊上和其他场合发表过多次，就是一直没怎么在意。）

歌词里有一句"政罗教网无羁绊"。是当年白话诗人、中文系教授、歌词作者刘大白先生的美好愿望，还是师生努力奋斗的彼岸目标？只是摆脱层层政罗学网，达到像马克思说的"未来的理想教育就是让每个人的个性得到充分的自由发展"境界，当年（上世纪 20 年代）做到了吗？反正今天不可能，明天、后日可能吗？我看果哉难矣。一位学历史的老朋友最近以清代为例，说对眼下的各种社会弊端，一百年之内别去指望改变，有些类乎唐德刚先生"历史三峡论"里的估计。若然，那么这句歌词还是改掉，或是晒到"乌有之乡"的网上去。

还有一句叫做"沪滨屹立东南冠"。在学界集体虚火飙升、排名牵动敏感神经的今天，这一陈述句听上去像是自伐自矜，东南的兄弟院校，如浙大、上海交大、南大，必会质疑这个"冠"字。即便你这儿全是磊砢之材，高出时套，我看还是什袭而藏为好。

至于"学术独立，思想自由"之类的话，差不多各校校歌里都有，烂熟之言是也，但是"悬天八只脚"，唱过算数，不必当真。

这几天毕业生都沉浸在告别的感伤里，大学四年日复一日的生活中，我听到他们如何咒骂食堂、图书馆、不称职的教师等等，此刻自然不会提起这些。就像昆德拉说过的，黄昏的夕阳下，看绞刑架，也显得不那么狰狞。可我面对着他们，回顾四年，自己再不像做青年教师那时跟同学打成一片，而是一次也没进过学生宿舍，总觉得作为教师，自己本可做得更好些，更多些——即使仅为争论世界杯也行，耳畔于是常响起一句话：I could have done better。若把句中第一人称单数改成复数，不但教育，还有其他各种事业，即使疾疢顽固而非一丸可销，有些事情本是可以做得更好一些的。

2010年7月5日

抄袭总归是不对的

我故意替这篇博文起了个想来大家从发蒙以来都能接受的题目。

事情又要说到南大王与清华汪的那宗笔墨官司。昨日 CCTV 的新闻联播说到,有批学者就此事写了封公开信致中国社科院和清华大学。今天,“豆瓣”网上就有网友发文说:“联名信里看到陆谷孙的名字真是惊讶……想不到也凑进来了。”我作为教师,对抄袭问题特别敏感,为什么签个名就变“凑”了?

同理,前几日在复旦的毕业典礼上,我说:“多谢同学们看高我,其实你们会后去看看‘豆瓣’网上人家怎么说我的,就会有个比较持平的看法。”我是要他们看看“月光族”、“苏门答腊”等网友如何骂我——不但在王 vs 汪的问题上,还有责我不懂翻译,作文粗俗等等——义务替他/她们扩大影响,不料仍被斥为“‘毁’人不倦”,“让他的学生都来看看吧,心目中的好老师是如何撒谎,是如何欺世盗名的”。

除了自己手脚不干净的,多数教师都恨抄袭,抄袭到了信息技术高度发达的今天,又发展出 downloading 这一新的资源。若干年前,这儿一个外教发现有学生“下载式”抄袭,居然花了 3 个小时终于找到出处。恰好犯事的是我的一个小亲戚,便来问我如何处理。我回答:“该怎么办就怎么办。”这位外教逢人要说《飞越疯人院》是她家什么什么人拍的,可能有点饶舌吧,可我始终佩服她打击抄袭的决心和毅力。

因为社会上造假的事情太多,现在大家似乎不那么恨抄袭了,而界定抄袭的门槛高度似乎也在一降再降,说到过往事情,时常耳闻“当年规范不严”之说。这儿引用一段海外来信,看看此说是否成立(写信人是研究汉语的):

> Speaking of scholarship in old times, one only needs to open up a grammar book or an article on linguistic issues written in the 1950's or ere that, and he/she sees immediately how pathetically lame an excuse like "we got loose plagiary rules back then" is. (试译:说到旧时做学问,谁都只须打开一本上世纪50年代或更早些的文法书,或查阅一篇涉及语言学问题的论文,即可明白所谓“那时候我们关于剽窃的规范不严”的借口何其苍白可怜。)

王安石说,风俗之变,迁染民志,关之盛衰。学界带头的人,应该义无反顾地反对抄袭,既是爱惜自己的羽毛,更是垂范后来的学人。

2010年7月9日

同行评议与网络“众包”

见过这样的学术软广告吗?

强大的团队保障,6 年的成功经验,保证您论文发表少走弯路,一次成功!本站将根据客户自身不同情况提供有针对性的个性化发表方案,论文发表价格合理,见刊时间快速及时。如有需要请将个人情况及详细要求发送 EMAIL 至本站邮箱,本站承诺当日答复,不成功不付费!

要在学术圈子里混的人肯定都见过这类文字,为了在核心期刊、权威期刊上发表篇文章,掏钱买版面的肯定也不在个别。我发现,大凡那些核心和权威后面,往往都有个“腕儿”。完完整整的人不做,专好英文里“以偏概全”的 synecdoche,沦为一“腕”,我看是也够可怜的。可是据说这些做无本生意的,现在也可以数百上千万的身价跻身“富一代”了。而且著作等身,因为麾下的博士生军团发表论文或专著,全都得把“老板”的名字放在首位。明抢之外,还有暗偷,偷完国外的,连“窝边草”也吃。前几天一位朋友告诉我,一位恋栈久久最后不得不退下的某校长,贼胆够大,把北边一位皇城根下的教授和南面这位我的朋友等四人联名做成的某研究报告,抢先发在自己的“核心”里,据说把四位原作者弄得目瞪口呆,如何应对,半天回不过神来。

试想有如此寡廉鲜耻的人占据学术高地，操控学人的生杀大权，污浊如何涤荡，特别是学界的后起俊秀，即便再有勇气，能杀出一条血路来吗？

美国的学术生态优于我们，但是"同行专家评议"的话语权使用也不是没有问题。按照今年8月23日《纽约时报》文《学者试用网络替代同行评议》(Scholars Test Web Alternative to Peer Review)的说法，同行评议这一招并非"金本位"，只是某一特定阶段的解决办法，"而非完美的理想"。因此，已有六十年版龄的《莎士比亚季刊》已将今秋9月号的四篇论文用他们称之为"众包"(crowd-sourcing)的方式晒在网上，从41名网民处征得350条意见，以保证编者最后判断优劣时更有依据。明年，《前现代》等学刊也将参与这种试验。如此，学者和懂行且有兴趣的读者结合在一起，不但在网上评书判文，并开始考虑向各自的大学进言"在非同行评议项目的基础上，批准晋升和终身教职"(to grant promotions and tenure on the basis of non-peer-reviewed projects)。

如果在清理现时国内某些道德与学养俱有欠缺的专家权威队伍的同时，借用这种把学术从少数人的垄断下解放出来的办法，能否限制学霸的话语权？让网络参与职称提升等学术活动，对于扫除核心与权威期刊的束缚和盘剥，对于新进人才的发现和培养，是否都有积极作用？

2010年8月25日

上课真的那么痛苦?

又要上课了。昨天跟一位中年教师说起,好不容易考进大学的年轻人,何以过不了多久就厌恶上课,听说有人还戏仿小沈阳的《不差钱》,凑成这么几句:“眼睛一闭一睁,一堂课过去了;眼睛一闭不睁,上午就过去了。人生最痛苦的事你知道是什么吗?是下课了,但人没醒。人生最最痛苦的事你知道是什么吗?是人醒了但没下课。最最最痛苦的事你知道是什么吗?是上课了,但睡不着。”不管这是不是恶搞,当教师的听了自应惊心,反省。

我们不能一味指责学生功利,嗔怪他们要求上过的每堂课都严丝密缝地和今后的求职需要相衔接。但是在教学内容和形式方面,认真安排好每一堂课,让学生始终保持清醒和警觉,感受乐趣,并逐渐使课堂不仅仅起到职业养成所的作用,还是“头脑风暴”的发源地,是“工具理性”和“价值理性”并重的地方,学得技能和知识的同时,还有学术兴趣的自我发现、思辨修养的提高、人格塑造和精神追求的激励等功效。上好一堂课,不让学生发出“上课了,但睡不着”这种犬儒主义的牢骚,教师可以施展的余地大着呢。

当然,现今的大学弊病不少,作为一名普通的教员根本无力改变全局的现状,那就只好把自己能够做的事情尽量做得好些,带头让学生体会到学校不是官场、商场、寻欢场与名利场。教师有无这种示范作用,聪敏的学生在课上是完全看得出来的,至于是否认同,我不敢高估教师敌过家长、日后职场老板等各种社会合力的作用,只给自己设定有限的目标，譬如说在四五十名学生的班上，程度不同地影响到“个位数”左右，就算相当不错了。我看大学生今天主要的苦恼在于，学成之后的回报渺茫。“都说知识改变命运，我学了这么多知识，也不见命运有何改变？”2009 年上海海事大学法学系一位研究生自杀前说过这样的话。为什么那么心急地只去各种有形的物质存在中寻求“回报”和“命运的改变”？精神的地平线就狭窄得容不下一个鲜活的生命？而精神地平线的拓展，譬如说体味到读书能够抚慰烦躁的灵魂，开启原来容量有限的心智之窗，挑战稚嫩软弱的自我，可能一定程度上也有赖于教师把每堂课上得精彩且富有感染力。

铃声响过，学生课后的生活和思想，可能更需要教师的关心。我现在老了，没这精力再和学生打成一片。但在青壮年时代，一周 16 节课后，每晚接待两对四名学生练习英语口语，所以学生中间发生些什么事情，他们近时的思想兴奋点何在，都了解得比较清楚。师生打成一片的好处是平等互动有了很好的基础，即使拿上课用英文造句这么个技术细节来说，那句子使学生感到亲切易记。几年前，校友聚会时，当年的学生犹用绰号“Continent”（大陆的“陆”）叫我，居然还有人记得三四十年前我写在黑板上的例句。

2010 年 9 月 7 日

第一堂课

以 NYU 的 Phillip Lopate 所编 *The Art of the Personal Essay: An Anthology from the Classical Era to the Present* 为主要参考书,又以他为选集所作序言为引子,结合自己学习心得,开始本学期第一堂"英四散文"课。这门课是我敬爱的老师徐燕谋先生率先在外文系开设的。当年,这门课是文学鉴赏的一部分——其他三门分别是林同济先生的英国戏剧、杨必先生的英国小说和杨岂深先生的英国诗歌。今天完全继承徐先生的衣钵,培养 armchair aesthetes 和 connoisseurs 恐怕不行,所以除了让选文的 time window"与时俱进"之外,还强调英文的"工具性"。我的指导思想是"用世"的同时追求一点点儿的"超逸"。

听众挤满本来已经热得叫人发昏的教室,六架电扇无力地从头顶送下热风。我劝没有座位的学生离开教室,找个凉快的地方寻乐子去,并根据以往经验,让其中真正感兴趣的人两三周以后再回来看看,届时可能就有空位了。到得学期行将结束时,再来听课,可能还会有一溜三座的"卧铺"空出来,也未可知。

Lopate 选编并论述的主要是 personal essays,有些发现很有意思,譬如说写随笔的作家中多有 Charles Lamb 式的独身主义者;随笔不但像信笔漫游,即使直接以散步漫游为题者也不在少数……选文虽以英美为主,总算也包含了我们这儿正在舍弃的鲁迅;还有尼日利亚的索因卡等少数族裔。索君与我参加过同一届国际莎士比亚学术会议，身披大氅，是会议的 keynote speaker，我是无数发表 short papers 的小不拉子。十多年后，索得了诺贝尔奖，那是后话。

Lopate 的书出在上世纪末，怕学生嫌不够新鲜，于是再给他们一本乔姆斯基的政论集作为课外读物补充，既可尝尝 impersonal essays 不同的味道，又因老乔刚在北大做过演讲，学生可能发生一种间接的亲近感。

吼叫两个 45 分钟之后，“巨汗”下台，人像刚从水里捞起一样。回到家里，有中青年教师祝贺教师节的电邮，一一作复，希望他们早早置换我这个七十老物。不过只要还在教书，就要尽力“取悦”学生。（最近老有人骂教师“取悦”学生，在我看来，“取悦”这话说得固然难听，其理不错！）想请技监跟学生约好时间，去他们宿舍，来几次“打成一片”。

2010 年 9 月 10 日

也来说说教师“走穴”

杨玉良校长最近提出教师“走穴”问题，认为做教师的不但应学高为师，还应身正为范。何谓失范？杨校长提到教师“走穴”，说有位大学教授讲 40 分钟，“出场费”高达 20 万元。乖乖！

教授应邀到其他院校演讲本是交流学术的好事情。区区不才，也做过这样的事情。最早一次是在 1978 年，应朋友张叔强、叶逢夫妇之邀到江西大学，住在他们的招待所里，听着校广播台的音乐与师生一样作息，连续讲了三四天，有无酬金已忘，有的话，也是区区小数，好在远在夏威夷的叔强伉俪似乎还常看我博客，可以作证。讲完后，主方派个吉普车送我上庐山一游。我带去一本 George Orwell 的《1984》，竟被陪同的一位英文教师，一夜读完，交流读后感时慨叹：这书若是早些译出也不会有“文革”了，这才有了前几天博文中提到的那篇被《读书》毙了的《权当……》小文。可见游山时还在读书。那次江西之行好像还有助于激发人才向学，记得从此常改一位姓戴的年轻朋友的作文，后来他考上华东师大研究生班，论文答辩见报，可惜留英回来精神失常，英年早逝……

这样的讲学后来又有过多次，庐山又上过一回，那已经是有“穴头”的时代。须知这“穴头”也是大有好坏之分的。二上庐山的缘由是江西师范学院在那儿组织了一个暑期教师培训班，还记得“穴头”姓刘（？），好像抗战时和我的老师刘德中一起在大后方当过美军翻译，一位忠厚长者。讲员除了我，有胡文仲伉俪等，我还是在山上初识当时名满天下的 Mr Follow Me 的。说到坏“穴头”，拜我友翟象俊兄所赐，有一年他老家山东省某大学在青岛办暑期班，翟兄介绍我去讲课。谁知那“穴头”为了抵挡学员抱怨吃住条件不佳的抗诉，嫁祸于讲员，似乎讲员在强索厚酬，“穴”里的钞票全花在他们身上了。我听了大为堵心，便把讲员所得实际待遇公之于众，戳穿谎言。这下惹怒了“穴头”。他们也不立即给我点 color see see，而是等我讲课结束，诳称船票难买，晾过一天之后，把我往五等统舱里一塞遣返上海完事。

从此，对“走穴”便心生反感，特别是舆论谴责“叫兽”“出场费”之后。此后确还曾外出讲过几次，但对收受酬金已经变得非常提防。凡主方给钱，总是返回给学生听众，要他们用这酬金租辆大巴去春游或秋游；有一次，忘记在哪所兄弟院校了，正逢某处地震，讲完之后，径直把讲课费投入了捐款箱。今年开始，进一步自律，非“雇主”下令，再不到处夸夸其谈了。

此文可能被人责为自鸣清高，往自己脸上贴金。诸位尽管拍砖无妨。我只求传达一个不合时宜的信息给小字辈同行：如果可能，读书人与金钱还是尽量保持一定距离为好，“极俭可，略丰也可，大丰则不敢也”。40 分钟收酬 20 万，太明火执仗了吧？

2010 年 9 月 22 日

再谈“走穴”

上次写到“走穴”之后，被人诘责，其中包括我带过已学成的博士生。

我自然知道今天青年教师面临的窘境，所以绝不反对他们另辟蹊径，补贴生活。事实上，我在做系主任和院长的那些年，给他们介绍一点活计，曾是我工作的一部分。当年（上世纪90年代），香港《文汇报》要在上海开个什么会，需要同传，半天付酬3 000元，经我介绍接活的教师，现犹在此工作。只不过我是希望一次得酬如许，这个月其他的“走穴”活动是否能辞就辞了，把心思集中到教学任务上来。在全系会议上，我曾问那时人称外文系“首富”的某教师，能否一周至少有10个小时的时间花在教学上，他点头答应。鉴于学生到了四年级，使用外语好像很流利了，洋人的腔调甚至肢体语言学得蛮像，但如果仔细一听，准确性仍大成问题，我曾力主教师多布置笔头作业，而笔头作业必然占去教师较多的批改时间，影响到旁骛所得。初步的fluency或sham fluency是每一个二语习得的学生不难达到的第一步目标，对非外语专业的学生，也许走到这儿就可以了。但是外语专业的学生，对于像comparable，lamentable，confiscate，contemplate一类词的重音应落于哪个音节，还是要讲究一点规范读法的，整个的二语习得活动也必须向accuracy的第二步目标精进，而要走这第二步，不问对错，脱口而出，远远不够，离不开大量敛思过脑的笔头训练。（我年过七十，至今还得训练不息。）为达到这一步，教师不花大量时间去帮着纠错，分析错误成因，我看不行。

正是基于上述认识，我寄望于小字辈的同行在教学方面多些投入，“走穴”则适可而止。这儿可能还牵涉到一个人的金钱观：钱是挣得越多越好还是挣个大概足够（指足以维持衣食无虞，住行便利的小康水平）即可。看到小字辈有经济能力买房购车，我当然高兴；对到了适婚年龄尚买不起房的，我也替他们着急，若能从旁推毂帮助他们增加收入，我绝不犹豫援手。但是，不敢苟同的是“When it comes to making money, the sky is the limit”（挣钱永无止境）般的哲学，理由是人的关注总量是个常数，过度追求某个目标，必然忽略其他。

有人说，对应用学科的教师来说，“走穴”有利于增加知识，扩展视界，学用结合，同行交流。我想对有心向学的人来说，应该是这个理儿，“走穴”的同时宜有选择，不做纯粹的“口腔体操”，扪心自问是不是往这四个方面去努力了。但是高谈阔论 40 分钟，挟 20 万而归，那种口吐莲花、字字珠玑的腕儿怕是与上述四大积极效应，都很难扯上边儿吧。

2010 年 9 月 27 日

扩写形式主义名句

今天上课，又讲到乔姆斯基形式主义名句“Colorless green ideas sleep furiously”，回来大改学生笔头作业25卷。学生笔下，因为用词不当（譬如跑三家医院看病称之为odyssey，我宁可作者用saga）形成强充幽默的效果，有时反显得年轻人可爱。形式与意义的分裂，问题最大。有些是母语干扰所致，譬如该说attention span时，写作“concentration period”（？我打问号表示并非绝对永远不可以）；有些是对英语表达的习惯生疏，而成冗语，如getting smarter，已经用上比较级，再加上一个increasingly，等等。也有的是上下文不清，而致意义发生紊乱，导致歧解，如“The choice beam is lit dim or bright as you like”（硬译：“或暗或明，选择的光柱可以任你点亮”）。这一句颇有点乔姆斯基名句的味道了。

于是，吃晚饭的时候想到，这著名的乔句，如果给提供一点上下文，再作后现代解读，说不定能从“形式”这一端回归到“意义”那一边去。试“玩”一把如下：

no news is news lead:
so says eco-friendly.
idle thoughts leap
but pale beside deeds.
thus:
colorless green ideas sleep
furiously.

引进了“生态友善”（eco-friendly）这个主语，配上世人对环保问题知固不敦、行更不笃的上下文，这句天书般文字不就成了“暗淡失色的环保思想忿忿郁积，只能沉睡”？回头看看，这诗还押上了 ABAAAB 的韵脚呢。

2010 年 10 月 9 日

I Like This Interplay

Altogether 25 papers were turned in plus a trickle of late arrivals delivered through good offices of Smiley, who regularly checks my pigeonholed mailbox. I would not have been able to handle such an enormous volume if everyone of the eighty-nine had written and asked me to take a look. As matters stand, some 30 papers are already quite a handful. Especially when there is only a four-day intermission instead of a week to do it and some zealous writers have produced over four or five pages in single space. I feel I must do my job in time to give the students to understand that their work is being taken very, very seriously. That is easily translated into an urge to write more in the future.

I had expected it to be drudgery most of which unfortunately was until I came across a few that are exceptionally sophisticated. For instance, one wrote about the making of a Chinese fortune knot. The writer apparently has a hyperactive imagination, combining handicraftsmanship with mathematics (binary function), geometry, poetry (Blake's tigerish symmetry) and philosophy (convergence of the opposites). Then inadvertently he knocked down a bottle of water over his keyboard, incapacitating the laptop in an H_2O bath. So he followed with an account of debating with himself: should he set to and salvage the hardware or write something anew? The question quickly became an intellectual probe on his part. Another confided in me a sad story of the past year, beginning, alarmingly, with the writer contemplating death. The shrink's diagnosis was "emotion cognition failure." It then fell upon Jim Pickens of Hollywood to refuel the writer — although bits and pieces, I suspect, may be a download — and now it falls on me to tell the writer to complement emotion with reason that "The sky doesn't fall" and "The sun also rises." I don't know if my advice will be taken seriously but I hope it does.

Besides, oh, what a smorgasbord these young men and women cook! There are predictable ingredients, to be sure. But I am also invited to explore new tastes and smells: what JM stands for, what Umeshu is, and how many of the listed eleven types of expensive perfumes I know of. I figured out JM is short for "jiemei" (姐妹?) on my own, commandeered help from Boarhead that Umeshu is a kind of Japanese plum-flavored wine, and as it happened, only heard of Dior and Chanel of the fragrant assortment. It seems the students date and party in fancy places (or do they fancy they do and are they only trying to appear cool?) while I have to date never set foot inside a KTV room. As interns, they eye a future IT job in an office cubicle. Nobody expresses an interest in a teaching lectern especially now that they have seen me soaked in sweat while shouting at the top of my lungs.

Quite a few had had experience with English-speaking environments before they signed up for my course. To point out the deficiencies, inadequacies and/or downright errors in their English expression, I have to first make them believe their exposure to and survival in native-speaking cultures does not entail unquestionable communicative competence. Often I have to write long passages of comments to hammer home pieces of advice even though it is unpleasant or demoralizing. How can I let go unmarked, for instance, grossly absurd dangling participial phrases like "My heart was so delighted when walking into those graceful places"? Wherever you go, whatever language you speak, your mind doesn't walk, does it?

Pauperdom in intellectuality is a bit disturbing in the 30-ish papers throughout which there are three or four literary quotes from, if I remember aright, Lord Byron, Faulkner, Whitman and Montaigne, two of which happened within an essay about their last lesson (Daudet-ish) before they were recruited as Expo volunteers and all classes suspended. The young writers, for the most of them, would rather log on to Douban or Renren for sanitized info or small talk with their buddies before they remember they activated their laptops in order that they have an assigned essay to write and a deadline to catch in the first place. To put it more accurately, visiting the virtual space and being irresistibly sucked into the black hole of it is quickly becoming their second nature. Likewise, as a group, they are shying farther and farther away from reality as they do from intellectuality.

Assuredly the humanities are on the wane. (Do refer to Stanley Fish's essay on 11th in NYT entitled "The Crisis of the Humanities Officially Arrives".) But I don't think I have got reason to complain. A month into the new school year now, there are still "standees" in the classroom. Calling a spade a spade (a dangling participle!), the papers are not top-notch. Maybe Phillip Lopate is right in identifying essay-writing as a "middle-aged" activity and the twentysomethings are unprepared for it yet. But the gunghoism with which the students write and connect to the teacher is simply admirable and merits reciprocity in the form of the present essay. I like this interplay.

13 October 2010

Eating to Live and Living to Eat

More and more papers. Today I examined one confessing a zoophobia. The author says she hates to see anything moving on wings or multiple legs in her household. But she did treasure her teddy bear, a fake animal, and go out to the Zoo at the insistence of her boyfriend. She described a geochelone, which I figured out to be a kind of huge *terra firma* — or better say amphibious? — sea turtle from geo- + -chelon, a present from the Seychelles Government for the World Expo in Shanghai. She identified it as a reptile. I changed that genus designation to testudinate or chelonian (Not that I know these technical terms but that I did a lot of googling). The creature was busy eating so that she didn't get to see how it looked. Then the inevitable panda. Her boyfriend read out loud from the caption signboard: "Bamboo only contains a tiny portion of nutrients. Besides, its nutrients are extremely hard to digest. Therefore, in order to compensate for this disadvantage, the panda ..." The author finished the sentence for the boyfriend: "Has to find other foodstuffs." "No," the boyfriend continued, "A panda has to eat a huge amount of bamboo every day to get enough nutrients." Sure enough, the panda they saw was doing nothing but chewing bamboo non-stop. Then they saw a chimpanzee, upset to beg for food from the Zoo visitors to no avail, turned round with its rump toward them contemptuously. Furious, it looked as if it were going to strangle itself with the rope used for a swing in its pen. Then upon second thoughts, it changed its mind and began to eat its own excrement.

It is a factual account per se, written in readable English with a view to inviting the reader to share the author's zoophobia. My comment: "Poor animals! Eating to live and living to eat. Is *Homo sapiens* any superior? If you had explored animal behavior along these guidelines, you could have made your essay much more interesting."

20 October 2010

故 人 旧 事

Xu Yanmou: An Eidetic Memory

— In Lieu of a Foreword to the New Edition of *Selected Modern English Essays for College Students*

Professor Xu Yanmou (徐燕谋), or Y. M. Hsü (1906–1986) by Wade-Giles, taught me Fifth-Year Intensive Reading in English and was advisor to me for three years from 1962 through 1965 when I studied as a graduate student at the Foreign Languages and Literature Department of Fudan University, Shanghai. The mentor-disciple relationship spanned the tumultuous years of the so-called "anti-rightist campaign," "the Great Leap Forward," and finally "the Cultural Revolution" from the late 1950s to the mid-1970s. Xu was a sanguine person by nature — what with his hallmark guffaw in classroom and office alike, the *laisser-aller* of a poet, and a repute of a gourmet big on such delicacies as long-tailed anchovy from the Yangtze — popularly known as "knife fish," but like all literati of his time, he was subjected to all kinds of brainwashing and micromanagement until he was reduced to a speechless and sleepless old man murmuring "No can do; no can do" all the time to himself in a secluded corner away from the crowd. After 1976, the year when the Gang of Four headed by Mrs Mao were dethroned, Xu partly recovered his ebullience — but briefly: the trauma was too deep-seated for him to get on top of. It was out of a progressive chronic depression that Xu chose to terminate his own life some time in the small hours of 26 March 1986 by drowning himself in a well in the courtyard of an old-style Shanghai building on Wuding Street, on the cramped ground floor of which the three old folk (Xu's couple and his lifelong single sister) and his books by the thousands found a humble shelter. I remember weeping that night out of a gnawing remorse that I had joined in mass criticism of him by *dazibao*, albeit mildly, in an early stage of the "Cultural Revolution," as was requested of every graduate student by the powers that be; weeping as if I had vicariously felt what a claustrophobic death it must have been for him in that vertical tube of a well. I wept myself eventually into composing a tearful poem in his memory:

留得孤危劫后身，
旧游多半委沙尘。
相怜惟有墙头月[①]，
磊落光明永照人。

Yes, Xu is a man of integrity. With an unwilling effort, he swam with the tide and managed to survive. However, deep down in him remained intact an esotericism of an ununiformed conscientious objector, a dissident forcibly made to consent and condone. Extremely fond of and prolific in writing poems, in addition to the occasional topical ones, in most of them the poet bemoaned the sheer waste of lives, his own nightmarish experience, and a lone soul craving for empathy. For instance, he wrote about his *bas bleu* colleague/friend Yang Bi (杨必), who had suffered abysmally during the "Cultural Revolution":

---

① As three tall walls encircle and overlook the lone well in the midst of the courtyard.

估铺狐裘稳称身,
心头冷彻总难温。
何堪重过邯郸路,
不待霜风已断魂。

(一日寒甚,遇君邯郸路上,披狐裘犹瑟缩,云冬衣已尽失,以六十元从估铺易得数裘御寒。)

and

我书未散苦无庐,
君屋犹存恨失书。
天上银河万斛水,
难求升斗活枯鱼。

(“文化大革命”初,君藏书尽失,我住房紧缩,书皆束阁,两人如鱼失水。)

About the tough time he had gone through the poet reminisced:

清谈何止十年灾,
虚耗英英一代才。
屈指今朝有为者,
阿谁不自白专来。

and

狂风吹散读书声,
学府翻腾似沸羹。
呼马呼牛呼老贼,
惟君依旧唤先生。

Woe worth the day when Xu managed to trudge through a strenuous life as delights were so few and far between, and petty too:

小院墙高日色微,
莳葱种蒜也难肥。

南邻养得牵牛好，
看罢归来露未晞。

（南邻牵牛盛开，花多过墙，侵晓往看，不须问主人也。）

or

嚣嚣扰扰两童孙，
夺果争糖晓到昏。
藻鉴颇闻今异昔，
不然为讲让梨人。

or

元夕儿时玄妙观，
广场提线洛阳桥。
岂知老去童心在，
夜半偷看匹诺曹。

（儿时住苏州玄妙观，有提线木偶戏《洛阳桥》。“匹诺曹”为《木偶奇遇记》中木偶名。）

We know that posterity have to read Shakespeare's sonnets, rather than his plays, to know more proximately about the Bard the person. The analogy would be too presumptuously offending to the unassuming poet if I should advise people to read Xu Yanmou's poems with a view to understanding him better. None the less, it is hardly an overstatement to say that Xu's crowning achievement lies in his poetry composed in keeping with classical prosodic norms in Chinese. For all I know, Xu may have been the only professor of English in China in his time who was indisputably a poet worth his salt. Prominent scholar-friends of his like Qian Zhongshu（钱锺书）and Su Buqing（苏步青）sang praises of him in glowing terms in their own poems. A Chinese professor of English, so enamored by and so well versed in his infinitely rich mother tongue, is nothing short of a phenomenon for a host of xenogenetic members of present-day Chinese young men and women who are head over ears into English often, regrettably, at the expense of needful linguistic equipment in Chinese. For me personally, I read his poems primarily for glimpses into the *sanctum sanctorum* of a broken heart of a modern Chinese man of letters and therefrom into the warp and weft of his time.

* * * *

It is my ex-classmate and friend Professor Zhai Xiangjun's (翟象俊) suggestion that we commemorate the one hundredth anniversary of the birth of the two late Professors Xu Yanmou and Ge Chuangui (葛传椝), to whom we both are much beholden, academically and otherwise. As part of the proposed commemoration, this present pre-1949 anthology of English essays edited by Xu Yanmou and the other two gentlemen and foreworded by Qian Zhongshu is being republished through the good offices of Fudan University Press. Teaching English essays to students at both the undergraduate and post-graduate levels used to be Xu's cup of tea. With an eye for what is tailored to the palate of an aesthete (e.g., beautiful but not bland; colourful but not gaudy; moderate but not nonchalant; determined but not bigoted; plain but not prosaic; friendly but not forward; buoyant but not unctuous), Xu had a penchant for the familiar type of essays *à la* Charles Lamb. As can be seen clearly from the writings hereby anthologized, Xu's taste can easily pass for being high-brow in the eyes of post-moderners. On a recent occasion when some of my literary friends in Hong Kong and I discussed Max Beerbohm with hearty gusto, we were scoffed at by a British professor in our presence for our "antediluvian taste" who alleged that few if any college students in Britain today would care to know of the essayist's name! Hearing that, I thought I saw Professor Xu turning in his grave.

So, as Xu's disciple, I now have a new tide to swim with if I wish to stay afloat: that of nouveau utility, of dogged accrual of knowledge about English as a means to a utilitarian end, and of anxious yearnings for material well-being. Taking over Xu's mantle, today I teach English Essays too. However, to ensure a sustained, robust interest on the part of the students so as to optimize the value of my teaching, deletion of previously much anthologized masterpieces in the Essay as a particular genre of literature has become a must, making room for adds that are written in the presumably more practicable and realistic English of the 21st century. The insouciant aesthete who sat back relaxed in an armchair pondering over what is beautiful must needs yield up the ghost, surrendering place to a restless and banausic soul ready to be slave-driven in a modern firm as a would-be white-collar. Literature as a Wonderland is but a sad anachronism. A no mean number of young men and women are ruefully bound, headlong, for a Wasteland: aesthetically barren and devoid of euphoria and ecstasy. Truth to say, I am often quite ambivalent about some of the sample essays I have lately selected — often with a sense of guilt and betrayal — for my students to read, not because they veer away from the traditional criterion of literary excellence, but because their topicality and the facileness of English with which they are written may, above all, help toward the making, say, of a tolerably informed bilingual CEO or CFO or whatever, rather than of a perspicuous connoisseur of art and literature with true aplomb. In short, the crux of the matter is that today we train rather than cultivate, looking agape at a ubiquitous realism taking the upper hand of idealism or disparagingly Don Quixotism.

Ecce, like teacher, like student. There is a stubborn destiny we have to be part of, however averse to it the participants are. Bound down by such a common destiny and looking always forward in vain to the *Jenseitigkeit* of an elixir for all men and women, Xu and I have a lasting like-minded rapport, and even though he is now a centenarian he remains my eidetic memory.

August 2006

(《现代英国名家文选》,徐燕谋等编注,复旦大学出版社,2006)

也谈邓丽君

中央党校主办的《学习时报》发表过一篇《歌声启蒙——纪念邓丽君》的文章;有的中国老百姓说起改革开放,不无调侃地把歌星与总设计师邓公相提并论,说老邓和小邓都功不可没。邓女士地下有知,怕喜跃抃舞,不能自禁呢。

犹记当年弄堂小儿跳橡皮筋时,用邓曲歌词“记住我的心,记住我的爱”作为调节动作的拍子,边唱边跳;老人聚在路灯下打扑克,可能嫌光线暗淡,会突然冒出一句“月亮代表我的心”;青年夫妇一方出国,另一方会对着远行在即的配偶,有意无意唱起“路边的野花,你不要采”。直到今天,出版界某位大佬还亲口宣称,听过摇滚、校园、嬉蹦(hip-hop)、饶舌等各种流派,邓丽君仍是他的最爱。

在邓丽君之前,“文革”歌谣常常是杀声震天,不时还掺入几句“滚滚滚,滚他妈的蛋”、“文化大革命就是好,就是好”之类的口号。也真佩服那些作曲的,给毛主席诗词谱完曲调——就数那个用弹词曲调谱《蝶恋花》的倒霉,“我失骄杨”一句招来江青嫉恨,于是祸漫整个吴侬软语的评弹,旗手说听那玩意儿要死人的——之后,语录歌大批出笼,连林彪(当然是爆炸前)那一长篇毛主席语录《再版前言》文字,也可从头至尾吟唱。我所在的“连队”曾上台表演过这个节目,所以那曲调,至今不忘。

邓丽君的柔性结束了一个时代的刚厉不假,但说她“启蒙”,仔细一想,不免悲哀,因为这从反面说明了前邓时代矇瞽之深。当代不再那么蒙昧的青壮们早已习惯了“重金属”之类的轰轰烈烈，音乐趣味换了一茬又一茬，笔者想觅一张早期“神秘园”这样的恬静音碟都不很易得了。可是面对一些十九不太如意的社会现实，我看网上的愤怒青壮常常怀念高呼“万岁”的时代，而并不那么珍惜改革开放的初级阶段成果。试想让他们回到听什么歌，看什么戏，读什么书，都有人在一旁管头管脚的时代，他们会作何感受？那时没有特权和腐败吗？（据我所知，以国宝熊猫做招牌的香烟早在上世纪50年代就开始在上海生产，只用于特供，叫做有货无市；悍妻一闹，出手就是三万——那时三万等于今日几钱？）我是至今也忘不了老百姓不烧到38度的体温，没有医院开出的证明，不得买西瓜的年月。当然还有饥馑的幽灵游荡在中国大地那些年的惨状。我时而有种“反面乌托邦”式的遐想：找个什么地方去搞个“票证满天飞，思想大一统”的特区，让老小中外的所谓左派念兹在兹亲历一番，或可实行轮训，三个月一期，只要不搞当年红色高棉波尔布特那一套，随便怎么折腾都行，不知结果如何？说不定三天一过，就有人要开小差了。

且不说中欧两种文化以及通俗和高雅文化之间的区别，我们要靠邓丽君来“启蒙”，而不是“披头士”甚或贝多芬的《自由颂》和《命运》，是不是多少也意味着改革和开放的大业，从一开始，起点就是比较低的，且注定一路行来坎坷多咎？

（原载2009年1月8日《南方周末》）

不折腾好!

“不折腾”三字据说有个“山寨版”译法,叫做“bu zhe teng”,把汉字变作拉丁化拼音,小学里就学,这也叫翻译? 有学生来考问我,我的第一个反应是:“Don’t toss and turn as in bed”(请注意“as”一词,倒译回去是 “别像在床上那样地辗转反侧”),学生嫌太实,不满意,于是我又往深处想: 如果主要是自上向下的要求,那么不妨译作“Up to no mischief”或“No monkey business”,倒译回去,就是“莫出花头经”或“别捣蛋”之类的意思;如果是从底层老百姓希望上面政策保持稳定的意义上讲,那么不妨译作 “No flip-flopping”(不要动辄“翻大饼”)。后来又想到思想界、理论人遇事好争论,像当年的姓“资”姓“社”,有时弄得剑拔弩张,民众莫衷一是,反而浪费了几许本可用于发展的大好光阴。如从这个意义上求译 “不折腾”,是不是可以说“No seesawing/wrangling over issues”(勿在争议问题上来回拉锯)? 小友毛尖已就这几个译法写过文章。为郑重计,不揣卑陋,将以上各种译法以及解读根据公开示众,求教于识者方家和大言炎炎的“高翻”们。

不管从何种意义上来解读,我觉得不折腾好,是当年邓公 “不争论”思想的延续和发展,顺乎民心。我这样说是有参照框架的,那就是“年年讲,月月讲,天天讲”以及过多少多少年“又来一次”的折腾日子。

就拿大学毕业生就业这一眼下热门话题来说,因为全球经济衰退，影响波及我们的职业市场，工作难找了，于是有的人便“满怀诗意”地回忆过去的统一分配。一个学生说，他投出70份履历求职，只收到一家单位的录用意向书，还有待面试，最后决出或纳或拒的结果。“你们那时，工作由国家统一包了，多好！”他这样说。我叫他去读读本人写过的一篇小文“追忆当年毕业分配”，设身处地尝一尝完全没有个人选择自由的滋味，想一想在那基本上不讲“量才录用”的环境中，家庭出身和政治标准——后者又往往表现在学生与系总支和年级支部的亲疏程度，成为主要的权重，毕业生要是作为“齿轮和螺丝钉”被装上错误的机械，那还不得折腾一生？或者更糟，毕业生是个发配到崇明岛劳动的“待分配”右派，非折腾十几甚至数十年后才得以“改正”，他还会羡慕我们那一代人吗？

我还要他别忘了，比他高几届的学兄、学姐，靠着改革开放的机遇，面临就业，曾有过“选择的过剩”：怀里揣着直升研究生的录取通知，还在忙着往什么“四大”会计事务所里挤，要不就是瞄准香港甚至英美澳的大学。盈虚盛衰，世之常态，始卒若环，莫得其伦，今日一时的困难，对年轻人来说，不但不表示事卒于此，焉知不是新一轮进取的始发触媒？能一遇到困难就怀念那折腾的岁月吗？

当然，不折腾不意味着思想就此偃旗息鼓。四百年前，法国哲学家帕斯卡尔说过人虽脆弱如芦苇，但却是一根“能思索的芦苇”，正是因为人自知脆弱，又知道宇宙强大，足以毁灭自己，人才比罔智的宇宙更伟大。

（原载2009年3月5日《南方周末》）

从“收骨头”到“骨头轻”

解放之初，在秧歌配腰鼓的热烈场面中，我们唱着《你是灯塔》和《解放区的天》欢迎革命大军进城，欢呼蒋、宋、孔、陈四大腐败家族倒台，特务学生横行校园、普通老百姓用大捆金圆券买草纸和火柴的日子终于到头。大哥哥大姐姐们，即便是资产阶级出身，唱着《我们是民主青年》争相参加军干校，随大军南下，解放全中国；我这个年龄的唱着《时刻准备着》，加入少先队，在夏令营的篝火边宣誓。回头想想，那激昂的民气多么宝贵可用，要是那建设新中国的五年计划一个个顺畅地实行下去，不折腾，真不知今日中国是啥模样了。

可是实际情况并非如此，经济经战乱后逐渐复苏，日子好过一点了，折腾也便开始，直到把知识分子们整得没了脾气，成了稀泥一摊，学会了夹紧尾巴“收骨头”做人（除了梁漱溟、顾准等有数的几位）。记得大二那年某日清晨民兵操集队，因为刚从热被窝跃出，睡意犹浓，“立正，向右看齐”号令传来时，精神有点恍惚，眼神有点迷乱，突被当时的支书（长我三届，后上调教育部）当头一顿近乎人身侮辱的臭骂：“陆谷孙，侬是斜白眼（沪语，指斜视）啊！”仇无大小，只怕伤心，正想回嘴，见全班同学都对着我看，终于还是忍气吞声“收骨头”算了。

平日里穿衣服必须低调随众，“水声冰下咽”的严冬季节，也是一件中式棉袄或中山装，外加罩衫，宁穿臃肿棉裤也不着呢料，脚下则一年四季踏一双宽紧可以收缩的北京式单鞋。老父恤子，把自己的羊皮袍子拆了,用那内衬给我缝了一件“派克”大衣,可我嫌这衣服太洋派,只有在后来“调整、巩固、充实、提高”的政治气候相对宽松时穿过几回。

有位青年教师素受总支器重,据说因为爱上了某位并非根红苗壮出身的异性,从此失宠。“文革”一来更不得了。家里对门住了一位里弄干部,听到我这儿传出的音乐是《圣母颂》而非《敬爱的毛主席》也要干涉。有一回,她颠着头——我怀疑她已患早期帕金森——指间夹根香烟,硬来摊派样板戏戏票,我那天刚喝过一杯啤酒,正有些 Dutch courage(虚勇,对不起,对荷兰人不敬了),与她争执起来,对方骂我:“侬灌了黄汤有种了,是哦?我这就去汇报派出所。”幸好我二姐闻声出来打圆场,向里弄干部赔了不是,事情才算了结。

这改革开放确实成果累累,但也免不了诱发一些反面的东西,当年的知识分子是大面积地“收骨头”,今天我们看到少数自诩为知识分子的人已不知自己几斤几两,骨头轻得可以。我听说这儿某院长带夫人出游,让老婆十指戴上九枚戒指;某权威演讲除了索天价,还指明要住五星级酒店,一日一瓶五粮液侍候;我本人亲眼见过某“海归”一信,自称英文之佳连英美人也承认难望其项背,所以他写的英文文章一个字都不许改动,可有幸听过此人说英文的朋友告我,“海归”那口母语地域方言奇重的英文根本听也听不懂。我还听说本来出身贫寒的子弟,经地中海海风一熏,回得国来,戴顶贝雷帽,穿条花格子红裤子,用一副马戏团小丑的打扮张扬个性。

这边是老土畸变洋派,在光谱的另一端,我们可以看到极度国粹身穿大花织锦缎唐装,嘴上却叼支洋雪茄的大牌教授招摇校园。现在有些大学里,休妻再醮(笔者用的是元明以前的本义,普适男女)成风,听说某系中青年男教师多数已完成第一次“糟糠下堂”,惟有某某与某某还在坚续琴瑟之好,就像贾府门口的两只石狮子,无怪乎有人说大学教师也快成“高危”职业了。凡此种种,看来“轻骨头”们还是需要修炼一点收敛的功夫才是。

最后，必须声明，骨头不收便轻，绝不是规律，也绝非笔者作文初衷。知识分子在社会上的形象还得取决于单个的人自己的信仰、思想、操守和修养。

（原载 2009 年 4 月 9 日《南方周末》）

葛传椝老夫子批《早春二月》

那几年,“文革”已呈山雨欲来风满楼之势,政治学习增加到一周两次。今日的读者肯定要问,哪来这么多的学习内容。回想起来,也确实难为当年的学校领导,“天下之理,不可穷也;天下之性,不可尽也”,要学的东西本没有穷尽,只是那时的政治学习,意在刺探、整肃甚于其他。大学是知识分子成堆的地方,而知识分子又是依附在资产阶级这张“皮”上的“毛”,一直是作为天敌一般提防着的,纵有历次运动反复洗脑,那异端邪说总要顽强表现。虽说科学昌明,毕竟还没人发明个“头脑解读器”(即英文里说的“mind reader”),所以惟有不停顿地让他们把心里想的东西说出来,始可掌控动态,于是也才有了每周整整两个下午无休止的学习、讨论和批判。

政治学习,顾名思义,必涉政治,像讨论反修的“九评”就是。大家比较喜欢这样的讨论,因为开会的程式总是先找个普通话说得比较标准的青年教师把那篇长文朗读一遍,一人读到精气不济,再找一人“接棒”继续。朗读过程中,听众思想开个小差什么的,一般难以被人发现。再说,讨论到古人考茨基或远在天边的洋人陶里亚蒂或铁托,毕竟难以攀扯到自己,一般触及不了灵魂。政治学习时发言踊跃与否,有点像今天研究生讨论班上参与积极与否,是个考量标准。诱使众人提出问题时,天真的葛传椝老夫子挖空心思参与一下,猛不丁往语法上扯:“帝修反三者并提时,用什么代词,it 还是 they?”引得我们捧腹大笑,可算是正襟危坐一下午之余轻松一刻的调剂。无怪乎,有位领导曾经牙痒痒地骂葛是个“政治白痴”。

政治学习偶尔也会“形而下”一番，譬如讨论课堂教学法和师生关系等等。一位教会大学出身、连“反右”的思想小结也只会用英文写的女教师作自我批评，说她从教数十年，都不知道还有什么“语法-翻译法”、“直接法”、“听说领先法”（当时还没有“交际法”、“功能法”之类的花头经）等等，使用的是“methodless method”（无法之法），而且好像也还奏效，于是受到一阵批判。这位老师不知是真的豁达还是佯装洒脱，同仁声色俱厉的批评，她会侧着头笑盈盈地照单全收。即使后来丈夫遭缧绁之灾，人被带走那天，从她嘴里说出来，虽然不无苦涩，总还不失幽默：“the day I was widowed”（硬译：我开始守寡那天）。又有一次，文学组戚叔含教授给某位工农速成中学升上来的学生打了个58分，被指导员报告上去，也给拿到政治学习会上来说事，言下之意，2分之差干嘛不拉一把？明明是歧视工农同学。戚先生平时一口绍兴官话挺健谈的，这时眯缝着眼睛，不吱一声。

最妙的是批判反动影片《早春二月》。还是上述葛老夫子，这次像是做了充分准备，煞有介事地说：“我讲三点。第一，二月是阴历还是阳历？如果是阳历，那怎么会是‘早春’？柔石的原作叫《二月》，乱改片题而致不通，必须批判。第二，萧剑秋（笔者按：主人公）同情孤儿寡母，如果后者不是反革命家属，我勿晓得错在哪里。我只晓得柔石是鲁迅肯定的，又是被国民党枪毙的，应该是好人。如此说来，好人美化坏人比坏人诬蔑好人更加恶劣？第三，这作品，不管是小说，还是电影，我都没看过，只是听大家说了才知道故事大概。”

这就是当年“文革”前夕政治学习给我留下的回忆。

（原载2009年5月7日《南方周末》）

挑灯夜战一亩地

老同学聚会,来一黄君。说起往事,大家都还记得,他是沪郊某地贫下中农出身,当年是我们年级的劳动委员。“大跃进”年代闹过不少今天看来颇有“黑色幽默”意味的笑话,其中之一叫做“深耕密植”。具体做法是,耕地不再用犁铧、锄头,而是用铁铲掘土至起码三尺的深度,然后一层碎土,一层肥料(人粪或从羊圈起出的“羊棚灰”),自下而上填充细作,直到地平作业面,准备以株距不超过“小半虎口”的宽度插秧密植。据说这是领导“从群众中来”的经验总结,现在要在全国农村推广“到群众中去”,如此则可确保粮食亩产超过千斤。

我们年级的同学在农村参加“大兵团作战”回来,本已人困马乏。谁知回到学校还要继续搞试验田,责任便落到本文开头提到的黄君身上。他到底是农村来的学生,觉得如此“深耕密植”有悖常识,可又拗不过领导三令五申的训示,就只好代表英文系三年级,在复旦大学今日第二教学楼的旁边,认下了一亩地。自此,全年级动员,女同学多数使铲子深掘,男同学挑粪,还到校外农户家的猪圈羊圈,借用“羊棚灰”。为了和其他年级竞赛,一连几周都要挑灯夜战。今天的大学生不妨想象一下当年的那种场景:几百烛光的灯泡把二教周围照得雪亮,铁铲飞舞,此起彼落,挑粪大队哼哟哼哟地喊着号子运来肥料;这儿突然有人大叫“不好,都掘到水啦”,那边劳动委员黄君赶来,探头视察之后,要大家跳进坑里像跳集体舞似的使劲踩踏,把冒头的水弄成泥浆即可——当然所有的同学都打着赤脚,那些日子里基本上昼夜不必穿鞋。时至午夜,趁工间小憩,众人涌往中央饭厅去领取两块略带甜味的蜂糕,匆匆充饥之后,赶回来继续侍候那一亩地……

待到秧苗密密匝匝插下,还有"后期服务",那就是或抗旱或排涝,还要"扒秧",亦即俯身拔去与秧苗齐长的杂草。这时"大兵团"已经化整为零复课。一应劳作改由学生轮流负责,碰到轮值,可以不向班长请假,理所当然地缺课。黄君缺课最多,同学们常见他愁眉百结地蹲在一亩地旁,大概在暗中祈祷秧苗快快生长。

"惯子出不孝,肥田生瘪谷",老话果然不错。"深耕密植"的一亩地,折腾到最后,基本上是颗粒无收。随之,那全国范围的三年大饥荒也便开始了。学生再也甭想吃蜂糕夜宵了。

老同学聚会上说到这事,有人纳闷:决策者明明也是农家出身,如何这样不懂农事?看来光有农家出身不够,还得脚踏实地真正务过农而非成天想着去干其他营生的。再有,"破除迷信"不见得是句坏口号,但决不可作为决策时头脑发热、异想天开的借口。古时候有邯郸学步的故事,要是学步未得其仿佛,遽失故步,又冒险腾跃,结果即使不摔成头破血流,可能也只好匍匐而行了。

(原载2009年5月21日《南方周末》)

“清官比贪官更坏”?

醒眼人着目这文题,准保认定笔者谵妄。今日里贪官迭见杂出,恶积祸盈,人人喊打;有的坏官这儿倒下,那边又爬起,竟然还有提升的。普通群众谁不期望吏治清明,巴望着多出些清官?说什么“清官比贪官更坏”,老百姓自然“不高兴”。

且慢,文题可不是笔者的意思。那是1965年深秋姚文元发表的《评新编历史剧〈海瑞罢官〉》一文中的观点,而此文又是翌年“文化大革命”的点火之薪。起初,谁也不怎么关心这又长又臭的文章,盖因姚文元其人曾在我们大一时来讲过“文艺学引论”,与周而复、以群等校外请来的讲课专家相比,不论内容还是口才,姚实在要劣去一大截。记得当年文艺理论中所谓的“人民性”是个表示资产阶级作家同情下层百姓的“好”的概念,“人性”则是资产阶级杜撰的坏东西。也许因为只有一字之差,也许讲课人语言智商有问题,姚文元在台上老是错置两者,听得我们大家掩口胡卢。之后也偶尔在报端读到姚的所谓杂文,从文艺、历史、哲学跳到“无标题音乐”,像是无一不知又无所不为的博士卖驴。文章老爱用“编者式的‘我们’”(即英文里的editorial we,以此代替个性化的“我”实为小品大忌)作主语,加上无数虚张声势的修辞问句,全无可读性。

这一回如此长篇檄文见报,再鲁钝之人也看得出来头不小;更加不同寻常的是要求我们讨论再讨论,讨论中又似乎特别注意诱导歧见。发表姚文的《文汇报》打破常规,一连几天,狂发“编者按”,几乎是“乞求”读者参加“百家争鸣”。那时我还是等待分配的研究生。说实话，我们中的多数人根本没有耐心去读完姚文，只好应景讨论诸如“岳飞比秦桧更坏吗”之类的问题，大开“无轨电车”。后来，时间跨入1966年，这位姚某人更不得了啦，再著长文批北京的“三家村”、“燕山夜话”，终于弄到我们被迫停课。记得那天本来是计划到虹口公园去实地上口语课的，兼带用英语议论清官是否比贪官更坏，师生都颇有期待，也作了充分的准备。停课令一下，计划泡汤。

除去体制性的大叙事不说，我至今不能认同清官比贪官更坏的姚氏论断。只是海瑞虽是南青天，还被皇帝下了大牢，听说天子驾崩，既不喜跃抃舞，也不自戕殉节，只是把吃下肚去的东西吐了出来，缺乏戏剧性和轰轰烈烈，有些让人恶心，可算是为官清正一生，最后的句号没有画圆（英文里可称anticlimax）。

（原载2009年5月28日《南方周末》）

群众的眼睛以及默契

“文革”期间进食堂打饭,有一套感恩祈祷的礼仪。走进中央饭厅,对着毛主席的巨幅画像先要一手端着碗匙,一手高举小红宝书挥舞,朗读一段语录。仪式始兴之时,有红卫兵监督,马虎不得,有人想逃过功课,从边门溜入,径奔饭菜而去,倘被发现,就会给抓到巨幅画像前,先虔敬认罪,继而罚读长段语录,由此耽误打饭,真个成了欲速则不达。更多的人往往斜眼瞟着那边打饭的队伍越排越长,这边不得不捺下性子,齐声读一段“最新最高”或是“世上什么问题最大?吃饭问题最大……”之类的相关“指示”。渐渐,为了早一点打到饭,吃到供应有限的菜,大家心照不宣地把语速急提,像今天唱 Rap 那样,匆匆读完,急奔卖饭窗口而去;而不知从什么时候开始,在巨幅画像旁实施监督的红卫兵也撤了岗,于是仪式变成了走过场的滑稽剧:只见三两人步入食堂,也不驻足,对着画像象征性地一挥膀子,连读三遍当时最短的语录“要斗私批修”,不知是自表忠心,还是算给那边的画中人一点面子。再往后,食堂请示仪式对大多数人而言,自动消亡,毕竟排队吃饭,填饱肚子是世上“最大问题”——除了像被关押在校的巴金先生,他在中文系红卫兵押解下,手提两个热水瓶(饭后打水为全天所用),照样要对巨幅画像行礼如仪,左焰最炽之时,还曾见老人被迫跪在食堂湿漉漉又沾满油渍污垢的磨石地上诵读语录。

然后仪式便移至寝室举行:大家把饭菜打回,若是夏季,先忙着把上衣和长裤除了,摆开棋盘,这时突然有哪一位想起还没“饭前请示”,便提醒众人,于是照样敷衍潦草地大嚎三声“要斗私批修”,接着一边进食,一边大杀车马炮。待到一局杀完,那穿着宽大纺绸衣裤(此人从不赤膊)的师弟甩着双臂,到盥洗室去冲洗饭碗,一边吼着自娱:“想当初,老子的队伍才开张……”(那是京剧样板戏《沙家浜》中的唱段)。

时隔四十多年,回忆起来,此情此景仍是缕缕清晰皎然。

是什么保证了这样一幕滑稽剧日复一日屡演不止?当年有句用烂了的警句,叫作“群众的眼睛是雪亮的”。这话隐含恐怖的杀机。谁敢不“请示”就张口吃饭,保不准哪位室友突然喷发革命肾上腺素,奏上一本,那是有可能老账新账一起算的。但与此同时,人同此心,心同此理,谁都知道这是演戏,于是才会把这本应严肃认真的程序,做得如此潦草、荒诞,像是彼此早已达成了某种默契。安插卧底,鼓励告密,迫使群众甚至包括亲朋相互提防,相互监督是“文革”政治动员、社会监控的一大法宝,当局用它已有得心应手之效,这一点其实群众也早已心知肚明,所以戏虽乖离幼稚,大家还是照演不误,以免生事招祸。另一方面,群众的默契和敷衍了事,“文革”当局当然也了然于胸,不过只要不出几个出格异类,门面还在勉强维持,懒得也无力去追究。这大概也算是众庶与权势的一种博弈吧,直到最后“请示”仪式被弃若敝屣,“文革”也以失败告终。

(原载 2009 年 6 月 11 日《南方周末》)

转弯子

1971年7月18日上午10时左右,学校的高音喇叭突然响起,传出不足百字的一段公告,宣布美国总统尼克松将于翌年访华。时非校广播台的寻常工作时段,而且公告无头无脑,播完就无下文。对毛主席《全世界人民团结起来,打倒美国侵略者及其一切走狗》的“五二〇声明”记忆犹新的革命师生,这时动不动还在唱“东风吹,战鼓擂,现在世界上究竟谁怕谁?不是人民怕美帝,而是美帝怕人民”这样的革命歌曲,自然被上述公告弄得一头雾水。美帝头子来访,不亦异乎!不亦惑乎!

于是,几天后,当时上海市革命委员会的第三把手徐景贤就来学校作报告,俗称“吹风”。请注意,这可不是什么移樽就教,而是“文革”当局知道,大凡知识分子成堆的地方最是难弄,每逢移宫换羽,易生腹诽怨谤,不派位大员来讲论大义,演绎丝纶,弯子转不过来。对有数的几个兄弟国家,帮助转弯子的重任由周恩来亲自担负,后来听说工作收效不大,还被“欧洲社会主义的明灯”和“天涯若比邻”的小伙伴给奚落了一番。

在我们学校的“吹风”会上,徐景贤从当年早些时候在日本名古屋举行的第31届世乒赛说起。因为“文革”,中国已经连续两届没有参加这项赛事,乒乓球界同其他地方一样,运动搞得轰轰烈烈,至少已经有曾为中国赢得第一座世界男单金杯的容国团和金牌教练傅其芳(其女正在我系学习)两人自杀。绝妙的是,徐景贤传达了要求乒乓运动员“一不怕苦,二不怕死”的最高指示,把第 31 届描绘得非常恐怖,好像如果中国派队参加,境外虎视眈眈的敌对势力就要对我运动员搞绑架甚至暗杀。其实,洋人似乎从来并不怎么把乒乓球看作影响巨大的体育运动,真想不出来谁会吃饱了撑的绑架加暗杀?(倒是后来有越来越多的事实证明,中国乒乓运动员“自己绑架自己”往外国跑,郁郁复离离,已足以组成一支庞大的海外兵团。)

徐景贤接着说,天下大事,必作以细。参赛事小,影响至巨,是伟大领袖高瞻远瞩,亲自批示了“我队应去”四个大字,事情方始定夺。由于担心抓了革命,忘了练球,跑到国际上打不出好成绩给“文革”抹黑,徐景贤曾不嫌其烦地解释“友谊第一,比赛第二”这句口号。一听这完全违反竞技本质又不无伪善的口号,果然腹诽顿起:那还打什么比赛啊,把人请来“排排坐,吃果果”开个联欢会不就结了?

接着,徐景贤重点介绍“乒乓外交”:毛主席如何在某日已经服过安眠药之后,挥动巨手,四两拨千斤,用小球推动大球,在美国乒乓球队访华要求未得响应而准备登机回国的最后一刻,决定邀请他们来华;美国人听到消息如何欢呼雀跃;来到中国后又如何爬长城,吃烤鸭,还蒙国务院总理接见座谈,最后感恩不尽而去,等等。其中徐景贤还传达了翌年接待尼克松时应当注意的事项,其中一条是态度要“不卑不亢”,要向名古屋的庄则栋学习:当时他看见一个鲁莽的美国运动员小子误登中国队大巴。正当一车的中国人像见了外星人一样目瞪口呆之时,庄跑上前去与对方接谈,还送了杭州织锦,从而打破坚冰。大家听了,觉得庄只不过做了一个正常人的正常事,这就叫“不卑不亢”?那也许是因为更多的“文革”中国人对洋人“亦卑亦亢”、“时卑时亢”已成了一种积习。

坐在听众席中的我,这时想起上一年翟象俊兄拿来叫我翻译的一个英文政治讽刺剧剧本(翟兄说是上海隶属于“四人帮”的写作组朋友所托):戈尔·维达尔作于 1970 年的《理查德·尼克松之夜》

（An Evening with Richard Nixon，笔者注：这种 an evening with …的标题已成俗套，即一夜阅读或演出，可窥主人公全豹）。剧本的所有台词全是剧中人在现实生活中说过的原话，把所有那些华言、浮言、曲言、伪言罗织排列，于串联并置之中可立见其妄。除了讽刺艾森豪威尔、肯尼迪等人之外，此剧矛头集中对准尼克松。剧中的尼克松，这个在 1950 年代狂热推行麦卡锡主义的反共老手，为从越南脱身，原来早从 1967 年起就向中国频送秋波，先是在《外交事务》上撰文："我们怎么也不能听任中国游离在各国之外，让她独自纵情妄想，蓄积仇恨，并威胁邻国。"如果说这段台词的语气还不够客气，那么从 1969 年推行"关岛尼克松主义"起，这位美国总统不但开始以"中华人民共和国"的正式国号作为称呼，而且提出破冰解冻和邦交正常化，直到 1970 年 10 月在《时代》周刊上放出试探气球："如果说我在有生之年还有什么未偿之愿，那就是到中国去。"这个在 1949 年曾责问杜鲁门"谁丢失了中国？"的冷战大王，就这样试图"找回中国"了。不积跬步，何至千里？木与木相摩则燃，原来中美是这样跳着小步舞开始接近的。只是老百姓不知就里，这才有了转弯子的必要。

"吹风"和"转弯子"从此成了我们政治词汇的一部分。

（原载 2009 年 7 月 16 日《南方周末》）

“驳壳枪”与“护心镜”

1967年下半年,复旦大学的革命委员会决定在郊县青浦朱家角一个名叫山湾的地方,开办“抗大战校”,将最近留校当教师的毕业生(包括本科生和研究生)集中到那儿去接受“再教育”。设校初衷,顾名思义,是学习延安时代的“抗日军事政治大学”。那时,“五七干校”尚未开办,所以这儿说的“战校”和后来设在崇明岛上的复旦“五七干校”不是一回事。

既是“战校”,自然实行连、排、班的军事编制。那是“工人阶级领导一切”的时代,连部首长以及各排排长由清一色的工宣队员出任,惟有班长才由工宣队指定学员中靠得住的先进分子担任。编制规矩既定,谁知领导上层建筑的工宣队在邯郸路校本部孵久了,都不愿大老远下乡去体验一下“工农联盟”中位居老二的艰苦生活,所以光连部组成这事就拖了又拖,我们这些学员便“待命”再“待命”,一直拖到接近年底的时候方始打起铺盖成行。

工宣队连长据说是个原来在工厂屁股就不大干净的主儿,不知这次下放是否与此有关。既然命令他出掌“战校”,他也就先从外表上来个“军事化”:足蹬大皮靴,又从生物系牵来一条大狼狗。听说他特别喜欢接近女学员,常破例恩准她们返回市区探亲以示照顾。我作为学员,原以为“战校”里将以农业劳动为主,反正大学五年加研究生三年,没少干挑担、插秧之类的农活,倒也还能对付,所以方寸并不大乱。

谁知到得“战校”,先是平整场地,第一天就忙着把校园里的一个坟包给挖了,白天挖不完,天黑之后继续挑灯夜战。明明是座无名氏的普通坟茔,自己吓自己,说什么定是大地主的墓葬,里头有宝,挖坟已惊动校区四周的阶级敌人,因而整夜轮流值班放哨。

工宣队确实不喜欢艰苦的农业劳动,所以“战校”生活基本上就是三个内容:1)把校区漆成“红海洋”,就是把所有墙面画上“葵花向太阳”之类的东西(最近看央视六一儿童节庆祝晚会使我有重返“战校”的错觉,瞄了一眼,赶快换台);2)背诵“老三篇”,人人必须通过测验;3)民兵操和夜间突然紧急集合——后者常发生在连部领导开夜车打扑克并吃过夜宵之后。供学员用于“整理内务”的空余时间倒是不少,学员或三五成群信步 15 分钟到淀山湖畔徜徉,或像我这样补补业务,练练笔头,记得曾写过题为“鹅步集”(因无休止的民兵操练而得名)的不少小文章,可惜后来因怕文字获罪,统统付之丙丁了。“战校”接受“再教育”生活中最值得纪念的一课是,那一年 12 月 25—26 日从青浦徒步走回复旦给毛主席庆祝生日的活动。25 日吃过午饭,学员集合,每人领到两件“宝”。一个是量体裁衣可正好装下语录本亦即“红宝书”的塑料小包,须知当年这种斜背小包也是一种 status symbol (身份象征),工宣队就是背着这种身份证似的小包进驻上层建筑各领域的,后来才慢慢普及开来。第二件是一块铅皮,上印当时极为流行的《毛主席去安源》油画。学员们就这样斜挎语录包——我觉得像武工队的驳壳枪,前胸挂着铅皮画——我觉得像古代武士的护心镜,踏上“长征路”的(其实,从青浦“战校”到江湾复旦校部大概也就四五十里路吧)。一路行来,始终有辆大巴跟着,名叫“收容车”,谁走不动要掉队了,可受“收容”待遇。其实那车主要是为我们的连排领导安排的,他们在车上打扑克,不时下来检查队伍步伐是否齐整,歌声是否嘹亮,再就是领呼几句“下定决心,不怕牺牲”的口号和“一二三四”之类的口令。

你别说，这样一支“驳壳枪”加“护心镜”的队伍，从郊区走进大上海，一路上还挺吸引眼球的。走到虹口游泳池是凌晨三点，这样的步速太超前了，不能使队伍恰好在校区早晨广播响起的那一刻走进校门。偏偏这时天公不作美，淅淅沥沥下起雨来。大家只好在寒雨里原地休息“倒时差”。待到重新集队，“收容车”已先行开回复旦，原先车上的工宣队这时都和学员打成一片了，雄赳赳、气昂昂地朝着复旦大学进发。时间掐算得非常精确，就在12月26日6点半，复旦大学广播台早广播信号“东方红”乐曲响起的那一刻，队伍走进校门，在巨大的毛主席塑像前站定，高歌并齐颂语录，向伟大领袖表忠心，给他老人家祝寿。那已被雨水打湿的老棉袄压在身上，沉沉的，滋味很不好受，但“文革”版“朝山进香”活动终于结束，接下来就是跨越元旦的差不多一个星期的假期，学员们还是挺向往的，想来给我们施行“再教育”的工宣队老师傅们亦然。

（原载2009年8月6日《南方周末》）

歌的流变

年轻的朋友，你听说过这些歌名吗：《你是灯塔》、《我们是民主青年》、《新民主主义进行曲》、《解放区的天》、《团结就是力量》……可能有几支听说过，但并不会唱，即使会唱，大概也不曾细细琢磨过歌词，诸如"民主政府爱人民啊，共产党的恩情说不完啊"、"向着法西斯蒂开火，让一切不民主的制度死亡"等等。即使琢磨了，也会发生疑问：法西斯就是法西斯，干嘛后面还加个"蒂"字？原来法西斯主义的始作俑者是意大利（当时译作"义大利"——与"美利坚"、"英吉利"等一样，用尽褒词，不知出自哪个"汉奸"译人之手？）的墨索里尼，所以用复数 Fascisti 指称法西斯分子们。此外还有借用高尔基的散文长诗《海燕》意象，歌颂毛泽东的《毛泽东之歌》："密云笼罩着海洋，海燕呼唤暴风雨，你（指毛泽东）是最勇敢的一个，不管黑夜茫茫……"记得当年，我们这些小萝卜头跟着大人，都是唱着这些歌，箪食壶浆，欢迎解放军进城的。这些歌的多数可能都诞生在解放前蒋管区的进步学生运动中，虽有伟大领袖与黄炎培那段"兴不勃，亡不忽"的"窑洞对"（仿"隆中对"？），从在野到执政，毕竟是个天地大翻覆，这些歌于是也就成了历史的回声了。

当然，解放之初的"一边倒"时代，苏联歌曲也曾大行其道，记得中学时代每周日还到黄陂路上当年的上海图书馆（现为上海美术馆）楼下，跟着苏联专家学唱俄文歌。今天的小友们可能知道《莫斯科郊外的晚上》、《红莓花儿开》之类的软性曲目，而如果听到斯大林时代进行曲之类中的歌词:“我们没有见过别的国家,可以这样自由呼吸”,不笑得喷饭才怪哩。“文革”把上面提到的这些歌作为十七年(1949—1966)修正主义文艺黑线的派生物,一股脑儿扫进历史的垃圾堆。除了《东方红》、《大海航行靠舵手》等有数的几首,就是不可胜数的语录歌加上“杀杀杀”和“就是好,就是好”之类的“中国式快板”。偶尔也会听到十七年黑线时代的东西,譬如“抬头望见北斗星,心中想念毛泽东”,凡听到这样的哀诉,那必是某支红卫兵或造反派队伍自认受了不公待遇,管他听得见听不见,要向毛主席呼吁了。就像1967年初复旦“红革会”炮打张春桥不成,反被中央“文革”杀了个回马枪时候那样。《代国歌——义勇军进行曲》唱的是“不愿做奴隶的人们”,“中华民族到了最危险的时候”,还要鼓动他们用“热血”去筑“新的长城”,岂止是迹近反动,简直是不折不扣的大黑话了,所以就必须改词,只是对于会咏(“四人帮”时代“文化部长”)式蹩脚透顶的宣传嚎叫,群众不买账,这才没有传檄而定。《国际歌》是党歌,纵令你有再大的无产阶级革命气魄,也没人敢下令作为“四旧”处理。可那歌词,不管是瞿秋白还是萧三译的,实在不合时宜:我们讲“大救星”“太阳升”,《国际歌》偏唱“从来就没有什么救世主,也不靠神仙皇帝”以及“全靠自己救自己”,这不明明唱反调吗?于是,就开了“曲可奏,词不能唱”的先例。时至今日,不妨做个实验,看看有几位党员能唱出《国际歌》的三段歌词。倒是我们这一代人,即使不是党员,还背得全歌词。这不,我友翟象俊兄读到这段文字,立刻用中、俄、英三种文字唱将起来。

接着便是改革开放,邓丽君、李谷一、朱逢博、张明敏等诸位的软性反弹,大受欢迎。记得有次学生聚会,邀我这老师参加,当年“文革”时极为激进且把我骂得狗血喷头的一位,突然放声唱起“我拿青春赌明天”,使我顿有时空给任意裁剪而恍如隔世之感。再往后,什么“你是那么咄咄,你是那么乖乖”、“月光放肆在染色的窗边/尘烟魔幻所有视觉/再一杯那古老神秘恒河水”(“谷歌”搜来),老古董们听了,懵懂之余只有吐血的份了。说到正儿八经的政治性歌曲,中国人毕竟讲究的是传承,轻易不标新立异。记得《歌唱祖国》这首歌,笔者还是上世纪50年代在敬业中学的大礼堂里学的,谁知道,这一唱就是半个世纪,一直唱到现在,真可谓弥久弥光矣。

(原载2009年12月3日《南方周末》)

她不是“假洋鬼子”

她死了。虽已活到逾九高龄,但上次在美国见她的时候,不说活蹦乱跳吧,至少还是精神矍铄,胃纳是胜于我的,幽默感也一如既往。那次,我们一起去巴尔的摩城当年美国总统罗斯福的孙女家作客,没进门前,她先向我介绍那对美国夫妇生育有问题,于是妻子就到医院去“借了一个蛋”(她的原话,我想是 borrowed an egg 一语的翻译),好不容易生下一女。进了那人家,她不管我是否需要,硬要我先去盥洗室,原来那儿的抽水马桶上方,悬挂了一张蒋介石亲笔签名送给小罗斯福的一张陆、海、空军大元帅戎装照。用她的话说,老蒋成了罗斯福后人的“toilet god”(守厕神)。

她是我的老师,好像是天津的买办家庭出身。学生时代只听说,当年追求她的人开来的豪华小汽车,在她家门口排长队,其中有蒋夫人的幼弟。后来的夫婿虽说也是圣约翰大学的大牌教授和最后一任校长,可是座驾最是不上档次,排在末尾。后来在美国,我问过她的身世,她也不详细回答,只是叫我去看她住在华府的朋友郑念写的英文传记 *Life and Death in Shanghai*(好像有人译作《上海生死劫》)。

其实两人很不一样,因为她一直在教育界。她的母语与其说是汉语,不如说是英语,故而常被人哂称“假洋鬼子”。今日复旦外文系图书馆的藏书借书卡上,一定还留有她的蟹行式中文签名,名字缺了居中的那个汉字,大概是因为笔画太多的缘故吧。教研室开会,大家都爱听她发言,既像是练习英语听力,又常被她的幽默妙语弄得哄堂大笑。这些在以前的多篇回忆文章中提到过,不赘。

比较惹人同情的是,她那位夫婿解放后最初定位在爱国教授,1951 年还曾把家藏的善本书“景宋本《礼记正义》”七十卷捐献给国家文物局。(据说这批稀世典籍曾有美国人出价 50 万美金购买。)她的夫婿决定捐献后,着人从香港把书运回上海,再由当时的政务院特批专列,由上海直运北京,入藏北图。但是 1957 年反右运动开始,这位“爱国教授”捐书的义举再无人记得,很快成了我系文学组的“四尊大炮”之一,被打作右派。作为右派家属的她,自然变得“火烛小心”,只是可能生性直白耿介,“无厘头”的话还会不时冒出来,例如说到戒烟,就来个譬方:“那痛苦是慢慢儿慢慢儿的,就像思想改造一样。”发现我这个学生对侦探小说与她有同好,某次在来校电车上,曾提议我们来合写一本,内容是某系教授们连环神秘被杀,抽丝剥茧,最后侦得元凶,乃是那个系貌似弱不禁风的头头。

这家人的厄运其实还刚刚开始。夫婿摘帽后,常跟老朋友酬酢往还,叵料当时最忌结社,说他们是组织反对党,连夫婿外交部长的职务都封好了,于是一概捉将官里去,家人从洋房里被逐到 14 平方安身。(我去过那斗室,多个箱笼都不知怎么弄到天花板上结缚着固定,还有一张四脚朝下的藤椅。)“天晓得,”她说,“还说我是他们开会时负责望风的。”下面这句用英文说的话“the day I was widowed”(译成今天流行的汉语就是“我‘被守寡’的那一天”),当然指丈夫被捕,她说得轻描淡写,像在就事论事,可在我听来,怎么就蕴藏着那么深沉的悲凉呢?那时正值“文革”,大儿子已毕业离沪去外地工作,小儿子似乎还在读初中,眼见家庭变故,从此自闭,直到后来改革开放,去了美国,也读了学位,但始终只愿在一家中学当门房,不与世接,直至今日。她赶到那所中学,谋得一个代课教师的职位,为的是在异乡陪伴并照顾幼子。就这样,一直工作到八旬高龄!

最后一次见她,是她从美西到美东来看朋友。去她借居的公寓接她时，我原以为总有些拉杆箱之类的行藏，谁知道她只拎着一只酒店的洗衣袋作为行囊。分手时，望着她远去的身影，我想到的不是她曾享受过的荣华富贵和青春美貌，而是浸透在骨子里的唯我中国人才有的超强抗压能力。她不是“假洋鬼子”，她确确实实是个中国人。

（原载 2010 年 1 月 15 日《联合时报》）

步行乐之二

先允我说明：文题中加上“之二”两字，是因为2001年曾写过一篇同样的小文，收进了集子。这阵子究责“代笔”的事儿闹得很凶。有人剥丝抽茧非证他人文字之伪和人品之劣不可。笔者可不愿卷入此种是非。同理，今日的我不能替昔日的我代笔，所以“之二”两字非加不可。

捡出过去写的文字一看，嚯，不得了，这散步的习惯真是有年头了。无怪乎，校长大人曾说，留脚印于复旦土地上最多的可能就算我陆某人了。其实难说。散步途中，我常遇见熟面孔，中文系的陈允吉兄就是一位。还有的——显然也是退休教工——虽然互不识名，因为经常遇见，擦肩而过时也会颔首致意；更有一对家住校外公寓的伉俪，开着汽车，到相辉堂这儿来，下车踱上几圈，消食之余，想必也是喜欢校园大草坪这边幽静的氤氲。

几年前的文章中，因为写到美国的森林公园，说过：“散步助人荡累颐景，散赏悟衷，渐收贪进之心。”若单就校园散步而论，轻车熟路，无揽新胜，这话说过头了。惟见一位不避寒暑，企立树下，若有所期的奇士，算是新鲜。因为路线既定，“颐景”、“散赏”云云，便无从谈起。我不爱热闹，尤喜假期中空旷少人的校园，每年除夕夜，都要计算自己一路碰见几位徒步或骑车而过的人，然后将“途遇三人二骑”之类文字写入日记。有时无聊，便计算跨出的步数，计有：长程5 200多步，短程3 500之谱，与2001年时“日行平均三英里”已不可同日而语矣。可见旧文中写到的吕蓓卡·索尔尼特(Rebecca Solnit)当年新作《向往漫游:步行的历史》(2000年首版)所述不谬:步行者往往爱作毫无意义的单调统计,计步器之类的小机件于是应运而生。

当然,更多的时候,寻觅幽邃,为的是"荡累"、"悟衷",头脑里的活动远比机械计步来得活跃。譬如说,因为教英美散文,走着走着,就会想到英国19世纪文评家赫兹利特(Hazlitt)的著名随笔和小品(其中好些都已由学弟潘文国教授译成中文),是赫君把散文这种文学样式比作信步漫游,而且指出不少欧美散文干脆都以散步作为文题或主旨;想到赫君,又会延伸到他的莎评、他与柯勒律治(Coleridge)的争论,还有他个人命运的坎坷和他的咎悔;想到散文大家,又会不免纳闷,为何这些作家中特多独身主义者(最突出的人物自然当推兰姆[Charles Lamb]),往往又都是中年成名——这些身份特点是如何影响作文的?想到散文,不禁要问:何以没有一个散文家可得诺贝尔文学奖?无怪乎散文家都爱在自己的文字中引经据典,掺入哲理或诗句,提高文品,使自己不致在文坛永远被边缘化。脚步落处,思潜于内,迹应斯通。我然后又会想到,为什么二战后的西方思想大家,如法国的罗兰·巴尔特(Roland Barthes)和德国的阿多诺(Theodor W. Adorno)都会属意于一种开放、流动、无定向、碎片化的前卫书写,亦即散文体裁?是不是这种古老的载体将会越来越多地容纳厚重的哲理内容,而不必像康德、黑格尔那样高议长篇立论?从这个意义上说,中国古代的"子曰",西方文明源头上的对话体和语录体,还有现代的钱锺书先生,不都已含有一定的后现代元素?有时还可以在头脑中做完日间尚未完成的功课,譬如说"不说白不说,说了也白说,白说也要说"怎么译成英文——那是学生问我的。

遐想无禁区。散步一路,意识流不断,什么都会从大脑闪过。这几日正读龚选舞描述汪伪汉奸末日的回忆录。那个《色·戒》里的特务头子、现实生活中的丁默邨被拉出去伏法时,已经吓成半死,瘫作一堆稀泥,非由法警挟持着去刑场不可。这场景到了张爱玲笔下,或在导演李安手中,能不能敷衍成作品的续集?抑或这时的人犯已是cerebral palsy病人甚至brain-dead了?由此激发出要去把金雄白写汪伪的长篇弄来一读的欲望。再譬如,就拿散步这种活动说,2001年那篇旧文提到,这是一种"艺术",于是想到所谓艺术,当指温饱无虞者的"闲暇散步",不包括登山运动家在稀薄空气中的弓身跋涉,不指"行人刁斗风沙暗"中的征夫,不指役使耕畜营田的农人,也不指闪聚到华盛顿纪念碑去的茶叶党。但"步行"毕竟是人类这两足动物特有的活动。不然,怎么不见有人写部"呼吸史"或者"声音交流史"?

美国作家比尔·布赖森(Bill Bryson)说,步行已是一种"失传的艺术",说的是汽车文化入侵人类生活后以车代步的现代生活方式。于此,笔者也有些体会。上世纪80年代开始在复旦这一带散步的时候,周围还有好些土路,偶尔从小径那边的田畴还会飘来粪肥的气味,在农业文明中长大的人对此颇有一些亲切感。就在日复一日散步的过程中,我也能感知城市化睥睨一切的盲目蛮力,直到校园及其周边统统成为柏油丛林的一部分。如今,即使在校园之内散步,不时也有汽车擦着你的身边驶过。有的驾车人全无"行人友善"(pedestrian-friendly)意识,小角度转弯,从不鸣笛(可能是学洋人),遑论礼让,行人如是手脚迟钝的老物,或者一不留神,极有可能出事。看来,在校园主干道上设置交通灯、停车标识和"睡眠警察"(sleeping policemen,指减速路凸)都该列入议事日程了。

可能是怕步行艺术"失传",也可能是护师心切,现在常有学生陪我散步。挪动脚步的同时,用嘴巴也可切墨箴规,被我谑称为walkie-talkie。交流读书心得,评论学生长短,追述校系往事,有时甚至以轶事八卦互娱,颇有些把个人"艺术"转化作同好讨论的效果。师学生之所工,生不用师之所拙,愚智互补,其乐融融。应当说,我这当教师的是主要受益人。譬如"金斗"(Kindle)怎么用,如何跟Siri对话,都是从学生那儿学来的。从亚马逊购来的美国上年畅销书 Eric Metaxas 著 *Bonhoeffer: Pastor*, *Martyr*, *Prophet*, *Spy*,就是大学士给输入“金斗”的。于是,一“斗”在手,一会儿看周佛海如何写密信向蒋介石输诚,一会儿又是德国神学家如何参与刺杀希特勒的密谋,生活因此颇不寂寞。至于 Siri 小姐,偶尔对话试试 iPhone 4S 的神奇智能(我说“You are an asshole”[你是个 xx],Siri 答“None of your profanity”[不许说脏话]),有趣,要全功能物尽其用,自己还差得远呢!

(原载 2012 年 3 月 4 日《文汇报·笔会》,有修改)

Sunset, Mother and Home

— An Attempt to Interweave Inner Reflections with Nature*

It is said that everyone must have some unforgettable experiences in his childhood. Such experiences, sweet or unpleasant, like a magician's finger, will touch his heart string often enough even when he grows old. New experiences, however numerous and fresh, are not likely to have the old ones effaced.

Such is the case with me. When a child, I lived in my hometown for some two years, and those were the very last years I ever spent with my mother. True, two years are but a short period. Yet, these particular ones, owing to their association with my hometown and my late mother's dear image, are never to escape my memory.

Of all things I like my hometown's sunset best. Many a colorful summer evening, after a refreshing bath, mother and I would walk up to the Yao River and watch the setting sun gradually dipping into the far horizon. Our hometown is noted for her abundant production of beautiful legends. Therefore, the sunset there was all the more suggestive. The place used to take on a touch of poetry even when the rural quietude was ruffled by an occasional call of a distant night-bird,

* 本文是作者二十二岁时的习作,由作者的好友叶扬教授提供。——编注。

whose plaintive note was the only music of the twilight country. Losing ourselves in a fertile and romantic imagination, we would sit on a large rock near an abandoned joss house for hours till the lonely distant bark of a watch dog or the now seen and now lost cottage lights reminded us of home. Then, mother would stand up, utter a gentle ecstatic exclamation. And I was very happy.

Shortly afterwards mother died of cancer and I left my hometown. All these years, I have been living in strange places. But whenever a sunset exhibits all its grandeur and poetry before my eyes, my mind, however otherwise occupied a minute ago, will infallibly turn back to my rosy childhood, to the Yao River, to my old home; my ears will again ring beautifully with that familiar ecstatic exclamation, while my heart overflows with a melancholy pleasure. I really can't help it.

Last year, in late autumn, I made a trip to Nanking. I visited many beautiful spots. But none of them gave me a deeper impression than the Swallow Strand. Some of my friends teased me for my infatuation with such "a shabby little hill" and felt sorry for me that I should have missed the magnificence of Sun's Mausoleum and the mellow beauty of the Xuan Wu Lake. For all that my partiality to the "shabby little hill" remains unalterable.

It was at a dusk that I came to visit the Strand by a feeling of familiarity. Its decaying walls, its clay statues of hideous gods, its surrounding bamboo grove, and even the few chubby and leisurely hens, which were waddling about, all of a sudden, brought me back to my old home. Natural and clean, calm and simple!

When I reached the top of the Strand, I was literally intoxicated by the scene which, with its dazzling grandeur and naked beauty, unfolded itself beneath. The Yangtze was seen gliding smoothly, its surface sparsely dotted with a few little white sails, light as gulls. Behind my back, stood solemnly the Purple Gold, whose bald peak, when the homeward sun had already withdrawn itself from everything else, was still being lavishly caressed by its lingering beams. The smoke of supper cooking was hovering about the small fishing village below. Its chimneys, thinly veiled in the light blue mist, emerged from a thick grove, around which a group of urchins were chasing one another. A woman with a bundle of hay on her back, was walking towards the village. In her wake followed her little son. They were going home!

A crisp night breeze had already set in, wafting a sweet balminess. The pine forest, a certain distance away, sent forth a complaining murmur as the breeze skimmed over it. The sun was now below the horizon. The shadows of twilight were rapidly setting unnoticed, melting their various features into one tint of sober grey.

A little sparrow, too much fatigued with flying, alighted on the only tree nearby. O! Little bird, art thou feeling lonely too? It gazed upon me for a while with its head amicably tilted, as if very much appreciative of human companionship. Then, perhaps half awed by the shadowy dimness now creeping over the country, half dissatisfied at the unearthly stillness of rural twilight, in which its cheerful carol would find no echoing listener, the bird flew away, flew to the domestic embrace, to its smiling mother. The leafless tree was trembling feebly and I was again left alone. Amidst such an unmeasurable depth of tranquility, out of the melancholy purple of evening emerged the bell for night worship of the joss house. Its dull heavy sound, coming at regular intervals, inspired sublime meditation. All nature seemed to repose. The finest emotions of the soul were alone awake!

Suddenly, a familiar sound caught my ears. Mother seemed to be with me. "Ah! Ah!" Wasn't that her ecstatic exclamation? And again I was very happy.

…

So in my mind sunset is always associated with my childhood, with mother, with my beloved native soil. I like to watch sunset. I love mother. I treasure the memory of my childhood. I long after home.

附:

Yang Ye*

Sent: Thursday, June 19, 2008 7:56 AM

To: Gusun Lu

…

By the way, I'm so glad Ye Ling found that early lyrical essay of yours. I also vaguely recall another one you wrote "a la Katherine Mansfield" which was about an incident you witnessed on the street. Do you still have it?

YY

---

* 叶扬,美国加州大学河滨分校比较文学系教授。——编注。

Gusun Lu

Sent: Thursday, June 19, 2008 8:55 AM

To: Yang Ye

o as i read the essay i was overwhelmed by shame. the affectation, the over-effusiveness, etc. combine to make me want to disown it. i don't think other essays will turn out to be any better! but then one has to make allowances for the fact that it was written by a 22-yr-old.

...

A Fake Collar or What?

Literally it was called "fake collar" as in the phrase "a collar and tie." But a misnomer it was because the collar was real and cannot be realer — be it made of cotton or Dacron lately in fashion. It was fake in that it made believe that the collar was the entire shirt — chest, back, sleeves, tails and all. With an outer coat the nothingness below the neck was concealed from the eye. So more accurately, it was, as it were, collar-only or collar-and-nothing.

Necessity is the father (or mother? or parent?) of invention. In those badly needy days, cloth was in acutely short supply and had to be rationed. Smart people who did not have extra coupons for a shirt or two came up with the idea of wearing the neck part of it to feign respectability of having worn the whole. There were special tailors who were good at making such "fake collars" with odds and ends of material.

If it was funny, it was tragically so. I remember seeing bean-sized drops of perspiration breaking out of the forehead of a professor of Japanese from this department when he had had a glass of beer too many in a drinking spree with a group of visiting counterparts from Japan. Remember it was in the late 1970s, and the country had just opened its doors. Poor man, he kept brushing the drops aside, first surreptitiously and then in desperation, but never bothered to take off his coat while his Japanese peers, short-sleeved, had long let their hair down. The poor Chinese professor of Japanese sweated like a pig until sweat showed unceremoniously in a damp patch on the back of his coat.

I asked him afterwards why he had not taken off his coat but should instead have allowed himself to go through this "diaphorestic tribulation." With a wry smile, he unbuttoned the coat to reveal to me what he wore under it: a fake collar that was about one fourth of a normal shirt, something like a man-made bust one frequently sees at a jeweller's to show off the effect of a necklace, remarking: "It is expensive to save face, isn't it?"

Who says we Chinese only clone what others do and are never an innovative nation? Give me a "fake collar" made elsewhere in the world to convince me.

24 February 2010

上海街头的乘凉大军和"小肺炎"

年轻的朋友,你能设想一下河南路和延安路交汇处中汇大厦(当年是上海博物馆所在地)底下的街道上,横七竖八躺满男女老少纳凉的情景吗?那年头,上海人住房困难,一到气温升至37℃左右的盛暑,"鸽笼"般的家变成了蒸笼,即使太阳落山,暑气一样不退。于是,在一片"热煞哉"的抱怨声中,你拖一把竹椅,我抱一条凉席,到马路上"乘风凉去"。大楼底部一般都是物理学中所谓的"风洞",是最吸引人的场所。中汇楼下,麇聚鸟集,足有二三百人之众,男女不分,手脚横陈,露宿风餐,堪称大上海一景。其中老幼,因为怕沾浃夜露得病,一般到得午夜时分便会各自撤回屋去,惟有少壮放心逍遥,至多往腹部随便撩上毛巾被一角防御寒气。所谓"逍遥",当然也是相对而言,上海这座城市早就吹不到海风了,倒是热岛效应日益戾虐,大团热焰笼罩不散,户外过夜更多的只是心理纳凉而已。有时,中夜突然电闪雷鸣,随即雨如瓢泼,乘凉大军狼狈逃窜,惟见一张主人来不及拆走的帆布床,孤独地在街头承受着雨点的暴打,似乎很有象征意义,从此竟成镂骨记忆。

那年酷夏,居委会托儿所的阿姨在给出生不满六个月的小女洗澡后,往春凳上一放,自去领取福利冷饮。小毛头骨碌一滚,掉下地来,摔成医生所说的"青枝骨折",打上绑带固定复位。痛苦加上痱子瘙痒,虽有父母挥舞大蒲扇送风,热浪滚滚的季节里,孩子整夜整夜悲啼而睡不成觉。因陋就简,我们只好把床铺改放到通风一些的位置。谁知那身体根本感觉不到的穿堂风还确实厉害,几个夜晚一过,孩子伤风咳嗽不止,终至高烧不退,送到东方红医院(即今天的瑞金医院)就诊,断定肺炎,立即住院。孩子太小,输液只能从额头进针,陪护人只能拖来两根木条打地铺。想给小病人榨点西瓜汁,必须来回跋涉几次,持医院出具的体温38°以上的证明,始能买到西瓜,而且一证一瓜,断不能多买。轮流通宵陪侍的父母,第二天起来,一个急着去做“六进六出”(早6点进厂,晚6点离厂)的车床工,接受“再教育”的同时,支援越南“同志加兄弟”的反美斗争;另一个去学校一边自我批判,一边编写阅读这篇博文的你可能使用过的《新英汉词典》。当然,对这家人说来,最苦的日子还在后面。

2010年2月27日

Have Learned My Lesson

The lesson learned is not to accept interview requests from overseas media. Reasons are manifold. Reason one is level-headed judgement of oneself as an interviewee inclines or disinclines one to such requests: whether one is outspoken to a fault or one is good at and given to hemming and hawing. Reason two is unless one toes a certain accepted line and speaks nothing untoward one is apt to unruffle somebody's feathers and arouse ire. Such ire almost always takes itself out on the interviewee, ending up with harsh persecution as a ten or eleven years' term for all one knows.

The newspaper whose interview request has been turned down is *The Washington Post*. But it is the same newspaper whose request for an interview I gladly accepted once. For documentary evidence, the interview took place back in 1983 during my second visit to the United States. The date the story was published was March 19th[①]. I'm not quoting the story verbatim for fear of being accused of gloating.

So, likewise, the lesson learned is also that times and people change. So does the newsworthiness of individuals. The haunting question is whether these are changes for the better or worse.

---

① 1983 年《华盛顿邮报》的采访见本书附录。——编注。

Also for documentary purposes I'm posting the Post's recent letter with all personal information suppressed by a So & So.

On Tue., 4/6/10, So & So wrote:
Subject: urgent: interview request from *The Washington Post* Beijing bureau
Date: Tuesday, April 6, 2010, 4: 38 AM

Hello Professor Lu,

This is So & So from *The Washington Post* Beijing bureau. We are currently travelling in Shanghai for EXPO story. We understand that you have different opinion on "no pajama notice" issued by the government. We'd like to interview you and learn your opinions on EXPO-related topic.

If you see OK, will sometime this Thursday morning or Friday morning work for you?

Could you let us know how to contact you?

Best,

So & So

8 April 2010

两员大将

前一段给《南方周末》写“回忆和随想”专栏，往事故人提到不少，给历史打打小补丁，语气不总是，甚至有人说，总是不厚道的。于是，就有人来教育我，说你陆某人即使做不到教徒那样“送上另一半脸颊”由人掌掴，至少也要学学勃朗宁——是诗人Robert，不是他夫人——“Good to forgive, better to forget”。何奈基因、血型以及人的一应chemistry构成了性格，很难服从管教。我倒宁可牢记Edmund Burke的话“There is, however, a limit at which forbearance ceases to be a virtue（容忍过了限度决不再是美德）”！

今天给学生说往事，说到曾经在外文系叱咤风云的两员大将，着实又不“厚道”了一把。对这样的人物，不写上一笔，咱们的系史好像总缺了些什么。

两人之所以成为“大将”，都与“文革”有关。第一位好像并非“红五类”出身，但在“清理阶级队伍”时负责一个专案组，一鸣惊人，挖出了教职工队伍中极其凶残的“阶级敌人”，立了大功，被工宣队作为“文革”时代绝对稀有的派往英国留学的一分子，后来又作为择优留校任教的唯一一位69届。“大将”确实了得，不知给专案对象上了什么手段，迫使对方交代，说是解放初期，对象和他的几个小兄弟（那时最多不过十一二岁吧）曾亲手杀死一名人民警察，而且掀起窨井盖抛尸灭迹！专案对象原是从某所兄弟院校分派来复旦的，被供出的朋友们当时仍在那所院校做教师。敌情信息一交流，据工宣队长说，那边也“揪出一串大闸蟹”。这功劳自然是大了去了。只是在今天第一教学楼1237召开的批斗会上，作为听众的我们，怎么也不相信，觉得像是在听神话：“国民党潜伏了军统、中统，难道还有童子军！?”后来“四人帮”打倒，开始强调学业务了，“大将”搞专案的特长无所用其技，精神上似乎受了一定的损伤，听说在来校的公共汽车上几次朗声说起夫人受流氓侮辱的细节，绘声绘色，用我那位英语比汉语更娴熟的老师的话说，那是一种变态的“voyeurism”。再往后，“大将”削尖脑袋去了美国。

第二名“大将”是跟台湾陈水扁差不多的苦出身，但借用“文革”语言，说他坏得“头顶生疮，脚底流脓”一点也不为过。大饥荒年月，偷了图书馆的书，除去标签，抹去印记，拿到五角场废品回收站去卖，曾被现已从东华大学退休的某学兄抓了个正着。改革开放后，当局有意派他出国进修，这时一个退休老教授站出来揭发“大将”了，原来“文革”期间，老教授被他屡屡敲诈，自行车在当时属“大件”动产，被“大将”掠去，人民币自然更不在话下，就连洗澡费之类的小数，也被一一拦截。复旦托儿所阿姨也来控告，说“大将”如何图谋不轨。“大将”出国之计于是泡汤，一怒之下，跳槽去了近处某所小学院摆上大王。不久，那儿又传出丑闻：说好跟人合译的“×××童话”待到出版，名利全由“大将”一人独吞。那位合作伙伴真叫冤枉，除去劳动被剥削，反目之前曾自愿给“大将”提供寓所，由他在那儿玩弄女人，直到忍无可忍，才将“大将”告上法庭。我最后一次见到“大将”，是在英国驻沪领事馆的某次招待会上，当时，一口不知什么乡音英文的“大将”，已是中国×××（英国某作家）研究会的会长一类角色。再往后，与上面那位一样，“大将”削尖脑袋去了加拿大。

写这些往事除了备忘，还有一个目的，那就是让今天的少壮们知道,许多丑恶并非改革开放之咎。至于是什么造就了“大将”们,找信史来读读,再像张志新、遇罗克那样自己去深入思考求解吧。

2010 年 5 月 7 日

人是可以貌相的?

扬兄和他在夏威夷的姐姐、姐夫回应“两员大将”博文,说起“人是可以貌相的”,与我的见识颇合。虽阔别多年,今天回忆起来,第一员大将的眼睛在镜片之后,只剩“一”字形的细线,可见再多的知识也难以令其启瞀,且多避免与人“目接”,说明从本质上讲,神经并不坚强,倒是可能虚弱而缺乏自信。偶尔看人,目光聚焦只一两秒钟就迅即跳开,眼球骨碌碌转向另一端,所谓眸眊而心不正是也。当然,后来“文革”祸起,又另有一副面目。第二员正好跟上面这位相反,看人的时候直勾勾的,使人瘆瘆然顿生“利心中鸷,贪目不瞬”之感。还有,与人交谈的时候,说着说着会突然无端嘿嘿两声,让对方无法接住他的“球”(conversational ball)作出反应,可能是思想已移往其他什么好事去了。反正当年与两员大将打交道(我都教过),总觉得不很舒服。

最近结交了一位小老板,是修理手机的,半个门面的营业部就设在国年路北端商业区头上。第一次“貌相”,他就给我留下好印象:留寸头,嘴唇厚厚的,长一张老实巴交的贫下中农忠厚脸。我看得出,与陌生顾客打交道时,他依然对上海人有些心存戒备,就事论事,不多说话,说完就别转头去,这时倘恰见我走近,他会突然咧开嘴巴,送来真诚的笑容。他要我帮他儿子入学,我根本无法办到,可这一点儿不影响我们的友谊。每次做完生意,我都想多付一点小钱,有时搁在他柜台转身就走,他必大步赶上还我,倒是反而常常只收我的“成本费”和“优惠价”。今天上课，课间在 Gentlemen's 遇见他，小老板是来解决“自然召唤”的，又带上一个热水瓶来五教打水。我们说了一阵子话，听讲开世博了，他在找人证明沪上居住合法。

看人写的字有时也可“貌相”。豪者字健，逸者字放，苦者字寒，奸者字诈。方圆利钝，轻重浓淡，伸缩偃起，多少看得出一点人的特性。我有个学生，不管正楷，还是行草，一概直立。为人方正自然没有问题，但肯定不善机变。

2010 年 5 月 13 日

追悼会后话旧人

前天参加译文出版社老领导、翻译家孙家晋(吴岩)追悼会。孙公有段革命经历可能因单线知情人早殁而始终不得官家承认,所以最后只获退休而非离休待遇。来到遗体前三鞠躬时,我细细打量死者遗容,生怕看到口眼不闭,结果,遗容安详,看不出生前有何不公遭逢,遗体覆盖党旗,也算是种旌表了吧。倒是家属致辞时简短说到那段往事,凄切声咽,可能听到的人也不很多。据说现今殡葬化妆术高明,可穿针引线,缝合应该紧闭而未闭合的窍隙,不知是真是假。

越一日,从北京传来范用先生去世消息,从报上读到范回忆三联创刊《读书》杂志的文字。原来创刊号李洪林先生的文章题目《读书无禁区》是范用先生亲自改定的。相信看到这么篇文章,这样个文题,许多读者像我一样,无不击节叫好。因为打倒"四人帮"不久(那是1979年),余勇可贾,我就写了篇《权当"警世狂言"如何?》,主张翻译 George Orwell 的《1984》,托因公途经上海的董秀玉女士捎去投稿,结果稿去如泥牛入海,准是给"和谐"掉了。上世纪90年代,我把董乐山和他那位做了美国人的兄长以及冯亦代请到复旦来参加"白菜与国王"讲座,方才知道,第一,冯亦代当时负责的《读书》,因为《无禁区》一文据说日子已经很不好过,哪会由我这个小巴拉子再去碰"禁区"? 冯对我那带点针对性的"有些右派改正以后比左派还左"的说法颇不以为然。第二,董乐山兄当时实际上已在翻译《1984》,可是只在外文局的《国外作品选译》中内部发表。第三,董乐山兄在中学时代即倾向革命,在上海的圣约翰大学从事地下党的秘密工作,可是因为直接领导人被捕不知所终,关系中断,解放后不久就成了革命的敌人——右派分子。第四,董乐山兄从善如流,为人诚笃,我斗胆提出他参与翻译的《第三帝国兴亡史》中一句"这是丘吉尔和希特勒两人玩的游戏"可能是误译,英文定是"It is a game that two can play"(意为"这套你会我也会"),长我一辈的老"约大"欣然曰善。两人相忘于道术,我正想跟他通信求教,谁知一年多后董就撒手人寰了。董君又使我想到他们美国所的另一员大将施咸荣兄,肃反时就吃了多年苦头,所幸病蚌成珠,后来译出了《麦田守望者》和《等待戈多》这样的新经典。我俩在 Berkeley 一起向山姆大叔报税那一幕尚未从我脑中淡出,施兄不到七十已经没了,痛哉!

翻译出版界的这些老人一个个凋零,译协啊,你们急急匆匆评什么资深啊?!

2010 年 9 月 16 日

在美国坐“黑车”

今天上课讲到英国人生性有点 inhospitable,而美国人又特别 sociable,脑中突然蹦出自己经历过的两件实事。关于美国的那件事是这样的:

1984 年某夜,我在 Berkeley 的 Shattuck 街等公共汽车。站牌上的到车时间已过,仍无车来,就问一恰好过路的美国老者这站牌时刻表是否准确。老者见我是亚洲人,说了“不能不信,不可全信”之类的话后,顾自行去。我续等几分钟后,突见一车在街沿停下,居然鸣笛招呼我。一看,原来是刚刚那位老者。他招呼我上了他特地开来的私车,专程把我送到记忆中好像设在 Dwight 的大陆学生会(我是去送家信的,那时国外的中国人常靠学生会找使领馆帮忙投发家信,贴上 8 分国内邮资即可)。美国“老雷锋”当然没收我一分钱,到了目的地,等着我把事办完,再载我驶回。文题说“黑车”,打了引号,打诨而已。

讲完之后,突然想到应当把这事写进文章。二十多年前的事了,那美国老者恐怕已经作古,可他那闲适隐逸的模样,清风朗月的义举,我不应忘,也没有忘。

由此联想到眼下我们这儿的黑车成灾。我不明白,买得起车的人怎么还非得暇时跑出租挣钱不可?识者告我,买得起车不等于养得起车,更何况有的车主暂时还只是“半主”,按揭尚未付清。也有公车被司机开回家过夜,泊着也是闲着,何不用来拉客,做点“无本生意”？看来这黑车绝对是中国特色，要整治还真不易。前一阵“钓鱼执法”忙乎了一阵，也没刹住黑车这股歪风，反而弄得众口哓哓。

我由此又想到，上海人怎么那么善于捕捉商机：买了房，吃租金；买了车，开黑车；世博展馆图章吃香（为什么吃香至今不懂），就私刻馆章；打火机不能带上飞机以后，浦东机场外向下机“老烟枪”旅客兜售打火机，居然也成一种营生！是因为穷？还是像这儿某些网友说的，钱这东西，当然多多益善。

2010年9月30日

梦见故旧高望之

一点没有白昼清醒意识的暗示,更不是 wish-fulfilment,也不是“前意识”(preconscious)检禁“无意识”(unconscious)的结果,反正昨晚突然没来由地梦见《英汉大词典》编写之初浅识的同人高望之先生。那时他还没转往中国社科院,是北大派出的两位编写人员之一(另一位是西语系的王式仁,至今仍偶有联系)。那时只知道高通多国语言,所以大词典的“辞源”一项工作就请他一人包了。所以在我的印象中,就是这么一个孤零零的“闪回”镜头:老高一人占着一张游离在外的写字桌,桌上和膝边全堆着书,宽大的背部佝偻着,整日一动不动地孤零零敛神工作,一支接一支抽烟,往往是编写组最后一个下班的人。后来稍熟,知道他做过北大前校长马寅初的秘书,就缠着他讲些掌故来听听。高先生沉默寡言,给逼得没法子了,只得用鼻音很重的声音说上几句。记得他说过某次马寅初校长作报告,北大学生递条子,问他“姓马克思的马还是马尔萨斯的马”,校长不卑不亢回答说:“我姓马寅初的马。”我还记得他说过,解放前的学生运动在教会学校里最为高涨。问他原因,他谨慎地王顾左右而言他了。但是说到陆平打倒马寅初(连带他高望之)出任北大校长,陆平后来又被聂元梓打倒,而聂元梓最后被“最高”打倒,老高也只有连连摇头了。高望之革命历史长(网上讯息:1947 年,高望之曾是清华大学文理学院地下党负责人),学问好,不久就奉调回了北京,留下一大摞手工做成的辞源卡片,直至今日。

昨晚梦见他，老高戴了一副用橡皮胶布勉强粘住支架的破眼镜，鼻音很重地告诉我，他结婚了，说着摸出一包喜糖送上。你别说，这梦还真有某些现实投射的元素，似乎并非完全无稽。他婚姻不幸，这个当年在词典组就私下传开过。今天上网查阅，才知道"文革"初期他被红卫兵毒打，一副眼镜曾砸得粉碎。

高望之托梦赠糖，使我想起不少词典组故旧。有位 J. L.君，沪江大学产品，在词典组一直没怎么受到重用。后去香港任教，继而出国定居去了。某年，此君听说我在香港中大，多方联络，等找到踪迹，我已他去，失之交臂。前些时候，突接他来信，说是七年前给我发过 email，可能地址有误，一直没有联系上。七年后再发一次，主要为了感谢我曾替他写过的一封推荐信"改变了他的后半生"——显然夸大其词，但是为证不谬，技监读过此信，存疑者可去问他。信稿一保存就是七年，这一点让我异常感动，于是终又恢复联系，现正等着他 11 月份来访。还有一位据说曾经犯过生活作风错误的王君，在词典组专踏黄鱼车运书做苦力，但我认定他中英文俱佳，所以曾与他联名发表过文章，而因此被领导狠批一通。王君后来也去了美国，换了个名字，撰文专门抨击大陆，所以也便失去了联系。再有一位名门之后，也曾暂时栖身词典组。国民党特务刺杀其父时，把他的脚也打伤了。前几年出了一本书，蒙他送我一册。书中涉及乃父与某位伟大女性交往时的来往信札(都用英文)，有些段落有意经过阴影化处理，想必坊间传闻其父与伟大女性关系暧昧，"委员长"非要杀了他不可云云，并非完全空穴来风……

一个梦引出回忆多多，激成意识流，难怪睡眠质量每况愈下。

2010 年 10 月 29 日

J. L.来访

上次博文中写到的词典组故人 J. L.君今日来访。原来，我搞错了。所谓给了他后半生很大影响的并非一封推荐信，而是替他改过一篇英文文章，写 China accounting 的。他说凭这篇文章，他被美国学校接受读完硕士，后又被香港科技大学录用，一聘就是十年。香港的大学薪酬之丰，全球有名，这十年也许为他打下了殷实的经济基础，使他在美国衣食无虞。当然，J. L.之妻犹在工作补贴家用。（我不记得改文章的事，更不信经我修改，文章会增色多少。如果这篇文章的确有助于他的后半生，我相信——因我对读过的 J. L.文章尚有模糊记忆——那是由于文章里本来就多“干货”，绝非无验浮辞。）

门启处，阔别二十年有奇的故人依杖而入。宾主坐定说话，这才知道他是由另一位我尊敬的前辈姚奔先生介绍进《英汉大词典》编写组的。当年我利用午休时间为他改 China accounting 一文的细节，这也才回忆起来。他又说，某日中午，他伏案假寐时想起种种不公待遇，悲从中来，暗暗垂泪，我听到 J. L.座位处传出噎唼之声，曾跑去安慰他，据说是“伸手轻抚”他的肩头，使他觉得温暖。

在美国定居之后，他说常在夜晚睡眠中惊醒，那是因为梦见了当年受迫害的经历。渐入老境之后，他也会偶尔从梦中哭醒，那是故国和故人在梦中重现，客居飞蓬，顾有怅然。我说过，人出了国，有的忙于生计前途，再也不去关心国内发生的事情；有的听闻不公事实，虽也惊心，但距离带来的宽容度常胜于国内的人。且听 J. L.君下面这几句话:“贪污腐化何朝何代无之？前三十年除了整肃知识分子,官场就那么干净？强国才是奇功。”看来定居国外的 old hundred names (老百姓)更关心的似乎是中国如何处理钓鱼岛之类的事,柴米油盐涨价毕竟离他们太远了。更何况还有发改委专家掷地有声的豪言:“中国不存在通胀,再涨四十年也赶不上美国。”撒开脚板追吧。

J. L.八旬老人还好学不倦,这次复旦会计系请他来讲学,可见他腹笥不虚。对中国会计行业的 case studies 做得很有心得。其实,这一行里的 practice 或 malpractice 何用劳动颐养天年的美籍华人不远万里来讲？我们自己不是已有庞大的 CPA 队伍,连我教过的英文系学生考出“持证会计师”资格的,双手也已数不过来。兴许有些话还是得由外人来说,方始安全。除此之外,我们还像当年在词典组那样,切磋语言,讨论茶叶党(Tea Party)。后者是今天的大新闻,报上连篇累牍介绍。其实,听听他们给自己的党名拆字“tea = taxed enough already”以及他们的口号“Dissent is patriotic”,“茶叶”得势,并不一定值得我们欢迎。

2010 年 11 月 3 日

悼国强兄

噩耗传来，国强宗兄沉疴不救，昨夜殁于中山医院。正好今天寒流来袭，北风大起，满地枯叶，催人凄然伤怀！

一度，说到复旦外文系，曾有人爱提“两陆”，即国强兄和我。又有人称“两陆不和”。“性相近，习相远”，一定要说两陆是完全一样的人，当然不符合事实。但入学之初，国强兄已是我辈老师，业务能力强，是大家公认且为学生崇敬的。后来我做研究生，他是在职研究生，在同一课堂，上过列宁的《唯物主义和经验批判主义》和俄文，师生之外，又添一层同窗之谊。上世纪60年代，国强兄、任治稷兄和我过从尤密，成了挚友（详见拙文《我的父亲》），常常是写了文章，都要交换一读，相互“吹捧”一番，他写的那篇 On the Pleasure of Being a Father（是时继东初生），至今记得。国强兄英语的口笔能力俱佳，自然在我之上，尤精于词汇研究，这方面的著作丰硕，所以成为外文系首席教授和国务院学科评议组成员，皆是实至名归。

尤其使我难忘的是国强兄贤伉俪“收留”小女陆霁。那是1983年的事。我从市区老屋移居学校，复旦的宿舍尚待装修，但小女学籍已经先行转来。为免霁儿日日远途来回，国强兄夫妇主动扫榻奠枕，邀她住入他们在复旦第七宿舍的家，不但视同己出，日常生活待遇之佳，竟使我有女儿养尊处优，骄纵过分之忧。须知当时“两陆不和”的舆论已时有所闻。今天追述这段往事既证流言之伪，也可略见国强兄贤伉俪的宽厚宅心。

与国强兄伉俪打桥牌最有意思。那是因为他们夫妇俩都精于此道,打牌既是与对手方一比高低,两人之间还要“内战”,从叫牌到出牌,再到打完一副事后检讨,意见常常相左。切切偲偲,夫妻怡怡,争论乃是这一对同样好强的夫妇特有的精益求精方式,被我戏称为“桥牌桌上国强与小朱(嫂夫人之姓)的‘卿卿我我’”。在我安顿初定的复旦宿舍里,记得有多少个周末,一打桥牌便不可收拾,到得凌晨,终于不支,人仰马翻,倒在沙发上便沉沉睡去。呜呼,载笑载欢的青壮年月,如今已是记忆残片,临纸情塞,但有哀愍!

2010 年 12 月 6 日

An Attention-getting Child

Every parent would agree that an attention-getting child is a handful. It is prone to pull monkeyish tricks one after another to claim attention. I abhor snakes. My child when she was at a tender age and felt somehow neglected by a father absorbed in work, would let loose a bamboo toy snake from behind my shoulder to scare the shit out of me. Having succeeded once, she would repeat the trick again and again. Oddly enough, knowing the snake to be a mere fake, I was unfailingly frightened and then became obliging with attention duly given to her. Reasons are two-fold: one, the snake was a realistic imitation, what with the forked tongue and a neck — that is, if a snake has one — cleverly made telescopic that can now stick out now draw back like real; two, she knew Reptiliaphobia to be my worst vulnerability or "soft rib" as we Chinese are wont to say. She was emboldened by her sure-fire success so much so that she took to trying her snake on family and friends and then on guests when we happened to have any. Invariably, she was up to her mischief when adults were deep in their own conversation leaving her in what she saw to be, as it were, the "dog house." Invariably, the sight of the snake would fetch an argh or an eeeek from all around, flabbergasted. General panic over, when grown-ups resumed conversation and started to wonder why kids all play with ugly, gross things, my daughter would retire to her play corner, triumphantly, knowing now she had created a hub-and-spokes effect.

Sick — I mean mentally sick — old people can be attention-getting too. They love to make a scene, blustering and pestering, until they think they've become unnegligibilities in others' eyes. I've seen one inpatient, a Lilliputian by statue who always wants to act La Fontaine's swelling frog. Undaunted by sure failure, he arm-wrestles with the Oxen in the ward. His purpose? To appear on a par with them so that nobody dares to look down upon him. Life in the ward is uneventful. But he knows how to enliven it with his chicanery: wetting beddings only in order to force the nurses to change sheets for him, ringing for docs for complaints he shams.

On one occasion he even spit into the uneaten rice of a fellow patient. After much ado is taken about nothing, he would bury his face in the pillow to stifle a snigger. Then, fortuitously, his hands happen to land on a paring knife on his bed table. He picks it up, flashes and brandishes it as the worst WMD in a menacing attitude until his relatives and paramedics all rush in to check him. Thereupon, he gaffaws with abandon. Some suggest they file a case of misdemeanor against him. "With the security council of the hospital or with the police?" he asks nonchalantly. "Then I get more attention." A knowledgeable inmate hits upon a stratagem of pooling all victims of his knavery and suing him at a court, petitioning for a freeze of his bank account. Holy mackerel! It hits home. The swelling belly of the frog gets deflated and he's heard muttering to himself: "So what? Passive-aggressiveness gets me as much attention as aggression."

Freezing a bank deposit is as effective as taking away the fake bamboo snake from my daughter's hand.

26 December 2010

世 间 百 态

新编《动物庄园》

之一

某日，动物庄园里，疯牛、瘟鸡和病猪聚在一起聊天。

猪最得意，因为这几天，它惹事最多，惊动了全世界，成为注目中心："瞧见没有，阿嚏，因为我老猪，人类都戴起了口罩。阿嚏，平日里吃我们的肉，熬我们的骨头汤，还剥了我们的皮当鞋穿。哼哼，你们也有今天！"

老牛哞哞两声，不以为然地说："你别高兴得太早。几年前，我们被人类宰杀了四百多万兄弟姐妹呢。天下本无事，我吃我的草，你吃我的肉。可人类偏偏自作聪明，一会儿放莫扎特给我们听，一会儿给我们灌啤酒，又在饲料里放添加剂，这东西下肚，日积月累，脑子便坏了。哼，叫我们疯牛，我看是疯人作孽。"

鸡婆婆闻言不高兴了，因为禽流感暴发时，整舍整棚的鸡被屠宰，还殃及整塘整塘的鸭子兄弟，数目无计，牺牲远非牛群可比；而据人类自己发表的数字，死于禽流感的人虽分属十几个国家，毕竟不满三百。这不成比例的生灵殒灭，不但使鸡婆婆忿忿不平，而且萌生了歹毒的报复念头："等着吧，哪天我们身上的'流感 A 病毒'畸变，跟人体病毒来个适应性的零距离接触，有好看的。"

老猪一半出于同情，一半也是显摆，因说："阿嚏，鸡阿姨啊，不要难过，复仇有我们。这不，小试身手，墨西哥一国已经死人一百开外啦？阿嚏，那儿一个当官的还在怪中国把疫病传了过去，到处检疫严防，都不敢来往走动了，说不定我们还能把‘全球化’戳几个窟窿，玩玩国际关系，让人类去相互猜忌，哈哈……”

李媛绘

老牛咕哝一声：“怪不得都说猪比人聪敏。看来，你们不会像当年闹‘非典’时的果子狸那么惨。”

老猪更得意了：“知道吗？阿嚏！我们这次发飙可不比寻常。听说过1918年的大流感吗？都闹进北极圈和太平洋去了，据说死人近亿。阿嚏，告诉你们一个秘密，这次的流感病毒HIN1同1918年那次的病毒一模一样。”

鸡婆婆说：“这人类是越活越没样子了。糟蹋环境、破坏生态、浪费资源不说，贪赃枉法，权钱交易，金融崩盘，诈骗横行，自定高薪，滥发钞票,告密光荣,见死不救,随地吐痰。昨天我接到天上打来电话,说是还要弄出几场‘马流感’、‘狗流感’、‘猫流感’之类更凶险的时疫来警醒人类呢。”

(原载2009年5月10日《东方早报》)

之　二

那日,我去采访。老牛因见我写过它们的对话,状甚友好。

“可惜啊,”又是哞哞两声之后说道,“我们说的好些话,你都漏写了呢。”

“譬如?”

“我们不是说过实验室里正日夜开工研制疫苗吗?那年,你们惯称的那个发达国家不是手脚奇快,一下子发明成功?可注射进去,一百个人当中,风瘫一个,这就叫副作用。再说,一场时疫从夏天首发,到秋天袭来第二波,势头往往更加凶猛。那病毒也狡猾,善于畸变。疫苗研制总不能老在后面跟着吧,没等派上用场,就又淘汰。”

“牛兄,你倒挺会替人着想。想当年,我读大学那功夫,邯郸路上常见牛群被人赶着走过,往屠宰场去。你们走一路,屙一路,五角场一带生产队的农民据说都把你们的粪便当个宝。学校里有位物理学教授觉着好玩,说了句笑话:倘使火星上有生物,拿架望远镜一望,准以为是个‘老牛大游行’的奇景呐。不料后来给打成右派。我说你们哪来那么多的排泄物啊?”

“这你就不懂了吧?我们打老远从内蒙古直立着挤货车来到大上海,到了大场站偏不给下,一定要开到江湾,再 death-march(想不到老牛还懂英文,还会把名词当动词用)回大场去。据说是嫌我们脏,别破坏了市容。憋的时间越长,大小便自然越多。”

“邯郸路一景如今咋就见不到了？”

“人啊，人，你们多精怪呵，说是走过长路的牛掉膘。现在的办法是下了火车，用木板一隔，辟出条‘牛道’，一头头通过，免得大家交头接耳。不知道咱们牛身上有没有肾上腺素，反正走近你们的‘杀牛公司’，大家体内都有条件反射，据说都会分泌一种有害的毒素。这不，如今你们的击颅大锤不到最后一刻不亮出来了。让我们到站以后，先休息一两天，让大家放松，不知死之将至。大限一到，牛体还没反应过来，毒素没来得及分泌，乘你不备，猛地给你的天灵盖来上一锤。”

“牛兄不要难过，你们比猪兄猪弟的待遇总要好些吧？前些年街上还跑着装猪猡的大卡车，那一路哼哼哧哧再加不时的尖嚎，听着可凄惨呢，叫人想起丰子恺老先生的漫画‘妈妈不要走’，虽说当年他画的是羊。”

“猪可聪敏了。这哪儿是哀嚎？它们是在诅咒你们啊。什么难听的话都让它们说尽了。有的是学着你们的样，在唱戏呢：‘咚咚呛，二十年后又是一条好汉！’”

“牛兄啊，做人也不易。就说上次写你们对话的那篇小文吧，差一点就给毙了！”

“怎么会呢？老牛这几天闲来无事，出于对‘改造身体’的好奇，在看一本东洋小说，写的尽是裂舌啊，文身啊，性虐啊，细节一点不落，也不见有人去毙了它。这人怎么以作践自己的身体为乐？莫非这就是‘万物的灵长’？”

本想给老牛讲讲啥是所谓的“纯文学”，还有在西方，“身体穿刺”如何曾是时髦——穿个鼻环特像老牛——现已渐入衰迟等等，因料定都是对它弹琴，遂止。

我嘿然。

（原载 2009 年 5 月 24 日《东方早报》）

之　三

第二个采访对象是鸡婆婆。

她先给我讲了一个故事，那是上次2003年之后禽流感暴发时的一件真事。说的是土耳其有个年仅八岁的小姑娘深爱小动物，玩伴全是小狗和小猫，尤其钟爱家里一窝毛茸茸、黄灿灿的鸡雏。一天，鸡雏死了，小姑娘哭着抱着亲吻那已经变了色的喙和羽，结果自己染病，不几日，一个夜晚，跟着小玩伴去了。父母哭她鲁莽，她却被天使接去，那境界空山月明，清旷无尘，多好！

“土耳其有‘鸡城’，‘鸡城’门口矗立着高达四米的‘鸡雕’，”鸡婆婆告诉我，“可那儿的人不给这小女孩封圣树碑。这才由我递上提案，牛兄、猪弟联署附议，经‘动物庄园’中央执行委员会投票通过，在这儿立了个‘鸡之友苏梅娅（土耳其女孩名）牌位’，一会儿带你去看看。”

“这种H5N1病毒袭来时，”鸡婆接着说，“我们头颅肿得像笆斗，一双细腿染红，只有等死。哪有什么动物医院可去治疗？你们人类为防传染，还对我们实行灭绝性大屠杀，管你瘟或不瘟。1997年在香港，三天之内就杀了我们一百五十万啊。”

“人类实在也是无奈。”我说。

“你们都是忽悠大王，同类间一边高唱‘伙伴关系’，一边忙着你灭我，我亡你；对动物也这样：一边杀鸡，一边还假惺惺给鸡做道场。日本九州地方一个高官说得最妙：‘我们要对鸡说抱歉，由于瘟疫蔓延，我们不得不将它们大批扑杀。我们还要对鸡表示感激，因为它们为我们提供了享之不尽的美味。我不知道鸡是如何看待这些事情的，但是我认为人类应该对这些生灵有所表示。’你们是怎么表示的？”

我提到前几年在柏林电影节获奖的短片《来份鸡肉》，说看得很不是滋味。鸡婆反驳：“哦，那还不是针对你们自己作孽造成的贫富不均？富人吃鸡肉留下多少泔脚，穷人捡回嚼鸡骨。观众中有谁会看着下单入厨，鸡坠油锅而唱起‘你的欢笑带出我的眼泪’？”

正谈着只见那厢拱着嗅着地面、跨着碎步走来老猪。等到把头扬起，竟是一头眉开眼笑的快乐猪，令人不由想起奥威尔“所有动物都享平等，有些动物有更多平等”的名言。老猪眯起小眼睛说：“知道吗？从本年4月30日起，猪在全球大平反了，流感正式改名为‘甲型H1N1流感’。这次WHO那位香港老太真积了德，这称呼一改，少杀多少头猪啊。”

我向猪表示祝贺。

“本来嘛，十到五十年发生一次流感大暴发已是规律；即使流感暴发，瑞士人不是利用你们的八角茴香研制了达菲特效药了吗？记得我们的猪哲说过：‘恐慌源自脆弱’，有些地球人风一吹草一动就怕，许是自觉特别脆弱的缘故吧？”

（原载2009年5月31日《东方早报》）

之　四

昨晚在人类一家饭店看到惊心动魄的一幕，一道叫做“活蛇咬活鸡”的招牌大菜是如何真实制作的。在人类众目睽睽之下，那蛇似乎并不愿意表演，第一条被撩拨半天，也不攻击，于是只好换上第二条。这第二条眼镜蛇同样被拍打怂恿好一阵子，才两腮鼓气，头部膨胀，终于懒洋洋上去咬鸡一口，全无平时电掣般的桀逆放恣。过后蛇头即被剪下，和死鸡一起送进厨房。据说蛇毒经高温处理即成上好的高蛋白，卫生部门专家对于如此做菜，只表示“不规范”、“不应提倡”而已。在饭庄食客的叫好声中，我看得胆战心惊，落荒而逃，一头钻进动物庄园。

我把所见所闻告诉了一只正在雄赳赳踱步的公鸡,不料它对同类之伤全不上心,反而教诲起我来:“有啥稀奇?见过烤全猪吗?见过蒸螃蟹吗?见过吃猴脑吗?见过活剥袋鼠皮制鞋吗?”

我试图以人类间也自相残杀的事实,来说服自己接受人类对动物的残忍。不料公鸡嗤笑我迂腐:“人间厮杀属于‘人与社会’范畴,虐杀动物属于‘人与自然’范畴。全然不同的两码事。凡属前者,规范、戒条、律法、禁区一应俱全,人都紧紧盯着,不得胡来。至于‘人与自然’,前些年闹‘非典’时,开始还有禁区,后来发现这事毕竟不属‘人与社会’范畴,死人再多,都可归咎果子狸闹腾,而处理好了,反可有利‘人与社会’的稳定,于是大可放松,禁区不妨暂撤。后来的大地震也好,眼下的甲流感也罢,都证明这一点。‘蛇咬鸡’和你们人类历史上早年的逗熊、斗鸡、猎狐一样,足证人在自己可控小范围内横行无忌已成积习,也不必顾忌谁会因此给钉上耻辱柱,弄出份劳什子白皮书甚至联合国安理会决议什么的。”

看着一副王者派头的大公鸡,我有些不服。“就拿蟋蟀来说,”我反驳,“与其被你大公鸡一口啄食下肚,人类捕来趋之互斗,从中取乐牟利,胜者喜跃抃舞,最后虽也总是一死,但那可算死有所值了。”

“什么话!?”公鸡怒了,“万物以自然食物链生存,唯独人类自作聪敏,要扭曲甚至打碎它。以德国佬施本格勒式‘人定胜天’的实用主义,挑战造化的自然规律,这是你们人类恣意掠夺宇宙资源的一贯伎俩。造化的报复已经开始了。谓予不信,去看看那层出不穷的矿难吧。连小虫也不放过,可以用来赌博赚钱,你说你们已经堕落到什么地步!”

我想起,虽然不赌,自己儿时也曾是个捕斗蟋蟀的好手,不觉赧然。时届暮年,每当溽暑,还要买来蝈蝈,囚在笼子里听它们声嘶力竭地鸣叫,窃取所谓的野趣,直至虫儿衰竭而死。今夏再不做这样的事了。

回头看那骄傲的公鸡，不禁想起莎士比亚说的："那报晓的雄鸡用它高亢的啼声，唤醒白昼之神，驱赶漫游的有罪死魂灵。"特别是圣诞的前几天，传说西方的公鸡都会彻夜啼鸣，于是，"星星不再以毒光射人，妖巫的符咒也会失去魔力"。

（原载2009年6月7日《东方早报》）

之　五

"不得了啦，"狗弟弟歇斯底里大发作，边跑边叫，引得庄园里的动物们都围上前来探看究竟，"人类大开杀戒了！有的说我们传播狂犬病，要创建'全国第一无狗县'，一周内宰狗两万多；又有消息说，某地某位领导在河边散步时给狗咬了，恼羞成怒，对狗下了'必杀令'。刚刚又听说，在口口声声文明至上的大城市，我们一个黄毛同类被穿官衣的吊在树上当众暴打致死，死后还剥皮吃肉。"

"瞎恐慌，"我把狗弟弟叫到一边，跟它说了陕西汉中屠狗只限于流浪狗和病犬的事，转述了当地政府辟谣的内容。至于黑河那边，"必杀令"已经撤销，"打狗队"已经解散。暴打黄毛致死的官衣，据说是出于迷信，已受到严厉批评，有无下文，不知。

"不得了，不得了，"狗弟弟还是一个劲儿地嚎叫，双目发直，口角流涎，貌似它也得了狂犬症，"你们自己说死于狂犬病的总共不过七八人，这就要两万条狗命去抵偿，这人狗还怎么和谐相处？大巴燃烧，山体崩塌，矿井埋人，死伤远不止七八，是不是也要我们去抵命啊？说到流浪犬，你去过意大利庞贝遗址吗？那儿多的是野狗。说不定都是火山喷发后幸存狗繁衍的后代。怎不见狂犬病流行啊？你们学校不是多流浪猫吗，据说都是被毕业离校学生遗弃的，不是一样自成群落，吃得体胖肚圆，自称'解放猫'吗？也没听说闹出什么咬人致病的事来。”

我承认有些地方对狂犬病反应过度。

“这还不是最可怕的，”狗弟弟说，“事发后网上有不少人为屠狗叫好，把养宠物的一族骂个‘我们的血’喷头，好像宠畜的都是无良有闲阶级，借机宣泄仇富心理。还说最佳屠狗时节是冬季，活杀活吃，狗肉滋补，下肚还可御寒。我好像听见人类已在那儿磨刀霍霍，看到他们全像得了狂犬病，露出了獠牙。”

我试图对狗弟弟说说华夷“狗观”的不同。我们的确骂人“猪狗不如”、“狗仗人势”、“狗眼看人低”、“资本家的乏走狗”等等，英文里却说“爱我，也爱我的狗”。

狗弟弟不以为然，反驳说：“可是不管中文还是英文，你们骂人时都说‘狗娘养的’！关键在于对生灵的尊重。听说对狄更斯的小说《艰难时世》，你们的安迪公子觉得理过其词，干巴巴的，读不下去。替我带句话去，还是希望他读读马戏团演员瞿普先生和他的爱犬‘飞腿’的故事。瞿先生把狗打得遍体鳞伤后流下一脸自责的热泪，狗儿却不计前嫌，爬上膝头为他舔去泪水！到底是条名叫‘飞腿’的狗啊，跟诺亚方舟里的动物同名，不管方舟在亚拉腊山巅，还是黑海海底，毕竟是六百岁的义人奉上帝之命建的啊。”

我给它说了一件洋县的真事：一条有证又有疫苗注射记录的金毛犬在家被乱棍打死，狗主老农始而跪地为狗求饶，见狗既死，转过身来哭狗。“这不比瞿先生和‘飞腿’的故事更感人吗？”我问。人和狗毕竟是会和谐相处的。

狗弟弟消息灵通，又说国际爱护动物基金会亚洲区的总代表在接受记者采访时，抗议屠狗。我却担心那人不知是啥背景，该不会是海外敌对势力来离间人狗和谐吧。

（原载2009年6月14日《东方早报》）

之　六

照片怵目惊心，河里漂浮着狗尸，成千上万的蛆，丑恶地扭动着身子形成白花花一片，“其欲逐逐”。不会是电脑合成的作品吧？我赶往动物庄园去求证于消息灵通的狗弟弟。

“这哪有假？”狗弟弟泪水涟涟，“动物庄园中心计算机正在统计确数，到今天上午十一点三十五分，河上浮尸已经过百。知道吗？那里杀一条狗可得五十至一百元的奖金，于是‘天下熙熙，皆为利来；天下攘攘，皆为利往’。宰杀以后，怎样处理遗体，就没人关注了，多数是随手往河里一丢，朝垃圾桶里一塞，听任腐烂。‘狗粉’虽多，也没见哪个富户站出来悬赏，譬如说掩埋一尸，大洋百块。我们庄园已开过发布会，问记者：‘你有孩子吗？如有孩子，也有爱心，为狗建一义冢，发奖章一枚，并报天上。’”

“这狗义冢可建不得，要占去多少面积的土地？弄得不好，还会像美国斯蒂芬·金先生写的《动物墓场》那样闹鬼。人类坟墓占地靡费已经是个大问题。没看见前不久有人看中了高级住宅区里的休闲绿地，自说自话，咪哩吗啦吹打着，来此下葬死者？你们的动物庄园能够存在至今，已是奇迹，说不定明天就勒令拆迁呢。”

老猪头这时走来，听见我们的对话后，插嘴评论道：“哼，你们人类对骂时都爱说‘你猪脑子啊？’其实猪脑比人脑管用。我们总不会‘宁可错杀一千，决不放过一个’地聚歼动物；即使杀了，更不会暴尸露天，让可能存在的传染病菌，加速散播，而遗尸江河，污染水源这类的蠢举，唯有人脑想得出来。”

我说我担心因为饮用了污染水会诱发瘟疫。“那又怎么样？”老猪头问，态度变得非常残忍。“你们不是抱怨地球‘又热，又挤，又平’吗？瘟疫暴发，正好减少些人口。我们的猪口、犬口、鸡口等等可是每天都在剧减，有的差不多快灭种了。这时，你们又假惺惺跳出来大谈保护濒危物种。哪一天要是发现'熊猫流感',看你们咋办?依我看,你们还是选择杀熊猫,以人为本嘛。"

狗弟弟劝我:"瘟疫这事可胡乱说不得,不然你会成为易卜生笔下的斯岛克曼医生——国民公敌。大家爱讲'绿色革命',大米、面粉、奶粉、火腿、月饼、豆芽、泡菜等等,甚至还有药品,你们一面掺假牟利,一面大肆宣传这也'绿色',那也'绿色'。我看你得随俗多写点'绿色'文章才是。"

我无语。

(原载 2009 年 6 月 21 日《东方早报》)

之 七

这天与动物们讨论庄园历史。出于好奇,我问"雪球"的下落。

"雪球"者,推翻琼斯先生曼诺庄园里人的统治的动物首领之一,曾与另一猪"拿破仑"(出于可以理解的原因,法国人最初翻译《动物庄园》时曾给它改名为"恺撒")齐名。因为"一国不能有两主","拿破仑"派遣警犬队追杀,驱逐"雪球",最后不知所终——虽说后来拍摄的动画片中暗示它已被杀无误。

老猪头说作家乔治·奥威尔是受了别有用心的"拿破仑"的蒙蔽,我又轻信奥氏而不明真相:"'雪球'这样足智多谋的聪敏猪,岂能死于几条'拿破仑'从狗妈妈那儿偷来豢养的小崽子?'雪球'逃亡啦!跑到外面在人间和畜群中朝餐草根,暮食树皮,几经沉浮,见了世面,受尽历练,几年后又回来了,隐姓埋名,繁衍后代,居然活了十八岁,几乎是野猪和家猪平均年龄相加除以二的最高值。"

鸡婆婆补充说:"老话说:春种一粒粟,秋收万颗籽。今天动物庄园中央执行委员会中，‘雪球’的后代就占了好几席。昨天，‘雪球’的一位曾重孙还就治疗甲流感，上电视演讲，说是欧美热衷研制疫苗，亚洲人不妨试试桑叶、菊花、薄荷、大蒜疗法，要不用韩国泡菜煮汤；再不行，可来个东西合璧，试试八角茴香配雪碧的方法。瞧，多有才啊！”

老牛似乎不太爱听大家一味把猪说得花好稻好，哞哞两声：“别忘了，暴君‘拿破仑’也是巴克夏猪，被它提拔起来的矮胖‘尖嚎猪’也是一路货。乱改庄园宪法，原来的戒条是不让喝酒的，偏偏改成不要‘喝酒过分’；明明是四条腿的，偏要学人两腿行走，还要睡人的眠床。倒是奇蹄类里多出类拔萃的动物：包科斯老马鞠躬尽瘁；母马克罗佛保护弱小；老驴班吉明洞察毫发。班驴子不但活得最长，动画片里还让它领导第二次革命呢。今天的中央执行委员会中幸亏有了班驴子的后代，这庄园里才有公平和公正。”

眼看猪牛拌起嘴来，鸡婆婆忙打圆场：“两位可都是偶蹄类的，同根相煎可不好。再说了，执行委员会里‘雪球’之后和‘班驴’之后切切磋磋，智能谋，力能任，民生和民主兼管，把个庄园治理得井井有条，人不敢犯，有什么好抱怨的？想想我们鸡啊，鸭啊，狗啊，羊啊，在委员会里不都没突胸目、雁形目、犬科的代表吗？”

“你们还要代表权？”老猪和老牛同时怒吼。老猪更加振振有词：“在‘拿破仑’治下，就是你们的蛋，还有你老牛的乳，喂肥了统治者。实在不甘心的鸡，至多把自己下的蛋啄碎罢了。起初乱嚷嚷‘四条腿好，两条腿坏’，后来见猪学人走路，鼓吹‘四条腿好，两条腿更好’的，不是羊吗？至于狗么，一群忘了本的‘拿破仑’畜牲而已。”

“怎么这样说话呢？难道有蹄类就高出其他动物一头？”鸡婆婆发怒了。“日本专家考证，从DNA分析，有蹄类的马和蝙蝠还是近亲呢。最近，蝙蝠要求加入动物庄园的申请不是被否决了吗？你们俩不也投了反对票？……”

“凡有生灵，就要争斗，即使在理想国也不例外。”离开庄园时，我这样想着。

（原载2009年7月19日《东方早报》）

之　八

动物庄园中央执行委员会选定在瀑布城开会，邀我列席旁听。瀑布城在瀑布山顶，委员们由劳役动物们利用人类的手摇脚踏原理，由索道送上山顶。已有十八猪龄、年高德劭的委员长（“雪球”之后一员）是坐着轿式滑橇拖上去的，拖橇的由警犬班十条彪悍的伯尔尼高山狗、瑞士大山狗和纽芬兰黑狗混编而成，都是当年“拿破仑”行刑队成员之后。据说为使橇行平稳，狗儿们训练了一年。

我是客人，给安排在一处野猪头草屋客栈，饭管饱，酒管够；除此之外，散步由一头野猪引路兼作保镖。走出客栈几步，只见山木益稠，蝉声益清，白云高屯，叠嶂毕露，真是个消暑佳处。不远处的青瓦宾馆原是人类中的王侯避暑行宫，此刻动物委员们正在嬉闹宴饮，吭吭、汪汪、哞哞、咯咯之声不绝于耳。听随行的野猪说，不管奇蹄还是偶蹄还是长爪子的，现在都学会了人划拳罚酒那一套，只不过用叫声来代替手指运动罢了。

山早已被封，满山只见乌鸦。野猪指给我看：“这是‘直升机’，这是‘战斗机’，这是‘歼击机’。”原来，它们都是“糖山”摩西乌鸦之后。摩西乌鸦曾靠说教，劝喻庄园里的动物安命驯顺向善，不然只有死后去那谁也没见过的“糖山”。时过境迁，后裔早就撇弃了祖宗，把“摩西”的名字翻个个儿，变成了“希魔”，个个把喙琢磨得似尖刀一般，尚武好斗，故而被派来守山。

之所以择址瀑布城，据说是因为今次的议题是水。动物庄园为自建风车闹过事，此后便向来缺水，一直靠弗莱德里克和匹尔金吞两处的人类庄园支持。作为万物之灵的人有什么善类！？弗先生狠刻毒辣，匹先生工于心计，两人一合计，决定联手染指庄园水务。委员会开会就是研究对策。

"水是庄园的命脉，"委员长主持会议并作开场白，"现在全球缺水，据统计，缺水的人类已达十亿，再过四十年，还要翻一倍。另一方面，科学研究证明水的功用无穷，一个名叫F.巴特曼的美国博士说，一天喝二至三升的水，分多次喝而不是等到口渴时才喝，心脏病、糖尿病、白血病等都可治愈，甚至对预防最近发生在中国青海的肺鼠疫也有作用。他的著作《水是最好的药》和《水这样喝能治病》，已被翻译成十六种语言，有人还把前一部与《圣经》相提并论。我们需要水，我们急需水！"

水务委员接着解释"水务"二字的涵义，说动物们处于天然散养状态时，各自自然取水，随地溲溺，供水和排污都不成其为问题。自从建起庄园，划定地界，凡事都学人类，要以蛋类、乳品、皮毛等购买或以徭役充抵水源提供，这才发生水比油贵的问题。前几天，一只袋鼠跟一条母牛为了抢水就发生过斗殴。为此，水务委员提议，解散庄园，重返森林。

"怎么可以！"委员长训斥道，"自从1945年乔治·奥威尔先生建起这个庄园，苍黄翻覆，好不容易历经六十四个年头积累起这点家当，庄园还要一统丰饶，天长地老，万岁万万岁。你不设法与大家共赴时艰，主张散伙，是何居心？来狗！——（它当然不呼'来人'）——把它给我逐下山去。"

经济委员就此兼任水务委员。他介绍"外资"弗先生和匹先生介入动物庄园水务的详情，虽也提到两人在三十至五十年间控股百分之五十以上的蛮横要求以及如此一来水费必定大涨的前景，委员长连称"善哉，善哉"，同时甩下一句狠话："不能因为有些人喝不起水，就不提高水价。"众皆嘿然。

（原载2009年8月16日《东方早报》）

之　九

那天，偷听到牛大哥、狗弟弟、鸡婆婆和老猪头的对话，我觉得动物说人，时有新意。

它们是在议论人类高考语文卷里考生写下的雷人语句："进入高三，我就过上了'起的比鸡早，睡得比狗晚，吃的比猪差，干得比牛多'的日子。"

老猪头爱咬文嚼字，说这考生用"的"和"得"显然经过缜思，大致不错。"'吃的'二字权且算是名词，'起的'就不对了吧？叫我老猪写，肯定写作'起得'。这儿应扣一分。"

牛大哥说："抠什么字眼？咱看内容。哼，说干得比俺老牛多，还'确实'呢，鬼才信呐。俺送头儿去卡拉OK拉完车，急急去拖'牛转翻车'汲水，一干就是十几个小时。以负重论，一天好几吨不在话下，真像另一句高考答卷妙语说的那样，'载不动，许多愁，恰似一江春水向东流'。（李清照和李煜男女声混合唱？——笔者注）都说现在童肩上的书包沉重，拿一百个来压俺老牛肩上试试，还不是小菜一碟？以单调论，甩尾巴赶牛虻，对俺老牛来说，就算一乐啦，哪有什么'奥特曼'之类的调剂？学生娃不就做做xyz，背背英语单词什么的，俺老牛转圈汲水无聊得慌，也早就背出不少了。不信考考你：啥叫water wheel，windmill，hydropower？"

鸡婆婆也忿忿不平："我老公每天一早四点打鸣，夏季有时更早，那是因为户外树上'百家争鸣'开始——现在方始懂得有些人为什么那么讨厌'百家争鸣'了。渎扰清眠嘛——要是那高某人的'红色经典'《半夜鸡叫》所写全是事实,打鸣还要更早。读书郎的睡觉时间,根据妇联转述国家规定,小学生每天十小时,初中学生九小时,高中学生八小时。所谓'起得比鸡早'是临考抱佛脚吧,要不就是在电脑上跟相好QQ欲罢不能。指望他/她们长年天天如此,不就个个从人变鸡了?"

老猪头言辞激烈:"'吃的比猪差'?这些小王子、小公主在家锦衣玉食不算,成天出入什么麦当劳、肯德基、必胜客,被西方的各种'亡我'食物,搞成矮胖怪物,不到十岁必须开始减肥了。在咱这庄园,除了当年的'拿破仑'、'尖嚎猪'、在位时的'雪球',还有今天的委员长这些贵族猪,我们草根猪吃什么,娃儿们知道吗?我来出道题,可以列入高考卷:什么叫水浮莲?并评其用途及危害。且不管水浮莲的学名叫什么,今天,这东西淤塞河道,破坏环境,是世界十大害草之一。可我们当年都是抢着挤着,到塘边去争吃那绿油油的叶子,吃得肚圆腹胀,下行之气不断,最后浮肿而死。连人类那时也把水浮莲当作不要粮票的救急食物。他们吃水浮莲做的所谓包子,用小球藻做人造肉,煮蕉树皮、木瓜树头,搁上点辣椒,就算是上等佳肴了。"

动物们还在接着议论高考答卷中的雷人语句,我这边不禁陷入了沉思。教育逼人帖括应制,好名贪得,所以会悬梁刺股。还是旁观者清。你看诸动物随遇而安,自适之极,令我衷心窃慕。曾听一小朋友说,来生愿投胎做只小鸟,最好是属稀有物种而归入国际保护级的,可以尽享林壑之乐,可见苦读的学子也与我有同感。

(原载2009年8月23日《东方早报》)

之　十

这几天,人间老是有超速或酒后驾车撞死人的新闻,孰料动物庄园也被惊动,对此议论纷纷。

“车从来不是个好东西,”老牛摆出一副博古通今的样子,没好气地说,“人力车废了一阵,随着工人大批下岗要自谋生路,又卷土重来。畜力车可从没废止,从北美仿古景点到孔夫子老宅,人都不肯挪动双腿,安步当车,偏要坐上马车来一番复古体验。庄园头头也非要我老牛驾辕拉车树权威,充老大。人类发明了火车、电车、汽车,便也有了脱轨、接电杆‘翘辫子’、冲撞等各种各样的事故。人生性懒惰,加上会‘作’,所谓的进步就逼着自己付出代价。现在到处怂人买车,还有‘以旧换新’的招数。再往后,人腿说不定会退化成细细的麻秆,再也不能直立,跟我们一样,非四肢着地爬行不可。”

“你懂什么?”老猪头今天变成了“哲学猪”,讲过一大通是非、优劣、进退之类的辩证法以后,又转到天文:“知道啥叫地球磁变?地球绕太阳,太阳系绕银河系,波浪式的运行都有周期。目前的周期据说到 2010 年之后就要结束,迎来新周期。每逢这时,地球磁场变弱,保护地球的磁力圈破了个大洞,所以天灾不断,瘟疫流行。人体也有磁场,受地球磁场影响,相应弱化,所以行为失去准心,道德沦丧。车撞人算什么?驾车人的大脑和手脚协调出了点毛病而已。没看见高科技指挥的潜艇、地铁在海底和地下也会相撞,今年七个月就发生了九起空难。你说这些全是巧合?……”

鸡婆忙不迭打断他,而且显得比老猪头更哲学:“扯远了吧?庸俗的地球磁变论,这能解释飙车杀人?用天文来解释社会问题是典型的形而上学。本老太闲来无事,成天网游,见闻多,阅世深,宁可相信‘制度决定说’。”

老猪头不依了:“俺老猪话还没说完,你打什么岔?地球磁变是外因,‘本恶论’才是内因,就是荀子说的‘人之初,性本恶’或犹太教的原罪说。都说人的动物性加上社会性,人就变得比我们动物优越。殊不知,这两重特性相加,人变得比动物更邪恶。那是谁说的?黑格尔吧：'人们以为当他们说人性本善时，是说出了一种伟大的思想。但他们忘记了：当他们说人性本恶时，他们是说出了一种伟大得多的思想。'"

我真有那么恶吗？我一边走开，一边这么想。

一年之后，我重返动物庄园，不料动物们已经散伙，我见到的只是蒿草抵膝的荒园一座。动物们想是摆脱了制度的约束，回归自然去了。它们在本身的兽性之外，尝试并实验过人的社会性，结果失望加失败，终于选择了恢复本真。

草木萋迷，低空云断，我怀念动物们。

（原载2009年8月30日《东方早报》）

知道分子为什么不可以穿睡衣上街?

外出的几天一晃而过,星期五下午回到上海。

回来第一感受,空气真差!算是晴天,可就是雾蒙蒙的,远处的房子都看不清楚。浦东还因为迎接世博被挖得一塌糊涂,灰天灰地。这和前几天秋光明媚的纽约,形成了鲜明的对比。

他们说,中国人现在到美国来,都说,美国好土啊!在物质方面,大城市的中国人近来容易有一种后来居上的优越感。可是,我还是喜欢纽约造的房子,牢固敦实,有传统感,细节也很讲究,很少使用造成光污染的玻璃,更不像一个模子里捣出来的。陆家嘴的那么多高楼,亮闪闪的,好像未来世界,我担心土地要被压到海底下去了。

新闻里说,世博会期间,禁止上海人穿睡衣上街。穿睡衣上街,把隐私拿到公众场合展览,确实不妥不雅,我一向如此认为。老外问到我为什么,我总是窘得无以回答。但我又向来反对偏见固化(stereotyping),而且笼统说上海人穿睡衣上街,显然是以偏概全,不公平。

但是,又想请问:穿睡衣上街犯了哪条法?又不是裸奔(裸奔也未必犯法)。假使真的穿睡衣上街,难道要被拘留吗?世博期间不准穿,是怕给外国人看到,觉得丢人吗?

穿不穿睡衣上街是个人的自由,谁也管不着。所以如果世博期间,上海人民可以大大方方走上街头开个 pajama party(睡衣派对),那倒是“一道亮丽的风景线”呢。

(原载2009年11月3日《云南信息报》,有删节)

快递——新的“骚扰源”

快递，顾名思义，应该是迅速又便捷的投递。

但是，我现在一听到快递，有种莫名的恐惧。可能不少朋友与我有同感。

先说两件真事：其一，某出版社要召开一次座谈会，邀我参加，来过电话后安排原已舒齐。我还特别在电话上告诉对方，不必再花钱去买什么花里胡哨的请柬发来。然而，现代人做事自有规矩。对方不但将花里胡哨坚持到底，而且把请柬交由快递送上门来。那日下午 1:30，老夫午睡正酣，电话铃声大作，惊梦一听，原来是快递核对地址，并提前五个多小时，预告当晚 7 点送到。那正是我铁定散步的时辰，无奈只好请钟点工胖阿姨滞后一点去下一个东家处服务，在此企足而待。等我散步回来，快递并未如约送达，阿姨似已颇有嗔意。7 点不来，我只好不闭“洞门”（我自嘲居处为“散仙洞”）续等。直到近 8 点，送信人始姗姗迟来。本来都已说好的事，何用请柬，何需这慢吞吞的快递？心里有火，开始想拒收，后见对方是位外来工，说不定除快递之外，还做着其他的营生揾钱，啰唣了几句之后也便罢了，不料对方火气更大，怒目金刚，与我似有睚眦之隙似的。

其二，孙辈索中国龙明信片和玩具，由小友代我从网上购得，说是我只需在洞内坐等快递上门。这次定购的物事共五件，麻烦可就相应增大：没完没了的手机电话加短信。一会儿问 A 商品递到没有，一会儿说 B 商品是否已经签收；再隔片刻，有人恶狠狠责问，上门按铃,何以无人应答——这纯粹是讹诈兼嫁祸,因我整日不敢出洞。如此拉锯通讯一天半之后,五件小东西始陆续送达。地方难找,路上塞车,联络失误,快递员莫不骂骂咧咧而去。

此前,还收到过错件;有的则拖拖拉拉,从徐家汇到杨浦,走了两天半才送到,比 6 分钱的“蜗邮”还慢。不去说它了。

上海的建设有赖于 1 800 万之众的外来务工同胞,自问对他们从不歧视。保姆也好,手机小摊主和他的儿子也罢,我都引以为友,决不主张他们“团成一团,以一种比较圆润的方式离开上海”。只是干一行有一行的规矩,快递业讲究速度、效率和准确性,雇主似须给从业者一点最起码的培训,更不能剥削人家,弄得他们个个态度生硬,东西递到,甩下一张冷脸子而去,仿佛我欠了他们多少钱似的。

2010 年 1 月 29 日

介绍《换局》

刚读完两名美国记者写的一本畅销书《换局》(*Game Change*, 2010 年哈珀/柯林斯出版),把 2008 年美国大选中鲜为人知的内幕揭露得淋漓尽致。原以为大选那年过程中,美国媒体穷追猛打,跟踪爆料,已无新鲜内幕可写;更何况新一届政府上台逾年,民众的注意力都已转向医疗、失业、反恐等问题,对虽是近事毕竟已成历史的话题定是兴趣渐衰。谁知这本书竟会高踞 2010 年 1 月 31 日《纽约时报》硬面非虚构类畅销书排行榜的第一位。

读完此书最强烈的感觉是,在大众传媒显微镜式的全神贯注之下,公众人物的人格缺失暴露无遗,这会有助于读者进一步读懂人性。就拿奥巴马来说,2006 年 1 月 22 日,在"会见报界"的节目上,曾斩钉截铁声称自己一定做满任期 6 年的参议员,绝不旁顾。"这么说,你不会在 2008 年竞选总统或副总统?"访员问。"我不会的,"奥巴马言之凿凿。事后,一位助理问:"你要是改变自己的决定呢?""决定是随时可以改变的,"奥巴马不假思索地回答。身居高位的政治家,碰到开会"马拉松"议事,听得实在腻烦了,会像小学生一样做怪脸,骂脏话,给旁座递条子:"开枪打死我吧。"希拉里为自己《亲历历史》一书旅行签名,尝到了被粉丝追捧的甜头,暗暗下决心竞选总统,可是丈夫比尔 · 克林顿绯闻又起,敌手还要为此开电话会议,于是只好着力清理自己的竞选班子,控制事态,但就是没法控制比尔的"利比多"。更不堪的是 2004 年民主党副总统候选人、2008 年总统候选人的原北卡参议员约翰·爱德华兹,原来是个包“二奶”的角色,被媒体揭发之后,先是抵赖,后又指使手下替自己“顶杠”,不料“二奶”不干了,河东狮吼了,手下反水了(也要写书,下月出版),最后只有掩面而退。共和党那边,麦凯恩一样有品德问题,媒体要拍个夫妇俩比较热络的镜头,非浪费大量胶片不可。他捧出个阿拉斯加州的女州长佩琳来做竞选伙伴,女州长说是在阿拉斯加可以看到俄罗斯,弄得选民哭笑不得。本书介绍,对佩琳的弱点,其实麦凯恩了如指掌,但是一边以她吸引攻击火力,使麦本人压力减轻,同时女州长自有她火一般的激情魅力,而且揽财有方,这才将她拉入团队。为政治而扭曲人格的许多细节,如克林顿夫妇在安桂拉海滩的谈话,如爱德华兹夫人大闹机场停车场一幕,书中都有精彩的描述。

写书的两名记者叫 John Heilemann 和 Mark Halperin。人家倒是颇有一点无冕之王的做派。

2010 年 2 月 1 日

Eddie

This writing may not befit the occasion, this being the turn of years. But I feel obliged to tell the story of a death before the year expires.

When the final big C diagnosis came in, we knew Eddie's days were numbered. He was put on steroids by the vet. The efficacy showed: he started to bark again after a silence of weeks. (How many times we used to hear "Eddie, shut up!" — a shouted signature command at Pulley Court.) When we skyped, if he heard his name paged through the microphone, he flicked an ear, and would scramble to his feet and look around inquiringly.

Then deterioration day by day. In deepening doldrums he started to lose large patches of skin which soon became exuvial sheets revealing ugly pussy and bloody messes. Steroids must have outlived their usefulness. Unable to gauge what dying dogs go through but using such terminal human cases as a frame of reference, they decided to "put him down," a euphemism for euthanatizing him. Sane decision as the mercy shot was ministered before Eddie lost all his canine dignity. He was in her arms reposing and then in a minute he was gone.

She wasn't thinking of having kids until she was into her early thirties. Prior to that, the emotional vacuum had been filled by first Roman and then Eddie. Roman is patrician, being a pure-bred golden retriever the couple had driven out to buy at over one thousand. He was the prideful puppy of the household. I remember getting up at dead of the night to let him out of the crater and the house to pee or poop in the back garden. My flashlight might have disturbed the she-dragon of a neighbor who would come up and lodge an official protest the next day.

She acquired Eddie at a much cheaper price because Eddie is a hybrid plebeian rounded up as a stray in the first place waiting to be terminated at a kennel if nobody should claim him. Growing up, Roman always behaved while Eddie was the rogue. He must have had the German shepherd in his blood but is much more hairy. When I looked at him and especially at his unkempt hair, I sometimes thought I was looking at a yak or a mendicant friar out of Giambono's paintings. He would steal all my watermelon slices on a bedside table while I was in the shower for three to five short minutes. One Christmas the family dined out. When we came home, all the bulbs and trinkets on the tree were bitten and gnawed — now all in a bad litter on the floor. She said that the knavery must have been at Eddie's instigation so he was punished with a lengthy timeout. I felt amused, imagining, Orwellian-fashion, the disgruntled Eddie saying to Roman: "Dog food again while they eat nice things? An insult to our gustatory sensitivities. Let's give 'em a hard time clearing up the tree debris!"

I was the early riser so it fell on me to let the dogs out to answer the call of nature and then feed them. Roman learned to wrinkle his nose to express delight. Eddie would often come downstairs in a noisy tumble, gliding headlong to a halt before the door with a screech from his paw nails. Once he even put his forelegs upon my shoulders — the Chinese say only wolves do that because when you turn your head you expose your respiratory duct down pat to the fangs. Is there wolfish blood in Eddie? I wondered. "Paws down!" he always did my bidding.

Wolf or dog, Eddie is no more and I am a friend minus.

Wherever he is, whatever form he takes, who can tell me if he is happier than he was at Pulley Court?

13 February 2010

蠢人和恶人，谁更易坏事？

这也算问题？当然是恶人更易坏事了。

我原本也作如是想，直到后来阴错阳差地做了一回谁也看不上眼的某个项目的主持人。那时与我共事的人中间，一个被我暗暗称之为蠢，什么样的稿子，一经他手，错误发现不了不说，对的也会改错。更可悲的是，他懵然不知自己有几斤几两的膂力，却偏好揽活，还爱臧否他人，说话时"they is"和"cutted"之类的错误会滚滚而出。另一位精明过人，甚而至于有点险恶，损招不少，常在私下开导我如何瞒骗领导，糊弄他人，同时信奉"不做不错，少做少错"的道理，推诿工作有术，轻易不说话，更不冒险说英文，一副深水潜流的模样。共事久了，我竟然发现，两相比较，自己宁可选择后者而非前者。你要get things done，就需要招儿，损招不也是招儿？而且总比昏招要强。你看，做了个小头头，这理念也会大变，居然觉得用人时宁恶毋蠢也成了一条经验。直到今天，小字辈里有谁当了什么事务所的合伙人，还会给他们以身说法。

纵观今日官场，坏事的常多蠢人，这点太值得用人的领导们正视了。像昨天博文中写到的瞒报运动员年龄，让人抓住"8年里只长3岁"的把柄，这类蠢官如何可以再用？今天又看到一条关于毒豇豆的消息，海南官员指责揭发问题的武汉方面"太不够朋友"，"于国于民都无益"，如此敢道人之所难言，如何可能不犯众怒？想想现在的官员都有高学历，连那23岁就要出任副局长的女孩也是大学本科毕业，原不该颟顸至此。可是从“你代表党说话，还是代表人民说话”开始，昏官蠢话不断，这就使人不得不怀疑学历是不是造假。要不，这些官员本人原来的智商实在太低？建议用人之前，除了看学历，加一道测验智商的考核，商数不到 100 的，决不大用，因为蠢人有时比恶人更易坏事。

2010 年 3 月 1 日

A Referendum?

I'm sure when someone sees the titular word "referendum" he/she becomes extremely uptight, thinking this blogger is up to some monkey business again. Nothing of the sort, pal. Relax please. No need chasing your own tail.

Fact is, I was approached by an editor for translating what was described as something very touching about the father-son relationship adapted for the screen. The editor is an adroit lobbyist, having succeeded in making me work for her (for the editor is a she I've never met in person) on two previous occasions. For the present commission, her persuasion first-off sounded plausible and powerfully cogent: 1) the thing to be translated is the handiwork of a University of Chicago professor teaching Shakespeare; 2) he wrote the novella when he was over seventy; 3) the story is about father and son — notably my notorious soft spot; and 4) the novella consists only of 100-odd pages and the grace period is generous. Sure enough, the first three arguments created a sense of affinity or an urge to do a peer joust. The length of the book or the shortage of it finally served to clinch the bargain as I had tackled much longer texts with a much more demanding schedule.

So the book was express-delivered. Giving it a hasty once-over, I waded in. My, no sooner had I begun to test water and warm up than I hit a submerged reef: paragraph upon paragraph about fly-fishing technicalities. I was cursing under my breath and at once thought of a friend/fellow townsman Professor Huang Yuanshen (黄源深), who is given to angling and whose name itself is watery enough. He would have found it much easier to translate such stuff than one who has never picked up a rod. I bumped and splashed through the difficult passages reassuring myself that after this expanse of troubled water there might be plain sailing. Who could have expected that after some fifteen pages, I hit upon a no mean amount of fly, leader, line, rod, loops, side-casting, roll-casting, and so forth again. By now I had developed a conditioned aversion to fishing: the sight of these words killed whatever appetite there was for translation. So I admitted defeat and sent the done part to the editor, asking her to "ling qing gao ming" (seek help from someone better qualified). I didn't forget to mention that the 15 pages already translated is a freebie; no remuneration was needed.

She wrote back to say how much she liked the done part of my translation in terms that make it difficult to doubt her sincerity — don't think I easily succumb to ego-boosting compliments — and begged me to go on to the bitter end now that over 15% is done. Meanwhile, my friends all say I made the sane decision in quitting; one of them even made a strong point of one having to leave some things undone in order to do other things well. Family and friends (students included), what do you think I should do?

That's what the referendum is all about.

10 March 2010

忏悔意识,你在哪里?

朋友聚餐,说到诗人、学者、翻译家吴兴华之死,无不扼腕。今人说到中国现代文坛大师,钱锺书、陈寅恪的名字耳熟能详,吴兴华则可能已经成为"被遗忘的缪斯"。其实,吴的先天才具和后天学养,可能不在两人之下。钱二十几岁为洋人翻译的苏东坡诗词用英文作序,吴十六岁发表长诗《森林的沉默》,并以初中学历跳级考入燕京大学西语系,发奋攻下六七门包括古典语言在内的外语,人称"神童"。译过《老残游记》的美国老师认定,吴的才华和学识绝不在他康奈尔学生中的佼佼者之下……

如此一件国宝先是被划作"右派",在"文革"时期更是受尽非人摧残。大热天里,牛鬼蛇神在红卫兵皮鞭下从事超强度的体力劳动,渴若枯鱼。吴乃取阴沟污水饮下,俄顷腹痛如绞,又得不到及时有效治疗,终于死在当天。年仅四十有四!

说吴兴华之死,是受迫害而"仰毒而死",我以为一点也不为过。对此应当负责的当年北大某红卫兵,居然前几天就出现在两会荧屏上,沐猴而冠,像煞有介事地扮作恺悌君子侃侃而谈,看得吴兴华先生的遗孀肠断眦裂。据说这样的主儿还要写回忆录出版,不知国宝因他而殇这样的旧事,作者提或不提,悔也不悔?

还有那些亲自动手打过人甚至打死人的,什么横行京城的"联动",沪上因四肢发达而臭名昭著的"上体司",什么现已躲到美国去的"要武"小姐们,你们今天也许可以稳稳当当地做官,开饭店,当富婆，做什么金牌教练等等，但是当年的暴行即使未载入史册，已深深积淀在民族的集体记忆中。你们现在尽可对往事讳莫如深，可你们那种用特殊材料制成的良心会一直平安到死？

忏悔意识，你在哪里？学学剧作家沙叶新吧。人家当然从来不演全武行，与上述打手毫无可比性。沙就是在“文革”前后写过为数不多的几种“遵命文学”，他自己不提，人家怕是早忘记了，只会记得他那被禁演的剧本《假如我是真的》以及各种直言谠论。可是沙先生至今还在忏悔，就凭这一点，还不值得大家学习？

2010 年 3 月 24 日

保安行军礼——滑稽

朋友,你见过守门保安对着出入豪华小区的汽车行军礼的场面吗？我算是从电视上饱了一回眼福。解放军有内务条令,里面规定“营门卫兵对出入营门的分队、首长和上级应当敬礼,分队带队指挥员、首长和上级应当还礼”;还有,“进见或遇见党和国家领导人时应当敬礼”。保安学军警,都想成为 paramilitary 或 para-police, 好像非此莫显权威,可惜学成了个“半吊子”。设想一下,出门车里如果坐着个最近闹得沸沸扬扬的挂西安“陕 0”牌的通缉犯,你也一概敬礼恭送吗?“被”敬礼的业主,这会儿是什么感受,因不曾受过如此礼遇,我不知道,也许有个别的因此意得志满,想来大多数还是不免忸怩,或像某位年轻朋友说的那样:总觉得“怪怪的”。幸好复旦和周围宿舍区的“兵营化”程度尚不算太高,保安的手臂不必过劳,物主可免尴尬。

我始终没有搞懂,给乘车而出的业主行军礼,对于“稳定压倒一切”有什么好处。

自从三天出了三宗校园弑童血案后,除教育部下文责令加强校园安保外,媒体已不约而同地减少后续报道,据说是怕担上惹出学样犯罪(copycat crimes)的罪名。各地安保新招屡有所闻:增设法治副校长,一校派驻一警,持钢叉防范歹徒(据说从日本学来),安装 CCTV(非指其他,而是 closed-circuit TV,即“天眼”),家长组织“护校队”,等等。最多见的一招是增用保安。根据我看到的数字,粗粗算一算，增用人数多的地方，一校可以摊到4–5名吧。某些地方可能矫枉过正心切，或许是特别爱护祖国的花朵，保安协警被赋予权力，可在校门口或校区附近截停“形迹可疑”者。上海办世博排铁桶阵也没搞成这个样子，是不是太过了？保安从给人敬礼到有权截停行人，其中一定有人自我感觉很爽。殊不知，这一条如果真的付诸实行，还不知会闹出一些什么新的“突发事件”来。

2010年5月2日

"One-eyed Dragon"

It must have been the internal body heat running amok inside me to find an outlet that caused it. I woke up unusually early feeling an excruciating pain in the left eye. A tremendous sty had developed, now pricking and now pounding.

Result: a cascade of tears followed by an over-abundance of mucus from the nose wetting a roll of face tissues soon, and more alarmingly, a racing heart. It being Sunday and rainy, I know the school clinic is closed and no eye specialist in any hospital is available. Even though he or she is on duty, he or she would not look twice at my problem before off-handedly prescribing some eye drops I've bought myself and applied on my own. It is at moments like this that I feel the harmful effect of a combination of a fiery disposition, incessant anxieties and over-fatigue of the eye. The human body, if and when magnified, is like a human society that needs safety valves. When boiling water produces too much steamy heat, putting a lid on the pot is bad policy. So better let the sty run its own course lest a more serious complaint should come to pass. Being "one-eyed dragon" is after all a petty nuisance and presenting myself to the students as a sorry sight is no big deal. Meanwhile, isn't cutting myself off visually from the outside world via the internet, who knows, a blessing in disguise? So that I turn blind to "the law's delay, the insolence of office, the despised love" and so forth — "a weary life" in short. Sharpened sensibilities bring about frustrations, dementia, and angst in no mean numbers. To dull them in sepulchral quietude may be a win-win: for those who don't feel comfortable with my presence anyway a pain in the ass minus and for myself imperturbation.

9 May 2010

培训班的那些事儿

有个叫山木培训的机构,最近因头儿涉嫌强奸被拘,方才引起我的注意。山木这名字使我误以为班主是个日人,后来才听说是同胞。照片也在网上登出来了。一看,嗨,除去了那把大胡子,真还有点像我前几日写过的“两员大将”中的第二位。就老爱上“春晚”的做派而论,也像。

改革开放之初的1984年,我就在沪上一家培训班里教过英文。那位班主是一家中学退休教师,以100块钱做原始资本,目标对准要考“托福”的学子,搞英文培训。起初,班主还挺“礼贤下士”的,记得他第一次来寒舍,坐了辆吉普车,头戴法式贝雷帽,印象奇深。我则是因为经济拮据,他那儿讲课费给得丰厚而欣然应聘。(因此,我至今完全理解青年教师去“新东方”兼职的不得已。)应该说,此人办的培训班,对于青年学子留洋确是起过积极作用的,所以他本人得过改革开放风云人物之类的称号;经过他处培训的学生,对他也“×校长”、“×校长”地叫得亲热。后来,事业做大,脸就有些变了。名片印成了三联式,那头衔多得要溢出纸面。最令我无法忍受的是,办班之初“迂回伏击”、“死缠烂打”请来的英语教授都成了他的“垫脚石”。接受采访时,为了凸显他既重视培训质量,又是老板,可以轻易决定打工仔的存亡,径向媒体爆料,如何炒了一位与我同姓、无论年岁和资历都胜我多多的兄弟院校教授的鱿鱼。可能是“兔死狐悲”吧,我闻讯也便拂袖而去了。

由沈昌文君介绍，认识了“新东方”的所谓“三巨头”之一的王强，读过他寄来的《书之爱》，又在某次饭局上听到台湾的郝明义先生说到，王强请他淘购关于书报检禁的某种绝版书之后，我对“新东方”一直是刮目相看的。有这样爱书的人经营其中，培训当不致太“豁边”吧。后来，小侄女去那儿接受了15天的培训，回来汇报说，短期合作结束，师生唱起 Auld Lang Syne，挥泪而别，更使我觉得这培训颇有些人性化的特点。我们这儿学生上学四年，到了毕业，有几个会与老师洒泪而别？更多的当然是赶快绝裾而去。自然，“新东方”现在变成什么样了，是不是也有“山木化”的趋势，已非我等外人得以知也。

同所有的事业一样，培训肯定也有良莠之分的。

2010年5月15日

劝生勿“辟谷”

某生告我周末开始“辟(读如避)谷”,我答以“哼哼”二字。今天问他,说是未抵挡住荤腥诱惑,不说自己意志力薄弱,反怪慈母治菜慰劳一周工作辛劳。

我之所以会“哼哼”,一是出于我本人所谓戒烟的教训。当年,心脏早搏大发,曾戒烟数年。后来,痼疾已成,感觉麻木,反而破罐子破摔,又吸起来。主要不怪学生送烟,而是自己心魔作孽。发誓之类一点没用。想起莎剧《爱的徒劳》中埋头苦读三年的誓言,还是哲人看得透彻,如英国研究“言语行为”的奥斯汀(J. L. Austin),就把发誓之类称作语言与超语言的现实相交时的一种“表现性”(performative)动作。还有我的一位南京甥女,若干年前迷上了叫做中华什么什么的功夫,沉湎不能自拔,投入大钱不说,还专门躲到黄山去“辟谷”一周。(那时我真怕她饿死了回来。)大概,时间确是最好的医师。几年过去,甥女现在已闭口不谈功夫,起居饮食与常人无异。我也不好意思问她当年“辟谷”修炼的体会,谁知道留下的是美好记忆还是一味的尴尬。

劝生勿“辟谷”,也不要像Carpenter兄妹那样节食弄出灾祸。修生保真,情虚澹泊,都应归之自然。忘记是哪位高僧说过“如厕则知进食之妄”,可他不也得出去化缘吃斋吗?

2010年5月15日

What Are You Driving At?

A friend's son is sitting for the GRE writing test. He asked me to help improve the writing wherein he is supposed to decide an issue: of competitiveness and cooperativeness, which is more important? The poor lad argues back and forth, treading the trodden, with the result that eventually his readers are at a loss whether both are of equal importance or whether one (and then which one) is slightly more important than the other. As he kept talking now about the society growing more and more competitive and now about more team work is called for if you want to have things done by multitasking, I was led unwittingly by him to a maze of arguments and ready to go crazy, really wanting to shout to the writer: For all your assurances and attestations, what after all are you driving at, son? The issue remains as if unaddressed.

Through the confused smorgasbord of the language I seem to have detected a built-in logic or the lack of any logic: The crux of the matter, it seems to me, lies in that modern people, being favored sons and daughters, think in terms of all-inclusive possession. Like a net-fisher, they think they are entitled to everything and can bag and take home every marine life — big fish and small scallops alike. This logic may enable them to be ahead of the game or out in the front, featuring one day perhaps in Fortune success stories, for all I know. Wouldn't the same logic, on the other hand — so I wonder — find them empty-handed in the end? That is, if they fish in the wrong waters or cast their nets while they are badly entangled to keep fish away and let the scallops at large through loopholes.

My advice to the lad, therefore, is to think in Kierkegaard's Either/Or terms — of course divested of the Danish philosopher's intended choice between the aesthetic and the ethical. I don't know any of the GRE examiners. But common sense tells me that they like to read writings in which a decision is boldly and sanely made and powerfully argued for than those with the issue hung and the writer in two minds throughout. Better to the point than around the point.

22 May 2010

老头过“六一”

英文里把老年叫做 second childhood（第二个童年）。今日是六一儿童节，一早收到出版社小于短信，祝贺节日快乐。那自然是调侃，要我别忘了自己已有多老。

果然，接着传来北外某君尽管已折一股防扩散，但健康状况继续恶化，跑到成都求专家开了第二刀，惟结果仍不容乐观。此君次我一辈，在我看来，犹是矜壮，良医尚且不能施功（张悟本的绿豆汤更不在话下），于是，“死生之穴（指穴道），乃在分毫”一语，即使在儿童节，听来我觉得尤其真实。

接着听张大编辑说，东北列车上有人持铁器行凶，滥杀无辜，性质跟幼儿园弑童有点类似；湖南永州（该不是柳宗元写《捕蛇者说》的地方吧？）法院开庭时有“当事人”持枪扫射法官。怪不得有人统计说，中国精神病患者人口已经逾亿。这叫我们的孩子以及孩子的孩子们如何健康长大成人？

又接南京国关刘生信，这是位“性情中人”，补看了许多关于德国人卢安克的影像和文字资料，看得这位曾经出使维和的汉子堕涕吞声。我想他们贤伉俪正值育儿阶段，卢安克爱孩子，在这儿童的节日，便尤其会触动他们做父母的心弦。

俄顷，复有一位曾去耶鲁接受“future leaders”训练的某校领导，发来短信，说“用儿童的眼光看待问题，会多一些真诚；用儿童的方式分析问题，会多一些善良；用儿童的真诚对待别人，会多很多朋友。

祝你六一节快乐。”领导看了我的博客，觉得我不“真诚”，不“善良”，朋友都已渐行渐远了？

至于我本人，一方面翕然景从“死生有命”的古训；一方面要动员起“第二个童年”所有的资源，努力造福于学生——他们在我眼里仍是应该好好过一过儿童节的孩子。是的，有的学生不喜欢我，因为我曾给过他们“不及格”的分数，给他们制造了痛苦，洋派一点的称我是“伊凡雷帝”(Ivan the Terrible)，青年国粹派叫我“关公”。值此儿童节之际，是该好好反省。莘莘学子苦恼已经够多，教育也已病入膏肓，干嘛苛求复苛求，执着于老一套，而不让他们活得开心一点？这样，自己也才有“第二个童年”的感觉。

2010年6月1日

Looking Old

Gao and the Boarhead dropped by.

Gao stuck out her tongue tip impishly, remarking that I look as old as my "trophy wife" looks young who can easily be mistaken for being my daughter. Gao must have been the nth person who has ever said such things that throw into bold relief the ill-assortedness in appearance between man and wife.

Likewise, an ex-classmate of mine, an age peer, is frequently used as a frame of reference in reminding me how I look older than my age. When friends from abroad respond to my query "Ain't I looking greyer?" with a "You look more dignified," I seem to have seen an antiquated me in the mirror that is their faces. How do you think I would feel? Upset? Discombobulated? No, not a whit. Instead, I take delight in having lived an apparently more taxing life which has left its marks behind. Also I can tell whoever has commented on my silvery crown, a newly developed bent back, a "chop-fallen" look with missing teeth and what not that I AM old. But I have never dyed my hair, have stopped wearing jeans and other adultescent stuff as I did in the US to appear less elderly, or have wasted more time than is minimally called for in front of a toilet glass. Nor have I ever in this life set foot inside a karaoke or a KTV to expose myself to the contagion of a youth culture, not to mention joining in the crazy stampeding rush on Super Junior the other day at the Expo. I think I am cozy and comfy in my cave or cocoon as age creeps on.

What is wrong with looking old? I abhor Dorian Gray the person more than his picture and join Hamlet in warning: "God has given you one face and you make yourselves another." An ex-student of mine is engaged, big-time, in bio-medical research and pharmaceutics. He adjured me the other day to use one of his cutting-edge products called the E.P.O. interferon to stave off ageing. I was nearly scared to death when he told me this new-fangled drug costs USD100 an ampoule, telling him to sell it to suckers and doofuses or go to hell.

Earlier on when I spoke of a taxing life, I had in mind failures and frustrations galore plus experiences at once enriching and impoverishing, elevating and lacerating, as well as work that is not always fun or labor of love. Cicero asked, "Give me an old man with something of the young," and said, "A man may grow old in body, but never in mind." I need a youngish mind by, say, watching the World Cup, taking pix with a formless smile on face with my students like we did yesterday afternoon, and remembering that twentysomethings could have perished some twenty years ago while older people survive. So looking old is fine with me.

4 June 2010

“围剿”可悲

最近,几位颇有影响的媒体人对一些“非诚莫扰”等所谓情感相亲类电视节目,万炮齐轰。鄙人从来不看这类以中国特色掺假的所谓“reality shows”,只听说有个拜金女大言不惭宣称,宁可在宝马里哭,不愿在自行车上笑。虽说我的人生观恰恰与此人相反,但我暗自思忖,此人恐怕说出了相当一部分女孩深藏于心的爱情观(当然,我宁可相信大多数女孩更希望在自行车或宝马豪车里都能笑)。现在,媒体人出来“围剿”拜金女了,使用的主要武器是提倡真实。太滑稽了。敢问这些“围剿”大军,你们都真实吗?你们又真实得了吗?人家只不过在本质上属于娱乐的次要节目上,挑了几个想露脸出名的男女,也许还替他/她们写好了台词脚本,把“reality shows”弄得违背主旋律或出格的“unreal”而已,而作为主干电视节目主持者的你们衮衮诸公,有几位说过几次真话?记得多年前有位黑衣女主播,也并未在荧屏上说什么大逆不道的真话,只是在说几句不那么真实的话时,神态有点不主流,就此从镜头前消失,不知所终。真是太搞笑了,那位地球人都知道的头戴假发的“聊发少年狂”的低俗“老夫”,还刺刺不休地扬言:“这是一个容易被克隆的时代。”先将足下的头发 de-clone 如何?

再说张悟本。第一次听到这个名字,是从一位从医的甥女处,她向我灌输食用豆类的好处。我常年吃豆制品多于肉类,自然不疑张语有诓。当然,“把吃出来的病再吃回去”,这个确是够邪乎的,我不相信。可是人家只不过发表一家养生之言,又不像××功之类搞什么结社,而强调食疗,也算是种预防医学(preventive medicine)吧,说不定还可在一定程度上缓解医保的压力。没想到张某人可能是因为赚钱太多而暴发,又不知踩着了谁的脚跟,哗,一下子从卫生部到新闻出版总署,全都围上来讨伐了。这番折腾的声势,就好比是张悟本一手抬高了绿豆的价格,给通货膨胀推波助澜,破坏国民经济。至于吗?稍有头脑的朋友,都想想吧。

“围剿”是上世纪30年代蒋委员长发明的,最终没有什么好结果。在今天的和谐社会,动不动一批人涌上重试“围剿”故技,我看一样会徒劳无功,而且影响稳定。要反对虚假,与其冲着对方骂不绝口:“虚假!虚假!”不如出以真实,反以止之。老子说过,“揣而锐之,不可长保”。“围剿”者们三思。

2010年6月8日

“哈韩”、“哈日”的背后

前几天，上海世博因为“粉丝”哄抢一场韩人音乐会入场券而酿成混乱。有此前车之鉴，原拟举行的另一场日人音乐会宣布取消，惹得“哈日”一族很不高兴，网上出言不逊者有之。愤青一见，民粹主义激情大贲张，把“粉丝”骂了个狗血喷头。这日本人也真厉害，几个歌星来不来唱上两句，居然可以激起中国人如此网上内斗，当年的军国主义者们可曾能想像到？

我看不懂这个“哈”字，深层原因有待社会学家们挖掘。从表面看，我只是觉得这潮流可能与小青年们的反叛有关。一是我们的学校和家长把他们压抑得太过分了。从幼儿时代开始，就被自己并不擅长此道的家长们逼着去学钢琴、英语、书法等等，然后是动员各种资源择校入学，从小灌输优劣成败的意念，接着就是没完没了的测验和考试，书包越来越重。（美国人发明了一种既可肩背，又可手拉的书包，咱们还不快去接轨？）压抑之下，日、韩——或许还包括港台——那些歌星貌似轻松自如的打扮，加上他们纵情恣意的放歌狂舞，都像是打开了一道安全阀，提供了一种释放。小青年们把这些歌手视作文化的 icon（偶像）也就没什么奇怪了。

二是小青年又在经历从朦胧到清醒的性成熟阶段，家长、学校、社会一方面困心衡虑地“绿色护航”，一方面又奈何不得前赴后继的贪官恶吏，乌烟瘴气的两性关系随着道德沦丧而变成街谈巷议之鄙事，无时不在侵袭着幼嫩的灵魂。孩子们就这样被夹在冰炭之中，性取向发生畸变也成了反叛的途径之一。国外厕所除了男女之别，现在出现了第三种 unisex（无性别差异）；甚至填表时“性别”一项，已有人选中“neutral”（中性）。此种畸变，使得孩子们中的某些人，特别容易钟爱并模仿那些伪阴柔的男子和伪阳刚的女子，而韩、日的歌星里恰好多出这样的人物，很快便能成为“角色模范”。中国不也有个出名的女“春哥”，最近还出了“伪娘”？

不知“有关部门”意识到了这种“哈韩”、“哈日”背后的深处隐藏着什么没有。不要泛政治或泛意识形态化地看待这种反叛姿态和审美取向，还是像德国志愿者卢安克那样，深入到孩子们的心灵里去了解他们。不要时不时地总想着“护航”和“导向”，苦心孤诣地去阻挡孩子们进网吧，封杀韩、日。还是把城里的孩子们从钢琴、英语、书法等等他们并不喜爱的课业中解放出来（真正喜欢的自当别论），带他们进入大自然，眺望广阔的地平线，还有隐隐青山和迢迢流水；让他们谛听鸟啼虫鸣，观赏花开花落；帮助他们读地图，看罗盘，扎帐篷，燃篝火，放手让他们自己学会存活，学会珍惜，学会审美。

2010 年 6 月 9 日

何谓“世博一代”?

上海某报日前发一长篇,题为“世博一代”,随后几日续以名家评论。

“世博一代”这四字,我琢磨良久,实不知其所指。是指昵称“小白菜”的志愿者们,还是所有“小白菜”的同龄人?在汉语里,“代”字表示父子相继或新旧交替,一代人,亦即英语里说的 generation,从幼儿成年,再到他们自己长大做父母,大约总在二十五到三十年左右。即使 2010 年上海世博会的确给“小白菜”们留下了不可磨灭的印象,他们就可从此终身成为“世博一代”?世博也可就此附着于整个一代人的人体身心,长存不衰?何况世博可是各国轮流着主办的,还不知道什么时候就寿终正寝了。所以,为求准确计,至少也应说“2010 上海世博一代”,对不对?

细读长文才知道,报道写的其实是我们寻常讲的 90 后,只不过以世博志愿者引入而已。且看文中所引《人民日报》1990 年元旦社论“满怀信心迎接九十年代”中的一段:“我们所做的一切,都是为了我国经济的发展,为了人民生活的改善。经济是基础,什么时候也不要忘记经济建设这个中心。”此话如果是针对改革开放以前的“年年讲,月月讲,天天讲”有的放矢,那就是继续拨乱反正的集合号,在特定时期可能是有指导意义的,然而如果整整一代都成了经济人,脑子里惟有“民生”,这误导就大了——特别是当经济被狭化为 GDP,民生等同于金钱的时候。

请看恩格斯是怎么给经济定位的(见《马恩书信集,1890年》中恩格斯于1890年9月21日致J. Bloch信):

According to the materialist conception of history, the ultimate determining element in history is the production and reproduction of real life. More than this neither Marx nor I have ever asserted. Hence if somebody twists this into saying that the economic element is the only determining one, he transforms that proposition into a meaningless, abstract, senseless phrase.

(译文:“根据历史唯物主义的观念,历史的最终的决定性的因素是真实生活的创造和再现。马克思和我的论述都没有超出这一点。因此,任何人对此曲解为经济因素是唯一决定性的因素,他就是把我们的观点更改为没有意义的、抽象和无聊的片言只语。”)

恩格斯说的“真实生活的创造”,按我的理解,就是现实;所谓“再现”,就是历史。我们的90后绝不能也不会只是精明的经济人。他们必定关注并介入现实,虽说由于樊篱太多,信息不足,他们有时会陷入现实的误区;同时他们会有理想主义,不容青史成灰,对谜团疑案总要探究个水落石出,虽说他们有时会摆出犬儒的姿态。过来人应该做的是把他们当做自己的子弟,多些理解和扶助,少些唠叨和指责,帮助他们做个经济人和道德人的结合体,有冰一样的理性和火一样的热情。权力应该做的是让“封杀”之类的词汇在他们的生活中逐渐消失,改善他们成长的社会生态。

2010年7月7日

事实细部有魔鬼

看到方舟子对“打工皇帝”唐某伪造学历的揭发，后者在自己的公开出版物里白纸黑字写着“但凭借语音识别方面的应用性研究成果，我最后还是拿到了加州理工学院的计算机科学博士学位”（摘自唐骏《我的成功可以复制》）。经方揭发，媒体追索，唐某被迫拿出了一张夏威夷野鸡大学的证书来搪塞。人家拿上面的白纸黑字质问他，唐居然说可能是编辑错误，“我手上的版本并无这样的提法”。耍赖了。

有趣的是，有人出来为唐某抱不平，说能力和学历是两码事，怀疑唐某学历打假是假，妒忌是真。今天上海的《新民晚报》更妙，以转载《沈阳晚报》评论的方式，说是“学位门”愈演愈烈，足见公众潜意识里不健康的名校崇拜。

上文第一段是关于事实的陈述，第二段是对事实的解读和判断。或者说，第一段说的是两造在法庭上应做的事，第二段才是法官的职责。同是今日的《新民晚报》上，另一页有个标题叫做“只说事实，好坏自断”，意思无非也是：说事实和断好坏是两码事。可悲的是，我们这儿经常有意无意地忽略前者，事实还未陈述清楚，两造话没说完，甚至一方还没说，匆忙跃进到第二步，解读兼判断，忙着做法官。这实际上带有很明显的历次政治运动中罔顾事实一味批判的语境色彩。以发生在我本人身上的一件往事为例：×××，你早在大一的作文里就狂呼“法兰西万岁”！不容我说明那是都德短篇小说《最后一课》的读后感,这“狂呼”的事实已经歪曲认定,然后劈头盖脸的解读和批判。你若是试图指出所控不实,那边群众的口号声已经大起:“×××不老实!”非把你要讲的话淹没不可。

照说现在的政治—社会生态宽松多了,大家可以心平气和按照毛主席的教导,摆事实,讲道理。请注意,那是先要把事实交代清楚,然后判断是非。可有些人偏不,如事实于己不利,有的狡辩,有的“闷声大发财”,总之赶快跳过,或者把事实弄得云谲波诡唬人,然后横加判断,对你钳口封嘴,怕的就是藏在事实细部里的魔鬼。

可是瓶口已经打开,你能把魔鬼塞回去吗?

2010 年 7 月 8 日

Stopping at a Red Light and Getting Paid

I was incredulous when I learned that in a northern city the police had initiated a new practice of offering a money reward of RMB ¥500 to a person who duly stops at a red light rather than jump it. A former student who is currently teaching in that city dropped by to say hello during the summer break. So I asked him about the matter, wondering aloud how much reward money from public coffers the police must needs blow since law-abiders no doubt outnumber law-breakers. He said "nope" (did he mean those latter outnumber the former?) and told me to remember the same city now enjoys world notoriety of adulterating powdered milk with chemicals.

"Do you mean to say law-breaking is the order of the day?" I asked. "Up to a point, yes," he answered. "How about beggars thronging in to plant themselves before a light? Are they entitled to the reward money? They can easily make a decent enough living out of it," I said, remembering a cartoon wherein in a pair of greedy eyes the three circular traffic bulbs metamorphose to three blown-up dollar signs. "The authorities have foreseen that so they dispatch discerning police agents to man all crossroads who can tell purposeful pedestrians apart from aimless loiterers. Besides, they have set a very short time limit for the experimental practice. Rewarding is not valid for ever, but remains so only within a specified window."

In a flash, an English phrase "affirmative action" flitted across my mind, although I was fully aware that I was giving it a laborious semantic wrench. Affirmative not in the sense of promoting the interests of those discriminated against on racial or sexual grounds but in the sense of rewarding those who don't deserve it without penalizing those who deserve a fine. "不应受奖的受奖,应受罚的不罚"— this is the logic of "affirmative action" with Chinese characteristics.

I'm reminded of the motorcycles and scooters swooshing through a red unashamedly almost without exception in town. They are especially hazardous to a person walking across a zebra as these vehicles mostly use the inside lane, hidden from view by rows of the stopped cars on the outer lines. Any such vehicles, a moped driver told me, which don't jump a light will be looked upon as an outlandish aberration!

Something must have gone wrong when normal behavior which is to be taken for granted calls for an undeserved reward and when the abnormal has become all the rage and goes unpunished.

22 July 2010

海外的“隔岸观火”派

海外有些人看中国颇有些“隔岸观火”的味道。光“隔岸观火”倒也罢了,还喜欢指手划脚。我的这一观感早在上世纪80年代初就形成了。那时是第一次出国,恰好是紧随国内审判“四人帮”之后。在美国,第一次看到了“江青像章”,佩戴这东西的多数是美国的女权主义者。记得曾跟其中一位发生过争论,那人自诩“亲华”,穿了一双脚背左右两处都有紧宽的“北京布鞋”(她称之为“功夫鞋”),把江青推崇到“妇女解放和文化革命旗手”的高度,进而认为“文革”本应是中国之福。当然,对于逮捕并审判“四人帮”大不以为然,说了许多难听的话。我跟她说得唇焦舌敝,毫无作用,不由得想到中国的成语“隔岸观火”四个字。如果“文革”期间,这位女士从头至尾都像个中国的普通老百姓,在这儿生活,接受洗礼,恐怕“美帝间谍”这把火还没烧到她身上,就会溜之大吉了,焉有此等隔着太平洋观赏熊熊火势,连称壮观的胸魄?

时间过去了约三十年,我们的“外包式”工作成效比当年自然显著许多,虽然中资的报纸在海外销路依然有限(连大陆出去的留学生对赠报也兴趣缺缺),海外的“隔岸观火”派队伍倒是在不断扩大。最能说明问题的是,最近就清华某教授是否涉嫌抄袭问题,海外一大批左派学者联名写信干预,说话的口气非常居高临下,颐指气使,好像他/她们对于中国“大学内部的日常文化政治”全有痛切的感受,并可发号施令。海外不少“新左”由他们的历史语境所决定,一见到中国某些人的理论话语与他们的在字面上接近或雷同，顿时就会激情贲张，本能地把这些人引为同道，然而中国的事情，包括“大学内部的日常文化政治”，岂是“隔岸观火”便可遽下结论的？真希望这些有头有脸的人物跳槽到中国大学来，并能利用霍金式的时间机器，回过头去亲历中国学术六十年之后，再慎重发言。同理，我也不喜闻“站着说话不腰疼”的一些海外报人的高论，诸如“错过世博就是犯罪”。根据这个逻辑，没去参观过世博的是不是都得“投案自首”去呢？

你愿隔岸观火，我们中国人也没有办法，只是请你不要对我们随便指手划脚。

2010年8月1日

机场梦魇

多时不坐飞机了，在“城市，让生活更美好”之后，近日有一次外地旅行，来回分别乘坐东航和上航的班机，一共应是4个半钟头的航程，结果不是虽然上了飞机却因“空中交通流量控制”而成一只sitting duck，就是据说来港飞机脱班，下完客后打扫工作又延误，再加上技术故障，延伸成为9个多小时，整整增加一倍！某日在外地某机场枯坐4个半小时，领教了机场广播里传出频率最高的一句话，那就是：“各位旅客，我们抱歉地通知……”闲得无聊，我就计算脱班与正点之比，4个半小时里，竟成4∶11！还不算被取消的那一班。待到延误的航班终于到得登机时，突然又宣布更换登机口，于是候机大厅顿时大乱，人潮左右反向涌动，而听到先前延误的消息走开的某几位“潇洒”乘客，不知道上哪儿找乐子去了，被一遍又一遍地点名登机。多数人等着极少数人，凭我有限的经验，这做法极有“中国特色”。飞机终于开始滑行了，你可别高兴太早，还有“流量控制”这一说非叫你刹车不可。令人费解的是，制定航班时刻表的难道都是木头人或病毒电脑，“流量控制”不在计算考量之内？

后来问了老在空中“跑码头”的人，被传授经验如下：发可乐，三钟头；送盒饭，等夜班；上大巴，赔两百。说的是民航那免费饮料和盒饭以及“维权”半天才到手的赔款，都得以大把大把时间为代价。在“我们抱歉地通知”公告以后，延误时间一长，照例会有人跑到登机口柜台去责问原因，那站柜台的小伙子或小姑娘，别看他/她们像煞有介事地拿个对讲机叽里咕噜，其实我看大多并不知道航班延误的真正缘由，只顾递上可乐，在你的登机牌上打个钩，以防你复领。不知道掌握确切信息，了解实情的究竟是谁，躲在哪里，又何以不能实话实说。莫非那实情难以向公众披露？我由此发现，机场小社区里航班延误信息的不透明，在某种意义上，可说是大社会中信息不时遭到封杀的缩影。难怪忿怒的乘客有时也会闹出点群体事件来。

中国民航总局的一位高官近称，中国航班的平均正常率一直保持在80%左右，居世界中上水平。如此看来，我五天中两次机场梦魇，定是自己运气不好，硬生生挤到那20%里边去了。

2010年8月11日

疯购外国奶粉

40后的中国老人可能都还记得美国的“克宁”牌奶粉。“克宁”两字是英文milk倒拼之后的音译，牌子老，信誉好，市场大。前几年，雀巢的“克宁”拿到黑龙江来生产了，不料也被查出含有三聚氰胺。牌子于是做坍。

40后的上海老人当然都记得现在淮海路上当年的“可的牛奶棚”。那是在居住在天津的德、俄、意、日等多国商人开始经营乳牛场之后，在上海最早开始安装巴氏消毒设备加工牛奶的地方。国人经营奶牛场在上世纪20-30年代也开始兴起，其中传说中以牛奶洗澡的蒋宋美龄也曾起过一点作用。那时，牛奶是富裕阶层的消费品，牛奶订户家门口都安一个信箱一样的小匣，骑车送奶人一早送来，订户取回后一般都是煮熟后饮用。这样的情况一直维持到解放后，没听说过中毒之类的事。

2008年的“三鹿”事件一下子沉重打击了中国的乳制品乃至整个食品工业，只要看看连“箭牌”口香糖都不肯拿到中国来生产了，就知道三鹿制造商和庇护者们给中国制造了多少负面影响。本来这事如果处理得好，很可能发生如美国作家阿普顿·辛克莱（Upton Sinclair）在1905年小说《丛林》（*The Jungle*，指屠宰工场）中所要达到的效果，让总统进早餐时读着小说恶心呕吐，从而迫使国会和全民从此切实注意食品安全。但是出于种种原因，我们的处理不但偏软，而且显然漏洞不少，三聚氰胺继续在一些外省的乳制品中出现。现在又出了圣元的激素丑闻，不管最后测试结果如何，国人对国产乳制品的信心由是进一步受损。你让那些口头高叫“抵制洋货”的初为人父人母的80后用问题奶粉哺育他们的宝宝，谁敢？

于是就出现了从网络由海外代购卖家经手，大批邮购原产地洋奶粉的奇怪现象（连国内大卖场的相同牌子的洋奶粉都怀疑了，宁可舍近就远），从报上看到有的父母一口气从国外买进6大箱，足够宝宝吃上一年。咱们的海关见你如此趸批，当然不会闲着，于是明令“9月1日起进出境个人邮递物品关税免征额度将调整”，说白了，你要往国外买奶粉入关，就得付比过去多得多的税款。不过上有政策，下有对策，据说有些年轻妈妈已在空姐中物色随身带入的渠道；当然更多的是瞄准回国的亲友。不敢想象，会不会有一天，海关要像查毒品一样，严查入境奶粉？

都是三聚氰胺造假惹的祸！说到造假，我这个年纪的人当年喝奶，从未想到过奶中是否含毒。莫非自从有了亩产万斤、大放卫星的荒诞剧之后，造假就牢牢粘附在我们的灵魂里了？

2010年8月30日

上天入地造假

这是一条好消息："据民航局有关人士透露，2008 年到 2009 年，民航局曾在民航系统对飞行人员的资质进行了全面检查，查出来飞行经历不实，甚至飞行经历造假的多达 200 多人。"问题是前两年就发现的问题，怎么直到今天才透露？幸好是伊春摔了架飞机，引起重视了。但愿是亡羊补牢。回过头去想想，过去两年，多少乘客坐过造假人掌握驾驶杆的航班，居然都全身升空又落地，造化小儿待人不薄哇。

同一条消息又称，民航总局局长李某说："如何通过这次伊春的空难，痛定思痛，适当地控制发展速度，要以质量求平稳的发展。"说得好！嘿嘿，这正是我这个乘客在博文"机场梦魇"中所想表达的意思，指导思想是胡锦涛同志提出的"科学发展观"，有几分力，办几分事，不要想钱或是想在国际上出头而昏招迭出。机场枯等时，我就在疑问，你买一两架旧飞机开家航空公司赚钱，我为什么就不能？难怪出现如此大面积脱班甚至撤班停飞的中国民航。这样办事业，能持续发展到何日？

网友跟帖说，发达国家不是一样有 delays 和 cancellations 吗？摔飞机的事也够多的。不假。但是人家重视，把乘客的投诉当回事，游说集团已经把事情提到国会去了。说到中外飞行延误及失事比例，请勿忘计航空总量。有网友说芝加哥 O'Hare 机场每 5 分钟起降一个航班，恐怕是误导。据我知道，那每 5 分钟应该是每 90 秒钟。

上天造假，性命交关。地下造假，贻笑大方。我说的是曹操墓的真伪问题。一方说有铁证是造假，为此当事人还花大钱无中生有建碑，另一方凿凿有据指责对方学历造假，互相咬得一地鸡毛。七八百年前的一座坟是真是假，毕竟并不直接影响国计民生；往裸山喷绿漆，至多有碍观瞻；假装残疾坐轮椅，走世博绿色通道，损害的毕竟是全民之中的小众利益。老百姓更关心的是大米、食油、牛奶、豆芽、小龙虾之类“祸从口入”的东西。马上要过中秋了，今天看到一条报道，记录了星级月饼是如何制造的。当心啊，那些装潢精美的月饼，不少是在环境污秽的草棚子里制造的，饼馅在你品尝之前，蝇群已经捷足先登，大啖为快了。

2010 年 9 月 6 日

看不见中秋的月亮

又是冷空气，又是台风，今年中秋看不见月亮。本来月的阴晴圆缺，古来难全，没什么了不起的。报纸原本并不缺少“人咬狗”的新闻，但宁可牺牲 newsworthiness，正儿八经地报道“中秋无月可见”。读者自己没眼睛吗？还有的预告明晚有“彩云追月”，不妨把观月仪式像某国党代会那样延它一延，纯粹是吃饱了撑的。

中国古代的文人骚客都爱拿月亮说事，即使时至今日，写旧体诗的，也常离不开月亮，就连当年的伟大领袖也概莫能外。我在想，这是不是也从一个侧面，说明中国文化阴柔的特征。要去国外孔子学院演讲的朋友，以月亮为题，做个象形的“月”字的 ppt，再说说“亮”字下方的“几”原作“儿”，人的两条长腿一伸，可见高处的光称之为“亮”，用来唬唬外国人，不也蛮好的？

中国文化阴柔，那可是老前辈林语堂早说过的。光是阴柔，倒也没有什么不好，遇事淡定，谦和，貌似柔仁，任你矢石并下，我自有“黄金甲”护身，说不定还能把那张牙舞爪的阳刚给“克”了。可是我们毕竟生活在电声光的时代，那份阴柔会不会已随之以险刻，会不会被暴戾取代？看到责在司法的某省高院副庭长杀人之后还分尸，看到曾无限接近“院士”队伍的专家，学着黑社会，雇凶教训方舟子先生，我看对这阴柔论大可质疑。这月亮也不必老被国人捧着当个文化符号，中秋节过或不过，实在关系不大。放假益旅游助世博，本是好事，因为紧接“十一”，假日被拦腰一截，劳逸节奏被打乱，周日上课险些错过，想想后怕！

但我还是要感谢向我送来良好祝愿和月饼的亲朋好友。你们可能怕我觉得孤独，殊不知有言道，孤独可以是个人的狂欢，狂欢也可以是众人的孤独。

2010 年 9 月 22 日

被剥夺之后

听说写了小说《余震》的旅加华人作家张翎曾是我的学生，现在多伦多从事言语障碍(speech impediments)治疗。老师惭愧，没读过张的大作。不过看完电影《唐山大地震》，我觉得小说的内容可能与书题更为熨帖。电影被冯小刚用商业化的大手笔一点化，膨胀成了“中国心灵史诗”，可首先这片题就大成问题，因为拍摄的主要元素并非全景式的灾难，把几次复现的蜻蜓群飞镜头计入，据说涉震只有区区3分钟，故事的大部分都在渲染个人和家庭的震后悲情。看电影前，有人警告说，这部片子是个“催泪弹”，用陈旧的美语说法，叫做“three-handkerchief movie”，现在都已不用织物手帕，恐怕该叫“three-facial-tissue movie”了。

有了思想准备，倒并没用上三块纸巾，只觉得冯导把中国人在被剥夺之后的反应刻画得相当着力，痴迷于真善美过了头，原著中涉及人性和现实的恶被斧削一尽。所谓剥夺，无非是天灾人祸带来的丧失和创痛。被剥夺之后，如何反应？唐山天崩地裂，在丈夫生命被剥夺那一刻，只听得徐帆撕心裂肺仰天大啸一声：“老天爷，你混蛋！”自此，被剥夺者就噤声了，至多故作深沉地说一句“没了，才知道没了是啥滋味”，再也没有对剥夺的抗议。(应当说，这种描写语境是中国人，包括笔者，非常熟悉甚至认同的。)接着就是“太阳照样升起”，天各一方的儿女和厮守家园的母亲各循自己的轨迹生活，最后轨迹相交，母跪女(冯导看过莎剧《科里奥兰纳斯》?)，母女对跪，一连串的

“对不起”声中，滴滴答答的泪雨中，被剥夺的亲情重新回归。如果说这部片子有什么“主旋律”意义的话，看来就是诗化这种节哀顺变，敦厚宽宥的民族性；催人落泪不过是提供了一个安全阀门，诱使观众宣泄对于被剥夺的无奈和怨愤。影片提倡我们发挥这种民族特性，以歉疚、悔恨和宽恕，以“对不起”三个字和眼泪来稀释剥夺，解读历史，再加上一点时髦的“国学”点缀，把其中不那么积极却又为许多中国人接受的内容，搬上银幕，诸如吃个西红柿也要男尊女卑；死了丈夫不忘报恩，不去追求“花红柳绿”而是“从一而终”，等等。地震的剥夺是不可抗力的作用，如果说对于老天爷，人类无法“与天斗，其乐无穷”，那么对待任何形式的剥夺，对于弥合所有的历史伤口，规劝观众一律采取这种态度，冯导的用意可谓深矣！

我喜欢陈道明和徐帆两位演员，可惜他们都没赶上姜文和刘晓庆演《芙蓉镇》以及更早几年张瑜和郭凯敏演《小街》的年代，觉得屈了他们。这儿说到的两部影片，还有若干其他的，如《便衣警察》和某部描写“四五”运动中一位小提琴手命运的片子，电视剧《寻找回来的世界》和稍晚的《人到中年》，等等。虽说技法不如今日之精致，我这个年龄段的人当时也曾被这样的“催泪弹”击中过。内容一样是小故事，怎么从中就能读出被剥夺的历史大叙事？可惜，现在这些作品不是已经就是渐趋湮灭，网上查找，常得“本页不能显示”的结果。

我估计，经改编的影片已与张女士的原著大异其趣。据说张女士认同改编，如见此博文，能否回母校来给学生做一场演讲？

2010 年 9 月 26 日

闷声大发财好?

网友雅意，劝我抛弃琐碎，去做“千秋功业”，譬如说翻译 Dr. Johnson。我本常态细人，兼之编了多少年的辞典，变得更加实用微观。学出世法，非出格丈夫不能。明明是躁进之徒，非要自我检禁，回到书斋，专营冰雪文字，我怕做不到。

就像殷海光说过的，一个思想的人必须有学人的训练和学问的基础，但他的思想方向和重点，毕竟和学院派不同，正如康德和伏尔泰不同一样。对我来说，迷恋于思想，即便是鸡零狗碎的断想也不后悔。“文革”可能是第一个转折点，国外和境外读书问学可能是第二个，上世纪 80 年代末期可能是第三个。除此之外，还有一点经世致用理想主义的残余：以真情与人，总不致卒至自陷。

本来，在一个健全的现代而非中世纪的学术环境中，多数知识分子都应各就各位，经营自己熟悉又爱好的专业领域。对他们价值的评价也应由规规矩矩的专业圈子来决定。然而，无情的现实是，学术政客和学霸们垄断了学术评价，把持了学术资源的分配，启动了一个与“优胜劣汰”恰好相反的机制，少数人富得流油（网上看到也是搞外语的某庞然大物身价过亿，也许是夸大?）的同时，老老实实做学问的人得不到相应的回报，争不到课题，提不了职称，可能有人穷得在滴血。就是网友要我学习的“角色模范”某翻译家，我知道他也在出版商的罗网中挣扎维权。这些年，应友人邀约，本人也做过一点翻译。与过去不同，译时老是不能自已地急赶，没有一次不是在对方规定的时限前缴稿的。(也没有一次是会按期出版的。)那回译毛姆,恰好看到一部关于清代皇帝雍正的电视剧,一味歌功颂德,戏里没有文字狱,没有白莲教,巴不得马上提笔写篇评论求教于编导,更想写信责问熟人焦晃,就因手头译事未竣,终未写成。我当时就自问:雍正和毛姆都与你无关,干嘛陷在里面拔不出来?后来想通了,毕竟还是雍正的关系大于毛姆。都说中国人普遍缺乏宗教信仰,没什么东西是神圣的,如果对历史一样上下其手猥亵,那就真没有什么值得虔敬的事物了。

尽管缺乏宏大叙事的功底,给正被集体失忆的历史打上几块小补丁,自问还能做到。至于"闷声大发财"的境界,道行尚浅,难以达到。更何况真的"闷声",你也发不了大财。不信的话,去问问你认识的翻译家们。

2010 年 10 月 1 日

Were Gates and Buffett Impressed?

As the Gates/Buffett charity dinner in Beijing, China, hit the headlines, the twosome stopped over in Shenzhen on their itinerary. As it happened, to the dismay and embarrassment of the city authorities, a throng of disgruntled prospective condominium buyers took to the street, choking the traffic around the city's Exhibition Hall, to protest against the alleged foul play of real-estate entrepreneurs on the previous day when a property block had been launched in the market with an incredibly cut-price quotation of RMB 11,000 yuan per sq.m. As there was a huge fiery green-eyed crowd of about ten thousand, lots were drawn to decide who were lucky enough to buy. But somehow and for some unsaid reason, the condos were soon sold out, leaving many of the lucky ones empty-handed and agog. Falling from the height of starry-eyed excitement at the prospect of becoming propertied class to a low of abysmal disappointment, they felt shortchanged and then incensed. Hence the sit-in.

Media say that such a mass scene must have been an eyesore to the No. One and No. Two richest men in the world, wondering why the "chengguan" (城管 city law and order management?) beef squads were not dispatched to interfere. My view is different, for

(1) "chengguan" squads are already overburdened with relocatees

holding out not to move, ambulant unlicensed vendors, and indefatigable plucky appellants with their complaints. Should the "chengguan" jurisdiction be further extended over condo-buying malcontents? How can one make a pair of full hands fuller? and

(2) with RMB 11,000 yuan per sq. m. as a bargain price — although it sounds astronomical to many — and with a massive feverish run on housing like bingo, weren't the two magnates impressed with the potential of China's real-estate industry and with the fabulous wealth of the nation so that they might readily dip into their pockets for big bucks to input hither? After all, they are getting on in years — one of them is an octogenarian — and aver that whoever dies rich dies disgraced. Say it again and please live it.

1 October 2010

小草、鲜花和大树

河北大学学生对校园车祸案一度集体噤声之后，听到不少舆论，在责问学校当局的同时，对青年学子多少也有点微词，诸如“怎么像板结土壤中的小草?”“鲜花咋不愿开放?”“如何成为参天大树?”等等。

诘问不是一点道理也没有。从倒金字塔结构（四祖→父母→本人）的家庭中走出，承载了太多的爱和期望，千军万马挤过“独木桥”，好不容易进入大学校园，面临的却是年复一年萎缩的职业市场，能指望孩子们幼嫩的肩胛有多少担当？为同学的横死，激情贲张之下，把自己当下甚至未来的利益置之不顾，一起搭进去？加上大环境商业化的蛊害，钱和权二字强行霸占了核心价值的地位；为减少或抵销“挫折感”，电脑游戏也许是个不错的发泄渠道，娱乐化又来给商业化“为虎作伥”，诱惑学生成为年幼的“犬儒”，结果使他/她们对于投入-产出的性价比（cost-effectiveness）计算得非常精明。河北大学噤声的同时，二三线城市出现了学生反日游行的事——北京、上海、广州的平静自然另有缘由，可见年轻人对成本风险的计算，已经相当老到。但是，等他/她们踏进社会，面对人间丑陋百态，被迫“蚁族”化，不能不有所担当的时候，也许就会出现卉木萋萋、鲜花怒放、大树参天的景象。

抛开体制不说，该受更多责问的其实是师长和家长。我们固然没有能力给学生提供一个好职业，可我们能为他们创造什么样的大学生态,足以让他们选择进取而不是退守,可以使他们不必忌惮打压和要挟而勇于担当;我们自己到了这把年纪有担当了吗?又有什么样以及多少励志树德的经验和真正用世的学识可以同他们分享,有什么样的品格可以去感染他们,有何资格做他们的角色模范?

河北大学又有一条不可复制的年轻生命陨落了,人们可以就“我的爸爸是李刚”写诗打油,那真有点犬儒狂欢的意味。我却视这句话为严厉的拷问,至少对我这个做教师的是如此。

2010 年 10 月 28 日

“寻死啊，老骨头？”

世博会结束了，据说市民的文明素质大有提高。

我却在宿舍门口的国顺路上，险遭横冲直撞的逆行摩托车撞上。

话说这条国顺路，机动车只准由南往北单行，所以我在上课去的途中穿马路，已养成一种“不文明”的习惯：只看单向是否有车过来，如果没有，便放心穿越，而不会舍近及远到路口去走斑马线。那日，正是上班高峰时分，北行汽车因为拥挤排起长队，形成目障，看不见那边半条路的交通情形。我仍按平时习惯泰然穿过马路，行未及半，嗖的一声，一辆逆行的摩托车由北向南飞驶而过，我赶快收住脚步，才算没被撞上。受惊不说，高速激起的“衣带效应”（coattail effect）险些把我刮倒在地。摩托车手显然一样没有预判，被突然钻出来的这个白发老头吓了一跳，于是回过头来，恶狠狠扔下一句：“寻死啊，侬把老骨头！”一边毫不减速，扬长而去。

不知是显规则还是潜规则，在上海市民和交警的文明行车意识中，“摩托车不属机动车”已是约定俗成的共识。那天，市里假座复旦正大体育馆开中秋节庆祝会，因有领导莅临，国权、国顺、邯郸、政修等五六条马路早早派有警察把守。可是过街时，照样见摩托车在交警身边乱闯红灯，谁也不去干涉。邯郸和国权路口的一盏行人止步或通行的信号灯，一年前不知被什么东西撞歪，扭过头去，成为安全隐患，至今不见有人来拨乱反正。莫非要等出了事，才想到“整改”？

从我本人不走斑马线穿马路，到单行道可以双行，从摩托车不算机动车,到歹毒骂人,上海人的文明有待改进之处尚多。穿不穿睡衣上街,事涉面子;行人车辆不按规矩横冲直撞,弄得不好就是性命交关,兹事体大矣。

2010 年 10 月 31 日

人之初

记得最早读到的一本关于“关系”的书是上世纪80年代初美国麻省理工学院教授Lucian Pye(起了个中国名字叫白鲁恂)写的,当时作者还未意识到“关系”一词的能指潜力。二十年来,“关系”在中国大行其道,与其用上不甚确切的nepotism(裙带关系)、cronyism(“哥们”关系)、favoritism(优惠关系)、networking(搞关系)等等,干脆就把拼音文字“guanxi”引入英语,前几年有两个红磡理工的港人Y. H. Wong和Thomas K. Leung甚至直接用“关系”做书名了:“Guanxi: Relationship Marketing in a Chinese Context”。最近屡闻一些外商举报中国官员受贿,深感中国“关系学”的为害已越国界。国内打笔仗或打官司,拉一批洋人专家形成压力集团,写公开信,来替一方造声势的事儿似乎也开始多了起来。我原本都以为是中国“关系学”走出了国门。

最近听说三件事,发现自己有点夸大“关系”的中国特色了。一件是,想进条件好一点的美国幼儿园,除了愿做“冤大头”,浪掷学费之外,跟校长保持良好的人脉也很重要。作为家长,为使自己的娃儿受到照顾,逢年过节,给幼儿老师送礼物也早成了“潜规则”。带孩子出游回去,送上一些旅游地的土特产,也很平常。这可不是亚裔家长特有的关照,waspish(正宗白人)家长们一样这么干,而且有一种不必明言的攀比竞争。第二件事,听某位旅外华裔前几天告诉我,我们视作“大外宣”一部分的孔子学院,院长都是请有点儿影响的洋人出任。有些洋院长花起中国纳税人的钱来眼睛都不眨一下,出手海威。譬如说,重金请来几位评论家,好吃,好住,好玩几天之后,或明或暗提示来客善评、褒评院长大人新出的书,帮助促销并扬文名。第三件事,学生告诉我,现在外资企业招人,非常看重"家庭背景"这一项。说白了,就是看你父母是否有权有钱,有无可以利用的资源价值。

我本人曾在海外的所谓"学术交流"中碰到过尴尬,失去过朋友。有的洋人把你请去讲学,完了送上几百美金的所谓 honorarium,我以为对方真的在乎我讲的内容——虽然某次演讲只有 7 位听众,演讲完毕,事情也就到此为止了。现在回想起来,他/她请过之后,要你明白"来而不往非礼也"的道理,而我未得学校授权,岂可个人做主;真请来了,谁掏钱?所以往往因为没有回请对方,"一锤子买卖"过后从此就再无进一步的"交流"了。当然,西方严肃、认真、一心向学的人,我也遇到过,为数还不少,他们并不索求"等价交换"。

所有这些事情,使我明白人性是普世的。我不同意儒家"人之初性本善"的论断,倒是墨子关于自然人"本性如丝",有待作为社会人之后任由各种颜色漂染的说法,显得更有道理。西方不是也有 tabula rasa (blank slate,即"白纸一张")论吗?夏娃没吃禁果前不就是这样的"白纸"?可撒旦那元始之恶,又是从何而来?莫非就是自然人"本恶"的形体外化?小小年纪的外孙为什么特别钟情于"利维坦"玩具和动画(张牙舞爪的恐龙、蛇怪、鳄鱼)?如此说来,我倒开始倾向于荀子的"人之初性本恶"了。

2010 年 11 月 1 日

争取更好,结果最糟

周末,经历了静安大火的某前学生来讲失火的来龙去脉。据他说,事起那栋教师公寓前方,计划要建造动迁安置房,居民说房子既大又高,会遮挡教师公寓的阳光和空气(即所谓 daylight robbery 是也),妨碍退休老师颐养天年。于是,几位维权意识特别强的老教师站出来,不辞辛劳向政府部门投诉,还找施工单位交涉。大半年之后,终于达成妥协方案:动迁安置房事关"拆出一个新中国",不能不建;晒不着太阳,新陈代谢和血液循环固然会变慢一点,毕竟不是性命交关的事;再说,铁杆"太阳粉丝"们远一点尽可跑静安公园,再不堪,搬张矮凳下楼到路边向阳面坐一坐,照样可以摄入钙和磷不是?最后,政府部门拗不过这些固执的老倔头,也做了让步:由我们出钱办实事,给教师公寓做外墙改造,加隔热层,改门窗。要知道旧楼改造排着长队呢,优先照顾你们,就满足吧。

于是,脚手架未经批准一下子就搭到了七楼,架上的走道仍是可燃的竹片板;为施工安全和观瞻效果,脚手架还用易燃的尼龙网密密匝匝包住。因为是节能综合改造,工程所使用的聚氨酯泡沫不但可能导致火势猛烈,还会散发毒气。这样,施工经过三次分包,弄到最后落到市里几次批评、区里却当做"宠儿"的某家弄堂公司,找来几位路边散工,不计后果地违规干了起来,终于酿成 11·15 震惊中外的一把大火。

亡羊补牢,未为晚也。现在旁边的兄弟楼(出事公寓为三栋楼房之一）和全上海的建筑、监理界一片鸡飞狗跳。但是440位住户中死了58人，比例高达13%+，任你如何封锁火场和殡仪馆，这事毕竟已经钉上耻辱柱了。对直接受害的教师公寓老弱住户来说，就像我那位前学生所说的，要是当时抱着“多一事不如少一事”的态度，阳光被挡，空气流通不畅，都认了，那么今天还应当是太太平平活着的人，而非冤魂。

前学生因此得出一个颇有哲理的结论：好多事情，别去争取较好或更好，因为争取的结果可能是更坏或最坏。他说现在已在准备迎接“赔偿”大战，与各方角力，人家如果“上路”，适可而止算了，可千万别再来一次“争取更好，结果最坏”。盱衡社会现状，我觉得他说的不无道理。中国的阿Q们也许就是这样养成的。

2010年11月21日

We're Growing Chemically Savvy

What is melamine（三聚氰胺）? Not until, I bet, the poisoned "Three Deer" powdered milk scandal was brought to daylight had few Chinese known about the word and the substance. The repercussions are still being felt today: a parent of a victimized baby, protesting that the damage had not been adequately redeemed, was sentenced behind closed doors for "disturbing public order" a few days ago and the blacklisted products have zigzagged their way through a network of banning and recalling and reportedly been found in remote provinces such as Qinghai. As if the havoc weren't bad enough.

The word melamine now leads off a long list of chemical words quickly being absorbed into a nomenclature with local Chinese characteristics, making the nation more and more chemically aware and savvy: acrylamide（丙烯酰胺 or 丙毒）in instant noodles, aflatoxin（黄曲霉素）in hogwash oil（地沟油 or 潲水油）, sudan one or oil-soluble yellow（苏丹红）in salty duck eggs made in brine dregs, fructose syrup（果葡糖浆）passing for pure natural honey, sodium formaldehyde sulfoxylate（甲醛次硫酸氢钠，俗称"吊白块"— a cubic chemical substance to highlight whiteness? [translation mine]) or benzoyl peroxide（过氧化苯甲酰，漂白剂）to make stale rice or flour look good, to name but a few. Most recently, the list has spilled from foodstuff items to the building industry, the most frequently quoted term at the moment being polyurethane foams（聚氨酯泡沫）— the No. One culprit in addition to inflammable scaffolding materials for the Nov. 15 conflagration of a high-rise condo building for teachers in Shanghai.

Thickeners, sweeteners, dyestuffs, pigments, preservatives, antiseptics, additives, residue disinfectants: over recent years the Chinese who are used to taking in hazardous chemicals along with their food have been well initiated in such terms — at least legibly so (meaning when you espy the terms you know what they mean even though you don't say them fluently). A professor friend of mine told me he is thinking of posing some of these terms as questions in an oral exam meant for applicants for next year's enrolment to see if they are with-it enough. "That would be too technical and difficult," I said. "Pooh! ABC of survival skills living in China," was my friend's retort. More viably and usefully, I'm thinking of poring over A Complete Food Hazards Encyclopedia of 55 inedibles on the net to make sure that the technical terms are entered without fail in the dictionary we write.

God bless China. I wonder if sustained exposure to toxics helps develop an acquired immunity to them and finally would succeed in remaking man. Otherwise how can one explain away longer life expectancy of the nation and the quick accrual of medals in sports events at the Asian Games these days in Guangzhou?

23 November 2010

When I Saw Her Picture Again

She used to be the Oriental Beauty Queen on Oxford campus. As is seen from her early pictures, hers is a kind of quiet, graceful, intellectual beauty. In between those and the latest one she took recently after she had emerged from confinement — mostly under house arrest plus occasionally in prison — some twenty years have elapsed. She now looks like an old dame with a tangled web of crow's feet around the eye corners on a gaunt face. Nevertheless, the exquisite grace is still there. If anything, beauty of fine features has metamorphosed into seasoned maturity bordering on, in my eyes, celestial ethereality. Despite a smile assumed before a camera, her eyes are a bit sad but somehow continue to emit a profusion of benevolence, reconciliation, placidity, and above all, an unflagging determination.

She is five years my junior, this stubborn woman who refused imposed exile in exchange for freedom, who could not hold her husband's hand when he breathed his last because she was told if she left the country at all she was not supposed to come back. When I was put under campus arrest for five weeks during the Cultural Revolution, she was young enough to breathe the air of freedom and was getting married to her husband. Nightmare for her — a magnified far far cry from mine, of course — began when I was set free and sent to join in the making of a dictionary. She went back to her homeland to nurse an ailing mother and unwittingly meddled with politics. The military junta would not look on with folded arms when she had the guts to address half a million with the Shwedagon Pagoda in the background, a famous landmark of the capital where her father had spoken up against the British colonialists. The resultant cost was as dear as everybody now knows. The entire world protested except a few one can count on one hand. The UN intervened, even with a General Assembly resolution. The ASEAN neighbor nations adjured. The Pope John Paul II, whose words generally are unheard or unheeded in the lay world, preached. An aficionado even swam across a lake on the q. t. to her heavily security-policed house, uninvited, to express concern. Far away, the Irish singer/songwriter Damien Rice composed a song "Unplayed Piano" especially for her, as her instrument had broken down and the authorities would allow no repairman to enter her house to fix it. U2 urged their concert goers to all wear a mask bearing her likeness by way of support. But all to no avail. Look, her country is a small undeveloped country with little say in international affairs. In fact, but for her, the country would have hardly been in the limelight. But when it stands up against the rest of the world, it can conveniently forget our common humanity and proudly scoff at a thing mythologically called public opinion or good sense, going amuck but unpunished. Can we say man is born good and kind-hearted? She was right when she said those in power were really "amazing" because so often they were always the last to know what the people really wanted.

I gaze long and affectionately at her recent picture, my eyes slowly moistening. Her father was assassinated. Will she follow in his footsteps?

26 November 2010

考高中比考大学更难

长甥女的女儿明年要考高中，托我找关系，看能不能进所重点。我一点路子也没有，明知无能为力，心底对这种做法还有点反感，拗不过她，只好虚与委蛇，装模作样给熟人打了几个电话，果然无效。

长甥女告诉我，现在考高中比考大学更难。一位从事教育行政工作的朋友也告诉我，去年和前年的实际录取率是：大学达到 60%左右，但是普通高中只有 40%（其中约有一半是重点高中）。这与国家对教育的投入向高校倾斜，大学扩招当然有关。我却从中看出，我国教育改革的指导思想和客观效果，是逼着处于 9 年义务教育出口处 14-15 岁的少年（和他们的家长）接受竞争最为剧烈的一场筛选和分流。相比而言，其残酷性比之把竞争推迟到三年以后的高考，有过之而无不及。更糟糕的是，竞争还在日益低龄化，正从高中祸延初中、小学甚至幼儿园。我怕几代以后，中国人有朝一日都变成头颅奇大而四肢萎缩的外星人式怪物。

竞争剧烈的筛选安排在学生几岁时为好，关系到国家把教育资源向何处何人倾斜。义务教育一摊亟需加强，姑且不谈，决策者能否从我们用来兴建所谓一流大学和现代化“橱窗式”大学城的钱，用来重金聘请“海归”的投入当中，拿出一部分来，从师资到图书馆、实验室、运动场、食堂等硬件设备，花它几年功夫切实加强所有高中，帮助目前的所谓“非重点”逐步接近上海中学、华师大二附中、复旦附中等校的水平，从而有助于高中学生为三年后“竞争剧烈的筛选”做好准备？至少，到那时，青涩少年的肩头负重抗压能力总会增强一些吧。我还了解到，目前部分高中教师不是学养不够，而是靠一份干薪对付不了通货膨胀和“居者有其屋”的压力，加上全社会拜金成风，业余盛行上海人所说的“揩猪猡”，家教两节课可得400元（我猜了100元，被耻笑），于是“上课像条虫，家教像条龙”。不知道国家投入多了，用以改善高中教师的待遇（包括达到若干教龄，购屋优惠），扩大他们在社会上的话语权，开设选修课增加课时，辅以优胜劣汰的教职置换制度（例如聘请“海归”改善高中师资结构），会不会吸引师生“重返教室”？

都说发达国家的教育制度优于我们和其他一些受孔老夫子影响最大的亚洲国家。依我看，人家的一大优点在于把“竞争剧烈的筛选”尽量拖后到大学甚至研究生阶段，在尽可能长的时间里不以“苦学”去浇灭学生求知的兴趣。以我们国家现有的财力，全面加强高中教育，提高入学率，绝非难事，比之成天叫着办世界一流大学，成本要低廉得多。而把最残酷的筛选从14-15岁的少年身上移走，可能也才是真正意义上的“救救孩子”。

2010年12月5日

干脆废了四六级如何?

一位前学生来拜早年,说起他在某校负责英语“四六级考试”的考前训练和实施工作,前一段大忙。我问:“四六级不是早已跟学位证书脱钩了吗?”他回答我说与学位证书脱钩不假,可是跟求职的那只钩子还牢牢挂着。今天要找份好工作,四六级打底,最好还有托福、雅思、口译证书,所以每年考四六级的仍有七八百万人。庞大的考生群就是商机,“助考业”便应运而生,内含报名、考前探题泄题、考时作弊、考后制作假证等环节。

据来客说,仅报名一项就有油水。自规定“四六级”只对在校学生开放以来,京沪带头,二三线城市跟上,出现不少报名代理商,收费高出25元标准的4-5倍。瞄准的对象是求职一群和一些无处挂靠的民办大学学生。探题的多是“识途老马”,本人考过或多次考过四六级,再花重金买通命题专家(应届的搞不定,上一届的亦可,少给点钱就是了,为的是“摸路子”)泄漏一题,付酬多少,都有行情。就这样,半探半猜,弄出一份答卷,找学生做“跑街”,在校园里兜售,生意红火,只是炮制模拟题的代理商增加,近年来价位下跌。也有学生相信此类标准化考试的诀窍,就是对付题海战术(我很同意),所以搜罗各种模拟题和往年的真实题,全部做遍,据说后来果然考过了500分。

最赚钱的还是实时作弊。前些年靠手机内问外答,但是信号不稳,又容易被监考抓获,现在已基本弃之不用。目前最稳妥的办法,是往考场派入“卧底”，拍照传出，外面早有高级“枪手”埋伏，把题解信息传入考生的埋入式耳麦。据说制造这类无线埋入式耳机的厂商多如牛毛，广告都做到校园去了，而“枪手”中颇不乏“211”和“985”一类重点大学的高手，于是答题的准确性年年提高。

如果考生的英文实在太烂过不了关，莫急。因为上网只能查得考生最近一次的成绩，又无法验证其真伪，干脆找个“办证”的，付上一二百块钱，弄张足以乱真的四六级通过证明。我说与其前面如此折腾，用这最后一招，不全结了。来客说，假证使人处于“心理弱势”，求职时如果不幸要求测试英文，对方发现落差太大，顿时穿帮，那可正应了严复当年的名言：“华风之弊，八字尽之，始于作伪，终于无耻。”

来访的前学生又说，考出四六级的学生英语实在好不到哪里去，讲不出，除了可能是背出来的模型文，一写就错，只是揣摩出题套路的本事大有长进。既如此，为何不干脆废了这四六级？

2010 年 12 月 25 日

附　　录

诗　作

一

无　　题

偏向疏篱断处尽,亭亭常抱岁寒心。
消磨绚烂归平淡,独步秋风无古今。

二

九零年作于香港

清歌曼舞正繁华,我尚漂摇未有家。
身似孤鸿悬海上,心随明月到天涯。
春来花好无人赏,客里愁销有酒赊。
尘世论交今几个,漫将往事诉寒鸦。

清歌曼舞亦繁华
我尚飘摇未有家
身似孤鸿悬海上
心随明月到天涯
春来花好无人赏
秋里愁销有酒赊
尘世论交今几个
漫将往事诉寒鸦

憶年少與學[illegible]兄留念

陆谷孙
二〇〇九年二月十四日

LE MERIDIEN
SHE SHAN SHANGHAI
上海世茂佘山艾美酒店

(原载 2016 年 8 月 3 日《文汇报·笔会》)

三

无 题

飞腾犹忆少年场，廿载正字落叶黄。
命途多有羊肠险，物外优游鹤梦长。
孤藤不死天留爱，长篇苦成溢书香。

My soaring youthful aspirations I still remember,
When 20 years of dictionary making has reduced me to a yellow fallen leaf.
The life path is full of hazardous twists and turns.
Only my extramundane dream remains as long
As the crane's life.
The lonely ivy stays alive but for the heavenly love.
Long as it is, the compilation is painstakingly done and full of bookish fragrance.

截自作者致好友 Thomas Creamer 先生书信。

四

一九八九年七月二十四日，首见《英汉大词典》上卷印成，感慨良多

菡萏翩翻薄暑收，虚堂微雨逗清秋。

诗心欲往羲皇上，酒窟相将汗漫游。

自笑半身退飞鹢，谁怜中路失友鸥。

两当容与疏风里，同座高贤几黑头！？

英漢大詞典 编辑部

菡萏翩翻薄暑收
虚堂微雨逗清秋
诗心欲往羲皇上
酒窟相将汗漫游
自笑半身退飞鹢
谁怜中路失友鸥
两当容与疏风里
同座高贤几黑头！？

[illegible] 顺颂

近佳

谷孙
九月二十七日

（原载2016年8月3日《文汇报·笔会》）

此诗另一版本见于作者致好友 Thomas Creamer 先生书信：

菡萏翩翻薄暑收，陋室雨声逗清秋。
自笑半身退飞鹢，谁怜中路失伴鸥。
两当容与疏风里，同座高贤几黑头。

With lotus blossoms stirred in the wind,
A mild summer is drawing to an end.
In my shabby, empty room, the sound of
Falling rain invokes an early fall.
I laugh at myself for being a vanishing water-bird
And who deplores the loss of accompanying gulls?
Alas, let both be one with the passing breeze,
For who of us has not a grey hair yet?

菡萏翩翻薄暑收
陋室雨声逗清秋
自笑半身退飞鹢
谁怜中路失伴鸥
两当容与疏风里
同座高贤几黑头？

With lotus blossoms stirred in the wind,
A mild summer is drawing to an end.
In my shabby, empty room, the sound of
Falling rain invokes an early fall.
I laughter at myself for being a vanishing water-bird
And who deplores the loss of accompanying gulls?
Alas, let both be one with the passing breeze.
For who of us has not a grey hair yet?

截自作者致好友 Thomas Creamer 先生书信。

五

无　　题

小园木落尽荒凉，惟有邻圃残桂香。
满地寒虫鸣寂寂，吁哭应和悲夕阳。

My little yard — a sight of wilderness with fallen leaves.
From the next-door garden is wafted fragrance of remnant mums.
Loud but lonely is the chorus of chirping late-fall insects,
Crying as if lamenting the setting sun.

小园木落尽荒凉 — My little yard -- a sight of wilderness with fallen leaves.
惟有邻圃残桂香 — From the next-door garden is wafted fragrance of remnant mums.
满地寒虫鸣寂寂 — Loud but lonely is the chorus of chirping late-fall insects,
吁哭应和悲夕阳 — Crying as if lamenting the setting sun.

截自作者致好友 Thomas Creamer 先生书信。

六

无　　题

留得孤危劫后身，旧游多半委沙尘。
相怜惟有墙头月，磊落光明永照人。

（此诗为作者于徐燕谋先生自杀后所作，见本书“Xu Yanmou: An Eidetic Memory — In Lieu of a Foreword to the New Edition of *Selected Modern English Essays for College Students*”一文。）

七

咏　鹤

来往云霄体格清，砉然长啸震天惊。
胸无半点尘埃物，负有生平浩气行。

（原载 2016 年 8 月 3 日《文汇报·笔会》）

八

无　题

空拜雕龙催澍雨，难教肉马上瑶池。
几人得似钱夫子，锐卒花旗抵五师。

（原载 2016 年 8 月 3 日《文汇报·笔会》）

九

己丑元月十三学生来贺生日留饭细诉平生夜倾泻胸愫得句

竟作乘桴海外游，尘缘淘尽付东流。
功名福禄原知梦，踪迹飞鸿莫我求。
黄叶闭门安道径，白云高卧九号楼。
往事回望渺如线，一洗沧桑无限愁。

（原载2016年8月3日《文汇报·笔会》）

十

乙丑年九月初六酒后为挚友老汤作

万种尘缘绝，研经深闭关。
曼倩颜常驻，希夷鬓不斑。
旧交能有几，坚卧在名山。

Composed on lunar 6th of the ninth month, 乙丑 year; lubricated, I dedicate this poem to my bosom friend Tom!

Ten thousand mundane considerations
done away with,
We would rather shut doors and
peruse our scriptures.
Would that you remain handsome and young,
No gray hair'll show on your two sides.
How many old friends do we have?
One of mine is a stubborn hermit,
Hiding himself in a famous mountain.

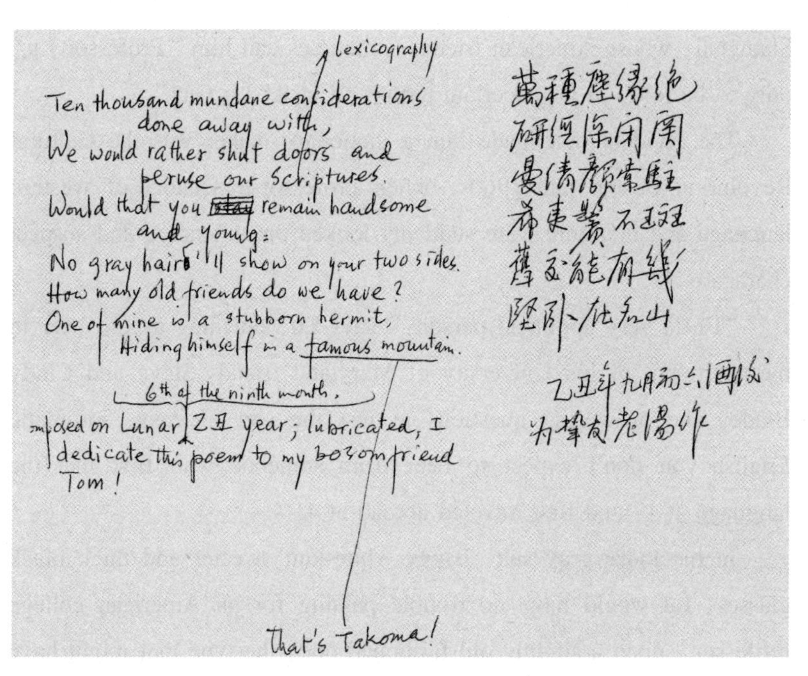

lexicography

Ten thousand mundane considerations
done away with,
We would rather shut doors and
peruse our Scriptures.
Would that you ~~stay~~ remain handsome
and young:
No gray hair'll show on your two sides.
How many old friends do we have?
One of mine is a stubborn hermit,
Hiding himself in a famous mountain.

6th of the ninth month,
[illegible]posed on Lunar 乙丑 year; lubricated, I
dedicate this poem to my bosom friend
Tom!

That's Takoma!

萬種塵緣絶
研經深閉関
愿儂顔常駐
兩邊鬢不斑
舊友能有幾
堅卧在名山

乙丑年九月初六酒後
为摯友老湯作

截自作者致好友 Thomas Creamer 先生书信。

访 谈

The Grand Master of "Chinglish"

By James Lardner

"I became a dictionary maker by accident," says Lu Gu-sun of Shanghai, whose American friends sometimes call him "Professor Lu" only to be told, in no uncertain terms, "Cut it! Lu Gu!"

The accident that made him a dictionary maker was the Cultural Revolution of the late 1960s, when professor-translators of western language and literature were suddenly looked on as strange and suspect characters.

"I'm a very apolitical person," says Lu, downing a cold beer in the apartment of his University of Maryland friends Steve and Cindy Bladey and answering questions in just the sort of easy, idiomatic English you don't expect to hear from someone who first met the language at 17 and first traveled abroad at 41.

In his loose gray suit, baggy white-knit sweater and thick black glasses, Lu would have no trouble passing for an American college professor, albeit a slightly old-fashioned one, the type that might have been played by James Stewart or Henry Fonda in the movies, and might have to contend with a campus full of rebellious teenagers.

The gang in Lu's life, however, was the infamous Gang of Four, which turned China into a place where, apolitical or not, he was regarded as a "budding revisionist."

"Sure, I got into trouble," he says. "But in retrospect that was a kind of experience, too, and because you were in very tough times — 'hard times,' as Dickens would say — you learn to be content."

Today Lu is a prolific translator of American criticism and fiction (including Arthur Hailey's *The Moneychangers* and Peter Benchley's *Jaws*), in addition to his regular duties as a professor in the foreign languages department at Shanghai's Fudan University, and head of the new Shakespeare Library there.

His lexicographic career got off the ground in 1970, when the study of Western literature was no longer an acceptable occupation in China. Lu was put to work preparing a mid-sized English-Chinese dictionary, which has now sold 2 million copies despite a hefty price tag of about $3, compared with as little as 30 cents for other Chinese books. Lu says the dictionary didn't really deserve the good reviews it received in the United States, because it was watched over a tad too closely by "workers' representatives" bent on purging it of slang, underworld expressions and "anything X-rated."

"They were thinking of producing a wholly clean and correct dictionary of Chinglish," says Lu. Just the same, he managed to "smuggle in" a few everyday practical terms such as "schlemiel," "schlep" and "schlock" — an achievement in which he takes visible pride.

His own conversation is laced with words like "newfangled,"

"viable" and "ubiquitously," reflecting the dictionary-maker in him, and also, perhaps, his experience translating popular American fare — some of it popular in China, too. His translation of *The Moneychangers* earned Lu the equivalent of a year's salary in China. His wife, who teaches English to medical students, has translated Daphne du Maurier's *Rebecca* — another hot seller.

As a professor, Lu earns a monthly salary of 82 Chinese dollars, or $45 U.S., which he calls a "so-so" rate of pay compared with that of, say, factory workers. He owns the family home in Shanghai, but shares it with an abundance of relations. Soon, Lu, his wife and daughter will be moving into a three-room apartment on the Fudan University campus — an unusually spacious establishment by Chinese standards.

Lu's firsthand knowledge of America comes from a year he spent here helping American scholars work on a Chinese-English dictionary. It was Lu's first trip overseas, and his first prolonged separation from his wife and daughter. "I did not have what they call 'culture shock'," he says. "I was very homesick, though."

Early in his stay, he remembers remarking: "I did not expect to see canines so widespread." But today that tale is told with a laugh about the offbeat phrasing.

Among the other American traits that first struck him: cold drinks, material well-being ("especially the housing"), serious work habits ("Work ethics are pretty good here. Work is work. Play is play."), and the fact that American drivers go easy on their horns — at least compared with Shanghai, where drivers have been known to commence honking even before they start up their cars.

And "this tenure system is pretty good," says Lu. By which he means, not tenure itself, but the period of competition for it. "We don't have a shadow of that sort of thing," he says. In China, tenure is early and automatic, and old professors rarely bother to teach. Nor can they be compelled to, says Lu, "because of the respect they command." The underlying difficulty, he says, is the generous policy the Chinese call "eating from the same big pot."

"That's one of the things China is trying to wrestle with," he says.

At the University of Colorado, Lu was stunned to learn that teachers were rated every semester by their students — an innovation he found so appealing that he proposed its adoption in China during a debriefing session with the Ministry of Higher Education.

But Lu has decidedly ambivalent feelings about the current "fever" of Chinese enthusiasm for America and Americana. "When I first came to live amidst such material well-being, of course, I could enjoy these things," he says, "but I kept thinking, well, these things don't belong to me." He looks on the United States, he says, as one big hotel, where he is emphatically a guest.

In Shanghai lately, Chinese youths have taken to carrying portable cassette players and riding motorcycles, and parents have begun putting the arm on their American relations to sponsor Chinese college applicants here. "The effort to understand English, to understand western culture, is largely healthy," says Lu. "But there are young people who have made it their lifetime goal to leave China and to settle down here. That's despicable!"

He flew to Washington two weeks ago to take part in a conference at the University of Maryland. In his lecture on Chinese-Western interchange after the first World War, Lu recalled that "some of the Chinese dramatists would lie prostrate before the feet of western dramatists." They complained, among other things, about the absence of a concept of tragedy in Chinese drama (which Lu believes to have been a misplaced criticism; there were Chinese tragedies, he says, but they tended to have abrupt happy endings tacked onto the end).

Today, he fears a return of that kind of national self-loathing. "China has a lot of good things," he says, "such as Chinese philosophy, which emphasizes patience and tolerance." (And, Bladey reminds him, Chinese beer, which "comes in bottles twice this size.")

When he defends his country and excoriates those who would leave it, Lu says "this is my father speaking through me." At the time of the 1949 revolution, his father worked for a Hong Kong shipping magnate, who urged him to leave Shanghai and move his family to Hong Kong. Instead, in the early '50s, Lu's father moved back to Shanghai. This was because, in Hong Kong, "life was so hectic for him — people were so material-oriented," Lu explains.

Lu's mother died when he was 8, and his father never remarried. "My father was father, mother, mentor and tutor to me," says Lu.

His father was also a scholar of French, and *The Count of Monte Cristo* and *The Three Musketeers* were two of Lu's favorite books as a boy. He studied Russian in high school, reading Turgenev and Chekhov, "and Russian music was played all the time," he recalls. But he hasn't had too much use for his Russian lately, what with the chill on Sino-Soviet relations.

At Fudan University, Lu has taught American literature as well as Shakespeare. The literature course goes from colonial writers through

Cooper, Emerson and Poe right up to what Lu describes as the contemporary "Jewish school."

"There's a lot of interest in the Jewish school," says Lu.

When he returns to Shanghai, Lu will start his Shakespeare course with a half-semester devoted to *Hamlet*. Shakespeare is catching on in China, he says. *Romeo and Juliet* was recently performed in Tibetan, and a drama class production of *King Lear* was shown on national television. Chinese audiences "like to be there even if they don't understand very much," he says.

Nevertheless, a Chinese Shakespeare expert remains a definite novelty in the West. Last year, Lu raised a few eyebrows when he delivered a paper on "Hamlet Across Time and Space" at a British Shakespeare colloquium. "I was the first Chinese speaker ever there at the conference," he says.

He looks for a parallel. He finds one.

"I was a panda bear."

（原载1983年3月19日《华盛顿邮报》）

“一江流过水悠悠”*

主持人：非常感谢大家今天来参加《一江流过水悠悠》的电影读书活动。我们今天非常有幸，请到了这本书的译者、复旦大学著名教授陆谷孙老师来跟我们交流，谈一下他翻译这本书时比较有趣的事情。陆老师自己很坦诚，他说自己不懂钓鱼，所以说这本书不应该由他来翻译，应该请黄源深老师来翻译，因为黄源深老师喜欢钓鱼。现在我们就有请陆谷孙老师上台。

陆谷孙：谢谢各位前来捧场，特别感谢我的 patron 陆灏。也感谢《文景》，还有曲阳图书馆的管理层，能够给我这么个机会，说实在的，说不出多少有趣的东西。本书翻译的事情是译林出版社当年的周丽华来约的。她第一次约我给一本小书《芒果街上的小屋》写序。然后第二本就是 Truman Capote 圣诞故事的译本序言。第三个任务就是翻译这本书。第四个任务是给她最近出的那本《阿弗小传》写序。

这本书翻译的经过大概就是这样。起初，我译到第 15 页就想住手了，因为全是关于蝇饵垂钓的，不甚了了。这个在电影里面各位大概看得很壮观，我自己连活饵钓鱼都没玩过，更甭说蝇饵钓鱼这么一个困难的技术活，所以实在翻不下去。老实讲，翻完了以后，对这技术活的户外运动，还是云里雾里，一知半解。所以各位在看这本书的时候，无论如何把我这句大实话也当作一个折扣打在里头。如果哪

---

* 本文是作者 2011 年 11 月 12 日在上海曲阳文化馆参加《一江流过水悠悠》与读者互动活动的录音整理稿，由作者的好友叶扬教授提供、编辑并注释。——编注。

些地方翻得不准确，欢迎大家指出来。

翻到第15页准备罢手了。结果周丽华说“你碰到那个钓鱼难段，我来替你翻”。我的感觉是，第一，这个人比较有诚意，的确是希望我翻的；第二，我也觉得，我是七十老翁，她那么个青年人，能够有这么大的勇气来给我翻一段，让我续完，所以我更应该接受挑战，于是接着就翻译下去了，终于一口气翻完。

我对翻译作品确有这么一条要求，非常希望英汉对照出现，这样，你所有的缺点、错误，你身体上所有难看的部位，全部忠实地呈现在照妖镜前面。所以我也跟有关方面建议过，我说如果哪家出版社准备出版翻译作品的，它必须建立它自己的资质信用。靠什么？就是靠出版原文跟译文对照本的读物。（最好是逐页对照。）几年过去，若没有什么人来提出太大的抗议和反对，就算是具备了资质，不然的话，总有人存疑的。而且现在翻译的劣品太多，比如说蒋介石变成常凯申什么的，这个不去说它了。

翻着翻着，我后来的确译出些趣味来了。为什么呢？主要是跟我对美国文学的爱好有关。我大学毕业论文写的是 Jack London，指导教师就是“文革”中夫妇双双投缳自尽的刘德中先生。我现在还记得我的论文里头有这么一句话：说起美国人的国民性，与其说来自“五月花号”的乘客契约，不如说更多来自蛮荒丛林和开拓新边疆的冲动。原始自然、草莽、新边疆、开拓先驱，这几个主题词我觉得是喜欢美国文学的人不能不注意的。当然，另外一个种族的母题也是不可忽略的。

我们还是先从形象破题来讲，你去美国国会大厦参观的时候，你就看到很多的风景画。风景画里面的阿帕拉契山道是 Bill Bryson① 走过的，走了两个礼拜败下阵来，鲜有人能走完全程的，从东北角的

① 布赖森（William McGuire “Bill” Bryson，1951 年生）：长居英伦的美国旅行家，以多部游记知名于世。

Maine,一直走到 Oregon。你到国会大厦去,还会看到落基山、大峡谷、大瀑布、密西西比河等等,而在欧洲那些博物馆或画廊里多见的是大教堂尖塔、古建筑的废墟。如果你到希腊,到意大利去跑跑,街头一个拐弯,突然看见铁条拦起几块古老大石,原来是某某建筑的遗物。这样的景象在美国比较少见,美国风景画里面见到的很多是悬崖峭壁,而不是教堂尖塔。

在美国经常见人背个双肩包,带上一条狗,远足度假,夜里钻睡袋,内急了,跨过篝火的余烬,爬到漆黑的户外化学马桶方便,听着远处的狼嚎。鄙人也体验过一次,只是走了不到三天,太娇贵,败下阵来。现在我们的黄金长假,都往人多的地方挤,亲近不到自然,不是拍照,就是大眼瞪小眼。有意思吗?当然,中国人太多也是一个问题。

于是我就想到美国从最早的 Washington Irving 的《见闻札记》开始,什么《睡谷传奇》,什么《瑞普·凡·温克尔》;还有 Cooper 的《皮绑腿》、《最后一个莫西干人》,文学来到了"户外",欧洲的宝塔形阶级结构给淡化了。然后有了新英格兰的超验主义,Emerson 的《自然》,有人说是奠定了美国文学独一无二的性格,而且跟我们这部关于"大河"的书有关,其中用了多少"水"的隐喻。说到自然,当然会想到 Thoreau 的《瓦尔登湖》,想到 Mark Twain 的《密西西比河上的生活》,想到 Melville 的《白鲸》,想到 Jack London 的《野性的呼唤》、《白獠牙》,想到 Hemingway 的《老人与海》,等等。Jack London 笔下的狗最后随狼群回归自然而去,可不像周丽华翻译的 Virginia Woolf 的"阿弗"那样的一条"文艺狗"。一直发展到今天,诸位可能不太注意当代的"自然"作品。我就推荐两位,一位是 8 岁开始学爬山的 Jon Krakauer[1],写攀登珠穆朗玛的 *Into Thin Air*,居然可以畅销;还有一

① 克拉考尔(Jon Krakauer,1954 年生):美国作家,登山能手。1997 年出版以他攀登珠穆朗玛峰的经历为题的 *Into Thin Air*(《进入稀薄的空气之中》),成为美国当年的畅销书。

位女士 Ann Ronald，三岁开始学滑雪，写了 *Rock*, *Water*, *Wild*，风靡过一时。[1] 我译“大河”就始终意识到自己是在这样动态的大背景前从事文化换码，而不是静态的语文作业。书里的水有情，会喁喁诉说历史；鱼有灵，不会那么容易让你手到擒来。至于人，就像 Ihab Hassan[2] 这些 post-humanists 说的，只是物种之一。爱默生说过，自然就等于 Not Me+Me。两者结合在一起，才是整个宇宙。译书的时候老想着这两者的结合，但两者又是不同的独立主体存在。

我个人觉得书比电影好。你不妨读一遍，其中对白并不特别的少，但基本都没有亲人间的称呼，好像亲情很淡薄，重要的是个体的尊严。户外露天决定了作品的基调和节奏。兄弟两个见面以后，感觉到有很多话要说，特别是哥哥，要规劝弟弟几句，改邪归正。但是刚要开口又噎回去了，而且为自己想开口这点感觉到非常内疚。你就是你，我就是我，我们两个都是主体，我不应该来干预你。所以在这本书里面，弟弟的死，弟弟平时生活的不检点，酗酒、酒驾、出车祸、赌博等等这些内容，都是一笔带过的，写得更详尽、具体而微的是捕鱼。不管怎么样，弟弟就是捕鱼的英雄。作者要详写纪念的是一个存活在自然界里的英雄。正因为如此，文字非常之洗练又阳刚。我记得有一个河岸场景，儿子问父亲读的是什么书，父亲答：“《圣经》。”儿子评论：“好书。”原文是“A good book”。编辑改作“一本好书”，完全没错。但最后我还是把“一本”两个字划掉了。你破坏了我阅读时候简约主义或称最简主义的语言节奏嘛。

再比如说父亲跟大儿子讨论到二儿子的时候，就讲我们真应该帮帮他，我们都应该拿出自己的一部分来帮帮他，那么拿什么部分

① 此处陆老师的记忆有误。罗纳德（Ann Ronald, 1939 年生）是美国内华达州的女作家，但是 *Rock*, *Water*, *Wild: An Alaskan Life*（2009）（《岩石、水、荒野：阿拉斯加生活见闻》）一书的作者是另一位美国女作家洛德（Nancy Lord, 1952 年生）。

② 哈桑（Ihab Hassan, 1925－2015）：出生于埃及的阿拉伯裔美国文学批评家。

呢,我可以拿出的部分,譬如说长老会的教义,他可能确实没有而又并不想拥有,这时有句话,大意是 what is needed may not be wanted。也就是说,在我们外人看来很清楚,他身上缺了点什么,需要什么,但是他本身要不要?不要,明明是他需要的东西,他并不要,并不想要,你帮不了他。这种亲情在个人尊严面前的无助,我以为是除捕鱼之外全书写得最妙的。而语言绝不枝蔓,点到为止,说句“政治不正确”的话,典型的男子汉叙事。以“阳刚叙事”的标准衡量,现在书的封面是不是太“小清新”了一些?

由于是英汉对照本,翻译的时候必须非常小心,以“信”为主。做没做到,请各位批评,上海人讲“捉扳头”,哈哈,欢迎“捉扳头”,一定有的。所以翻译的时候,基本上态度是诚惶诚恐,战战兢兢,穿着紧身衣。翻到最后的时候,这紧身衣穿得实在难受死了,想起维特根斯坦的语用“游戏”论和海德格尔的主体论,既然女性主义批评认为原文文本代表的是“父权至上”,那不妨也来个小小的颠覆。最后一句的原文是:I am haunted by waters,这时我终于挣脱了紧身衣,把压抑多时的自我释放了一下,翻译成“水啊,我的梦”。我自己觉得已经是最后一句了嘛,就从“信”字偏离一下也可以原谅,可是责任编辑不同意,一定要改成“魂牵梦系”之类的措辞。我这人固执,又改了回来。孰可孰不可,诸位明断。

下面我想说说翻译问题。翻译嘛,名声是一直不好,什么“象胥”,小吏一个;什么“舌人”,不就是鹦鹉?现当代地位更加卑微,郭沫若大人就说中国多的是媒婆,少的是处子。媒婆,多难听!还有更难听的,说什么翻译等于嚼饭于人,多不卫生!

其实,翻译在先进理念和新思想传入方面所起的作用,不论是圣杰罗姆、马丁·路德、廷代尔等在西方译经,还是“五四”时期的赛德两先生来华,甚至后来改革开放初期的思想解放,都是不可低估的。口头上承认翻译重要的人可能不少,实际上把它边缘化的人更多。

一个稿费低,一个翻译不算学术成果,把大批能做翻译、善做翻译的人驱赶得远离翻译。在我们这儿,翻译是理论和实践隔裂最甚的领域,可能与计不计入学术成果的计算也有关系。你译“大河”算什么学术?我别出心裁阐释翻译家有16种身份才是理论成果。我的天,16种身份(纳税人这一身份可曾计入?)!落笔翻译的时候,如果老想着我现在处于何种身份状态,怕是一个句子都写不出来的。要搞理论,也弄点新鲜的。譬如说,我老在想 Eugene Nida① 的两种等值差不多被人说烂了。What is beyond the two equivalences?有没有一种新天地?我称之为 overarching 的新天地。overarching 就是两边像“大河”里描写那样,树木参天,冠盖向对岸延伸,连成一片,形成头顶环抱,你中有我,我中有你。也就是说,你看译文所得到的激励、兴奋或者是悲伤、抑郁等等,都能与原文读者的感受无限接近。你读原文可能想象到译出来之后应是怎样;你读译文又可以揣摩原文大致是如何表达。给它杜撰个中文译名吧:“越顶环抱态。”这个“态”字算有点理论味儿吧?

对有志于翻译的青年说几句。一个是极度熟谙译出语——对我们来说,多数情况下就是外文。常听得翻译家自谦:鄙人汉语造诣不深,可没听人承认自己外语修养不行。其实翻译活动中第一位要求或者叫先决条件,就是理解——不,说理解还不够——要吃透原文。理解失之毫厘,译文还去添油加醋,失之何止千里!你说下面这句英文简单吗:It is the mother whose tongue is sharp, who sometimes strikes. 一次翻译竞赛中的句子。示范译文出来了,是某所外语院校专家们的译法,又经过杨宪益夫人 Gladys 的认可:“那做母亲的说话尖刻,有时还出口伤人。”我直到今天仍认为 strikes 是“动手打人”(上文中恰恰就有父母端着咖啡杯追打的情节)。说到理解,最好是

① 奈达(Eugene Nida, 1914－2011):美国语言学家、翻译家,以其“动态对等”(后改称“功能对等”)的《圣经》翻译理论知名。

有洋人供你咨询。不过,英文里常有每个词你都懂但整句意义可有歧解的情况。像上面这一句,我问过的洋人不下三四位,结果还是莫衷一是,写信去问作者,未得答复。前辈冯亦代先生当时说我 hair-splitting,我倒希望有志于翻译的青年人个个都是 hair-splitter。查问再三,仍无定论,怎么办? 做个脚注,把悬疑的理解问题交代给读者。

说到查问,现在搜索引擎可多了,要常用并善用。几年前鄙人的 patron 陆灏写到不用电脑的文化人中还有我,现在该除名了。何种问题大概可在哪个网站得到解决,这是我用电脑尝到的甜头,于是离不开电脑了。第二个当然是驾驭译入语能得心应手,最好游刃有余,就像我们编《英汉大词典》时特别要求编者汉语要好,现在编《中华汉英大词典》英语要好。第三,做翻译的人最好是一个杂家,知书习业,什么书都看的人。昨天上课有两大发现: 一,学生居然不知道 Ku Klux Klan (三 K 党)是个什么东西,那还是读过《飘》的学生呢;二,莫洛托夫鸡尾酒是土制炸弹不知道。这是常识啊,朋友。

青年朋友中还有出版人吧? 难为你们了,因为你们决定不了稿费标准,那是比你们更懂"性价比"的领导,譬如陈昕先生,说了算的。算不算学术成果,那更是一些自己可能从未做过翻译的学官们决定的。所以,约译的事也只能将就着做了。翻译作品也有好的出版人,就像排球出色的二传手,对自己掌握的译者人力资源了然于胸,某人属大刀阔斧、速战速决型,某人倾向于慢工出细活,某人合适译何种题材、体裁、长度,某人理性多于感性,等等。另外,对域外书情必须相当熟悉,更有自己第一手的阅读体会,有自己心目中的"新经典",别老盯着几个奖项的风向转。再一个,现在不是都说"大外宣"和"走出去"吗? 看来还有必要培养一支汉译外的队伍。

问: 我想问一下陆老师,《余墨集》会不会出第三集? 这是第一个问题,第二个问题就是以前读书的时候,像《草叶集》啊,还有看到的杰克·伦敦、库珀,看了不少,后来就基本脱节了,当下美国文学主流是什么？与当时可能是20世纪左右的状况相比有什么样的变化？大概的情况请介绍一下。

陆谷孙：第一个问题，《余墨三集》会出的，现在合同已经订了，但是好像没见下文，即便出不了，总有一天会有一本迟到的《余墨三集》吧。第二个，你叫我讲现在美国文学的主流，我觉得很难说，因为从上世纪50年代的麦卡锡主义搞得全社会“鸦雀无声”，到60年代的Counterculture，Black Power和FSM（free speech movement），到70年代的Me Generation，到80年代的“政治正确”，到“9·11”以后新保守主义崛起，直到次贷危机之后和最近的99% vs 1%，这种轨迹还有待于文学敏感地表现出来。

虽说保守派、传统势力攻击“政治正确”，说新派貌似尊重“他者”，提倡“多样化”，其实是搞“话语霸权”，但像你们这一代读者的思想和情操，是被“政治正确”熏陶起来的。所以我觉得在文学里面，我至今还看不到新保守主义的回潮，但是在俗文学里头你都可以看到对现实和人性的诘责，只不过形式常转到魔幻和科幻。最近不是还有一个什么“猿猴星球崛起”吗？这不但使我们想起《人猿泰山》和《金刚》，还呼应了我前面说过的post-humanism，这种后现代思维同环境保护一结合，我估计力量远比什么“茶叶党”之类的强。

问：我现在自己也在从事翻译工作，您刚才提到说，希望有志于翻译工作的年轻人可以多花点功夫，我想请您推荐几本书给从事这方面工作的年轻朋友，比方说你觉得必须要读的翻译理论的书，或者是文学的，翻译得非常好的文学作品。

陆谷孙：翻译得非常好的文学作品太多了，我一时也难以报出名字来，我记忆当中翻译得非常好的，是我中学时代读的，那时候偏重于看俄罗斯和法国的，草婴和傅雷这样的名字记得很牢，但是英国作品看得并不是太多。吴劳打了一个多小时的电话给我，祝贺我拒纳“资深翻译家”的称号，引我为同道。我是真实感到自己不称，翻译家就应是草婴、傅雷他们,吴劳也应该算。我充其量是个资深教员。说到翻译理论,可找 Jakobson[①], Newmark[②], Bassnett[③], Lefevere[④] 等的书来一读。

问:其实您刚刚那句话没有改掉,还是“水啊,我的梦”。

陆谷孙:没有,是我改回来的。

问:就是说也还是尊重老师您的意思,没有再改了。

陆谷孙:而且我给她说明了,我说周大编辑,我知道,这句话是翻译得太活了,但是我实在是紧身衣穿得太压抑了,让我最后一句话放松一下,可否?这样跟她商量,她还是铁面无私地改掉。我又冥顽不灵地改回来。

问:陆老我想问一下,这个作者也是教诗歌的,您对现在诗歌翻译怎么看?

陆谷孙:诗歌翻译是最难的,我一般不敢碰。真的,诗歌翻译太难了。那个打油诗都那么难翻,我翻译的打油诗都被人骂,说你怎么不甘寡淡,文字总要出花头,其实人家 Edward Lear 的“胡诌诗”是非常寡淡的。比如说第一句 There was an old man of Venice(威尼斯有一个老先生),然后隔了三句以后,最后又回到老先生:How stupid was the old man of Venice.(多蠢啊,威尼斯的这个老先生。)就是说翻译时不要有任何变化。他讲得也对,不是没有道理,他讲儿童就是靠你不断地重复才能从里头得到诗要传达的意思,我也承认。但是我没有回应他的批评,我也不敢回应,心里却在想,我给海豚翻译这本书,不是给中国孩子们看的,我估计买这本书的基本上都是中国的

① 雅可布森(Roman Jakobson, 1896-1982):俄裔美国语言学家。

② 纽马克(Peter Newmark, 1916-2011):出生于捷克的英国翻译理论家,生前在萨里大学任教。

③ 巴斯奈特(Susan Bassnett, 1945 年生):英国翻译理论家、比较文学学者。

④ 勒弗菲尔(André Alphons Lefevere, 1945-1996):翻译理论家,出生于比利时,生前执教于美国得克萨斯大学。

成人,而不会是中国的孩子。寡淡到第一句到第四句句句一样,全是老头多滑稽,小姑娘多有才,我也能做。但是这就涉及翻译的受众和目的,你不能一点没有商业考虑。你的对象是谁,究竟是中国幼稚园的孩子们,还是中国学了点英文的人,你若寡淡到这个地步,他肯定不愿意买来看。因为我们已经试过了,我们在《万象》上发表过几首,发表了以后,就有人骂我们两个,两个都姓陆:“两个姓陆的吃饱饭没事做了,拿这种东西出来。”

所以诗我是不敢轻易碰的,我劝你也慎重,因为你先得把诗的格律弄得非常清楚,几个音步每一行,五个音步,那么你要有五个强读的中文字;第二行跟第一行不押韵,另外一个韵,四句的韵脚可能是 ABBA,那你必须另用一个汉字,然后第三句你还得用 B 韵,第四句再回到 A 韵。同时不断地要注意它的复制的作用,以这样的标准衡量的话,我觉得翻译得好的还是卞之琳先生,他是很注意这些方面,这个的确是太难翻了,而且又不失它的意境,你往往为了押韵,你要在自己头脑的中文词库里面“碧落黄泉”地找,但是一押韵,原文的意象就跑掉了,所以两全的事情难得啊,太难得了。所以这个我不敢弄。

问:陆老师您好,我想请教您两个问题,第一个是您刚刚先讲,美国人的文学里面蕴含美国文化,可能美国人比较喜欢跟大自然相处这种孤独的旅行,喜欢跟大自然有一种相互交流的过程。但是我觉得还有一个美国人的文化,他们很强调一种开拓精神,换句话说征服自然的一个过程,他整个西进运动也好,到整个自己所说的“美国梦”也好,其实都是在不断征服的过程,所以我觉得有一点点是矛盾的,一个是像您刚才说的,他们是希望跟自然有一种非常和谐的、孤独的融入过程,另外他也希望征服一切,或者是征服自然,这两个文化中心,在美国文化里面我不知道您是怎么看它们之间的关系。还有第二个问题想请教您,第二部分也说翻译的事情,您也总结了一些，您说原文里面说的是 a good book，您翻译成“好书”，但是她改成“一本好书”，我觉得这样作为一个翻译过程，就太过于强调翻译，我觉得译者也有自己个人创造的一部分，我不知道您做这么多年的翻译，乐趣是在哪里？如果是从头到尾，可能像您说的紧身衣穿到最后，还很难有自己一点点创作的发挥空间的话，是不是很难找到翻译的乐趣？我就这两个问题，谢谢！

陆谷孙：第一个问题，我觉得这个不矛盾，我应该先补充一点，就是在美国文学里面，实际上还有一大块，我刚刚只提了一句，很大的一块母题是种族问题，特别在南方；这个大家都知道，我一提这个纲要，大家都知道我所指的是什么，这个 racial issue 到现在没解决，现在更多的不一定表现在黑白之间，而是表现在非法移民（特别是 Latinos，就是墨西哥人）和美国人之间了。关于自然，一个是被自然所吸引，一个是征服自然，淘金啊，铺铁路破坏自然，然后驾驭自然，驾驭意味着一种特定的融合，最终的就是融合自然，Not me 加上 Me 了。

至于你说翻译的乐趣，我觉得经常有，这个有点自吹。我最近想到一个例子，就是当年在 Berkeley 翻译这个《蒋经国传》，江南，台湾的报人写的《蒋经国》传，因为写了《蒋经国传》被国民党刺杀了，然后他妻子，也就是后来陆铿的妻子崔蓉芝出了一大笔美金，要人把这个传翻译成英文。那时候我正好在 Berkeley，我想赚钱，我就翻译。这里头有一句话我记得蛮清楚的，就是说，“在很多方面小蒋是传承了老蒋的衣钵的”。这么一句话，“衣钵”大家都知道是 mantle，我翻译的是 In many ways，小蒋 is his father’s son。翻完以后我好不得意。那时候葛传椝先生还活着，我就跟他讲。葛先生说，很好，这个可惜词典里放不进去。词典里确实放不进去，放进哪个词条去？son？father？都不行。所以这种时刻是非常愉快的，不是你稿费给我多几个钱我就能享受到的愉快，经常会有。有时候发现人家的翻译里面有个错,我虽然还没看到原文,但是我一看到他的中文我就猜到他的原文是什么。有次看到"好一股妖风"。我想肯定是 an ill wind blows nobody good 的缩略,意思是没有一阵妖风是吹得人人晕头转向的,也就是说世界上没有绝对的坏事,对你是妖风对我是好风。"一阵妖风"能穷尽这层意思吗?发现这种东西的时候挺愉快的,挺有满足感的。这个不知道是不是回答了你的问题。

问:陆老师,我想请问一下,你这次的小说题目翻译得很漂亮,叫《一江流过水悠悠》,让人想起乔志高先生翻译的尤金·奥尼尔的 *Long Day's Journey into the Night*,翻译成《长夜漫漫路迢迢》。您在翻译这个题目时,措辞上面的选择是不是放开了很多呢?

陆谷孙:谈不上放开。文艺类书名的翻译,我是觉得要下功夫的。第一还是个"信"字,不走样。我第一次翻译 *Rebecca*,用的文题就是《吕蓓卡》,而不是《蝴蝶梦》。在忠于原文的基础上,你能够把文字弄得跟书的情调接近的话,上乘。但是忠实还是第一位的。我记得我翻过一篇文章叫"Ms Directing Shakespeare"。Ms 是个双关语,翻译还是求忠实:《新派女士误导莎剧》(Ms 这用法最早也是上世纪 40 年代后常用的,所以叫"新派")。但也有因忠实而失落意义的,如 *The American Way of Death*,那是据 American way of life 化出的,你如果翻译作《美国死亡方式》,人家以为书里写的是因心脏病死的有多少,自杀的有多少,等等。其实不是,是讲死一个人现在要花多少钱,殡仪馆要敲你多少钱,所以我后来翻译成《美国殡葬业大观》。这个就只能活译了,不然的话容易引起误解,或者无解。本书文题好像我们争了几次的。大概编辑方面坚持要"大河恋",我说不行,因为这有歧解,特别是现代的情况下,以为是男女两人在 Mississippi 碰到了,游轮上面碰到了谈恋爱也可以。

问:陆老师您好,我是一名在校大学生,我有两个问题,第一个问题是时下非常流行外面报班学习英语,而且好像生意非常好,对学校教育和外面培训，您有什么看法？第二个问题是，我一直认为您是中国的乔姆斯基，如果您当上了中国的教育部长，你会对中国的教育采取哪些措施？

陆谷孙：第一个问题，对现在的学校英语教学，我觉得问题确实比较大，好多人都要翘课的，我估计跟教材有关系。这个教材呢，太死板，一味推销成功学，对挫折和失败讲得太少，而且这些教材里面，说情感的成分太少。我一直引以为豪的是，我曾经参编过《21 世纪大学英语》，里头有一篇《洗衣妇》，写一个贫穷的洗衣妇，视诚信如命，临死也要把自己接下洗净的衣服送还顾客。那个 affective index（情感指数）非常高。教材里边一定要有这么几篇是震撼灵魂的，你读了想哭，想仰天长啸。另外，当然也跟我们的老师怎么教有关系。这中间原因太多了。至于外面培训班的英语，我也不知道他们怎么教的，反正李阳最近名声不好。

但是他的疯狂英语，我倒是要给他讲一句话，不是没有道理的，就是说脸皮要厚，这是学外文很重要的一点。根据我同班同学的一句话来说："陆谷孙为什么英语学得比较好，就是脸皮厚。"你必须要脸皮厚，不怕出丑，那么李阳精神不怕出丑这一点，我觉得还是有可取的地方。至于其他的培训，好像更多的人都在说这个培训不好，老师在课堂上就是讲一些离题的，跟英语没有什么关系的，发一通关于时事的牢骚，然后就走掉了。是不是有这种现象我不知道，我没有去那里侦探过，所以我不知道。但是我想你自己靠自己的阅读，就像我讲的，如果你大学四年，阅读量能够达到一百万字，自己的产出，包括你的翻译，包括你的英文写作，能够达到一万字，我想你的英文再糟也糟不到哪里去，这要求并不高。

至于第二个问题，我跟 Chomsky 完全是霄壤之别，他是非常张扬的一个人，也有人说我比较张扬，什么霸气外露，这是周丽华的评价，我想自己没什么霸气，你觉得有吗？Chomsky 在 MIT（麻省理工学院）也非常霸道，容不得不同意见，提问环节时会无礼地打断别人的话，所以我想我跟他不一样。还有，我成不了教育部长，你这个问题的前提不成立，恕不回答。

主持人：今天非常感谢大家来参加这个活动。

身在丝绒樊笼，心有精神家园

采访整理　金雯

不要把自己当作了不起的存在，你不过是整个世界很微小的一个粒子，生命本身是种偶然，个体的 to be, or not to be（生或死）实在不会在时空长河留下什么影响的。

我们这一代人已经在悬崖边上排着队，等着一个一个掉下去了。

我是 1940 年出生的，历经多次政治运动，可以说成长于“高压锅”。年轻人之间总是有竞争的，现在表现在学业上，那时候就是比耐压和抗压性，开始逼着自己，算勉强跟得上。但我本性喜欢在大原则指导下率性地生活，最好是“leave me alone”（让我一个人待着）。下乡劳动可以挑百十来斤，但那叫“大力士挂帅”，说你没触及世界观。劳动休息时，因为爱闲步田畴，自言自语背两句普希金，得一诨号“田埂上的小布”（小布尔乔亚）。

我的大学：夹蛆、挑担、挤时间读书

1957 年到 1962 年，我在上大学。当时复旦外文系是五年制，大概有一年多在下乡、下厂、下建筑工地、下码头劳动。可以说领导脑袋一拍我们就得下乡，同时还说不要荒废业务，让我们写贫农老大娘的家史——用英文写。我也经历过最荒唐的劳动，大冷天跑到江湾乡间的粪缸旁边，用筷子夹蛆，这是为了防止开春后蛆变苍蝇。我不知道来年的苍蝇有没有减少，但我一直记得女同学手上全是冻疮。

在各种政治运动和劳动中，学习时间必须挤。难得享受一个完整的暑假，其他同学回家了，我却会从上海的家里回到学校。平时七人一室的宿舍里，就我一个人，物理空间不变，主观却有了一种解放感。我花一个暑假看书，刚开始是看比较刺激青少年的书，像阿加莎·克里斯蒂的书、《福尔摩斯探案集》、《梅森探案集》都看过；也看哥特小说，图书馆的 *The Mysteries of Udolpho*（《尤多尔佛之谜》）据说直到前不久，借书卡显示只有我一个人借过。

作为一个长在"高压锅"里的人，"文革"对我的思想冲击最大。有两件事情是我亲历的：四姑母家境困难，丈夫被打成右派在安徽劳改，自己在上海一家很破败的民办小学里教书。"文革"一来，她的学生把她当成地主婆批斗。她是一个自尊心很强的人，受不了迫害，上吊自杀了。傍晚，我去收尸，亲眼看到她是怎么自杀的：女厕破败阴暗，横梁很低，身体蜷缩着才死得成——她是抱定了必死决心的。我岳父是苏州第一人民医院的 X 光技师，割手腕自杀的，还割了颈部动脉，墙上、天花板上都是血，很是惨烈。

"文革"中被开除"人籍"

"文革"中，复旦大学小小一个外文系有十多位教师和所谓反动学生自杀。原来以为 5% 的教师被打倒，定额算完成了，后来发现达到了百分之十几。"文革"最后一波"一打三反运动"把我也打进去了。被抓之前的两三个月就已经没人跟我说话了，出入校园，像缀上了霍桑的"红字"一样，被开除"人籍"。我女儿满月那一天，工宣队终于上门了。

批判我的材料包括大学一年级时的开会发言。那时候不让上海同学回家过周末,我发了句牢骚:上帝创造万物才工作六天,星期天理应休息啊。1957 年说的话,在 1970 年被翻了出来,应该是当年被“记录在案”了。这些“反动材料”估计现在还在某个档案柜里放着。我们读书的时候要向党交心,最隐秘、“肮脏”、“反动”、“不良”的思想都得向支部书记交代。类似于向神父忏悔,只是神父会永远保持缄默,而支部书记是“钓鱼”——搜集你思想深处的黑材料,日后用来批判你。“反动”身份确定之后,就开批斗大会,当年带头喊口号的人现在还跟我住一个小区,不是他跟我有什么恩怨,只是他嗓门好,会唱歌,口号喊起来响亮。

被隔离了六个礼拜后,因为查不出什么问题就让我去编词典了,那时候复旦大学外文系有三十多个老师不能教书,被指派去编词典。第一届工农兵大学生进校时,我们被带到复旦大学 1237 大教室的右前方坐定,然后一声口令,我们起立,向后转。工宣队告诉工农兵大学生:“以后见到这些人不能叫老师。”我们是革命的对象,不能与人接触,一说话就要放毒,即便我一直是相当受欢迎的老师。现在想起来,绝望也是有的。我妻子还怀过第二胎,当时我们两个商量决定不生了,怕生出来让他受苦。

“文革”派性内斗时,托那时复旦写作组的福,他们跟踪外刊动态,翻译资料给高层领导看,找我这编外有问题的帮忙。比如美国中情局局长换人了,要搜集外媒资料将此人背景介绍一下,这样算是有了看外报外刊的机会,也算是我“学徒”阶段的训练。“文革”中要办家庭学习班,一家人坐在一起念毛主席语录,我不喜欢,躲到三楼翻译《蝴蝶梦》,自娱自乐。“文革”后,译林出版社要出版,就给了他们,但译者写的是我太太的名字。

1980 年后有机会出国看看,了解外面的情况,两相对照,更觉得政治运动荒废了中国人多少大好时光。过去我也会为了“过关”讲一些冠冕堂皇的话,但没有人格分裂,思想中也没有钙化的意识形态。

不像那些搞审查的意识形态"蓝铅笔",专门检禁。他们大概一直是革命动力,不像我们是革命的对象。我觉得他们一定有面罩的,只是我们无法了解他们的另一面。如果写一篇小说,我一定能写出这样一个典型人物:虚伪、廉价、怯懦、阴险。

做"规矩人"是家传

大学的老师将我引导入英美文学,特别是莎士比亚之门,工宣队将我推入词典之门。但是我最早的中文训练来自父亲,在家我受的是旧式教育——背书,背得最多的是家书类文字和诗词。做"规矩人"是家教,做人做事合法、合道德,负责任、有担当。我研究生时代用英文写日记,里面说到一些朦胧的三角恋情,谁知父亲也在做"蓝铅笔",受到他的严厉批评。严格管束会让人失去一些自由灵性,但能保证你不做越轨之事。父亲的管束还包括一些物质上的要求。上中学时,我喜欢听门德尔松、柴可夫斯基等等,想花 60 块钱买个唱机,父亲不准,觉得浪费钱,也怕影响学习。我喜欢打篮球,戴着父亲的手表满足一下小小的虚荣,父亲派表哥去学校找我,当着同学的面令我将表摘下,回家后还要写检查。我的所有检查以及民国时代起的成绩报告单,父亲都妥为保存,现在传给了我女儿,恐怕早就不知塞到哪个被遗忘的角落去了。

父亲对我最大的影响是精神不能矮化。最近看某位复姓人士的一个视频,展示的是复姓先生去看车展,对着中方工作人员大呼小叫,对方像是个刚踏上工作岗位的小女生,怯生生被复姓骂晕了。这时来了个意大利的外商,好家伙,复姓先生顿时换了副嘴脸,夹着几句破英文,谄媚不及。复姓先生是国内有名的"左派"。这个视频说明此人实际上标准一个"左皮西仔",外表是左的,内部却是西仔,就是当年父亲教我应该最鄙视的洋奴。他不是老骂"带路党"吗?真到了节骨眼上，还不知“带路”的是哪些人！

父亲言教加身教，使我不会低三下四地去取悦外国人。我自己是学外语的，现在妻子、女儿一家都在国外，但我还是不应他们的要求去申请绿卡。这跟从幼时的教育有关，特别是在农业文明的环境中长大，根子就扎得更深一点。一到秋天，秋虫鸣叫声大起，这时故乡的草木、风物、氤氲，那些说不出的牵引力就会催着你回来。现在骂知识分子的人很多，但也就在这批人中间有化解不开的“故园情结”。这是很难描述的情感，像脐带一样无法割断。

陈丹青讲的“民国范儿”已经没有了。（当然，民国也不全都是好的，就像我父亲说的，逛窑子就不好。）但那个年代作为人的总体风范，还有基本的美学标准，确有不少值得传承。特别在教育界，讲究精神富足，淡泊物质，至少不会穿上名牌，戴上名表，挎了名包，嘴上什么脏话都骂得出！有时我走过精品店，常常想起苏格拉底在希腊的市场里讲的话，“这里有多少我不需要的东西啊”。

我不是什么斗士，只是个遗老遗少式的人物吧

我现在还忙着给学生上课。上学期是每周介绍一本书让学生看，戏称“恶补”；这个学期我让他们写，每周 300 字都可以，允许下载，但不能占全部文字的三分之一以上，这叫“产出”。好多学生一听有写作要求，跑掉了，但是我相信剩下的学生对语言是有亲和感的。真希望每培养一届学生中会有两三个比较不那么功利。我希望他们语言功底好，英文说写读译流利，文学原著浸淫得深，知道西方文明是如何演变过来的，从希腊城邦到罗马帝国、日耳曼骑士、英格兰清教徒，都能弄清楚。

但是，总体而言，就其佼佼者比较，现在的学生不如过去，这跟整个大学教育的变化有关。大学培养的不是学士、硕士，或者讲技术的术士,而是一个初级的思想者和怀疑者。我当年至少有一点朝这个方向靠近。现在的学生,英文讲起来腔调可以,但是你让他写东西,一出手就看出问题来了,有的是错误迭出。单就技能型的要求说,也难合格。

我们的青年教师也自有苦衷,语言文字尚未过关,急急去专注各种理论派别,不看原著。无论是语言学还是文学都是各种主义,而且我觉得学也没学对,比如,“新左派”在国外是反对殖民主义、帝国主义的,反对“死白欧男”(DWEMs)垄断的,反对不光彩的过去,是有进步意义的;但是国内“新左派”却为并不光彩的过去辩护,虽说打的牌子一样,内里是一回事吗?再说,在欧美做文学,批评讲究 identity politics(身份政治),而我们搞欧美文学,首先还隔着外语这一个大障碍,能一点不读“死白欧男”吗?

在微博上,我是@陆老神仙,至少义务回答了一年的问题。也遇到有些孩子不太像话,连 supplier(供应商)是什么都要问,词典上一翻就能找到的。现在国家提出大力发展文化产业,但只看到“管制”,实名制、限娱令都来了。所以,我决定离开微博。开始是尝尝味道,现在尝够了,以后不打算上了。

在网上我还经常被骂,“死老头子”、“老不死”还算文雅的,一些脏话我都不愿重复。当然,你可以说让人家骂好了,但是,我不是斗士,只是一个遗老遗少那样的人物。前段时间,小宝在《东方早报》上写了篇文章讲 snob 怎么翻译,他认为应该翻译成“装 bi”,可以说他的翻译是很准确的,但是我这一代人绝对不会用这个词。用了这个词,似乎整个品格就降了一大截。我也会用“给力”这些词,但是我不会用这种带有脏词的网络语言。

生命只是偶然,最终 from dust to dust(尘归尘)

我喜欢孤独、宁静。孤独是灵感的催化剂。在一群人中,如果没有一个可以交心的人，那我就向内，回到自己的精神王国。或者外面热闹得不得了，比如在婚宴上，周围都是人，自己的元神会跳出肉身，看别人也看自己，看着自己的肉身活像一具傀儡。

我把我这简陋又老旧的住所叫做洞穴，人家问“回家没”，我常答“已经回洞”。每天晚饭后散步，路上不时与亲友、学生短信交流，我叫它“walkie talkie”。尤其大年三十，人少清静，每年我都会在日记中记下：今年遇到几人几骑。我的日记会在适当的时候处理掉，沪上某名人出日记时，我就劝过他不要出。日记必然有私密，必然臧否人物，也必然会触犯到制度性的东西。当然，可以删削、编辑，但是那样又有什么意思？

不要把自己当作了不起的存在，你不过是整个世界很微小的一个粒子，生命本身是个偶然，个体的 to be，or not to be（生或死）都不会对时空长河留下任何影响。对于这一点自觉悟得满彻底的。我们受了一些教育而离不开书本等精神享受，其他人在劳作之后洗澡就睡去了，也是一种存在，所以，写本书、编个词典这样的事情可能有点成就感，但过后一会儿就淡忘了。

现在采访、演讲尽量都推掉，我只想着 leave me alone（让我一个人待着），因为实在对外面的事情很绝望了。学生、学校、社会，这里强拆，那里冤狱，让人变得非常消极，想赶快度过余生。

朱维铮不久前去世了，还好葬礼上没有各种讲话之类。以后我的葬礼就是租一条船，从十六铺开到吴淞口撒掉骨灰，from dust to dust（尘归尘），然后大家洗洗手回到船舱开一个派对，不许说到陆某人生前如何如何，就这么结束。也省得后人一到清明还要来祭扫。

采访手记

与陆谷孙先生聊了两小时三十七分钟。从他称之为“洞”的家中出来，身处闹市，突然有点切换困难。接下来，“陆老神仙效应”开始大爆发，寻来金雄白所著《汪政权的开场与收场》，因为陆师最近在看。顺带找了汪精卫的《双照楼诗词稿》，为余英时一万多言的序所折服，又入手了《余英时访谈录》。甚至打算入手 Kindle 一台（陆师曰“金斗”，他正在用）。终于又有了修复“三脚猫”英语的动力，将 Elizabeth Gaskell 的 *Cranford* 买来潜心阅读，因为陆师说学英文要看原著。葛传椝先生的《英语惯用法词典》也被翻出来，这个样子简直要摩拳擦掌地大干一番。

（原载《新周刊》2012 年第 8 期）

你这一生离不开它

采访整理　戴燕

希望外文系是个好的求智场所

戴燕：陆先生现在还坚持上课，是每一学期上两门课吗？

陆谷孙：以前有一门隔一学期上，有一门贯彻始终的，这学期就是本科四年级的散文选读。学生好些是外面的，我自己的学生逃课的恐怕很多，你想嘛，到了四年级，有的要去找工作了。

戴燕：您读书那会儿，复旦外语系什么样？就您那一届，招了多少学生？

陆谷孙：有四五十个学生，就英语一个语种。

戴燕：这四十多个同学进来，会设想将来毕业了做什么？

陆谷孙：谁也不必设想，等待统一分配。到时候，暑假里学生都走了，毕业班不能走的，就在寝室里面打牌、下棋，等着。某一天下午通知来了，说开会，然后跑到一个教室里面，我们的支部书记穿个木拖鞋，就像日本人的那种木屐，那时候还不是塑料的。

戴燕：您毕业的时候是1960年代初？

陆谷孙：是1962年。

戴燕：您这一届同学毕业以后从事外语工作的有多少？

陆谷孙：一部分当了大学老师，比较少，多数都是到北京的各部，就是“×机部”等的。我们那班毕业前就陆续有人调进外交部去学所谓小语种，后来，1959 年西藏出事，中印开战，我们叫自卫反击战，那时候我们班就有六个同学提前分配到西藏，随军做翻译。

戴燕：其他分配出去的都做翻译和看资料？

陆谷孙：做翻译，然后，大概就是看些科技资料啊，跟他那个专业有关的资料，然后做摘译。还有一部分，就是像我们这种留校做教师的，留在大学里。那么最“差”的去处就是到中学做教师了，一个错划右派的分到偏远的小地方。还有的，像有一个党员去了高干子弟的北京景山学校。

戴燕：复旦的外文系，院系调整之前就有吗？

陆谷孙：以前就有。调整的时候，复旦是收益大户之一。就外文系而言，譬如说，刘德中、杨必、葛传槼、我的老师徐燕谋，都是外边过来的，有的是教会学校，圣约翰、沪江就来了好些人。以前的老复旦也留下几个，伍蠡甫就是。

戴燕：当时的外文系，比如跟上海外国语大学有什么不同？

陆谷孙：相当不一样。上外的外语系本来只有一门，就叫俄语专科学校。1949 年后一边倒，学苏联。你别说也蛮厉害的，像我中学的六年，全部是俄语，没有学过一年英语。所以我是凭俄语考英语专业的，那个时候可以这样。考进来以后当然跟不上，同学们有的是英语学过好几年的，那么我们就分在慢班里。

戴燕：当年的复旦外文系，重视的是外国文学吗？

陆谷孙：我们这里好像一贯比较重视文学。语言学呢，也学一点，只不过就是入门。譬如说研究生以后，或者是在高年级，有语言学概论。概论，再基础没有了，就是什么叫语言，什么叫言语，什么叫共时，什么叫历时，这种普通的知识性的东西。

戴燕：上世纪五六十年代的英语教材用的是什么？

陆谷孙：上世纪五六十年代，教育革命高潮那一时期，批判资产阶级，全学《北京周报》、《中国建设》什么的，以时事、时评为主。但是“非高潮”的时候，还有在校最后一年，就是“调整、巩固、充实、提高”八字方针那一年，也不光学《北京周报》、《中国建设》这类东西。不是三年大饥荒吗，后来就来一个“调整”时期，那个时候就比较宽松了，有“高教六十条”，西洋的东西就学得比较多一点。

戴燕：有西方文学吗？

陆谷孙：有，无产阶级的西方文学。比如说杜波伊斯（Du Bois），黑人的这种。其实今天在西方，人家也蛮把他当回事的，那么由于他是黑人，我们就学他的。还有《牛虻》、《穿破裤子的慈善家》这一类。有一个“同路人”，叫费里克斯·格林（Felix Greene）的英国作家，当年是跟中国友好的，我知道后来此人亲达赖了，这些东西，学了不少。这些都是临时性的、油印的。完整的教材，有一套高教部组织编写的，1－4册由许国璋主编。5－6册由北大的俞大絪主编，就是俞大维的妹妹。7－8册由我的老师徐燕谋主编。这个是全国统一编写的，这部教材的好处，就是不选中国人写的英文。

戴燕：所以，英文学习没问题。

陆谷孙：我们最后一年，就是八字方针以后，各个口都搞“六十条”，“高教六十条”是周扬他们搞的，开始强调“三基”，就是基本知识、基本技能、基本理论。强调“三基”以后，我就觉得比较正规一点，1962年毕业，还可以用英文演话剧，演的是《雷雨》，剧本是一个外国人跟王佐良他们几个一起翻译成英文的。到我读研究生的时候，也比较正规。到1964年又不行了，“千万不要忘记阶级斗争”来了。

戴燕：这么看，您算是幸运的，学了英文，然后留在系里。

陆谷孙：我进校的第一个半年，太太平平的，平静的书桌，没事儿。尽管那个时候高年级都在打右派，不过也已经打到一定阶段了，第一波反右已经结束，但我们还是要开会辩论。然后到1957年的年底，毛泽东发表了“党的教育方针”，就是教育必须为无产阶级政治服务、教育必须与生产劳动相结合,从这开始就有大量的劳动。我们是五年制,后来我们算了一下,劳动大概一年以上,不过就我自己来讲,英语学习时间还不能算少,我会自己偷偷挤时间。譬如说好不容易放个暑假,那时候寒暑假常常都要取消,要劳动,好不容易有暑假,我看人家外地同学都回家了,七个人的寝室只剩下我一个,我可以看书看到凌晨四点钟,然后早上广播喇叭响起,我也不醒,一直到中午才蓬头垢面地去吃一点饭,然后下午开始再继续这样……

戴燕:一个人的时候看些什么书?

陆谷孙:那时二十上下的年纪,大都是看刺激性极强的书,什么《福尔摩斯全集》啦,外文书店有卖的。上世纪50年代末60年代初,福州路外文书店楼上专门有这么一个地方,卖旧书的,很便宜,大概都是院系调整的时候,从教会学校图书馆那些地方搜来的,有些书上还残留着校图书馆的公章。除了福尔摩斯,还有阿加莎·克里斯蒂,这作家后来是红得不得了,还有那些哥特小说,全是悬疑,还有神鬼故事。当然也看一些正经的,但是我的趣味跟人家不大一样,大家书单上开的呢,我反而不一定去找来看,我去找那种图书馆没有人看的,从书卡看,没人借过的,所以今天我估计有些书,可能复旦大学只有我一个人借过,像 *The Mysteries of Udolpho*,18世纪安·拉德克利夫(Ann Radcliffe)夫人写的,古城堡里的魅影幢幢,刺激得很。

戴燕:那个阶段还是可以读一些东西的。

陆谷孙:那阶段还可以读,“文革”以后不行了。但是“文革”以后呢,一个偶然的机会,我还有机会读书。我在苏州,我小姑姑有一个亲戚是红卫兵,抄家抄来的很多东西都堆在一个房间里,她说你既然那么喜欢看书,我去给你拖一袋来。所以,我也沾了“文化大革命”的这点好处,看了不少书,而且看了以后,当天晚上就讲,那时候家里住了很多外地来串联的小孩儿,给他们讲故事,再后来当然也成为我的罪状之一。

戴燕：那个年代，一般人会考虑我学了英文，在中国有什么用吗？

陆谷孙：没想过，这个没想过。我的期待是教书。

戴燕：今天，当然大家都知道外文在中国越来越重要，甚至很多人都觉得外国的东西很好，是一个标准。那时候的风气怎么样？

陆谷孙：多多少少认为英语是帝国主义语言。

戴燕：不可能成为主流文化、主流价值？

陆谷孙：不可能。

戴燕：现在复旦外文学院有几个语种？还是外国文学占主流吗？

陆谷孙：七个语种，这是1990年代以后的事。外国文学也不占主流了，现在是语言学占主流了，但是这个语言学，怎么讲呢，也是完全朝理论靠拢的，真的。譬如说"绿色的草在愤怒地歌唱"，你说这是好诗吗？这是乔姆斯基想出来的一个有名的句子，然后分析形式与意义是不是可以割裂开来。还有的就讲你的脑子，说话作文是左脑还是右脑在活动，你的眼珠又是如何转动的，从中分析认知过程。大家都往这方面发展，反而忽略了语言的基本功。我是觉得你可以朝这方面发展，但是你先得把语言的功底弄好，爱读、听得懂，能说、能写、能译，这是最起码的条件。现在你去看看我们有的教师用英文上课，简直就像是钝刀子割肉，我说是用钝刀子割火鸡。英语里面有一句话，叫作"刀子切黄油"，那就是势如破竹。讲英文也应该要做到这个。

戴燕：您是说理论本身有问题，还是说语言不过关？

陆谷孙：我觉得引导也有问题，因为最后要写论文，你要提职称就要写论文啊。

戴燕：这样文学就减少了。

陆谷孙：教材里文学少了，应用文多了。连我都得每年把教材改一改,置换几篇,我不能老是这几篇一直教下去。我本来选的都是非常文艺的,基本上都是现代主义时期的,因为是20世纪嘛,我不讲19世纪的,一讲19世纪,甚至18世纪,好散文很多,甚至所谓"文艺复兴"(现在都叫 early modern),甚至更早的中世纪(现在叫 pre-modern),其实是好东西很多,当然诗体占主要。

戴燕:但是同学没有兴趣?

陆谷孙:兴趣不大了。散文,包含应用文,但又不等于应用文,可能派不了用场。所以我现在呢,第一,把教材全部改成20世纪,课的名字也改了,"20世纪英美散文选读",然后每年总要置换好几篇文章,有的是跟时事结合得比较紧的。譬如说今年我置换的一篇文章,不是马上要大选了,我就置换了《纽约客》上的一篇文章,叫作 Tea and Sympathy,不妨译作"以茶待客",专门讲茶叶党的,波士顿怎么开始有茶叶党。文中有历史,包括尼克松因水门事件下台,有今天的时事,有大选展望。文章又写到仿制当年倾倒茶叶那艘革命船,如何孤零零地停泊在那里,外面的雨水打入它的船舱,冲刷舱底,写得很文艺的,是文学、历史和现状都有的一篇好文章。

戴燕:您还是非常非常花心思在教学上的,而且不光讲语言,也不光讲文学,还讲文化和现实。

陆谷孙:我会花三个礼拜讲那个散文的特点是怎么形成的,讲流变。从古希腊的对话录开始,到古罗马的修辞、演说,一路发展下来,到法国的蒙田,然后从法国移到英国,讲培根,也讲约瑟夫·艾迪生(Joseph Addison)和理查德·斯蒂尔(Richard Steele),这一路下来,把它的流变讲清楚。两大派别的不同,一个是杂文、随感、小品一类,一个是论文、批评一类,都有各种各样的例子可以举出来,然后各有什么特点,为什么写散文的人多是在中年以后,为什么青年时代多写抒情诗,为什么写散文的英国作家"独身主义者"特别多,等等。

戴燕：真是这样吗？独身者写这种很多？

陆谷孙：对，人们首先想到的一定是查尔斯·兰姆（Charles Lamb）。你要有时间来抒发心中各种各样的思绪和感情，除了疯姐姐，又没有一个倾诉的对象，那就写文章跟自己对话吧。

戴燕：您认为写作其实是一种内心独白，总是要倾诉？

陆谷孙：我觉得是有一点。不光我这么认为，美国一位教授写了篇很精彩的文章，全面谈散文写作，我当作这门课的开场白，先给学生读。

戴燕：同学听完了，也许觉得这多没意思啊，这不像苦行僧一样吗？

陆谷孙：我觉得还是很有意思的，这是培养你对语言的一种亲和感、悟性，甚至灵感，然后你一生都离不开这种文字和语言了。我觉得学外文最主要的一条，就是你这一生离不开它。

戴燕：学生会不会想，我先得找个工作。如果他找了一个公务员、公司职员的工作，怎么还能有您说的那种心情？

陆谷孙：即使你是只被关在笼子里的鸟，这只鸟还得啼鸣，是不是？啼鸣发自内心。心里要有个精神家园。不读书我看是不行的。我现在上课，班上六十到八十个人，我像个牧师传教一样，这当中能够有个位数，两三个人被我说动皈依，我就觉得已经成功了。

戴燕：您现在一个礼拜要花多少时间在教学上？

陆谷孙：教学大概总归要八九个小时。两节课，八九个小时。

戴燕：您理想中的外文系是什么样子？学生应该怎么做？

陆谷孙：我期望当中的学生，应该第一语言和文字必须过关。我有时善意地讽刺他们，我说：You're very good at unlearning。你们各位的强项是什么呢？就是把过去中学时代学习的东西忘掉，unlearning。你看看我电脑上改的作业，那都是一片红啊。所以我要求：第一，你文字用不着老师再这样改，你讲出来的语言，你口音有错，音素有错，元音音素有错，无所谓，只要你错得一致，不会引起误解就行了。第二，是一个爱书人，不就是像我这么爱东看看西看看吗，至少有我这么一点精神，有点好奇心吧，对知识和思想的好奇心。正因为有这个好奇心，你有疑问，就会经常去看书。也不要给他去定什么书单，让他自己到书的海洋里去游泳，也可能就游出来了，没有灭顶，浮上来了。这是第二个。第三个呢，就是我希望这些人，从书本里不但得到知识，“于不疑处有疑”，至少成为一个初级的思想者吧。如果外文系能够培养这样的人，这个外文系就是个好的求智场所。

戴燕：这也是您自己成长的经验。

陆谷孙：我做中学学生的时候，看草婴翻译的托尔斯泰的小说，看傅雷翻译的法国文学作品。我记得那时候上海延安路有个沪江电影院，电影院旁边有个书摊，租书给你，一个月只要两块钱，《复活》、《红与黑》、《基督山恩仇记》啊，我就是从那里租来看的。我喜欢法国、俄罗斯胜于英国，可能就是看这些书的缘故，特别是托尔斯泰，又听柴可夫斯基，这可能还有当年“一边倒”的政治取向的关系，这些东西合成起来，所以我对俄罗斯一直是有一种难以名状的崇拜，这个民族不会垮的。另外还有一点，我觉得西方的，也包括俄国的 intelligentsia，永远就像 T. S. 艾略特讲的那样，尽管挫折加幻灭，“我不希望自己死去”，面对战后的社会问题，不少人在美欧间穿梭，寻觅加探究，他们很少有我们这里竹林七贤、陶渊明这样“悠然见南山”的退守主义。这种东西在西方知识分子里面很难找到，即使在检禁横行的时候。

戴燕：没有隐士。

陆谷孙：隐士，不得志以后就隐了，这种很难找到。西方知识分子的阳刚这一面，我觉得是他们在当年能有影响的一个很重要的原因。我爸爸那时候还在灌输我，还要我背这个背那个中国的东西，我当然也背啊，也要应付他，但是我已经感觉到这两个文化实在太不一样了。

要让词典反映出中国文化

如何接受英文、运用英文

戴燕：这样看来，翻译还是很重要的。从前说翻译文学作品是很了不起的一件事情，翻译家的名字大家都知道，现在怎么样？

陆谷孙：对，很了不起的事情。现在地位不一样了。现在，好多硕士生在校期间打份工就搞翻译，如果有什么家教之类的，翻译还排在后面呢，因为第一是时间花得太多，第二稿费也少，宁肯去做家教。

戴燕：这样一个翻译状况，您有什么评价？

陆谷孙：外国文学呢，老实讲，我现在不看。如果出版社要我翻了，我就只能动手翻，但是我强调要英汉对照，一定要两种文本都印出来。这也说明我的一个态度，就是说现在有些翻译的质量实在太差了。

戴燕：我有时看现在的翻译作品，有一个最大的意见，就是你对照以前出版的，包括"文革"期间的，哪怕它很政治化，但是总有前言、后记，有介绍、有评价。现在一看好多翻译，什么都没有，前无序后无跋，光杆一个，就让人怀疑你是从哪儿来的，不可靠。

陆谷孙："文革"期间少虽然少，但很认真啊，而且是发动了最精华的人。你看嘛，刚刚一家出版社给我写信，我翻了毛姆的一个短篇小说，他要出了，要跟我签个约，他说你的译后记我们能不能拿掉，我同意他拿了。

戴燕：为什么要拿掉？

陆谷孙：因为还有别人译的其他作品吧。自然也为了降低成本，现在什么都要考虑这个。

戴燕：因此现在翻译出版的很多是流行书。

陆谷孙：是，流行书也可以翻，因为流行书、畅销书，你从扩大的意义上来讲，从《鲁滨孙漂流记》开始就是了，这也不是不可以翻。

戴燕：您最近出版的译作《一江流过水悠悠》算不算流行书？

陆谷孙：那个还不算太流行，当然它也畅销过几个礼拜，但是它畅销不在于情节，现在的畅销书，小说类的多数是以情节取胜。但是你别说他们西方现当代作家，他即使写一部《达·芬奇密码》也有他的思想特点，弄得现在很多地摊文学都在讲共济会的问题。

戴燕：您的日常工作里面，教学是一块，翻译是一块，还有一块是编词典。

陆谷孙：对，现在就在做《汉英大词典》。最近开了个会，又给我比较大的一个鼓舞，这次得到几位专家的肯定。香港有位专门搞汉英平行语料库的先生，我们把 A 字母部分印出来寄给他，请他提意见，我特别要求他跟他的语料库对比，看收的东西有没有巨大欠缺，结果发现没有，基本上跟他持平，可能还多一点。我是想，一定要让这个词典作为一个记录，就是这一阶段的中国文化是如何接受英文、运用英文这样的一个阶段性总结，所以翻译上，比王佐良先生他们那个时代也要力争好一些，因为我非常讲究跟英语对接。你像"功败垂成"，他们过去就是按照字面翻的，就说失败了，成功已在眼前的时候失败了，当然是对的，但是我要给它翻成"失败在第十一个小时"，或是在这个杯子将要接触嘴唇的时候"砰"掉下去了，失败了。洋人可能会觉得更加亲和。

戴燕：就是"功亏一篑"的那种意思？

陆谷孙：对，因为这在英文里面也是有的。

戴燕：听说您这词典要给复旦大学出版社？

陆谷孙：对，现在叫《复旦版汉英中华词典》。我这个人，就是有一种乡土情结，对中国也是这样，对很多事情看不惯，但是我一到美国，有了距离感，就怀念这儿的草木和九舍的鸟啾虫鸣。复旦也同样，对我是口高压锅，"文革"中给关起来办学习班。当年学生时代，不准接待外宾，不能跟外国人接触，总觉得你们思想不好。

戴燕：不被信任？

陆谷孙：就是一进来的时候，不是说反右第一波已经结束了嘛，那时候叫我们也发言，就民主问题什么的讨论，我呢最恨的就是礼拜六不放我们回家，所以我就说上帝创造万物，礼拜天也是要休息的，这话就上了我的档案，后来把我关在学习班里头斗我的时候，都拿出来了。

戴燕：决定了您不是最受信任的。

陆谷孙：尽管是高压锅压的，但不知道为什么就是对复旦产生了感情，像散步的时候走过这些地方，想想以前我们在这个小棚子里面上过课，就有一种很强烈的怀旧和依恋。

戴燕：您是老复旦了！我看您毕业以后不久，“文革”初期就开始编词典了。

陆谷孙：对啊。我 1962 年毕业，大概太太平平念了一年半的研究生，上了四门非常扎实的文学课：英国戏剧、英国诗歌、英国小说、英国散文。

戴燕：主要是古典时期的？

陆谷孙：都是古典时期的。戏剧我记得从莎士比亚开始，经过王政复辟，一路到萧伯纳为止。小说也是从第一部《汤姆·琼斯》开始，一路下来到普里斯特利(J. B. Priestley)。当时的一大好处，就是你非念原著不可，不能靠二手的。然后，由于当时我们系里面教师不够，就把我推上了讲台，去教低我两届的英文系五年级“英美报刊选读”。

戴燕：那时候也能及时看到英美报刊？

陆谷孙：很及时。但你不能选太政治的文章、讲中国的文章。就找一些“无害”的，无害即可。那时周扬说选教材的标准，有益最好，无害亦可。我刚开始教书那个时候，要给工农同学开小灶，就是每天吃过晚饭，四个人，两个人一组，到我宿舍来练习讲英文，天南地北的就练口语。我一边这样教书一边写毕业论文,而毕业证书还没拿到的时候,“文革”来了,所以毕业证书也一直不发,等到“文革”以后才发的。1970年“一打三反”,说我是“白专典型”、“修正主义苗子”、“裴多菲俱乐部成员”,把我关起来,一关关了六个礼拜,就在这期间,我曾一手拿过五个灌满水的热水瓶,此生中最厉害的。然后就是编词典,不能教书了。

戴燕:编词典跟教书有什么区别?

陆谷孙:教书有一种满足,教师有演员的某种元素在里头,满足表达欲。编词典是很安静的,很艰苦的,有时候是很机械的。

戴燕:当时编《新英汉词典》有什么基础吗?

陆谷孙:没有基础。之所以开始编词典,是因为运动实际上已经到后期,没什么杀伤力了,更多教师感觉到没事干,成天来上班,开个会回去,有人就提出说我们来编本英汉词典吧,开始也不是很认真的一个活儿。工宣队说好啊,你们就成立一个词典组。还是半信半疑的。而编者,除两三位领导外都是有问题的人,包括我。然后突然有一天,说是好消息来了,徐景贤批准了,说上海需要这样一本词典。这不就弄假成真了?从此开始编字典。

戴燕:《新英汉词典》之前,一般人用什么词典?

陆谷孙:用郑易里的《英华大词典》,主要译自日本的“英和”。那时“二战”刚刚结束,日本被美国军队占领,所以美国军队里面的俚语特别多。现在这本词典,商务印书馆正在修订。

戴燕:要把它重出?

陆谷孙:重出,我的一位前学生在做。我说一定要根据郑老先生当年的风格,他不求给你很多用法,他就是释义多,帮助求解。

戴燕:编《新英汉词典》的时候,要参考哪些东西?怎么选词目?

陆谷孙:我们以大批判开路,先批判这些词典。至于词目的选择,主要是从六部洋人的词典(三部英国的、三部美国的)里面勾出来，英美三四本有的，重合的，我们就选。

戴燕：这个工作，现在有电脑很容易，那时候就抄啊？

陆谷孙：那全是手工，那些卡片都还在。然后还要找例子，有的可能就是用洋词典原来的例子，这要看各位编写人的喜好。我一般喜欢用最近看到的最新鲜的例子配上去。

戴燕：一共多少词条？

陆谷孙：《新英汉词典》大词条有五万，不包括肚子里头派生的。

戴燕：一共做了几年？

陆谷孙：这个快，编了五年。在工宣队的领导下，一个口号就是"急工农兵之所急，想工农兵之所想"。

戴燕：前后多少人参加？

陆谷孙：也挺多的，总归有五六十人、六七十人。校样到最后主要是我看的，就是我一个人看的。我一天可以看十四张，我不是校对，我是往里头加东西。

戴燕：您这给人家出版社添好多麻烦。

陆谷孙：就是说啊，不但是出版社，主要是给排字工人，所以排字工人骂我是"打翻了墨水瓶"，工宣队还叫我到商务印书馆的工厂去搬那个字盘：你体会劳动人民多累啊，你画条线多容易，你画条线人家就要搬字盘。但是，如果你不这样做的话，《新英汉词典》一出来就没用了，肯定扫进历史的垃圾堆。因为它全是什么"反对修正主义"啊、"美苏两霸要统治世界"啊这种东西。由于我这样拼命地往里头"走私"，曲线救书，也不能说我一个人，这部词典总算没有被扫进历史的垃圾堆，还是卖出不少，出版社统计累计出了一千万册。

戴燕：那后来再编《英汉大词典》就比较容易了，轻车熟路。

陆谷孙：至少我们已经有经验了。像我派到词典组的时候，根本从来没编过词典，我只用词典，只有葛传槼先生编过。

戴燕：编词典是另外一种工作。

陆谷孙：另外一种工作，你要看懂每一本洋词典的体例，有的你看不懂啊，像《简明牛津》，那真是简明啊！它是用最简洁的话来容纳尽可能多的信息，这一套功夫，都是要慢慢练出来的。幸亏有个葛先生在那里，他编过词典，跟着他学吧，尽管葛先生后来早早退出了词典组，因为他被十七路电车撞了一下。词典出版的时候，署名叫作"《新英汉词典》编写组"，没有人名的，也没钱的，那也很自然。

戴燕：还是在"文革"。

陆谷孙：后来改革开放了，北京的《汉英词典》有署名了：吴景荣、王佐良等。周建人的女儿当年是译文出版社的头，叫周晔，她跑来专门征求我的意见，要把我陆某人放在主编位置。我说你这个于情、于理、于法都不对，我死也不从，坚决要把葛先生的名字放在最前面。

戴燕：后来您再做《英汉大词典》有年轻人加入吗？

陆谷孙：还是很多中老年的。一开始大家都愿意来，当时"五七干校"还没取消，弄得不好你要到"五七干校"去，两害相权取其轻，还是到词典组去吧。最兴隆的时候我们有一百零八个人。

戴燕：也得到学校的支持？

陆谷孙：是上海市。

戴燕：上海市专门给你们辟一个什么地方，有单独的经费，等等。

陆谷孙：对，在社科院。

戴燕：现在正在编的这个《汉英词典》，算是这个工作的延续吗？

陆谷孙：汉英呢，实际上是我不好，我太轻率……1991 年我到香港，见到一些朋友，他们跟我说：你《英汉大词典》编好了，现在应该编一个汉英，就可以跟梁实秋、林语堂齐名了。我小小的虚荣心就被刺激起来了。又碰到一位安子介先生，他是主张要搞一本好的汉英词典，方便外国人学汉语的。我给他翻过东西，他晓得我这手英文大概还可以，他就觉得我应该来编这个词典，这是理由之二。理由三呢，就是我当年到美国替他们一个词库搞过一个文字档。这个词库，就是个跨政府部门的，在中美建交以前，我估计他们要了解中国的情报，就靠看报纸，看我们的出版物，然后把一些词语放进这个档案，放进他们的计算机里头，然后找在美华人或者日本人，翻译成英文。他们叫我，还有一位薛诗绮同志，去干什么呢，就是从他那个乱七八糟的文档里面，看能不能挑出一些有用的东西，编成一本词典。

戴燕：那是什么时候？

陆谷孙：那是1980年，做了半年。我去给他挑，就觉得多数都不行，但是后来一查，又都是有根据的，是日本的《中文辞典》、台湾的《国语大词典》里面有的。这个文档，中美建交以后不就没用了？他们美国人不用，我就试探，能不能把你这个档案送给我，哎，他居然同意了。现在我们把它也列为我们的一个资料来源。

戴燕：您这个《汉英词典》打算要列多少词目？

陆谷孙：单字大概就有两万五以上，不加一个字下面统领的词，大概三千多页。

戴燕：主要是给外国人学汉语用吗？

陆谷孙：不，我觉得中国人也可以用。譬如"囿座之器"是什么？原来历史上帝王的宝座旁边都放一个盛水的东西，水往里头注满了，就要溢出来，它提醒君王做事情不可以过分。这个"囿座之器"，《汉语大词典》就有。我本人不看英文就不知道，更别说年轻人了。

戴燕：这个是很大的工作量了。会收很新的词吗？

陆谷孙：流行词我们要拳头捏得很紧，不会有闻必录的。现在网民喜欢按英语构词规律自己造英文词，有些还是挺精彩的，但我们要看这些词语在英语世界的接受度和频用度来决定取舍。

戴燕：有没有古汉语和现代汉语的区别？

陆谷孙：我们用标签区别古今。如果用古话作例证，像“温故而知新”，就在前面打一个五角星。

戴燕：您这是要古往今来，一统天下啦。

陆谷孙：是的，包括方言，沪语的“刮辣松脆”也能查到。所以，我写了篇文章，叫《志虽美，道难达》，专门骂自己。

戴燕：现在这个工作大概完成了多少？

陆谷孙：九千工作页里头，好像有三千五百页做好了。

戴燕：有几个人帮忙？

陆谷孙：主要是三个女将。

戴燕：可以想象工作难度不小，但是读者也很需要。

陆谷孙：是很需要。我自己在国外待的时候，跑他们的书店，就知道英汉词典是没有销路的，在美国，人家要的是汉英词典。

戴燕：您现在大部分时间都在做这个？

陆谷孙：我这个寒假大概改了两三百工作页，就是寄希望于这个寒假。现在做做倒有点兴趣了，原来的英译实在不够好，就尽量设法改进。

戴燕：现在您是在电脑上做？

陆谷孙：也是在纸上做，工作页小，贴在一张大纸上。

文学研究还是要以文本为主

戴燕：现在还有时间去做莎士比亚吗？看您在文章里说，复旦外文系藏有很多关于莎士比亚的文献。

陆谷孙：因为当年林同济先生和我跟海外的交流比较多。现在基本没人做了。

戴燕：莎士比亚太古典了，大家没什么兴趣了？

陆谷孙：难也有关系，我觉得语言难是主要的一点，他等于是现代英语的开山鼻祖啊。我上课的时候，一个《哈姆雷特》剧本，我要讲三到四个礼拜，不像有些老师那样教，一周可以讲四个剧本。不行，我是一个字一个字地讲。为什么戏开场时第一句话 Who's there？不按常规由守更的哨兵喝问："来者是谁？"而是来换岗的喝问："那厢是谁？"等。前面的二十五行都是散文写的，叫他们背出来，下一堂课谁上来背，背出来，或者再加上一个独白，两段能背出来的，我奖赏《牛津词典》一本。

戴燕：好厉害！

陆谷孙：剧本真是写得好，你要仔细去读的话，这里头蕴涵可真是丰富。譬如接着两个哨兵交换口令 Long live the king，"国王万岁"，这多讽刺啊，这个剧里面没有一个国王是长命的。为什么剧本从头开始就是反复颠倒的，要细讲的话，是不是很有讲头？

戴燕：您觉得学生爱听吗？

陆谷孙：爱听，那是极爱听。

戴燕：那为什么都不愿去做研究呢？

陆谷孙：就是说，人家听听是蛮好听的，就像听《隋唐演义》一样。

戴燕：像您这样下功夫琢磨的，现在不多了。大概像您那样去看不同版本的，也不多了。

陆谷孙：版本是很重要的，第一个对折本跟第一个四开本有什么不一样？同样的一段独白，为什么有不同的版本？这个是要钻进去的，中国人这些都不钻了。我佩服朱生豪也就在这里，当年哪有那么多版本看啊，贫病交加，他还能翻成这个样子，我非常佩服。你如果现在叫我翻，我也可以翻，我翻肯定很慢，我要各个版本一部一部地对过来。

戴燕：您这是做学问。现在国际上，莎士比亚这一行的情况怎么样，受不受重视？

陆谷孙：也不太景气。

戴燕：那如果让学生读经典，大学的文学课总要找些经典来教，教什么呢？

陆谷孙：我估计在英、美的话，中学就读了，像《威尼斯商人》什么啊，比较容易的剧本，中学就该读了。

戴燕：今天中国的念外国文学的学生，您觉得他还一定要过莎士比亚这一关吗？

陆谷孙：我觉得一定要过，或者说最好要过。将来你要搞19世纪也可以，浪漫主义也可以，现代主义也可以，后现代也可以，你根源上不懂不行。现在文学批评追求新颖，什么后人文主义就说，人没什么了不起的，人只不过就是各种各样的物种里面的一种，猴子也是，猿猴帝国不是也拍成电影了吗？随着环境保护主义的声音，这个越来越厉害。

戴燕：现在外文系的学生或年轻老师，他们也都接受这些新的东西？

陆谷孙：也不见得，文学课本身就在衰落。

戴燕：您自己不大用这些后现代的东西。

陆谷孙：我不用，像这种没什么意思的。像我看到有人用"模因论"（memetics）解释翻译，戴顶帽子、穿双靴子，内容还是离不开意译、直译等，有什么价值呢？还是文本为主吧。

戴燕：可是我看您编词典呢，又好像很注意吸收新的语汇。

陆谷孙：新的语汇我也是有选择的，绝对有选择的，而且不能随着网上的狂欢，跟着它走不行的，这个我宁可保守一点，拼命地想办法给它翻译成好的英文。

戴燕：像每年评选的诺贝尔文学奖或是这个那个奖的作品，您会关心吗？

陆谷孙：我会看一看，但是我觉得不怎么样。让我心动的，就是像艾米莉·狄金森（Emily Dickinson）讲的——什么是文学？两种东西：一个呢，就是像在最热的热天，“滂”一桶冰水浇在你背上，醍醐灌顶；第二呢，就是你感觉到你的头颅被砍了，还没下来。只有这两种感觉出现的时候，你才碰到了文学。她是这样认为的，我也有点同感。

（原载《书城》2012 年第 5 期）

书《余墨三集》后

叶　扬

陆谷孙老师的《余墨集》，问世于2004年8月。次年2月，在该书第二次印刷前，陆老师添加了一篇“自序”，将书中所收录的所谓“余墨”定位为“非学术类文章”，将之分为“读后感、时评、见闻和序跋类几种”；除此之外，他又说到书中也包括了“演讲、通信、日记类文字若干”以及“短小英文两篇”。《余墨二集》于2009年2月付梓时，陆老师在前一年12月所撰写的“自序”中，说到《二集》的篇幅“膨胀不少”，对收录文字的范围有所扩张，似乎不再以“余墨”为限，他自己提出的理由是：“……老之已至，敝帚自珍，巴不得把写过的文字，包括与正业有关而并非余墨的，及早盘点搜辑……”随后，陆老师又加了一段非常感性的话：“我觉得人越上年纪，对文字越有一种亲切的依恋和专注的痴迷，在天远月孤的伶俜时分尤其如此。”

陆老师的这两部书，我都有幸得到他亲笔签名题赠的原书。2005年6月我返回申江时，应陆老师之召去外文学院作了题作“电影与文学”的英文讲演，由陆老师亲自主持，我手边的《余墨集》，在扉页中题写着“扬兄闲读哂正”，就是那次见面时陆老师亲手赠送的。2009年3月我再度返沪，与陆老师两度餐聚，并且回外文学院作了题为“蒙田和英国散文”的英文讲演。陆老师于2月题写签名的《余墨二集》，晚了一个月，在见面时也到了我的手中。时至今日，我还记得他当时将新作递到我手上时，脸上所流露出的自然的喜悦。我当时就这两部书的内容,跟他有过许多当面或是通过电邮的隔空交流,时至今日,我还常常翻阅,聊当故人晤对。

晚明的徐青藤(徐渭)曾经自诩:“吾书第一,诗次之,文次之,画又次之。”青藤的自知之明似乎有些问题,因为几百年之后来看,他的诗文实在没有多少出众之处,书法也只能说平平而已,唯独他自己置诸自己造诣最末的画作,倒是造就了他的不朽声名。钱默存先生在《林纾的翻译》一文中,谈到林琴南对于自己的文相当自负,认为自己的诗与文相比,只是“狗吠驴鸣”,至于他传世的译作的地位,也许就更不值得他自己一提了。陆老师向来不怎么喜欢晚明名士的风尚,他不会像青藤和琴南那样,作类似的自我评判。不过,在复旦大学外文学院近日举行的一次学术讨论会上,陆老师的美国友人克里默(Thomas Creamer)在会上说起,如果有人问陆老师自己他的职业为何,他的第一个回答绝对不会是“词典编纂者”(lexicographer),而很可能是“第一,老师;第二,作家;也许第三才会是词典编纂者。”克里默先生不愧是陆老师的老友,他这个说法,我是完全同意的。不过,这只是就职业而言,根据我对陆老师的了解,他一定会把做人这一条放在他的职业之上。从这个意义上来说,我认为他首先是我国优秀传统中所弘扬的那样一位“弘毅”之士,也是萨义德(Edward Said)笔下所描述的、能够始终保持自己独立人格的“知识人”(intellectual),随后才依次是教师、作家和词典编纂家。

大约十年以前,陆老师从外文学院首任院长的职位上退下来之后,我在见面交谈时隐隐感觉到,他常有时日无多的紧迫感。陆灏老弟编辑的《人间世》一书于2008年4月出版,其中收入了陆老师在前一年10月写成的《我的父亲》一文(后收入《余墨二集》),文末有这样一段:“父亲只活了62岁,我今年已经68岁了。活得比父亲长,至今沐浴着他的遗泽。我深感自己不称不配,只是个德里达所称的‘逾期的苟活者'罢了。"在这些年来的许多聚会中,陆老师好几次流露出同样的想法,我当时觉得他这种说法未免太过消沉,几次以开玩笑的方式向他表示反对。但是,在他生命的最后数年,他几乎将全副精力,投入《中华汉英大词典》的编纂工作,好像在和时间作一场殊死的竞赛。最后,他就像盘马弯弓、战死沙场的将军一样,中夜伏案之际,飘然而去。《余墨三集》以"谈文论字"作为第一部分置诸卷首,我觉得好比紧锣密鼓的开场好戏。作为一代词典编纂家的陆老师,在这些文章里显示了他在数十年教学研究的过程中,对于中英两种语言之间各种异同的敏锐感觉,以及建筑在大量的实践经验上对于词典编纂的取径和见解。

"如果能够再次选择,我还是会做老师,因为我喜欢教书,喜欢学生。"对于自己的职业生涯的主要追求,陆老师自己说得再明白也没有了。他还多次跟我说过,当教师的人,应该要有一点"表现欲",甚至应该想要 show off ("炫耀,卖弄"),"每堂课至少要让学生笑三次"。上世纪 70 年代末,我进复旦外文系念本科的时候,由于种种原因,陆老师当时尚未能回校任教,我无缘亲炙。三十年后,我于 2008 年应邀回外文学院客座任课时,总算一偿夙愿,在他驰名的"英美散文"的课堂上,一睹他的丰采。记得陆老师每次总是很早就来到 5209 大教室里,静静地站在讲坛前面,等着那一百多个学生纷至沓来。一旦他开口,那风趣诙谐的语言、抑扬顿挫的语音语调、丰富的表情和肢体动作,立刻就把学生带进了课文内外的另一个世界。在此集中"三尺讲坛"这个第二部分里,陆老师跟我们分享了他教学生涯中的许多酸甜苦辣。我们都知道,陆老师是静得下来、坐得住冷板凳的,但是我觉得好静只是他的一面而已。作为一位优秀的教师,其实他还是喜欢热闹的。他大概不会在乎我在这里插上一句笑话:"人来疯"是我们这班教书匠的"书生本色"。集中的"附录"部分,收录了六年前陆老师就其译作《一江流过水悠悠》在上海曲阳文化馆参加与读者互动活动的录音整理稿，就是一个精彩的例子。从前面的讲话一直到后面的答问部分，他旁征博引，从英美文学的经典到当代的畅销作品，都有所涉猎；他妙语如珠，可以让人想见他当时逸兴遄飞的神态。

18世纪法国作家布封的名言“风格即人本身”（“Le style c'est l'homme même”），当然也适用于陆老师的文字。读着这个集子，尤其是那些出自他一度亲笔经营的博客的“博文”，常常使我想起多年来每次相聚时，他言笑晏晏、咳珠唾玉的情景来。在布封之后，下一个世纪的法国作家福楼拜别出心裁，在给一位友人的书信中说：“风格就是生活！她正是思想的生命线！”（“Le style c'est la vie！c'est la sang même de la pensée！”）我以为福楼拜的这个说法，特别适用于陆老师的作品，因为他虽然好静，却从来不是离群索居于象牙塔中的隐士，而是一位紧接地气的“性情中人”。《三集》中的“故人旧事”、“世间百态”这两个压轴的部分，字里行间，反映了他那种“位卑未敢忘忧国”、“一枝一叶总关情”的坦荡心地和博大胸怀，也充分表现了他那个写得端端正正的斗大的“人”字。

陆老师的弟子朱绩崧在应召为《余墨二集》撰写的序言里，曾经说起前面两个集子内容的时间跨度，《余墨集》为22年有余，《二集》则为9年有余。如今《三集》的跨度，则广达54年，当为其最。此集之所以能有这样的跨度，主要是因为收录了陆老师的英文小品“Sunset, Mother and Home”（《日落、母亲和家》）。这篇文章的收录跟我有些关系，应该在这里跟读者交代一下。

苏东坡曾说“凡文字，少小时须令气象峥嵘，采色绚烂”，而这篇文章正是陆老师青年时代的“采色绚烂”之作。我们从《我的父亲》一文中知道，陆老师虚岁8岁那一年初夏，母亲因病不治，他从学校被家人传叫，飞奔回家，与母亲已经阴阳永隔。除了这简略的数行文字之外，他的作品中提到母亲的，好像现在只有这一篇绝无仅有的英文作品了。根据陆老师自己回忆，此文当作于1961年（“22岁”）。陆老师那时是英文专业大四的本科生，与系里的青年教师任治稷老师相交甚笃，任老师当时也刚过而立之年，据说两人都喜欢以英文写作，而且都有争强好胜的个性，两人往往定下一题，埋头执笔，各显神通。这篇文章，大概就是这样一场以文字比试的成果，写成之后，很快在同学当中流传开来。次年9月，我的四姐叶逢进入英文专业，这篇文章就是某个周末她从学校带回来的，我读后非常喜欢，自己手抄一过。多年之后，侄儿叶尊在翻检家中旧物时，找到了这个劫余幸存的手抄本，重新打字，三姐叶令也从电邮将之分别发给了陆老师和我。当时关于他的这篇“少作”，我跟他还有一通电邮的交流。这一次，关于是否将此文收入《三集》，我先征询了智玲的看法，智玲回答说：“谷孙很幼小时母亲就去世了，他对母亲的记忆既有限，也遥远。发表这篇文章也是让他显示对母亲的怀念，我没有意见。”既然智玲开了绿灯，我就将文稿发给了编辑，这样读者就有了阅读这位大教授、大学者的学生时代的习作的机会。希望大家掩卷之后，会跟我同样喜爱这篇真情流露、抒情色彩极为浓厚的文章。

如今《余墨三集》即将刊行，按照陆老师自己的说法，她的篇幅比诸《余墨二集》又“膨胀不少”，不过就内容而言，则可以说是沿袭了前面两部，尤其是《二集》的旧例，附录中还收入了陆老师的旧体诗作和访谈，也可以说是终于完成了陆老师在《二集》自序里所表达的“及早盘点搜辑”的心愿了。

然而，此书的出版问世，毕竟是晚了，晚了，太晚了。在上文提及的陆老师参加“电影读书活动”的访谈录里，在讲话之后的提问环节，有读者问起，《余墨集》会不会出第三集，陆老师回答说：“《余墨三集》会出的，现在合同已经订了，但是好像没见下文，即便出不了，总有一天会有一本迟到的《余墨三集》吧。”如今回想起来，他当时随随便便的回答，真是“一语成谶”，因为从某种意义上讲，《余墨三集》确实是“迟到”了。迟到了——此书刊行之后，我已经不可能再收到作者亲笔的签名题识；迟到了——作者已经无从再一次闻到自己新书的油墨的芳香；迟到了——我们已经无法请作者自己决定文章的取舍，向他请教文字上最后的修订。唯一可以告慰陆老师在天之灵的，就是英语里那句成语，better late than never（《英汉大词典》译作“亡羊补牢，未为晚也”）。想来陆老师也应该会感到欣喜：他所“依恋”、“痴迷”的这些文字，虽然迟到了，毕竟最后还是跟读者见面了。

2017 年 11 月 27 日稿竟于美国加州华山市猿影斋

图书在版编目(CIP)数据

余墨三集/陆谷孙著. —上海：复旦大学出版社，2018.3
ISBN 978-7-309-13306-6

Ⅰ. 余…　Ⅱ. 陆…　Ⅲ. 散文集-中国-当代　Ⅳ. I267

中国版本图书馆 CIP 数据核字(2017)第 245671 号

余墨三集
陆谷孙　著
责任编辑/于文雍

复旦大学出版社有限公司出版发行
上海市国权路 579 号　邮编：200433
网址：fupnet@fudanpress.com　http://www.fudanpress.com
门市零售：86-21-65642857　团体订购：86-21-65118853
外埠邮购：86-21-65109143　出版部电话：86-21-65642845
上海盛通时代印刷有限公司

开本 890×1240　1/32　印张 15　字数 357 千
2018 年 3 月第 1 版第 1 次印刷

ISBN 978-7-309-13306-6/I · 1071
定价：58.00 元

ISBN 978-7-309-13306-6

定价：58.00元
www.fudanpress.com